About this book

David Whitmarsh was the winner of the inaugural Science Fiction Debuts Prize for his "exceptional, compelling and instantly engaging" novel, *The Measurement Problem*.

Launched by Hodder & Stoughton and the Science Museum in 2022 to celebrate the museum's exhibition "Science Fiction: Voyage to the Edge of Imagination", the writing prize aims to champion science fiction storytelling and discover some of the exciting talent of the future.

As the winning novel, *The Measurement Problem*, was described as "a near-future high-concept science fiction thriller, told in a noir style" and set in the late 21st century, in which much of east London is being abandoned to the rising sea. Against this backdrop, Detective Inspector Lewis Drake is tasked with solving a murder linked to a new drug, *implicitins*, which allows the user to experience alternative quantum realities.

Of the competition, Molly Powell (Hodder & Stoughton), said: "...All of the entries were of the highest quality, and selecting a winner was no easy feat, but Whitmarsh's brilliantly realised ideas, hugely engaging writing and a tightly plotted mystery stole the show."

SCIENCE MUSEUM SF DEBUTS PRIZE WINNER

THE MEASUREMENT PROBLEM

DAVID WHITMARSH

Published by David Whitmarsh.

ISBN: 978-1-0681586-0-5

Cover design and interior formatting:
Mark Thomas / Coverness.com

'[The Many-worlds interpretation is the] only completely coherent approach to explaining both the contents of quantum mechanics and the appearance of the world.'

—Hugh Everett III

CHAPTER 1

Tuesday 12th November: Marek's Café

We've all heard of Schrödinger's cat, sitting in a box with a vial of poison and a trigger controlled by a quantum event. Theory tells us that before we open the box the cat is both alive and dead, in a superposition of states.

Open the box, however, and you will find either a living cat or a dead cat. What is it that causes the nebulous superposition of states to collapse into a single, definite result? Is it some magic that exists in the human mind that forces the physical world to conform to our expectation? Does the cat's own mind suffice?

This is The Measurement Problem.

The arguments over the solution raged for more than a century even though the answer was revealed as long ago as 1957 in the doctoral thesis of one Hugh Everett III. For decades his work was widely ignored, scorned, or derided. But follow Everett's reasoning and you understand that when you open the box and look, your own quantum state is entangled with that of the cat. You, too, are in a superposition of states. There is a you that sees a dead cat and a you that sees a living cat. Each unaware of the other's existence.

That used to be the case. For some of us, it is no longer so.

A K Amari - *The Measurement Problem, A Guide to Entanglement*

Where to start. For me it all kicked off the day I was murdered. Most people don't notice things like that but it turns out I'm sensitive.

I was in Marek's café that dismal November morning. Ten past eight, Marek had only just opened and the place was empty. I'd been going there three years, any day when the vagaries of traffic meant I arrived early for my shift. I liked Marek's. I liked the sounds and smells of shabby leather seats and soft jazz. I always ordered the same thing, and every time Marek acted like he'd never seen me before. In a way I liked that, too. In my line of work it's better not to stand out. That morning I sat at my usual table with the usual macchiato in front of me. Outside, the pre-dawn drizzle on the narrow cobbled street sparkled in the light from the window.

My thoughts ranged over the usual ranks of problems: the divorce settlement and my precarious finances were the most urgent, but as always it was Alice's condition that was at the forefront. All avenues to find what had happened to my sister and who was responsible had turned into dead ends, and if this latest round of treatment didn't effect a cure I had no clue how I could cover the cost of her ongoing care.

Amongst all that I could barely spare a moment to consider our hopeless failure at Canary Wharf, three weeks of careful exploration and surveillance with the robotic rats and absolutely nothing to show for it.

A shadow moved in the glistening darkness of the alley, dragging me from my despondency. A tall figure in a long coat, shoulders hunched, face shaded by the brim of a hat, came along the alley, stopped a few seconds and headed back the way they had come. The receding shadow vanished in a glare of bright light, Marek's reflection in the window as he pushed through the swing door from the kitchen with a tray of pastries.

You could say I have a suspicious nature, but you'd be wrong. Suspicion isn't in my nature, it's a skill learned the hard way from fifteen years in the service. Someone had come looking for someone. They'd seen me and turned away. My best first guess was that they were looking for someone else.

My speculation was curtailed by a ping from my phone signalling another missive from Vittoria's solicitor, this one claiming that their investigations suggested I had undeclared assets, shares in VirGenTech and various other pharmacorps. If only. If only I'd had the sense to put my meagre savings in companies like that ten years ago and caught the tide of the biotech revolution. Those who did have done very well. But I had only my UBI and the supplementary stipend for performing an allegedly useful function for society. Everything else was gone on legal fees.

I penned an appropriate reply:

> *Not in this world.*
> *Regards, Lewis Drake*

I bore my ex no ill-will—I'd long ago abandoned my resentment for the way it ended—but her solicitor had access to someone entangled and an exaggerated impression of the usefulness of entanglement. The resulting barrage of claims and accusations was getting a little wearing. The reference to VirGenTech in particular was unkind after their treatment of Alice. The solicitor knew that and was trying to needle me. I had to give Vittoria the benefit of the doubt and assume it was an idea churned out by the solicitor's devious algorithms, but damn, I needed it settled. Until it was all final, she would have a claim on my service benefits. I'd assigned them to pay for Alice's care if anything happened to me, but if Vittoria got a slice it wouldn't be enough.

I still had time to kill before my shift started and the news feeds provided a suitable distraction. A story about Hubert Neuville, a junior minister in Paris who had been arrested on espionage charges, held no interest for me. Next was a piece on the high court declining to prohibit Sunday's anti-entanglement protest march from Parliament Square. An accompanying video showed the protest organiser, Winsford Saïd MP, standing on the high court steps with his legal team, fists raised like a victorious prize fighter. That story stirred deeply mixed feelings so I moved quickly onto the next: the Metropolitan Police said that arrests were expected imminently in connection with the murder of Sir Roger Wyndham, now twenty-four hours since he had been found dead in a hotel room in Milton Keynes, shot twice at close range. From the rumours circulating in our department imminent arrest seemed unlikely.

I gave up on the news and steeled myself to start reading the book I'd been recommended: *The Measurement Problem*, about entanglement, by one of the entangled. I needed that perspective for the work; so much criminality and corruption, so much personal tragedy stemmed from the use and trafficking of implicitins. More importantly, I needed to better understand my sister's situation.

The anxiety crept up on me while I read, starting as a vague disquiet. I cast my gaze around the café and peered out at the dark, wet street. Nothing. Nobody. I was alone. Marek was back in the kitchen doing whatever he did after opening.

I turned my attention back to the book, but my eyes wouldn't rest on the display. My pulse climbed, my fingers flexed like they wanted to do something. I had to suppress the urge to reach for the Glock beneath my jacket. I found myself gripping the edge of the table, staring at the glass door, at the worn arc across the floor where the bottom edge always scraped. I could almost hear the squealing sound of that ill-fitting door swinging open, but the only real sound was my own gasping breath.

It hit me. I couldn't breathe, my throat tightened like steel bands. I couldn't move, couldn't think, my mind paralysed as much as my body. Overcome with a chilling dread, my vision shrank to narrow tunnels. The table and empty chair opposite dwindled to distant points. There was a presence, cries of pain and grief, desperate fingers clutching my hand, then darkness filled me: utter emptiness that might have lasted an instant or an eternity.

Vision came swimming back through dark shadows. I eased my grip on the table edge. What had happened, I had no idea, not until some time later.

I gulped down the rest of my macchiato and stood.

'Goodbye Sir,' said Marek from the kitchen doorway with his usual anonymous deference. Nothing had happened to disturb him.

As I pulled open the door the bottom edge screeched across the tiles like it's been doing all the time I've been going there. Maybe one day Marek will get it fixed.

My heart rate had returned to something like normal by the time I'd reached the end of the alley and walked the two hundred metres to the back entrance of the station. Twentieth century glass and steel, showing its age more than the stone edifices of earlier centuries that stood on either side. Lifts with sliding doors opened on glass-walled lobbies and open-plan offices on every floor. I stepped from the lift on the fourth and through the glass door into Organised Crime. The pale clouds of the morning sky framed DS Harris's compact silhouette at the window. I locked my weapon in my desk drawer and joined him. He was holding a paper cup of what passed for coffee in the canteen two floors down.

The drizzle shone in the lights of the vehicle compound below, empty but for a couple of patrol cars charging in their bays.

'Cambridge?' He looked up at me, that look of concern on his face. He didn't really need to ask; he knew that on nearly all my days off I was up at The Grange, visiting.

I nodded.

'How is she?'

'Hard to say.' Complicated was the real answer, too complicated for a five minute chat at the beginning of the working day. There weren't many people I could really talk to about Alice but Jack Harris was one—at the right time in the right place. He took my answer at face value, for now.

'Any progress on Canary Wharf?' I asked.

A raised eyebrow was his answer.

'What?'

He took his time with his drink, then lowered the cup. 'We've been looking the wrong way.'

'Show me.'

I followed him to his desk where he pulled up the plan of the complex. The obsolete docks crossed the neck of the Isle of Dogs from east to west, lined by the more recently derelict skyscrapers, their lowest levels washed by the highest tides. The raised Docklands Light Railway crossed from north to south, the underground Jubilee Line and Elizabeth lines east to west. Harris pointed to the Jubilee Line station, and the passage that led from it north into the Canary Wharf shopping centre. 'Our informant said they were in an abandoned shop at Canary Wharf, so that's where we've been looking, but there's another underground complex.' His finger moved south to the other side of the station, to another maze of shops and passages labelled *Jubilee Place*. 'I reprogrammed the rats and sent them scurrying this way.' He opened a video excerpt: grainy green of low-light imaging from a perspective close to the ground, a half-dozen shadowy shapes carrying boxes between rows of tables in some form of eatery.

Some of the crates were long, carried between two men struggling with the weight. Others were smaller, lighter. 'Freeze that.' I leaned over his shoulder and zoomed in. *VGT*, the VirGenTech logo, large and clear on the side of the box. 'Jackpot.' Guns and drugs. 'Good work.'

It had to be a Red Claw hideout. They were the strongest of the London gangs and they ruled the East End flood zone, especially the Isle of Dogs. Nothing happened there without their consent, and without them getting their slice of the action. And from there they ran their protection rackets and their trade in guns and black implicitins.

'We sent in a couple more rats yesterday to keep a watch. We're going to plant trackers on the goods.'

That was the way, slow and steady. Follow the goods, follow the people, piece together the network. The ultimate prize was to locate and identify their entangled leader *Vidmar*. I might have wished the breakthrough had come while I was in the office but I was just happy we were making some progress.

'Have you given her the news?' I said, nodding my head towards Detective Chief Inspector Baxter's corner office.

Her door opened before he could answer and Baxter leaned out. 'DI Drake! DS Harris! My office! Now.'

'Yeah, yesterday,' Harris muttered under his breath as we made our way between the lines of desks. Two and some years since DCI L Baxter had taken over and she held things tight, always correct, always formal. So formal that none of us even knew what the "L" stood for, but she was okay. Never a misplaced word, never a word of reprimand or of praise that was not deserved.

'Sit,' she said without looking up from her screen. 'Close the door.'

When we were settled she leaned back in her chair, steepled her fingers, and fixed us in turn with her iron glare. I admired her drive and determination. A couple of years younger than me and a rank above, I resented that she had overcome a personal tragedy a hundred times worse than mine to do that, and I felt bad about my resentment. What else could she do but work to bring down those who had killed her partner and her children.

'You're aware of the Wyndham case?'

I hadn't been living under a rock, neither had Harris. 'Yes, ma'am,' we chorused.

'We've been sent the file. I'm assigning it to your team, Drake.'

'Why has it been sent to us?'

'Forensics reports he was killed by two shots, close range, ten point two mil.'

Ten point two mil, point four inch in the old units. The weapon had to be an antique, the ammunition custom-made. We'd seen the same thing a dozen times in the last two years. 'Ballistics?' I had to ask.

She nodded. 'No serial number on the firing pin but it matches the cartridges retrieved from the other killings. This was a *Rdeča Kremplja* hit.'

Rdeča Kremplja. Baxter pronounced the Slovenian name like a native, the only one who could wrap her tongue around it. To the rest of us they were just *Red Claw*, who were the biggest of our problems and if they were behind the killing of Sir Roger Wyndham, then that, too, was our problem.

'So what's the motive?' Harris asked. 'What dealings has he had with Red Claw?'

'He's chair of the Docklands Redevelopment Corporation,' I said. 'There's got to be some contact for the DRC to be able to operate in the Isle of Dogs.'

'Very good, Drake. Take a couple of hours to get up to speed on the file. Set Penfold to trawl Wyndham's tax and bank records. Look into his business interests, movements, phone and other comms, contacts, especially anyone known to be Entangled.'

Yes, she spoke the word *Entangled* with a capital letter and it set my teeth on edge. 'Is there any indication that Wyndham was Entangled, ma'am?' She had me doing it, too.

She gave me her most withering look. 'And how would we know that?'

It was a dumb question. The entangled mostly didn't like to give themselves away, and those who got past the initial confusion soon learned how to hide it from us poor simplexes. 'I thought that someone as high up as Wyndham dealing with Red Claw might have dealt with Vidmar directly.'

'Part of the famous conspiracy of the Entangled?'

'No, I don't believe…'

'Enough. There's work to be done. Wyndham had friends in high places. The commissioner is putting pressure on the chief constable's office. We'll need to put on a show. Give us a breathing space to do the real work, and send *Rdeča Kremplja* a message that they can't operate with impunity even in the flood zone.'

I didn't like the sound of that. 'What did you have in mind, ma'am?'

Out of the corner of my eye, I saw Harris twitch. He knew as well as I did what was coming.

'We're going to raid Jubilee Place.'

Harris's frustration exploded. 'But watching it is a chance to gain valuable intel. We'll lose it if we go in.'

Objecting was pointless but he was right and I had to support him. 'We'll be messing up our own investigation, burning our leads. We'll be lucky to get a few low-lifes.'

She stood, and leaned forward with her fingers splayed on the desk. Harris and I hurriedly shuffled to our feet.

'The decision has been made. I will take care of the arrangements.'

We were dismissed. So much for slow and steady.

It was going to take a day or two for her to set up the raid, so we headed for our desks to get up to speed on the case. Twenty-four hours the murder squad had been working on it with nothing to show. I had my calendar call the widow, Lady Wyndham, to set up an interview. It came back in under a minute, 2pm that afternoon at her home. That done, I skimmed through Sir Roger's file. While I read, Harris opened the interface to Penfold and set it digging into chains of beneficial ownership through corporate registries in various countries, some of which were officially shared with us, others where the access was not so official. The fact that Penfold was given access to those channels said something of the profile of the case.

'Have you seen this? Jazila Limited?' He called over the low partition that separated our desks.

I knew the name, it was plastered at intervals along the flood wall from the Tower of London up to Canning Town. Jazila was the prime contractor. 'What about it?'

'Wyndham's been building a stake, just in the last few weeks.'

I drilled down in the Penfold chart. Wyndham's holding had gone from zero to at least forty percent via a tangled web of nested companies, trusts and funds. It seemed an elaborate structure if it was done for tax reasons, but it was a mundane company. The docklands flood wall had brought in a pile of cash in recent years but now it was feeding on maintenance work on the wall and smaller flood defence projects around the country.

More interesting were his holdings in companies with close ties to the Docklands Redevelopment Corporation: consultancies, specialist underpinning and marine engineering firms.

'So what's the DRC trying to do?' Harris asked me.

'They want to turn the old Canary Wharf complex into a kind of canal city. Let it flood to whatever level the sea eventually settles at and build locks to manage the tides. They're buying up the properties for pennies and getting government grants for the feasibility studies. More to come when they start the construction, grants and government-backed loans.'

I had Penfold draw it up: boxes for each of the companies involved, lines to show ownership, trading relationships, flows of cash. My screen was rapidly covered with a rat's nest of boxes and lines. Money percolating down, millions siphoned off via salaries and bonuses and dividends and expenses—likely some of those were kickbacks—and a substantial slice going out to other companies. I pulled up our list of known and suspected Red Claw front companies. Plant hire, gang masters, transportation and logistics. Penfold slotted them into the diagram at the bottom, tying in a whole new layer.

I beckoned to Harris and he came round the desk to peer over my shoulder. 'Well, there's the link to Red Claw,' he said.

'Looks like they're getting their due so where's the motive for murder?'

'Buggered if I know.' Harris straightened. 'What are you doing for lunch? Marek's?'

The mention of the café brought it back: the panic, the blackout, the inexplicable terror. 'Not today, no.' The realisation I had somewhere else to be gave me a chance to breathe, to calm myself. 'Going to talk to the widow, Lady Wyndham. I'll grab a sandwich in the canteen.'

*

The concrete canopy over the station entrance gave some shelter from the drizzle while I chewed my way through a rubbery cheese and pickle roll, waiting for the car. A Dongfeng pulled up, its light blue paint faded and peeling, and a disconcerting whining sound coming from the front nearside motor. The thing was as old as me. Every expense was spared on the transport budget, so any non-urgent vehicle request was always channelled to the lowest bidder.

The plastic seat was hard and the interior cramped. My elbow banged the door panel when I took my phone out to review the file. Lady Wyndham—Monica—was independently wealthy, heiress to the Harcourt brewing conglomerate. At fifty-two, she was fifteen years younger than her recent spouse and had been married to him for twenty-five years. They had two children: Bentley was at medical school in Tripoli, his younger sister, Sarah, was a budding actor. Lady Wyndham had one older son, Aiden Harcourt, from a previous relationship. The transcripts of interviews by a pair of inept murder squad detectives provided little illumination. They had focussed on the will, and on the stepson. Lady Wyndham's responses to that line had rapidly turned from monosyllabic to viperous. Aiden himself had not been interviewed, his whereabouts currently unknown.

The drizzle had turned to a more definite rain by the time the car pulled up in Kensington Square outside a substantial town house. Iron railings protected a small flagged courtyard decorated with half a dozen dense evergreen shrubs in glazed pots. The house behind, rendered and painted grey, had rows of wood-framed sash windows of elegant proportions on three floors, capped with a grey slate roof and a set of dormer windows. Early eighteenth century, at a guess. A small blue plaque affixed to the wall by the grand solid door celebrated some once-famous former occupant who I had never heard of. The brass doorbell button in its ornate surround was bright, polished by the pressing of innumerable thumbs, now by mine. Old money, privilege and power. I expected to be greeted by an overworked, underpaid minion and presented to a pompous matriarch.

The door opened. The figure that greeted me, in the simple grace of her posture, in the elegance of her dress, hair and makeup, undermined my expectations at several levels.

'Detective Inspector Lewis Drake?' Her voice was clear with an unaffected home counties accent. 'Please come in.'

'Thank you, Lady Wyndham.' Fifty-two years old, the file said. I wouldn't have said she looked younger, but she did wear her years well.

She led me into a drawing room where a small chandelier and elaborate plasterwork on the ceiling contrasted with furnishings in a turn-of-the-century minimalist style: chairs and couches of straight lines in black leather, a coffee table with a simple glass centrepiece. As I sat on the couch she indicated I saw the faint crazing of the black surface. Originals, genuine leather.

She took the seat opposite, the coffee table between us, and sat with hands clasped in her lap. Stiff, reserved.

'First of all, Lady Wyndham, may I offer…'

She held up a palm to stop me. 'Save your sympathies and condolences for someone who needs them. My husband and I were not—close, and have not been for many years.'

'And yet you have remained married?'

'It was convenient. Roger and I had interests in common, he had contacts who were useful to me and vice versa. And our children of course, they have remained close to us both. Roger is… was very protective of them, even Aiden, my eldest, his stepson.' She hesitated and raised a finger. 'A new line of enquiry, your message said. I take it my children are no longer under suspicion?'

'I'm sure they never were, Lady Wyndham, but we have to pursue all avenues.'

'Hah! They as much as accused Aiden to my face. First so he could claim his inheritance, then, when I pointed out that he stood to receive nothing, it was supposed to be in revenge for that.'

'And it was at that point that you, ah, terminated the interview.' I kept a carefully neutral tone and a straight face—the transcript had been scrupulous in reporting Lady Wyndham's precise choice of words.

She relaxed her clenched fists, and snorted out a heavy breath. 'Indeed.'

'I have no reason to suspect your son, but should the question be raised, it would be helpful to understand why he had been excluded from the will.'

'Still pursuing all avenues, Detective Inspector?'

'If only to ensure they are thoroughly closed off, Lady Wyndham.'

She gave me a look like the ticking of a time bomb, then leaned back and let the frown melt away. 'It was Aiden's choice. He confronted Roger last year and told him he had neither the need nor the desire for his money, having learned too much of whence it came. Roger was quite upset, but eventually he acquiesced and changed the will.'

Having seen what Penfold had found of the whence of Wyndham's money,

I could understand Aiden Harcourt's reticence. His principled stand deserved some respect. 'And where is Aiden now?'

'Here and there. He doesn't keep me informed of his movements.' Her hand waved in little circles and her eyes flittered between the corners of the ceiling, as if she might find him there like a prodigal spider. 'I'm told it may be some time before the body can be released for cremation.'

'I'm afraid so.'

'I'm arranging a memorial service, next Monday. Bentley and Sarah will be there, and I hope Aiden will, too. I shall send you the details if you would like to attend.'

'Thank you, Lady Wyndham.' I jotted a note: *Monday 18, memorial.* 'You mentioned that you and Sir Roger had interests in common, would that be because you are on the board of the London Flood Management Commission, while your husband was chair of the Docklands Redevelopment Corporation?'

'That was certainly one area.'

'Isn't there something of a conflict of interest there? Do the FMC award redevelopment contracts to the DRC?'

'Less than you might think. We set strategy for the flood defences, manage relocation programmes and such like. Tendering of flood defence works is handled by another department, while the DRC operate outside our walls. There were some areas of common interest but Roger's influence worked more at government level. He saw an opportunity. Abandoning so much of East London to the rising sea has been a career-ending move for enough politicians that the survivors will snatch at any straw. The grant money for studies and remedial work in Docklands has already run into billions with plenty more to come.'

'And how is the redevelopment project progressing?'

'Oh, it isn't. Never will. Those buildings were never designed to have their ground levels beneath the sea. Some of the taller skyscrapers on deep pilings might survive a while but concrete cracks, the steel reinforcement rusts and expands, cracking the concrete more. Roger and his friends take the money and do just enough to persuade the treasury that progress is being made and the politicians turn a blind eye because as long as the money is being spent, it shows they're taking action. By the time the project collapses those responsible will have moved on to other posts.'

Her voice curled in disdain over the last sentence.

I shook my head. 'It's an old story.' That earned a somewhat cynical smile from her. 'Lady Wyndham, do you know of anyone who might have wanted your husband dead?'

Her face dropped. She stood, hands flapping. 'I beg your pardon, Lewis. It is Lewis, isn't it? You must forgive my appalling manners, I haven't offered you any refreshment. Tea? Will you take tea?'

'You're very kind, but no. Thank you.' She was already opening the door. 'But, please, take a few moments to gather your thoughts.'

The door closed and she drifted back to sit again by the small table. I kept my silence, waiting for her to continue, wondering what was behind that little piece of amateur dramatics.

'I don't have any names but I know he had dealings with some gang in Docklands. I assumed he must have crossed them in some way.'

'Red Claw?'

'Is that what they're called?' She looked down at her right hand, which rubbed at her knee.

'Does the name *Vidmar* mean anything to you?'

A brief shake of the head.

'I have to ask you—was Sir Roger entangled?'

She looked up, eyes wide in surprise. 'No.'

'Can you be sure? I'm told it isn't always easy to tell.'

'I am familiar with entanglement.'

'You know someone entangled?'

'I have a close friend who followed that path. I've seen how, for those who take to it, it broadens their outlook, opens new depths, brings wisdom. When I first met Roger he was a dynamic and charming man, but never *deep*. Of those attributes, the absence of depth was the only one he retained in later life.'

'It sounds like you admire them, the entangled.'

'Yes, I do. Elijah, the friend I spoke of, took the treatment ten years ago. He is the brightest, most reasonable man. He does so much good work.'

Elijah. Not a common name, but there was little chance of it being *that* Elijah, and not particularly relevant. But ten years ago… 'He must have been one of the first.'

She gave a nod of affirmation. 'One of the first, and one of the lucky ones. He came through without any adverse effects.' She shivered and looked down at the carpet by the side of her chair. 'When I think what happened to some of them in those days.'

'Not just those days.' The words escaped me before I could stop them.

'Detective Inspector?' She reached over the small table to rest her hand on my knee. 'You know someone entangled?'

'I do,' I said. 'I do. It didn't go so well for her.'

*

On my way back to the station I ran through all the things Lady Wyndham had told me. She'd given me more than she intended, and much more than she'd revealed in her first interview. I'd have liked to credit my good looks and innate charm, but as I lacked both those attributes it could only have been the other detectives' incompetence. For all her bluster, behind it all she was grieving, if not for the Sir Roger of recent years, then for the dynamic, charming man she had married twenty-five years before. She most certainly knew more than she let on about her husband's nefarious dealings in Docklands and I wasn't convinced she was telling me everything about Aiden Harcourt. We'd need to track him down for interview, but there was nothing to link him to the crime—ballistics had shown the weapon was the one used in other killings known to be related to Red Claw, and we had a growing pile of evidence, admittedly circumstantial, linking Wyndham to them.

What little daylight we'd had was gone by the time I got back to the station. Harris was still at his desk, head down, fingers twitching, weaving patterns of data on the displays before him. The blinds were down and the lights off in the corner office.

'What've you got?' I asked. He jumped and twisted round to look up at me.

'Oh! Hi. Yeah. Drawn a blank on the comms. All the addresses and accounts registered to him are full of fluff. Family, golf club. His secretarial agent is locked up tighter than a duck's arse. Without his keys we've get nothing. So I'm working through the Vehicle Licensing Authority logs on Wyndham's vehicles, tying it up to his diary and his contacts lists.'

I pulled up a chair and squeezed next to him in the narrow space between the desks. 'Anything?'

'Most of it's mundane. Attending DRC board meetings, dinner with his wife, nights with his mistress, drinks at his club. Almost everything ties up, except once every two to three weeks he stays one night at the hotel where he was killed. Nothing in the diary, and I've done a sweep of all the vehicle logs the VLA has anywhere at the hotel on the same dates. None owned or rented by anyone on his contacts list.'

'The widow told me they had interests in common. Try her contacts.' That was one thing the murder squad had done: followed the procedures, ticked the boxes, pulled all the contacts of relevant persons.

Harris's fingers worked, his eyes fixed on the screen as he loaded the contacts list and matched it with the list of users of vehicles in the area at the times of the meetings. One match: a vehicle that was there for all of those dates, a 1952 Rolls Royce Silver Dawn, retrofitted for electric propulsion, privately owned. The name on the VLA registration was one I was too familiar with.

'Who the hell is Elijah Cloake?' Harris asked.

There was only one Elijah in Lady Wyndham's contacts and it *was* that Elijah. A name I'd seen more than once in documents my solicitor had extracted from VirGenTech. I could have got angry, but angry hadn't got me anywhere in the three years of Alice's condition. I pushed the rage and frustration back into their box.

In my silence Harris's fingers rattled the keys and Elijah Cloake's file appeared. Former chief executive of the Genetic Therapies division at VirGenTech, but that wasn't the datum Harris jumped on. He twisted around to look at me. 'He's entangled.'

I had only one response to that. 'Let's get a drink.'

'Sure,' he said. 'And you can tell me how it went yesterday with Alice.'

*

Harris is as particular about his ale as I am about my whisky, and it was his turn to try and educate me, so he led the way from the station, down the alley past Marek's, turned right, left, left, and I was lost.

'Is it far?' It was cold, and the rain had started again.

'Ten minutes.'

Twenty minutes later down a crummy back street he pushed open a battered green door with an engraved glass panel and the noise leapt out to engulf us. The place was jammed solid. Somehow, he squeezed his way to the bar and returned minutes later with two pints of Harcourt IPA. He always manages to get served quickly no matter what. I guess it's his winning smile and boyish good looks.

We were pressed elbow to elbow in a corner, leaning against the old wood panelling beneath a ceiling so yellow it must have had a hundred years of tobacco smoke left to mature another hundred.

'Entangled, eh?' He was still talking about Cloake.

'Yeah.' The beer wasn't bad. Pale amber colour, fruity, kind of a citrus tang to it.

'What do you think?'

'About what?' All the woodwork looked original. Victorian, maybe Edwardian. Stained glass panels above the bar matched the design on the door.

'Cloake.'

'Some poor sod is going to have to interview him. But, entangled? Nightmare.'

He put on his serious look, the one that was not going to be fobbed off or distracted. 'You've got to face it, Lewis.'

'What?' I studied the cloudy beer in my glass, but I knew what he was talking about.

'How long is it since this new doctor...'

'Stebbins-Reese.'

'Since he told you Alice is entangled? Two weeks?'

'Three.'

'Three weeks. If he's right, if she is entangled, how are you going to square that with the way you feel about them?'

Trust Harris, always ready with the awkward question. It had been easy while Alice was speechless, immobile. Lost, as I thought, in the darkest recesses of her own mind. Easy to blame the entangled Cloake and VirGenTech, the company that made her that way. Easy to resent the power and influence that the successfully entangled gained through their knowledge and experience of other worlds. Three weeks ago, I'd been full of hope when, under the first experimental treatment administered by Stebbins-Reese, she had opened her eyes and spoken.

One sentence, not even a full sentence: *There are tigers…*

'He's right. She is entangled,' I said. 'She's talking more and more every time I see her. I thought it was just incoherent rambling.' I'd managed to kid myself it was just incoherent rambling but deep down, I'd known it was cerasthesia, the confusion of senses across realities. 'Yesterday she was much clearer. Lucid.'

'That sounds like real progress! What did you talk about?'

'Not me, her. She was talking to a friend she knew before, *Beets*, but there was only Alice and me in the room.' It was easy to blame the entangled, until I heard Alice's side of a conversation she was holding with someone in another reality. For a moment I'd wanted her catatonic again, and hated myself for thinking that.

He gave me a sidelong look like he knew what I was thinking, like he was waiting for me to figure it out.

'Whatever she is.' I swirled the last of my beer around the bottom of the glass. 'She's still my little sister. I have to look out for her.' I downed the last of my pint and held up the empty glass. 'My round.'

'Let's find somewhere less busy.'

It might have been the cold night air or the lurking anxiety from the incident in Marek's that morning, but once outside the thought of another long trek to another pub lost its appeal. I cried off and we said our goodnights.

Barely a minute later the car I summoned arrived to take me back to the delights of Limehouse. Cold cones of luminous drizzle hung from the lamp posts on my street. Light shone from the windows of half a dozen houses. The rest were dark, some with windows boarded or broken. More people abandoned this area every week. The Thames Barrier had over-topped too often. My flat was upstairs, above a hairdressers. The power might fail when the storm surges came, but at least my feet stayed dry, and the rent was a fraction of what I'd pay north of the flood wall.

The door lock clunked open at my approach. The steep stairs squeaked as I ascended with my mind churning around the incident in Marek's that morning. Panic attack, heart palpitations, brain tumour. I'm not a hypochondriac but the sheer weirdness of it had me on edge. I hunched down in the bathroom and rooted around in the dark recesses of the cupboard under the sink to find my scanner, still in its dog-eared box. Shirt off, left arm raised, I probed with my fingers to locate the tag buried under the skin of my armpit. The scanner read it and found no sign of problems with heart, blood or brain, and no toxicity that couldn't be ascribed to the ale. It just chided me gently about a somewhat elevated blood pressure. The generous dram I poured myself to ease my nerves wasn't going to help the b.p. Fourteen year old Linlithgow, delicately smoky, very palatable. It calmed me enough to debate with myself the relative merits of slinging a faux-chicken pie in the microwave, or popping down to Pisano's for a pizza, but Pisano had taken the relocation and moved out the week before. I was still contemplating the pie, without much enthusiasm, when the doorbell rang. Ten minutes I'd been in. She must have seen the light come on.

I hit the door release. 'Come on up, Kay.'

Kay, my landlady, ran the shop downstairs and lived across the street. Her heavy heels clumped up the squeaky stairs. I opened the door and there she stood, bright red lips, eyes shadowed in deep, dark shades of blue, geometrically precise eyebrows, cheeks a dusty pale darkened to brownish orange over the cheek bones. Every time I saw her I wondered what she was hiding beneath all the makeup.

'What happened?' There was a piercing focus in her eyes as she scrutinised my face. 'Tell me!'

My attention was drawn to the large baking tray covered in tin-foil held in her hands. One thing about Kay, she can cook. Proper, old-fashioned cooking. With ingredients. 'Nothing happened. I'm fine. Come in. Let me take that.'

She opened her mouth to speak again, but stopped and bit her lip as she handed me the tray.

I lifted the foil to reveal a lasagne, enough to feed eight. 'Thanks Kay. You really shouldn't have.'

'Leftovers.' A tiny piece from one corner had been sliced out. 'I made it yesterday.' She followed me into the kitchen.

I scooped a couple of generous portions into a dish and threw it in the microwave. 'How are you? How's business?' One time I'd seen a customer leaving the shop downstairs with hair carefully sculpted like Kay's. One time, in six months. I was out a lot during the day, on duty or at The Grange, but even so.

She stood close, looking up into my eyes with her hand on my arm. 'It's piss-poor, Lewis. Two more of my regulars moved away.'

'I keep telling you to take the relocation. I know, you've lived around here all your life, but this place is dying.'

Her mouth drooped. She was on the verge of tears.

'You are. You're taking it.'

She nodded. The lip pouted a fraction more.

I put a hand on her shoulder and squeezed. 'Good. Good. You won't regret it.'

The microwave pinged. I busied myself dishing up. 'How long?'

'I'm sorry, Lewis…'

'No, really, it's okay. I just need to find somewhere. It won't be hard.'

'Two weeks.'

I snagged us a couple of beers from the fridge and glasses from the cupboard. I'm a civilised man; I drink from a glass in company. She helped me carry the food and drinks through to the little table at the back of the lounge. She raised her glass to her lips and took a delicate sip and fixed me with those colourfully framed eyes. 'Are you going to tell me what's wrong or do I have to guess?'

'Apart from being made homeless?' I joked, raising my glass in salute. 'Really. Nothing.'

She frowned. 'I'm sensitive to these things. I know you don't believe me, but…'

She was right, I didn't. The one time she told me she was psychic I'd laughed. I still felt bad about that. She's a kind soul.

Her forefinger, nail bright and garish in glossy red and white curling lines, stabbed the air in my direction. 'You're sensitive too for all your black cynical heart, to what happens in other worlds.'

A suspicion crept up on me. 'You aren't talking about astral planes here, are you?'

'This morning I was skimming the news feeds like I always do, and my heart turned to stone, as if I'd read something terrible.'

Like the news every day. The look on her face killed the quip before it reached my tongue.

'What was it?'

She shrugged. 'It's like, I saw your name in a headline, but when I looked again there was nothing. All celebrity gossip and floods and famine. I mean, that's terrible, but…'

'I know.'

'And I know how you feel about the entangled and about the gammas and deltas and all the other drugs, but for some of us these things can leak through the walls and…' She stopped to wipe her eye, smudging the artfully applied mascara, 'I've been worried about you all day.'

Marek's Café, that morning. I relived that experience, the mounting anxiety, the terror, the blackness. I had no explanation, no rationalisation, just that deep, lurking horror. When I opened my eyes again Kay was hunched forward in her chair.

'Tell me.' Her voice was soft, but commanding, so I did. I recounted the episode in as much detail as I could recall and she listened attentively without question or interruption.

'In the moment before I blacked out,' I said at the end, 'it was like staring into the eyes of death.'

'I know someone...' Her gaze drifted to the darkness of the window.

'A friend?'

'An acquaintance.' She flipped her attention back to me. 'He told me something very like that, but he'd been taking gammas. Saw it coming—the knife, everything.' A shudder passed through her. 'Afterwards there was a whole thick strand of realities that were gone for him. He didn't live there any more.'

'Kay, I haven't been taking gammas or any other kind of implicitins. I was not and am not entangled, even temporarily.'

'These things can leak through. You're sensitive.'

'Other realities!' I heard the irritability in my own voice and took a breath to let it go. 'Even if something happened to another version of me in another world, it makes no difference to me in this one.'

'Oh, Lewis, whatever happened there, you might be in danger here, too. You have to be careful.'

'Always am.' I picked up my plate. 'Lasagne's getting cold.'

We ate the food and drank the beer, punctuated here and there by snippets of small talk. Half an hour or so later she got up to leave. I tried to press the rest of the lasagne back on her as she knew I would and she refused, as I knew she would. I was grateful, it would save me for a couple of days from bad takeaway or, worse, my own cooking.

I saw her down the stairs to the street door. The rain was gone, but it was still a murky night.

She stopped in the doorway and gave me a kiss on the cheek, lingering a second as her hand found my waist. 'When I relocate you could come with me,' she whispered, arching an eyebrow.

'You could tempt me with that lasagne.'

'The way to a man's heart...'

'Goodnight, Kay.'

She took one step then turned back to face me in the doorway. 'Be careful, Lewis.'

CHAPTER 2

Wednesday 13th November: The Raid

Entangled is a word most commonly used to denote those who have opened the door to other worlds but every living creature is a manifestation of a quantum wave function that has different values in different realities. Every conscious being is subject to a greater or lesser amount of leakage of mental state, of thought, of experiences from those other realities.

You may have lost someone close to you: friend, parent, child, even a beloved pet. In your own home (this usually happens in a familiar environment), while absently engaged in some mundane task, you catch a glimpse from the corner of your eye of the one you have lost. Is it grief, expectation, imagination, or did you perceive a fragment of another world where the tragedy did not occur?

An unfamiliar place, face, or conversation evokes a feeling of déjà vu. Perhaps it is a memory of an experience that has seeped through the walls from another reality.

Someone you meet for the first time evokes an instant and powerful emotional response: distrust, aversion or love at first sight. They may be someone that another version of you knows well.

Entanglement is not a fundamental change in the nature of consciousness, it is a question of degree. For everyone the door to other realities stands ajar and moments of high emotion can leak through like raised voices in another room. The entangled have thrown that door wide open. They live, not in a single room with an ear pressed to a door, but wandering freely through an immense mansion.

—A K Amari - *The Measurement Problem, A Guide to Entanglement*

Wednesday morning, my doormat at the foot of the stairs held yet another letter from the FMC, the Flood Management Commission, addressed to *The Occupier*, no doubt extolling the virtues of the various schemes to encourage people to sell up and vacate the area. Whatever they offered, I'd be left paying more rent than I could afford on the other side of the wall.

Outside, the clear sky was brightening, the street lamp on the corner flickered and went off, and there was no car waiting for me. I turned up my coat collar against the gentle, chill breeze that blew from the east, and listened to the twittering of unseen birds. The peace was broken by a door slamming shut four houses down on the other side of the road. Earl, I didn't know his last name, shuffled along the pavement bundled up in coat, hat, scarf and gloves. He raised his stick in quiet acknowledgement when I waved to him. Two kilometres to the nearest corner shop that was still open but he made that walk every morning, whatever the weather. Earl would never leave this place, no matter the incentives, no matter how high the tide rose. He'd never leave until they carried him out. Most of the remaining residents were like that.

Earl was a doddering dot in the distance when, at last, a car pulled up to the kerb. I say a car, it was a single-seat, two-wheeled pod, but during the morning peak you can't afford to be fussy. I squeezed in and tried to read my messages while it weaved and wobbled its way through the streets. There was another bill from The Grange. I didn't have enough to cover it and my credit was maxed out, but I reasoned they wouldn't kick Alice out before payday. Next month's bill would be something to worry about next month.

Vittoria's solicitor had sent a formal acknowledgement of my snarky message from the day before, and another message re-iterating the same claims. No doubt it was billing her for each message sent. I was so busy stewing over that one that I didn't notice that the pod had stopped in a queue at the Shadwell gate. It edged forward a few paces at a time towards the old Victorian brick arches that carried the raised railway. Nearly all the arches and other openings beneath the railway had been permanently blocked up to form part of the flood wall. Those that remained had strong steel sliding gates to keep out the water. With so few openings, the traffic often backed up during rush hour, which is why I always allowed an extra twenty minutes for the trip to the station, and more often than not I would arrive twenty minutes early and head to Marek's to catch up on mail and news over coffee. But today I wouldn't arrive early, for which I was somewhat relieved. After the previous day's episode I wanted to give Marek's a miss for a while.

Like the day before, I found Harris peering out of the window when I pushed through the office door.

'Looks like the show DCI Baxter was talking about,' he said.

In the yard below three APCs, Armoured Personnel Carriers, were disgorging their squads of AROs, Armed Response Officers, in full Kevlar body armour.

A familiar voice called out. 'Drake! Harris! My office! Now.'

The usual routine. We sat, she leaned back and steepled her fingers. 'I saw your report, Harris, linking Wyndham with this Elijah Cloake. Good work. What do we know about him?'

'We'll do the full background checks today, ma'am,' I said, 'but we know he's entangled.'

She fixed me with a silent stare and spoke without looking away. 'Harris, I need a word with Drake in private. Meet us in the briefing room in ten minutes.'

She waited until he had closed the door behind him before speaking again.

'DI Drake. We're all aware of your personal circumstances, but in these last years it has affected your previously excellent record. Twice now you've been passed over for promotion. If you had been able to carry on as you once did, it would be you sitting here now instead of me.'

Personal circumstances. Alice's condition, the divorce from Vittoria. Through all that I'd done my job, done everything asked of me. Competently enough, but no more than that. Baxter left a pause long enough to invite an argument or an excuse. I didn't give her either.

'This Wyndham case is high profile. I took a chance giving it to you. I need to know you have the commitment to see it through. More than that, I need to know that you can be objective.'

Commitment was simply a matter of juggling priorities. The veiled threat was enough to make this case my highest. I couldn't afford to lose the stipend.

'Objective, ma'am?'

'Now we find the investigation touches on one of the Entangled, this Elijah Cloake. I am concerned that you may harbour some prejudice against him that might impair your judgement.'

I had much more against Elijah Cloake than his being entangled, but I wasn't going to raise that if Baxter wasn't. 'I don't think the entangled should get any special treatment. Deal with them like anyone else, according to what they've done in our world.'

'Straight from the manual, Drake. But how do you feel about them?'

Her eyes were focussed on me like laser beams. When she got like that there was no hiding anything from her. She didn't need Argus and its high-tech monitors from the interview rooms to see right through you. 'I don't like them. They look down on the rest of us, consider themselves superior. Like the rule of law doesn't apply to them. But how I feel will not interfere with my judgement or my objectivity.'

Her head nodded three times. Slow, careful movements, but her eyes stayed fixed on me. 'Perhaps more accurate to say that they consider the penalties of law a minor inconvenience, a small price to pay for whatever they might want to do.'

We were saying the same thing but Baxter always liked to have the last word. 'I'll get the team onto a full profile of Cloake: Finances, contacts, movements. See if we can tie him into Red Claw. We also need to interview the Wyndham children and track down the stepson.'

'Wyndham was trying to keep his meetings with Cloake quiet, but Cloake is Entangled. If he *was* behind the killing he would have covered his tracks better. He will expect us to find out about the meetings. Go and have an informal chat with him. Let Harris deal with the children.'

She stood, I stood.

'But not now. Briefing room.'

*

All eight of us in the department were there with the three squads of AROs we'd seen arriving in the yard. Baxter's briefing was brief but thorough, though she didn't bother to enumerate the days and hours Harris and Marlowe had spent steering rats around the dark, damp voids under Canary Wharf and Jubilee Place. She described it as an intelligence-led operation against a Red Claw arms and drugs store in the derelict shopping centre. Marlowe, who had been monitoring the rats on the night shift, confirmed the goods hadn't been removed and said that four suspects had entered the premises and not been seen to leave. There were three entrances to the complex. A squad of AROs would storm the location from each one. Once the scene was secure the rest of us would enter to process any Red Claw survivors.

We went straight from the briefing to the APCs. Harris and I squeezed in the back of one with Sergeant Elphick's squad. Elphick: two metres tall with a face carved from granite, the only ARO I knew who looked more intimidating without his helmet. Unease rumbled within me. If Vittoria would only agree the divorce settlement then I'd know Alice would be looked after whatever happened. Not that I really expected anything to happen. Still, that thing at Marek's had left me on edge. And Kay's prognostications of doom still bubbled beneath the surface.

My nerves were not eased by the lurching of the APC as it sped through the streets and around the roundabouts, but once it screeched to a stop the adrenalin kicked in. Elphick and his AROs leapt out first, helmeted and visored, assault rifles at the ready. By the time Harris and I stepped down onto the bleak desolation of Bank Street, they were already disappearing through the arched entrance of the old Canary Wharf tube station.

The sun shone, but the cold wind funnelled around the monstrous old office blocks with the howl of lost hell-hounds. I shivered in my flak jacket and hunched against the side of the APC. Acres of cracked concrete and dirty glass, miles of grimy chrome and dusty marble surrounded us, the forsaken architecture of a power now vested in a handful of plutocrats and their software servants.

'South entrance secure.' A calm whisper in my headset.

'Station secure.' That was Elphick.

'Parking level secure.'

And that was our queue. In theory we had Jubilee Place bottled up. Harris and I dived into the station entrance and down the long staircase next to the grimy corroded escalators that hadn't moved for years. Our footfalls echoed between the concrete walls of the cavernous ticket hall as we descended deep into the darkness and stink, deep below the original ground level, until our feet splashed into the slimy detritus brought in by the last spring tide, slippery and freezing cold—I should have worn my boots. A train rumbled through the tunnel deep beneath us. They'd closed the station and sealed off the platforms years ago but the Jubilee line still ran down below.

In the dim light that leaked through the filthy glass roof the squad clustered by the exit to Jubilee Place on the south side of the ticket hall. Two covered from the doorway while the first four ran up the staircase to the shopping level, rifles at the ready. The other squads would be doing the same, tightening the noose.

Gunfire. Two rapid bursts were followed by the loud clattering of the AROs' assault rifles. The sound echoed and re-echoed around the ticket hall.

'Drake, hold your position. Elphick, secure the area.' Baxter's voice crackled in my earpiece. Elphick signalled the other ARO with a finger pointing up the stairs. Their boots stamped up the steps to the shopping level, leaving me and Harris waiting in the cold, dark ticket hall.

Harris's eyes were on his phone screen. 'This isn't right.'

'What isn't?'

'The live feeds from the rats aren't showing the AROs. They've been hacked.' He turned to show me, his feet splashing the wet muck. A wave of ice cold slipped over the top of my shoe onto my already frozen feet. I really should have worn my boots.

'Thanks, Harris,' I mumbled, my voice loud in the echoing void.

'Did you hear that?' He turned again, more gently this time.

Somewhere nearby a drop of water splashed, then a flurry of them. A soft creak like an old, stiff hinge. I took out my Glock, slipped the magazine, checked it, re-inserted it.

'I'll take that,' someone whispered behind me and I felt cold metal pressing the back of my neck. My headset was pulled none too gently from my head. A sound of something hard hitting something only a little less hard answered my next question. Harris fell to the slimy floor with a splash.

I was frogmarched slipping and stumbling to the opposite side of the ticket hall. My captors, two of them, led me by torchlight up the stairs into the near-total darkness of the Canary Wharf shopping complex. Dark passageways lined with empty kiosks, the smashed plate glass of shop fronts, concrete pillars, shorn of their marble cladding, cracked and stained rust-red where the water had penetrated to their steel cores. The floor here was dry now. The tides rose high enough to flood this level only once or twice a year, so far.

After ten minutes of stumbling through the rubble and debris, lit by the torches and by the pools of murky daylight from encrusted skylights, we ascended the cracked concrete stairs into the ground floor lobby of one of the skyscrapers. Most of the glass was intact, and what wasn't had been covered over with poly, so inside was calm, quiet and chilled as an overspill morgue. The whole ground floor was an open space three storeys high, lined with glass and marble that had lost its shine under years of crud. Four great lift banks occupied the centre, protected by broken security barriers. A desolate reception desk, a few broken chairs and a sparse scattering of torn paper and rotting cardboard were the only other features. The lights were working, and so were the lifts.

One of my abductors stayed in the lobby while the other encouraged me at gunpoint into a lift. He pushed the button for forty-eight. My first chance for a good look at him. One metre ninety, solidly built, late twenties or early thirties, short wavy dark hair, clean-shaven. The shade of his skin suggested time spent in the sun, or perhaps some Mediterranean ancestry. Jeans, sweatshirt, light jacket. Solid, but ordinary, I wouldn't have looked twice passing him in the street. The face was not one I recognised from the Red Claw files.

'What's this about?' I asked him, one eye on my gun in his hand. He held it easily, like he was used to it.

He didn't answer. The lift announced 'forty-eight, doors opening,' in that irritatingly calm voice that all old lifts shared. The doors opened and his spare hand gestured for me to exit. I did so, quickly pacing to the end of the bank. I slowed at the corner, listening for the sound of his footsteps behind me. I turned and reached to push aside his arm, but he was already stepping back. My momentum carried me forward as he moved aside. A foot against my ankle, an arm against my back, and I was down like a felled tree. He stepped back again before I could swing my legs to knock him down.

It could have gone worse. He made me look like an idiot, an amateur, but he didn't shoot me. He didn't even look that perturbed.

'Through there, please.' He pointed to the glass door at the end of the lobby.

I climbed to my feet with such dignity as I could salvage and went as directed into a corridor lined on one side with glass-walled offices and meeting rooms. Tinted glass with glass partitions and windows beyond; my eyes were disturbed by the broad, curving bands of moiré patterns that rolled and moved as I walked. At a closer look the glass wasn't tinted; embedded within it was a fine mesh of hair-thin wires. The moiré patterns came as I moved past, looking through two panes.

The glass door at the end of the corridor led onto a larger space. To my right was a plain door marked with an emergency exit sign and a large label: *Stair 3*. The room was empty but for a chair, a low table and a small black holdall beside it. Rows of hinged metal covers crossed the floor. One near my feet was half off, revealing power sockets and data ports of a style dating back to the forties when these buildings had finally been abandoned. The windows looked out to the north, to clear blue sky darkened by the mesh in the window. The flood wall stretched from the Tower of London in the west, following the raised railway line to disappear into the haze to the northeast.

Only the short fat man with receding hair, pin-striped trousers and mismatched waistcoat obscured the view. Him I did recognise from the files: Bennie Thacker, Big Bennie. Whenever his name cropped up it had been bad news for someone, most notably at the Leven Road massacre. Sadly, witnesses had a tendency to disappear or turn up dead.

'Drake.' He pointed to the chair. 'Sit.'

My minder guided me, now with extreme firmness, to where Big Bennie pointed. There seemed little option but to acquiesce with good grace. I regretted that decision when the zip-tie pulled tight around my wrists and the back support of the chair. Deft, proficient, the way that was done. I pushed my legs down on the floor to confirm a suspicion and yes, the chair was bolted down.

'Marek's Café, yesterday morning. What were you doing there?'

'Drinking coffee.'

'You were there to meet someone.'

'No. I was there to drink coffee. It's where I go if I'm early for my shift.'

'You were early because you'd arranged to meet her there.'

'Meet who?'

'Where is she, Drake?'

Either I was missing something, or Big Bennie was misinformed about something. 'I'm Organised Crime. Sounds like you want Missing Persons.'

I saw the fist coming and tried to roll my head away as it struck. He didn't look a tough guy, but there was some weight behind the punch. I counted my teeth with my tongue.

'There are two ways we can do this, Drake. We can help you, we can help you a great deal.' He turned away, walked to the window, and stood with hands clasped behind his back. 'The Grange. It's a good place, good people, competent, caring.' He faced me again. 'Expensive.'

That got my attention. That Red Claw in the person of Big Bennie Thacker knew about Alice and about The Grange was a new thing to worry about. 'I'm listening,' I said, stalling for time. At some point the squad would wonder where I was and start looking, but Canary Wharf was a big place to search.

He took a step closer to me. 'Where. Is. Erica?'

It was like a stage play where I had a leading part, but no-one had bothered to show me the script. I wracked my brain to try and remember if I knew anyone called Erica and came up blank but for a lurking disquiet that maybe I should know, and maybe I wouldn't want to say. 'Perhaps she doesn't want to be found.'

He took another couple of steps and crouched down, eyes level with mine. 'Drake, I know you want to protect her, but it's okay, all we want is to talk to her.'

'How do I know that?' *Keep stalling, they'll be looking for me.*

He smiled with wide, thin lips, then turned and lifted the holdall onto the table. Metal clanked against metal as he rummaged. If he was going to seriously hurt me, he'd start by taking out my tag before it could transmit an alert. My left armpit itched while I waited for him to bring out a knife and start looking for it.

Moiré patterns—micromesh in the windows, data ports in the floor. Data would have flowed here; sensitive data at a time when encryption and security protocols were being broken and rewritten daily. This place was screened, electronically isolated. Impervious to radio signals such as a tag in an injured officer's armpit might transmit.

It wasn't a knife he drew from the holdall. The blackjack slapped lightly in the palm of his hand as he approached me. The blow landed hard on my right thigh. I saw it, heard it, then the pain roared.

It was a good thing I couldn't tell him what he wanted to know. Standing up to pain was never a strong point and he had plenty of time to work on me. The deserted towers of Canary Wharf had millions of square metres of offices, shops, apartments, and then there was the maze of housing in the rest of the Isle of Dogs. All Red Claw territory. Without a locator signal from the tag, Baxter and the squad would never find me.

Big Bennie ambled back to the table. His hand rummaged in the bag and pulled out a blowtorch, an antique. Maybe it wasn't such a good thing I couldn't tell him what he wanted to know.

'They're in the lobby,' the minder said behind me. 'We need to leave.'

'When I want your advice, I'll ask for it.' Bennie held the torch up and turned a knob. A click, and it lit with a pop. 'What Vidmar wants to know, we must find out.'

The flame burned blue with flickers of yellow, its subdued roar grew louder, the blue jet brighter, as its bearer stepped towards me.

'You're wasting time. He doesn't know.'

I craned my neck round again. The minder had a gun in his hand. A Glock. My Glock. It fired. Big Bennie fell to the ground and lay staring at me, a neat hole in his forehead. Wisps of dark smoke and a stink of burning plastic rose from the ancient carpet tile where the still-flaming blowtorch had fallen.

'You need to be careful, DCI Drake,' my minder said as he crouched to place my gun on the floor. 'You could end up dead here, too.' He walked briskly to the door—stair three. His feet on the concrete steps reverberated from the stairwell.

'DI drake,' I said to the door, closing on its springs. 'I haven't made Chief Inspector yet.'

They're in the lobby, he'd said. There was no way he could know that, no CCTV, and this place was screened. I could be here a long time with a dead torturer and the noxious fumes from the burning carpet.

In the deep bowels of the tower a lift whirred into life. My face was sore from the punch, my thigh ached from the blow of the blackjack and my fingers were numb from the zip-tie tight around my wrists, but so long as that rising lift was bringing good news, I could count myself lucky. Beneath the jet of the blowtorch flame the last vestiges of plastic carpet tile bubbled away to expose the blackened concrete bones of the building.

A muffled sound of lift doors opening was followed by the rhythmic pounding of heavy boots, then the crash of the lobby door. Four ARO's fanned out to cover the room. Harris followed. His eyes took in the body lying in front of me, the Glock on the floor a way to my left. He raised a questioning eyebrow.

'The other one's gone,' I said.

Harris reached into his pocket, walked around behind me, and I heard the *snick* of the blade of his lock knife. The slightest tug as the tie parted and my hands were free.

'He won't get away,' Baxter said from the doorway. 'We have the exits covered. Which way did he go?'

'Stair three.' I pointed. I'd heard his feet pounding the concrete before that door had closed but there was something about the cadence… 'He was going up.'

It's a rare thing to see DCI Baxter looking nonplussed. At a shout from one of the AROs I turned and caught the last flicker of movement of something falling past the window. Some*one* falling past. I hobbled over in time to see the graceful unfurling of a rectangular parachute canopy below.

'Take him out!' Baxter shouted. A rifle butt smashed against a window with an impotent thump. Another of the squad stepped back, raised his weapon and fired. I couldn't quite see whether it was a small dimple that appeared in the glass where the bullet struck, or just a leaden smudge. This floor had been secured against more than electronic interference; to withstand a close range shot from an assault rifle, that glass was seriously tough.

Our quarry's parachute tipped and twitched as a swirl of wind caught it, then banked and slid from sight around the corner of one of the dilapidated skyscrapers. When I turned around a forensics bot was lifting the still-burning blowtorch from the floor. Its mechanical fingers turned the knob and the flame was extinguished. The bot trundled away, leaving me looking at the chair bolted to the floor.

I have never been burdened by an overactive imagination, but that day, with the chair before me, I had the most vivid image of Big Bennie crouching in front of me, unzipping my flak jacket and holding the torch up to my chest. The cotton of my shirt burned through in a second, and I heard my own screams as the skin burned and the flesh beneath cooked.

'You alright, Lewis?' Harris stepped in front of me, his hand on my arm. I wiped the cold sweat from my face and nodded dumbly.

I had to wait for forensics to check me for residue before I could get out of there. I guess they had to verify that I hadn't fired my own gun from five metres away from the chair where I was tied. Or that I didn't shoot Big Bennie and then run over and strap myself to the chair. I don't know. They bagged my Glock and took my phone from me, too. No big deal, standard procedure.

I hobbled to the lift, working the pain from my leg, fleeing the silent sound of my imagined screams. Baxter held the door for me, and punched for the ground floor.

'How did you find me, ma'am?'

Baxter smiled, a scary sight. 'We followed the muddy footprints all the way to this building.'

'How'd you know which floor?'

'You'll see.'

A minute later the lift slowed to a stop, the doors opened and I stepped out. It was one of six lifts in that bank, each with an old-school digital display above the doors. Five of them said *G*, the sixth said *48*. Anyone would think they'd wanted me to be found.

*

In the back of the APC heading back to the station I tried to count all the things that didn't make sense. I ran out of fingers. One thing stuck in my mind:

You could end up dead here, too.

Was that, someone else is dead here? Or, I'm dead somewhere else? This many-worlds thing was messing with my head.

They took me straight to the interview room. Big Bennie Thacker was no great loss to society but a death meant there were procedures to follow, questions to be asked. I was there for hours with Baxter and some independent uniformed Chief Inspector I'd never met before drafted in from downstairs. Over and over, I recounted all I could remember for the recorder. I knew the drill; stick to the facts, answer the questions, keep clear of speculation and supposition that might confuse or mislead Argus as it watched my expressions, my posture, and listened to my voice looking for any hint of untruth.

After we left the interview room with its cameras and microphones Baxter seemed satisfied. Argus must have approved my answers. Baxter handed me back my phone and walked with me as I limped towards the canteen, in need of a cup of coffee. I switched the phone back on as I hobbled.

'So what do you think that was about, Drake?'

There are times for bullshit, and there are times to say what you think. I tend to err towards the latter anyway. That doesn't always work out well.

'One,' I counted off with my thumb. 'I was set up, so they were waiting for me, knew exactly where I would be.'

She nodded for me to continue.

'Two, the minder. Did he leave a trail deliberately? Footprints, the lift. If so, why?'

'I think he did,' she said. 'It was too easy.' A troubled look nestled on her face.

'Three, how did he know when you'd reached the lobby? No CCTV, and the place was screened.'

'He would know if he was Entangled. If in some slice of reality he had stayed in the lobby and sent the other perpetrator up with you, he would have seen us arrive.'

And if he had been in the lobby, he wouldn't have been on the forty-eighth floor to stop Big Bennie having fun with the blowtorch. My hand went up to touch the swelling on my cheek. I had to focus on the case to keep my scrawny imagination in check. I paused by the canteen door. 'So what was his agenda? I mean, I'm not sorry to see the end of Big Bennie Thacker but I'm curious to know why.'

My phone warbled, the tone reserved for emergencies. 'Excuse me, ma'am.' There were a string of voice messages from Cecilia Watts at The Grange. Baxter entered the canteen with me as I listened, and she went to get the coffees as I sat. Alice had been distressed, really distressed, hysterical, and calling my name. Cecilia picked up right away when I called back.

'Hi, Lewis, we've been trying to reach you.'

'Yeah, I got the messages. How is she?'

'Asleep. Mid-afternoon she calmed down. Another visitor we think. She was talking to someone anyway. We could only hear her side of the conversation.'

I took her meaning. Whoever she was talking to wasn't present in our world.

'What did she say?'

There was a long silence before Cecilia spoke again. 'Can you come tomorrow, Lewis? She needs to see you.'

Baxter put two coffees on the table and sat.

'I'll be there as soon as I can.'

'Alice?' Baxter said as I put the phone back in my pocket. I nodded.

'Take the day tomorrow. We can pick up on Friday.'

'Thank you, ma'am.' I took a big slug of bad coffee. 'What happened at Jubilee Place? I heard gunfire.'

'Booby trap. No-one hurt. I think it was intended to keep the armed response unit busy while they grabbed you.'

'Did you find anything there?'

'Abandoned days or weeks ago. We picked up a few bits of kit they left behind. Nothing of any note.'

The formalities, the paperwork, dragged on. I watched the time creep past my nominal end of shift. Last thing was a trip to the armoury for a replacement firearm. My own was evidence but the powers that be get nervous about us wandering around unarmed.

It was late when I got home. A dark moonless night, starlit and frosty. I waved at Kay's twitching curtain as I opened my door. Reheated lasagne, a small glass of the Linlithgow—I needed to eke it out—then bed, and dreams of crumbling tower blocks screaming their agony as blue flames flecked with yellow seared the flesh from their bones.

CHAPTER 3

Thursday 14th November: The Grange

Twenty years ago the plague wars ended with no clear victor. They petered out as the relentless pressure to develop new technologies finally bore fruit. Full spectrum monitoring to identify new infectious agents of every patient at every clinic and hospital combined with the techniques to create custom vaccines, anti-virals, and antibiotics in days or even hours have consigned the spectre of infectious disease—natural or artificial—to history.

One infectious agent, a particularly nasty cytomegalovirus, CM-2057-phi-kappa, attacked the brains of those it infected, leaving those few adults who survived it in a persistent vegetative state, but children under the age of around twelve were unharmed other than a complete loss of memory. Post-war, researchers seeking to help the survivors discovered that the virus severed the link between the macroscopic transmission of nerve impulses and the quantum variations in certain nano-tubules. In the children that link was re-

established as they recovered from the infection. Pyotr Szylinski was the first to make the connection with the Everett many-worlds interpretation of quantum theory, recognising that human consciousness has always been shared across a thin, almost identical set of alternate realities and that the disease, by suppressing that sharing, destroyed the minds of its victims. That understanding led to the development of a family of drugs with the reverse effect, called implicitins. *In some realities, the pharmacorps that developed them were reckless in their early use, encouraging executives and researchers into their entanglement programmes, for how can you compete against a scientist who can conduct every variation on an experiment simultaneously, or a manager who can test the real-world outcome of every decision? Many of those who took them were unable to cope and are still paying the price. Nowadays, the process is gentler, more measured. We edge the door open a little at a time, ready to close it again at the first sign of distress.*

—A K Amari - *The Measurement Problem, A Guide to Entanglement*

Thursday morning, seven-thirty am. A red swelling on the cheekbone greeted me in the bathroom mirror. My face hurt when I washed, when I shaved, when I brushed my teeth, and when I ate the toasted stale bread that was my breakfast. By eight I was out of the door waiting for my car.

A young woman strode past, smartly dressed in a dark trouser suit and low-heeled shoes. She fumbled with the leather bag on her shoulder, looking for something.

Recognition arrived as she walked away. 'Samantha?' A year or more since I'd last seen her.

'Oh! Hi, Lewis.' She gave me a smile, stopping by the door of the rental agency next door. The one where she used to work before it closed down over a year ago. She turned to the door again and a look of puzzlement crossed her face. She raised a hand to press on the plywood that covered the door. A step back and her gaze ranged over the whole front of the building: the boards over the windows, the bare panel with screw holes where the company name was formerly secured.

'No!' she murmured. 'No, no, no.'

My own thoughts echoed her words: No, not Samantha. She was always so bright and cheerful, always ready to chat, interested in everybody's lives. She was going to need help now, but I had to get to Cambridge and my car would be here any moment.

'Did the barrage fail?' she said as I stepped over to her.

'The barrage?'

Her fingertips brushed the plywood once more. 'No. This is old. They never built it.' She turned slowly around, taking in the street as if for the first time, the signs of neglect and decay. 'This whole area's being abandoned.'

'What did you take, Samantha? How long ago?' Alphas, betas, gammas, deltas—which one, how long ago, how often, would determine whether this entanglement was permanent or would wear off.

'It's okay Lewis.' The smile she gave me this time was brittle. 'Big mistake. I'll go home until it wears off.'

'Where do you live?'

She opened her mouth to speak, closed it again, shook her head. 'Different places.'

A car turned the corner and rolled quietly along the street towards us, braking sharply when Kay's heavy heels clomped across the tarmac in front of it.

'Sam, are you alright, sweetie?' Kay took her arm.

The car pulled up at the kerb and the door popped open for me.

'Go, Lewis. I'll see she's okay.' Kay took Samantha's arm. 'You'll be fine, Sam. You're just confused for now. Come and have a coffee.'

I watched them across the street, one more thing to be thankful to Kay for. The car gave me an impatient beep. I got in, barely looking, and sank into the broad, comfortable seat. I had to agree with Kay's assessment: Samantha would be alright. She was confused about which reality she was in, about what had happened in the past, but she was coherent in the moment and not panicked or distraught. Even if she'd overdone it and become permanently entangled she might learn to adapt. I'd seen far worse on the streets and in the homeless shelters. I hated to see what implicitins did to those who couldn't handle them. I hated the kind of people that those who could handle them turned into: arrogant, secretive, manipulative.

The best hope for Alice was that she would become one of them. The knot in my stomach was the fear that she wouldn't.

The car rolled under light cloud lit red by the impending sunrise. A smooth motion, very smooth. The badge on the console was the ringed "M", an old Maxwell. The fabric of the seats was frayed and faded, but in its day it was the height of comfort with ample room to stretch out my sore leg. By the time it reached the M11 I'd calmed enough to start again on Amari's book. I needed every angle I could get, any insight to help me understand Alice's condition. Three weeks since Dr Stebbins-Reese had told me she was entangled, that rather than being catatonic she was in what he called *the Omega state*.

I thought I knew a lot about entanglement and implicitins from the service training. I knew about Hugh Everett's many worlds interpretation, saying that the world we see is one of a huge number of alternatives, and about Roger Penrose and how consciousness itself is built on the quantum world. I'd heard how Szylinski had developed the first implicitin drugs, taking Everett's theory from abstract speculation to incontrovertible reality. The training covered all of that at a basic level, but the bulk of it was about the different formulations of implicitins and their often devastating effects on users.

I came to a paragraph that said Szylinski's work in developing implicitins came out of research into CM-2057-phi-kappa, the virus that had robbed me and Alice of our childhood memories and left us wandering lost and nameless on Drake street. I had to read that three times before it would sink in. Then I had to stop and calm my ire when I got to the passage about the recklessness of the pharmacorps in the early days a decade before, as if that were history, as if it didn't still happen. It was going to be a tough read.

*

The Grange is an old manor house outside of Cambridge. You would pass by the tall wrought-iron gates never knowing what lay hidden at the end of the driveway. At eight-forty five the Maxwell turned in through those open gates, I'd have some time with Alice before Dr Stebbins-Reese arrived for her next treatment. I closed the car door and took a deep breath before marching in and up to the reception desk.

Cecilia was on duty. Cecilia of the crooked half-smile and the kind green eyes. She raised her hand half-way to my cheek before drawing it back. 'That looks nasty, Lewis.'

'It's nothing,' I mumbled. Some things you don't want to be reminded of. Big Bennie Thacker on the floor with a hole in his head, the burning blowtorch.

She booked me in, brows knitted, lips narrowed in her look of sympathetic concern. 'I'm so sorry to have bothered you, Lewis, but she was very upset.'

'Was? Is she okay now?'

'Dr Stebbins-Reese cut the medication yesterday so she's drifted back into the Omega state.' She led me along the corridor. 'She's calm, but, well, you know what to expect.'

I knew what to expect. It was all I'd seen of Alice until Stebbins-Reese started with his treatment. 'Do you know what triggered it?'

She stopped outside Alice's door and laid her delicate fingers on my forearm. 'Lewis, she thought you'd been killed. It might have happened in some other reality.' Her eyes searched mine, but I didn't know how to react. File it away, digest it later. So that cleared up what the Canary Wharf base jumper had meant by *You could end up dead here, too*. Another hint that, as Baxter had suggested, he was entangled. I gave her a small nod. She tapped lightly on Alice's door and pushed it open. Her eyes met mine again for a moment before she headed back to the reception desk.

Dim and dark, the morning light leaked from the edges of the curtains, picking out the shadowed shapes: the bed with the framed pastoral print on the wall above, the two tub chairs and small table squashed in one corner. It took a moment for my eyes to adapt.

Alice was sitting in one of the seats in the corner, her right arm crooked across her chest, the hand resting on the left shoulder. I knelt to kiss her cheek, took her left hand and squeezed the finger, careful not to disturb the cannula. She looked up, a startled expression on her face. Her wide blank eyes stared through me. Her head turned slowly back to look straight ahead.

'I heard you were worried about me,' I said, still holding her hand. A dark fuzz covered her head, a couple of days since they'd last shaved it. 'It's alright, Alice, I'm right here. Nothing to worry about.'

Her fingers twitched beneath mine. Maybe it was a reaction to my words, maybe coincidence, maybe I imagined it.

The way she was sitting with her right arm crossed and resting on her shoulder, I squinted my eyes and in the dim light I could imagine I saw the figure standing behind her with a hand on her shoulder, Alice's own hand clutching it, caressing the fingers.

She wasn't alone. Someone was here. Here, but not here. Here in another reality. My eyes searched that empty space behind her. Her friend Beets I guessed. Alice had talked about her in the weeks before it happened, her new best friend she'd met at work. I'd never got the chance to meet her myself. I guess in this world she'd moved on since then. Hard to maintain a relationship with someone who's been catatonic for three years.

There were those moments of near lucidity when I'd been here on Monday, when she was talking to Beets. In some reality she was there for her. Whoever she was, I was profoundly grateful for her support. She was, as far as I could tell, the only other person in any world who cared about Alice.

There was Cecilia. Her kindness was more than just professional.

I levered myself back to my feet and sat in the other chair and talked. I talked about anything and everything and nothing, filling the empty space between us; what I'd done, heard, seen, felt. Alice sat still as a meditating

Buddha with her lips curved in that all-knowing soft smile. I knew now that on some level she heard my words, perhaps on some level she spoke them. To be so connected, yet so disconnected, was the cruellest irony.

When I ran out of things to say I picked up the tattered hardback volume bound in green cloth. Our one link with our unknowable childhood, the copy of *Alice in Wonderland* that had been in my backpack when we were found wandering aimless along Drake Street with no memory of who we were or where we'd come from.

A few pages in, a tap at the door interrupted my reading. Dr Stebbins-Reese's portly personage followed the knock into the room. I turned back to see Alice's eyes fixed on my own.

'Hello, doctor,' I said without releasing Alice's gaze.

'Good morning, Lewis. I'm glad you're here, I hope your presence will calm Alice as we ease her out of Omega. Just some quick checks, first.'

He turned up the light enough to see what he was doing and busied himself checking her pulse and blood pressure while I quivered under Alice's relentless attention. I'd never seen her do this. She was *here*, more than I had ever seen without Stebbins-Reese's experimental treatment.

'Alice?' I reached across the table to touch her knee. Her only reaction was a slow blink.

'Blood pressure slightly raised, pulse eighty. A little high. Come Alice.' Stebbins-Reese held her arm at elbow and shoulder. She rose at the suggestion of movement and allowed herself to be guided to the bed. Like a motorised mannequin she responded to the gentle pressure to sit, turn, lie back on the bed. I lifted her head for him to slip on the skullcap with its fine mesh of sensors and wires.

Sitting by her bedside, I took her hand again while Stebbins-Reese hooked up the monitor.

Her head turned towards me on the pillow. *Lewis*, she mouthed silently.

'Hmm, interesting.' Stebbins-Reese glanced at her face and turned back to the monitor. 'She seems to have a degree of focus even though she's still deep in the Omega State.'

He hummed quietly to himself as he inserted the piston cassette into the infusion pump and hooked it up to the cannula on the back of Alice's left hand, then clipped a monitor onto her index finger. The display on the bedside table lit up. Eighty-four, her pulse. His fingers danced on the pump's controls, setting the flow rate. 'I'll stop the treatment if she starts getting agitated.'

Slowly, Alice's lips formed the shape of the word.

Stebbins-Reese hadn't seen. 'She wants you to bring her out slowly, doctor. Can you turn the flow-rate down?'

'Hmm? Oh, I don't think…' He hesitated. 'Yes, perhaps. She knows better than we do.' His hand reached to the panel and tapped again. 'Ready?' He hit the green button without waiting for an answer.

A minute, two. She stared at me, then I saw her eyes begin to glaze. The heart-rate monitor had dropped to seventy-two.

Stebbins-Reese reached towards the pump controls.

'Give her a little longer,' I said.

Her eyes closed, squeezed tight shut, she took in a deep shuddering breath through gritted teeth. 'Lewisssss,' she hissed. The green numerals on the monitor turned orange. Ninety-four

'Alice, tell me what upset you.'

Her eyes opened wide. 'No time. Losing the sight. You. Beets. At Marek's. It was him.'

'What? Who?'

'Too many names, too many faces. Which one is this one? I can't tell which world this is.'

Her hand gripped mine and squeezed hard. The monitor flashed red. One hundred and seventeen.

'I don't understand, Alice. What happened?'

'He killed you.'

'Who?'

The monitor emitted a shrill tone: one hundred and thirty-two. Her hand jerked across her body and slapped onto the back of the hand that held mine. She ripped the tube from the cannula.

'Lewis, the light is so bright, and the noise. I see through your eyes but you're hollow. It's you, but you're not there.' She flopped back onto the bed. 'I don't know who he is. It's gone, Lewis.' Her breathing was short and ragged.

Stebbins-Reese, flustered, muttered, 'No! No! No!' He closed the cannula, fiddled with the pump, checked the tube and finally turned to the monitor. 'She's out of Omega.'

I only glanced at him before turning back to Alice. 'What did you mean, too many names, too many faces?'

She shivered. She took a deep breath. 'I don't remember. I'm cut off from all that now.' Her eyes creased. She bit her lip. 'It's gone. Is it important?'

'Not right now. How do you feel?'

'Glad to see you safe and well. Did something happen to you?'

'Not in this world.'

'What about Beets? Is she alright?'

'I don't know. I've never met Beets.'

'Don't joke about that. Of course you have.'

Stebbins-Reese attached the monitor again. 'Now Alice, let me have a look at the cannula, see if I can connect you up again.'

'Please doctor, not now. I need to go back.'

Stebbins-Reese reached for the detached tube. 'Forgive me, but you seem quite at ease. I see no reason we shouldn't continue.'

'It won't help you get what you want, Doctor. You're breaking me up, blocking me in every world at the same time. Now my alternates can't see Lewis, I feel their distress, I have to join them.' She lay back on the pillow and closed her eyes. 'It will take a little while. Talk to me, Lewis.'

So I did. All the years I'd been coming here, talking to her, reading to her, knowing she couldn't hear a word of it, I'd carried on because it helped me to cope. How wrong I was: *I can't tell which world this is*, she'd said. All those years she'd heard every word I'd spoken, in every world where I'd come to visit. Once more I talked to her about anything and everything and nothing; what I'd done, heard, seen, felt. I left out much of the detail of the Canary Wharf incident, skipping straight to the look on Baxter's face when we saw the kidnapper sailing away from us under his parachute.

'Vidmar,' she mumbled. 'All the names, all the faces.'

Vidmar. The first time I'd heard that name was from the mouth of a survivor of the Leven Road massacre where six of the top dogs in Red Claw were wiped out. He was found dead in his cell the next morning. That was three months after Alice came to The Grange. For a second I wondered how she could have heard of him, just for a second. I grew up before there was such a thing as entanglement: ways of thinking ingrained in my brain from those years.

'She's going again,' Stebbins-Reese said. As if I couldn't tell.

'I'm worried about Lewis, Beets. He's so thin.' She sounded as drained as I felt.

'She's gone. Full Omega state. Would you mind?'

I lifted her head for him to slip off the skull cap. 'What did she mean?' I asked. 'You'll get what you want.'

'My research, Lewis.' He looped up the cables and packed away his instruments. 'Today, she hovered on the edge, lucid but still in Omega. Think of the things she can tell us if we can control that, maintain the balance.' He snapped his case closed and looked at me. 'Goodbye, Lewis. I'll be back to see Alice again on Monday. Will you be here?'

'If I can be. I'm going to sit with her a while now.'

He hovered in the doorway and turned back to me. 'We've come a long way in such a short time.' The door closed softly behind him.

I was under no illusions about his motivation. Alice was a research subject to him, but what he said was true, we had come a long way.

I hadn't really taken to the man in the beginning, but he had been persuasive. Our first meetings I sat and listened, arms folded, as he explained his theory about the Omega State, that Alice had gone far beyond the level of the Alpha entangled, whose personalities were permanently fused across realities that diverged years or decades ago. Alice, he said, was lost in a near infinity of lives and realities, branching from a common ancestor thousands of generations past. His description made her sound like a goddess from ancient myth. I was, to put it mildly, sceptical, but I saw no harm in allowing him to hook her up with his skullcap of SQUID sensors and his monitor with the incomprehensible multi-coloured graphical visualisations.

Afterwards, when he wanted to talk about taking the next step, Cecilia joined us. In a meeting room on the first floor of The Grange he showed me the equipment: the pump, cannula, monitors, and a glass vial of a clear liquid. The consent form lay on the table before me.

'It's a derivative of the toxin secreted by cells infected with CM-2057-phi-kappa.' He held the vial up to the light, gripped between thumb and forefinger. 'If my theory is correct, it will, in small doses, impede the connection between realities, and bring her back more into our own world.'

'Kind of an anti-implicitin?'

'An inhibitor.'

'What are the risks?' Cecilia had been sitting, quietly watching until that point.

'We'll begin with such a small dose that...'

'There are always risks.' Cecilia glanced at me. I nodded for her to continue, glad to have someone here who knew the right things to say. 'You need Lewis's *informed* consent. So, what are the risks?'

He put down the vial. 'Firstly, let us consider the risks of doing nothing. The median survival time for people like Alice is less than five years because of the physical decline caused by the lack of mobility.'

'I've seen the statistics,' I said. 'What are the risks of your proposed treatment? CM-2057-phi-kappa killed most of those infected. Alice and I were among the few who survived.'

'Indeed.' He clasped his hands and looked down at them. 'That is the unknown factor here. I need to determine whether it is possible to find a dosage level that will help her and still be safe.' He pulled himself upright and looked me in the eye. 'She *will* die if we do nothing. Next year or the year after, who knows when, but she will die.'

I signed the form. Two days later, Alice lay on the bed hooked up to the monitors. Cecilia and I sat by the bedside, me holding Alice's hand, Cecilia's hand on my arm.

'I don't expect any reaction today.' Stebbins-Reese held up the syringe, the steel needle shining in the sunlight through the window. 'It's such a small dose, almost homeopathic.' He let out a small chuckle like it was a joke.

As the tip of the needle touched her arm I looked away. Cecilia chewed her lip, a glint of a tear in her eye. I guess she realised she was gripping my forearm. She drew her hand away and looked down in her lap.

'There we are.' Stebbins-Reese turned to drop the used syringe in the sharps box. Alice let out a heavy breath and her head moved a fraction, barely more than a twitch. Even after Stebbins-Reese's warning I had trouble beating down the stirrings of hope. A breath, a twitch, they signified nothing. A minute passed, two. An irrational disappointment crept up on me.

Then Alice opened her eyes. She looked at me and smiled. 'There are tigers, Lewis,' she said, 'I'm… I'm…'

Her eyes closed.

We sat in silent shock, Cecilia and I, while Stebbins-Reese rubbed his hands together grinning gleefully. 'Well, well, well.'

Cecilia burst into a gentle sobbing that triggered the tears in my own eyes. 'Tigers.' I was laughing and crying at the same time. 'Do you think there are still polar bears and rhinoceros wherever she's been?' Cecilia rested her head on my shoulder and I put my arm around her. As so many times before I wondered at how dedicated she was to Alice, how deeply involved she was, how much I wished some of that warmth was there for me; a foolish, selfish thing to think about at such a time. Three years since Alice had spoken, since she had done anything of her own volition.

That first treatment was only three weeks before. I was under no illusions about Stebbins-Reese's motivation, but I was supremely grateful for the change he had wrought in Alice. Now I had hope that in time he'd be able to find a balance and she would be able to function, to make a life in our world again.

My rambling thoughts were interrupted by the creak of the door handle behind me. Cecilia edged in balancing a tray with two steaming mugs.

'Instant, I'm afraid.' She sat, taking one of the mugs herself and leaning towards me. 'I'm sorry, it was too hard to explain over the phone.'

I leaned in, too, like a pair of conspirators. 'That's okay.' The light from the edges of the shaded windows cast half her face in deep shadow, but her pale green eyes were wide, pupils dilated in the darkness. 'She told Beets I was *thin*,' I said. 'Seemed an odd thing to say.'

She cast her eyes down. 'Do you have the book I told you about?'

'The Measurement Problem? Yes. I've been reading it.'

'Amari explains it better than I could, but basically in all the worlds she lives, she sees you in only a few, like you're no longer there in all the others. It makes it harder for her to see you, to focus on you.' She picked up her cup and cradled it in both hands. 'I was worried this incident might set her back.'

This incident. Me being killed. 'Beets. She seemed to think I know her. Is she alive in this world?'

She set her cup down again. 'I don't know, Lewis. You know as much about Beets as I do.'

'It sounds like a nickname. You haven't heard her mention another name?'

'No.'

Alice stirred, murmuring incoherently. Still in that borderland, partly in this world.

Cecilia rose to her feet. 'We should leave her to sleep.' She picked up the tray with the still-full cups, and stepped briskly to the door. I padded over to Alice's bedside as quietly as I could.

'Goodbye, Alice,' I whispered.

The door *snicked* as Cecilia opened it.

'Goodbye Lewis, goodbye Beets,' her sleepy voice murmured behind me. 'Be careful.'

Cecilia pulled the door to behind me. 'Cerasthesia again. She loses track of who she's speaking to.'

I knew that. How could I not know? But Cecilia seemed tense, distracted.

She bade me a hasty goodbye and I watched her receding back as she bustled off towards the office behind reception.

*

The car that turned up to collect me from The Grange looked like a feral with its layers of dirt and faded and peeling paintwork. With not a little trepidation I got in. Not too bad at first but once we hit the motorway I regretted not calling another. It swayed and rumbled and whined as it hurtled along. I had to turn up my phone's volume and hold it close to my ear to pick up a message from Kay.

'Hi Lewis, thought you'd want to know how it went with Samantha. She's going to be fine but…' She paused, took a breath. 'I know you're not going to approve. Turns out she's been hitting the betas and deltas in small doses for months, so much that she's pushed her divergence point way back, joined worlds that diverged from ours years ago. No wonder she's confused. The good news is she's showing no sign of cerasthesia. Looks like she's permanently entangled now so she needs to learn some coping strategies. I've given her details of someone who can help her with that.'

Foolish woman to take such a risk. I'd only ever known her to speak to in passing on the street, but I'd liked her. One more good person lost to the ranks of the entangled. But the alternative, if she had not come through it so well, would have been an institution like The Grange, if she could afford it.

In a place like The Grange, she might have ended up like Alice. What I'd give for my sister to reach the same place as Samantha, where her biggest problem was learning the strategies to manage the confusion of many lives.

I put that thought aside and spent the rest of the journey on the crime scene report, beginning by rotating and zooming The 3D image of Wyndham lying on the hotel room carpet. As so often with Red Claw hits no-one saw the killer arrive or leave and there was no video; the hotel security system had gone down. Forensics had found slight indents in the carpet pile from the pressure of a pair of size twelve boots or shoes and nearby, a single frayed Kevlar fibre, most likely from an armed and armoured officer sent in to secure the scene. Harris was due to give the place the once over in person that morning, but by now it would all be clean, sterile, picked over in minute detail by the forensics bots. It was only just past noon so I diverted the car to the Bishopsgate station. Baxter had said to take the day but there was work to do, and there was another crime scene I wanted to look over.

*

Even in the early afternoon, even beneath a narrow strip of blue sky, that cobbled alley was as dark as my mood as I pushed my leaden feet towards Marek's door. A heartbeat's pause on the step, then I gave that door a hard shove. The screech of it across the tiles set my teeth on edge.

'Hey, Lewis. Here for lunch?' Harris was sitting at the table by the window, on the side facing the door. My usual table, my usual seat. The one I'd been sitting in when I'd had the panic, the blackout.

'Jack,' I mumbled. It was all the greeting I could summon at that moment. I scanned the room. A dozen tables, though the big mirror across the back wall made it feel much bigger. Lunch was Marek's busy time, one or two customers at nearly every table. Marek himself was behind the counter steaming milk. Three paces to Harris's table. As soon as I put my hand on the back of the seat facing him I felt a shiver. I pulled the chair out to sit.

Some people have a thing about sitting with their back to a door. It doesn't bother me that much but given the choice I'd always pick the one facing. I slipped off my coat and hung it on the back of the chair. Harris watched me with brow furrowed. I sat.

The door was behind me. The door that screeched on the tiles. I'd heard that screech before I was killed. The back of my neck tingled and the muscles of my shoulders tensed so tight they hurt. I had to turn and look. The door was closed.

'You okay, Lewis?'

I forced myself to turn back to look at him across the table.

This was where I'd been sitting when I died. I was here on this side of the table because someone else was on the other side, my usual seat, facing the door. I'd felt a hand clutching mine as I fell.

My chair fell over backwards as I stood. 'Let's get a different table.'

'Sure thing.' His grin said he was humouring me. I picked up my coat and followed him to the only other empty table, at the back. Harris took the bench seat behind, leaving me the chair opposite with its back to the door. No problem: I could see the door in the mirrored wall behind.

'Is Alice okay?' he asked.

I grimaced. 'She thought I'd been killed. That's why she was upset.'

'Another reality?'

'Yeah. She said a lot of things I didn't understand.' I found myself looking past Harris's shoulder at the reflection of the door. 'I had a funny turn while I was here the other day. I think that's when it happened.'

'That why you were acting so weird just now?'

'What can I get you, gentlemen?' Marek appeared silently at my shoulder. We ordered coffees and paninis.

'The Wyndham case: who was first on the scene?' I asked Harris before he could start pumping me any more about Alice and what she'd said. Not like I wanted to keep any secrets, just wanted some time to digest it all.

'Local police. Murder squad were called in after.'

'Their report wasn't in the file.'

'I'll look into it. You thinking of the Kevlar fibre?'

'And size twelve boots.'

'Half this job, chasing up other people's paperwork,' he grumbled as he made a note on his phone. 'The warrant came through. Wyndham's secretary had to give up what it had.'

'Anything useful.'

'It was set to auto-delete anything over a week old, so only drafts of documents in progress. Remember Jazila?'

'Flood wall contractor, yeah.'

'He was about to up his stake to fifty-five percent.'

'Majority control. Guess he had plans for the company.'

'And he's been buying land in Essex. Lots of it, south of Basildon.'

'Wetlands. Maybe he's a birdwatcher.' A memory clicked of when I was at Hendon training academy. I'd asked out this young trainee and she'd drank me under the table. 'You're from Essex, aren't you?'

'Yeah, I'm a Southend boy. I know that area. Another ten years and it'll be sea bed.'

Movement in the mirror: Marek with a tray ghosted up beside me with our orders, reminding me I was hungry after such a meagre breakfast. The panini was up to Marek's usual standard, hot, crunchy. Runny, stringy cheese, and tuna with enough flavour that I could have believed it came from a real fish in the sea.

'Anything on the Wyndham children?' I asked between mouthfuls.

'Sarah's been on location for a film shoot at Woburn Abbey. Bentley is, as we speak, flying back from Tripoli. No sign of the stepson, Aiden.'

'Anything on file for him?'

'No, nothing.'

'Passport?'

'Hah!' He picked up his phone, flicked and prodded and turned it to show me. A passport copy from thirty years before. The photograph was a small baby. 'That's the only record we have. Father's name is not recorded, and there's no record of Aiden Harcourt entering or leaving the country anytime in the last thirty years, though the first ten years of that were during the war.'

During the war. A lot of records were lost or corrupted in those days. 'Maybe he uses another name. Ask the widow for a recent picture.'

*

Back at the office I pored through the files on Elijah Cloake. Ten years ago he'd been an average middle manager at VirGenTech when he volunteered for the company's nascent entanglement programme. Back then it was a leap in the dark, too dangerous for VGT to want to risk sacrificing their best and brightest. Cloake was one of the lucky ones who flew through the process and emerged with all faculties intact and with the insights that only entanglement could give. Within a year he was head of the therapeutics division, within three he was on the board. With the salary, bonuses and share options from VirGenTech and with the astute investments he'd made outside, he was now a very wealthy man. His high-flying career had ended when he resigned without explanation from VGT three years before. Much of his time since had been devoted to his charitable foundation focussed on flood mitigation and relief efforts in the worst affected parts of Asia and the Pacific.

On the surface, a lucky guy trying to spread his good fortune. I couldn't square all that with his being entangled, involved with VGT, with Sir Roger Wyndham and the DRC, and by implication, with Red Claw. But mostly, I couldn't square it with his role in putting Alice where she was.

I rang the contact number.

A pompous-looking man appeared on the screen. Close-cut, greying hair. 'Elijah Cloake's residence.' A pompous voice to match.

'I'd like to speak to Mr Cloake, please. Metropolitan Police.'

'Mr. Cloake is very busy, sir. May I ask what you wish to speak to him about?'

'Now, Mr…?'

'Soames, sir.'

'Mr Soames, I believe he might be able to assist us in our enquiries in a murder case.'

'Just "Soames", sir. I will see if he is available. May I give him your name?'

'Detective Inspector Lewis Drake. Please ask Mr Cloake…'

Soames raised a hand to the camera. 'Mr Cloake will see you tomorrow morning at nine o'clock if you please, at his home.'

CHAPTER 4

Friday 15th November: The Cloake Residence

For the unentangled, it is not only the most intense emotional experiences that leak through the boundary between worlds, but also the most mundane.

I have an acquaintance in one world, a concert pianist for twenty years. I found her in another world working as a carer in a hospice, perfectly content with her lot. She took up my suggestion to take piano lessons. While she will never reach the perfection of her alternate, she did make remarkable progress and within a year surpassed her teacher.

Such experiences illustrate the benefits of a limited degree of entanglement. Even without conscious awareness, the expertise and intuitions that seep from other worlds can be of great help to those who are most sensitive. Most sensitive of all are those childhood survivors of the cytomegalovirus plague CM-2057-phi-kappa.

But to break the barriers further can come with a price, in confusion and mental illness. It has been suggested that entanglement was the primordial natural state and that evolution in the distant past erected the barriers to protect the vertebrate brain from the confusion.

—A K Amari - *The Measurement Problem, A Guide to Entanglement*

Nine am, that's the time Soames told me, so that's the time I told the car I wanted to arrive. I thought I was going to be early when, somewhere in the wilds east of Cambridge, it pulled off a narrow country lane to stop in front of a pair of massive iron gates set in a stone arch. They opened to welcome me in and after a good kilometre of unblemished tarmac threading the centre of a broad avenue of ancient lime trees in their winter nakedness, the drive curved around to run down a shallow valley between broad swathes of close-cut grass bordered with woodland. A dozen deer ambled along the margin of the wood. It was a scene from a historical drama, except for the house itself. A long low wall of dark glass spread before me in a gentle arc, tapering down to ground level at either end and merging seamlessly with the lawn, which extended up and over to form the roof of the building. The driveway ended in front of the glass wall in a gravel circle with a chrome steel fountain at its centre. Thirties *Diskret* school, ironically loud in its feigned unobtrusiveness.

The door opened before I reached it. Soames stood stiff and tall in the shadow inside. Behind me, wheels crunched on gravel as the car departed to find its next fare. From such an out of the way place it would have a long way to go.

'Detective Inspector Drake.' In person, Soames' voice lost none of its officiousness. 'Mr Cloake awaits you in the library. Please follow me.'

Once inside, the shadows receded to reveal an interior that matched the external style, post-modern blended with biophilic, clean smooth lines, floor covered in soft and deep drymoss grown in elaborate patterns of yellows and greens, walls panelled with waxed pale wood, sparse but elegant planting of shrubs and small trees in robust earthenware pots. Soames, in his long-tailed coat, black tie, shining black shoes and dazzling white shirt was as much an anachronism in this house as the house in its estate. The back of the entrance hall opened onto a long corridor that curved away on either side. More of the soft sheen of waxed wood. The dim winter daylight from long, domed skylights was augmented by a warm glow that emanated from the walls themselves.

The first room on the right was the library. Floor to ceiling bookshelves lined the walls on either side, every shelf packed with old-fashioned print and paper books of all sizes and colours: uniform rows of matched volumes, heavy hardbacks bound in cloth or leather or covered with glossy sleeves, garish paperbacks with creased and tattered spines. The far wall was a single sheet of dark glass, part of the façade of the house. Cloake rose to his feet from behind an ancient leather-topped oak desk as big as my bed.

He had thick dark wavy hair with flashes of grey, clean-shaven with wide, solid features and a broad nose. A serious looking man. I would have guessed older than the forty-eight years his file claimed. Such was the man whose decisions had left Alice needing twenty-four hour care, left her uncommunicative, helpless.

'Please, have a seat, Detective Inspector.' He came round the desk and offered his hand to shake. I hesitated only a second before taking it. I couldn't afford to let my resentment interfere with the case. Professional courtesy was required unless and until I could tie him to the crime.

He gestured expansively to the chesterfield couch at the side of the room. I sat and he took the armchair adjacent. The butler had silently departed and the door silently closed by the time I was seated.

'And may I offer you my condolences?' His voice was deep, his expression sincere.

'I'm sorry? Condolences?'

'I know how it feels to die. I think you do too. To suffer such violence in such a thick stream of realities. I understand you are a CM-2057-phi-kappa survivor—you surely felt it.'

... *a particular sensitivity to such experiences*, I'd read in Amari's book. I was back in Marek's café, overwhelmed with that stark terror. I shook my head, clenched my fists, looked at him. His eyes met mine.

'I'm sorry, I didn't mean to upset you.'

'No, no. It's fine. That wasn't me. Just someone like me. This is the only reality I know.'

He paused a few seconds, his eyes still fixed on me. 'If you say so.'

I didn't want to ask but Alice had seen it, Alice had lived it, and it might help me to help her if I knew. And I had the distinct feeling Cloake was waiting for me to ask.

'Do you know what happened to me?'

'I don't have all the details,' he said, 'only what I read in the feeds. A gunman surprised you in a café in London on Tuesday morning. He was himself killed before he could deliver the coup de grâce. Unfortunately you mostly died at the scene.'

'Mostly?'

His mouth twitched in a brief grimace. 'There is a strand where they managed to keep you alive but the prognosis isn't good. If it's any consolation, your wife's injuries are less severe. She is expected to make a complete recovery.'

I had trouble imagining still being married. A gulf had opened between me and Vittoria after Alice was first hospitalised. That was a rabbit hole to avoid if I wanted to keep a lid on my anger.

'Any idea of the killer, the motive?'

He gave me a sideways glance. 'The gunman's name wasn't reported but they did reveal that he was a police officer in the pay of an organised criminal group called Red Claw, whose leader you had unmasked. A DI Baxter arrived on the scene too late. It was she who shot the gunman. Red Claw's leader was killed shortly after, resisting arrest.'

I didn't bother to correct him on Detective *Chief* Inspector Baxter's rank because *Red Claw's leader* could only mean Vidmar. 'Was this leader named?'

'That's where it gets interesting,' he said. 'The reports identified him as Winsford Saïd.'

My mind went momentarily blank as I failed to fit that piece into the jigsaw.

'Winsford Saïd the member of parliament? That can't be right. The one thing we do know about Red Claw's leader is that he's entangled, and Saïd is violently anti-entanglement.'

'Indeed he is. The very reason I have so little information of what happened to you is that in those realities Mr Saïd has risen to the level of Home Secretary and I, like most of the entangled, am imprisoned. Fortunately he carries less influence in this world.'

This was spinning off in too many directions. Winsford Saïd running Red Claw made no sense at all in this world. His connections, associates, activities were all under far too close a scrutiny. I made a note and filed it away, intending to think about it later.

'Tell me about your relationship with Sir Roger Wyndham.'

'I've never met the man myself but Monica, Lady Wyndham, is a good friend.'

'Then can you explain why one of your cars, a retrofitted Rolls Royce Silver Dawn, was at a hotel near Milton Keynes at the same time that he was there on five occasions in the last three months.'

He froze, his forehead creased. 'I don't…' Then he smiled. 'No. It isn't possible. Not in this world.'

'It's there in the Vehicle Licensing Authority logs,' I said.

'Curious.' He reached into his pocket and pulled out his phone. His fingers swiped and flicked. 'The Silver Dawn hasn't moved since the beginning of July. It's in the garage being restored to its original condition. A hobby of mine. Someone has tampered with the VLA records or cloned the ID onto another vehicle.'

'Both are based on blockchain protocols. Tamper-proof.'

'Both are based on fifty-year-old blockchain protocols that were tamper-proof at the time they were created except by the most advanced quantum computers possessed by the intelligence services. That was before entanglement. To the entangled they are vulnerable. I could have done it if I'd wanted to incriminate myself in your investigation.'

'Not in this world?'

'I'm sorry?'

'When I asked you about the Silver Dawn being at that hotel near Milton Keynes, you said "it isn't possible. Not in this world." Did you mean it *is* possible in another world?'

He leaned back in his chair and clasped his hands together in his lap. 'How much time do you have, Detective Inspector?'

'As much as it takes, Mr Cloake.'

His eyes ranged over the bookshelves behind me, then he looked at me and began to speak. 'Entanglement confers on us certain advantages. We can project an illusion of intelligence greater than we really possess because we can try different answers to a problem in many worlds at the same time to find the right one. We can read, research, compress years of study into an evening by splitting tasks across realities. We can see the outcomes, good and bad, of decisions we take differently in different worlds, amplifying our ability to learn from experience. But there is a trade-off. I sit in this room with you in certain strands of existence, and my mind overflows with memories of people and events from many diverse pasts. So, when you ask me about something that has happened in this particular world, it is not always easy for me to answer. I remember the enjoyment I have from working on the Silver Dawn in some worlds, in others it sits waiting so that if I make mistakes I can start again using what I have learned. When I said, "it isn't possible. Not in this world," I was thinking aloud, trying to establish in my own mind whether the world in which you asked me the question is one in which the Silver Dawn is lying half-restored in my garage. You see, all the streams of reality are not conveniently labelled, named, numbered. They are simply there. We rely on notes and diaries and tricks of memory to help us keep track. For us the past can be as fluid as the future.'

Imagination failed me. I understood the words but I could not envisage how it might feel to live like that.

'I'd like you to focus on this reality, Mr Cloake,' I said, taking out my phone. 'Can you account for your whereabouts on...' I opened the file. It always feels more authoritative referring to the file even when you know what you're going to ask. 'The fourth of October?'

'I was in Delft in the Netherlands at a conference on flood defences, there are many witnesses, video footage, hotel registrations. I'll have Soames collate the records. Send him the other dates and he will check my whereabouts on those dates too. But let's not waste time on that. I'd like to discuss the reason for your visit.'

'I am investigating the murder of Sir Roger Wyndham.'

'That's the trigger that brought you here, but someone has gone to some trouble to link me with Sir Roger, injecting false information into the VLA records. It's the reason for that that intrigues me.'

'You believe you're being framed?'

'No. The link is easily disproved, but it served to bring you here. There are congruences.'

'*Congruences*?'

'I can recommend a book on entanglement: *The Measurement Problem*, by A K Amari.'

'I'm reading it.'

'Amari describes congruences where two or more facts are true in some set of realities and false in another set. It implies a causal connection, a past point of divergence between worlds. At some time in the past an event occurred that in one set of realities led to you being shot at Marek's, and in another to you being here today.'

'My being killed at Marek's is an obvious cause of me not being here today.'

'There are earlier differences. The causative link arises at the point of divergence from the common ancestor of those realities.' He stood and walked around the back of the chair to a small table that held several interesting bottles. 'Care to join me?' he said, pouring himself a generous dram of a forty-five year old Tamnavulin.

'Not while I'm on duty, sir.' There was too much spinning around in my head already, I didn't need anything to make my thinking any muddier. 'What earlier differences?'

He sauntered back to the chair and sat slowly down, taking a careful sip of the whisky. Ostentatious, but at least he gave it the respect it deserved. 'The earliest I've been able to identify is the fate of the Genetic Therapies Division of VirGenTech three years ago.'

The glass made a firm *clunk* as he placed it on the table and leaned forward. 'Why might someone want *you* here, Detective Inspector Lewis Drake? Why *you*, specifically?'

This was the taboo subject, the one I hadn't wanted to raise for fear of what I might say or do. The Glock hung heavy in its holster and I wished it were not there. 'What does this have to do with my sister?'

'Now we come to it.' He picked up the glass, cradled it in both hands and swirled the liquid. 'Alice Drake worked in the Genetic Therapies Division which some on the VGT board considered to be no longer our core business. There was a proposal to close it down and sell off those parts we could. I opposed it myself but in *this* world I was unsuccessful. In those worlds where you were killed, we retained the division and its projects. Alice had done such excellent work that I wanted to keep her in VGT whatever happened so I encouraged her to apply for the entanglement programme and I authorised her acceptance. Her subsequent treatment and misfortune were the same in all the worlds I'm aware of.'

This was the man who caused it. If not for him she would still be the bright, capable, joyful little sister I'd had as far back as I could remember.

'You may choose to believe me or you may choose not to, Detective Inspector, but I was deeply saddened by what happened to Alice. They told me that such tragedies were no longer possible, that the process was better managed and far safer than the early days.'

I cannot put into words how little I cared about Cloake's sadness. I'd had enough of VirGenTech executives telling me how Alice's reaction was unprecedented, how deeply they regretted the outcome, how they had taken every possible care, and it wasn't their fault, there's the door Mr Drake, don't bother us again. Being here, with Cloake, with a gun, it was like I was being tested. I guess I passed. 'You haven't answered the question, Mr Cloake. What does this have to do with my sister?'

'I don't know, but it has something to do with the Genetic Therapies

Division. In this world it was broken up, parts sold off. The congruence that brings you here now suggests some link with Alice, or with *Doctor Fallon*.'

He emphasised *Doctor Fallon* like he was dropping a bombshell. It was a dud. I guess my blank look served as answer.

'You don't know Erica Fallon in this world?'

Erica. Big Bennie Thacker with his blowtorch was looking for an Erica. 'No.'

'That *is* interesting.' He knocked back the whisky, draining the glass like it was a cheap blend. 'I am being drawn into a game here.'

'Am I playing this game, Mr Cloake?'

'You, Detective Inspector Lewis Drake, are a pawn.' His hand reached under the table and my fingers twitched, ready to reach for my weapon. 'And pawns are easily sacrificed, as you were in Marek's café on Tuesday.'

'You rang, Sir.' Soames stood in the doorway.

'Soames, how long would it take you to gather together all the old files we have on the VirGenTech Genetic Therapies Division?'

'I should think, two hours, sir.'

'Very good. Have copies sent to DI Drake today. And he will need one of the cars.'

I got the message and stood up. 'That's alright, I'll call one myself.'

'You'd be waiting twenty minutes for one to reach us here. Take the Saqqaf. Send it back when you're done.' He ushered me towards the library door. 'The files Soames will send you are all administrative detail, nothing of a sensitive nature, but perhaps there is something of value in there, something to do with Doctor Fallon or your sister, or the project, Furcifer, that they worked on together. With your particular involvement you might see something I have missed.'

'Is that your move in the game, Mr Cloake? What do you expect of this pawn now?'

He smiled at that. 'I expect you to be very careful, DI Drake. It's not what you discover that will get you killed. It's who you tell.'

Soames waited in the passageway. 'This way sir.' He led me along the curving corridor away from the entrance hall, past half a dozen dark hardwood doors on either side, some open or ajar. On the right, the front of the house, I caught glimpses of a large dining room and an intimate lounge. A door opened to my left and a knee-high cleaning bot paused on the threshold of a spacious uncluttered bedroom. After we passed, it whirred to life, closed the door behind it, then trundled back the way we had come. At the end of the corridor Soames pulled open a plain, heavy door, fitted at the top with a spring door closer, and led me into a museum, a gallery, a cathedral to the history of motorised transport.

The room was white, clinical, sterile. Plain white walls, plain white ceiling interrupted by more glass skylights. Six bays to the left, six to the right, each contained a vehicle. To the left they were all modern while those on the right were ancient but all looked to be the height of luxury for their time. The wall behind was lined with racks of tools and drums labelled *synthetic biofuel - petrol substitute*. The Silver Dawn was in the first bay, its folding bonnet raised, exposing the complex jumble of mechanical parts and pipes and blocks. It was, as Cloake had said, being restored to its original hydrocarbon-fuelled condition. Every vehicle on that side of the room was a burner, built to run on hydrocarbons. I peered into the window of a low sleek number, bright red, with a prancing horse emblem on its bonnet. A steering wheel, foot pedals, switches and dials. A miracle that anyone could ever figure out how to get it moving.

Opposite the red was a Saqqaf. I'd never seen one this close, each one hand-built at the Saqqaf workshops in Cairo. A smooth, frictionless profile, black as night, windows so dark it was impossible to see inside. It looked solid, like the cars from a hundred years ago, like some of those on the other side of the garage. In those days they had sturdy monocoque steel bodies to give the occupants a chance of survival when they crashed, as they so often did. Soames pinged me the Saqqaf's authorisation code and the door opened for me.

'You'll have those files by the end of the day, sir, and please send the car back when you have finished with it.'

I stooped to enter the vehicle. I've seen, even ridden in, bigger cars than this, but nothing so luxurious. As I sat in one of the two soft tan leather seats at the back of the saloon, a polished hardwood panel at the front folded up to make a table. A generous display screen above it partly obscured the view through the front window. Sets of buttons on the arms of each chair were marked with the usual icons.

Soames closed the door and I pressed the command button. 'Take me home, Saqqaf,' I said. With the authorisation code Soames had pinged me the car was linked to my phone, and my phone knew where I lived. Smooth and almost silent, it pulled out of the bay and accelerated towards the ascending roller door, timing its exit with split-second precision, and emerged through a concrete-lined recess in the low grassy slope of the side of the house onto a narrow roadway that curved around to join the long driveway at the front.

A premium news feed rolled across the screen as the car sped along the narrow lanes towards the motorway: a week before one of the highest spring tides this year, no storms forecast as yet. Erosion of the Ganges delta was accelerating, exacerbating the refugee crisis. The prime minister of Morocco demanded that Spain do more to stem illegal migration across the Straits of Gibraltar of Europe's jobless seeking work in the solar industrial belt of North Africa. The French junior minister, Hubert Neuville, at the centre of an espionage investigation, had been found dead in his cell.

It was distracting. I turned it off so I could concentrate on Doctor Fallon.

A search pulled up a list of references to Doctor Fallons, a physician in a small outback town in Australia, a quack selling yatapox virus treatments to those crazy enough to believe the plague wars hadn't ended twenty years before. Restricting the search to references that also mentioned VirGenTech gave me a bunch of academic papers whose authors included a Dr E B Fallon. Most of the titles were beyond my comprehension, but DNA and genes cropped up in many of them.

The most recent of the papers, *In Vivo Phenotype Reprogramming—A New Approach to Treating Genetic Disorders*, was three years old. Co-authored by Dr A Drake and Dr S Okorie. It had been published on the same day that Alice had been given the implicitins that sent her to The Grange. It must have been one of the last things she worked on.

A surname and an employer were enough to get Dr Fallon's address from the tax office database. Her last known residence was near the small village of Babraham. I'd be passing less than ten kilometres from it. I pinged the address to the car, and a minute later it swooshed effortlessly up the slip road off the motorway.

She lived in a barn, so-called. One of those stone and oak faux-barns that had never seen a cow or a bale of straw. Long, low flint walls and synthetic slate tiles on the roof. At first glance it could have been built anytime between 1990 and 2030.

Nineteen ninety-seven popped into my head from nowhere, as good a guess is any. In those days it was likely something of a status symbol but now the style had a dated look. The sun shone in through the glass wall of a generous living space revealing a bare flagstone floor, white plastered walls with stone features, oak beams and a few items of cheap panel furniture. It had that cold empty feel of a neglected house. The plant pots by the door were ragged and weedy.

The front door was oak, in an oak frame surrounded by glass panels. There was a bell. I rang it. Nobody answered, but the little light on the little camera up in the corner of the door frame blinked red.

'I'm looking for Doctor Fallon,' I said to it.

The light went out.

Round the back were two apple trees surrounded by rotting windfalls and what might once have been a vegetable plot, now overgrown with weeds. The lawn was cut to snooker table perfection. Beside the shed a robot mower sat quietly at its charging station. An elderly couple in yellow raincoats walked along the other side of the broken-down fence at the back of the garden, walking poles in hand, heading towards a stile by the roadside.

A patio outside the back door was peppered with more overgrown plant pots. I tried the handle of the door. Locked, one of those old mechanical locks that used a metal key. As my hand left the handle I had the strongest sense of déjà vu. My eyes were drawn to a small terracotta pot that held a clump of chrysanthemums suffering the seasonal cold. I reached down and lifted the pot.

A key. The key.

Déjà vu stayed with me as I picked it up and inserted it in the lock. That little reluctance to turn, a gentle press sideways, just so, and it opened like always. *Time we replaced that, before it gives up the ghost.* I opened the door, and shivered.

I put the key back under the pot before closing the door. The place was clean. I mean, there was a layer of dust over everything, and evidence of a cohort of industrious spiders, but it was meticulously tidy. Nothing out of place. The expansive hallway reached up to the open beams that supported the roof. A staircase led up one side to a landing with a chrome bannister, glass panels beneath. A sod to keep clean, greasy fingermarks every time you walked past it. There were no greasy fingermarks, only dust and cobwebs.

Beneath the stairs a door opened into a small study. Old wall screens, optical connectors ending in nothing where some kind of computer must have been. A rug, ochre and off-white, possibly hand stitched, oriental origin, lay on the flag floor. A small cupboard door flush with the wall attracted my attention on account of it having been ungently opened at some time in the past. The home security system was inside, a Sanderson, old fashioned but robust. There was a gaping socket where the memory once had resided. The little blinking light outside the front door blinked in vain. My fingers probed the sides of the plastic casing and felt an edge. Between fingernails I pulled out a yellowed card. A serial number and a passcode.

I wandered from room to room building a picture of Doctor E B Fallon. The furnishings were simple and inexpensive but tasteful: pale woods and gentle shades that felt calm amongst the stone and oak and white partition walls, a well-equipped kitchen, but old, decades old, with scratched and discoloured marble. Little food remained in the cupboards, a few tins and packets, nothing perishable, and the fridge and freezer were empty. There were ornaments on shelves: coloured glass vases, cheap but pleasing imitations of Venetian glass, a few oddments that could have only had sentimental value, like the pair of hideous toby jugs. The paintings were what really caught my eye, simple splashes of colour on white backgrounds. A couple of particularly impressive canvasses dominated that big front hallway, each hanging above a glass fish-tank with gravel and stones and little dead plants. No fish. There were lights in the top, but no pumps or filters, no algae, dry as bones and the dead plants didn't look aquatic. Spiders or snakes I guessed. A small snug held an old, battered, but comfy-looking sofa, a wall screen, and another of the canvasses. This one smaller, waves of blues and greens like a fading storm. That was her favourite. Her favourite? I kept making these assumptions, wild intuitions, instead of focussing on the facts. I tried to decipher the signature in the corner: *B Msquiggle.*

The clothes in the wardrobe and drawers of the main bedroom were all old, worn, or outdated. Very little underwear. The bed was made but the room felt incomplete. So much was missing. Not only her, not only her day-to-day clutter. I kept thinking I saw things out of the corner of my eye, but when I turned it was just another empty space.

I was heading back out when it struck me what I hadn't seen. I went back around the house, room to room, searching. Here on this sideboard in the dining room, a conspicuous gap, and in the cubic shelving in the living room, big square spaces that shouted their emptiness. A kitchen fridge covered with magnets holding three-year-old notices of village events and addresses of local services and a cluster of magnets holding nothing at all.

No photographs in the entire house. No photographs of Doctor E B Fallon or anyone she might have known.

I let myself out the front door. The Saqqaf was still waiting by the gate, dressed in silent black, like Soames. I told it to take me home, stewing in the back over an absence, an emptiness.

The news feed kept on. The crisis between Cascadia and the Christian States of America was escalating. The Sacramento government had threatened air strikes against the CSA's coal-fired power plants if they weren't shut down. The CSA said they'd retaliate with a nuclear strike. The editorial pointed out that those nukes dated back to the previous century, well past their sell-by date, but that a successful launch couldn't be ruled out.

The Gillibrand Institute announced that they had been commissioned to put together a proposal to stem the flooding in Bangladesh by building barrages to hold back the rising sea, using pumps powered by a series of tidal lagoons to lift the Ganges flow up to the new sea level. They cited the success of the smaller-scale scheme now operating on the Rhone estuary and earlier design studies for the Volga and the Thames.

Flooding, Cloake's pet project, brought my focus back. I was supposed to be investigating Cloake and any link he might have with Red Claw, and here, he had conveniently lent me one of his cars and given me its authorisation code. I wondered what level of clearance that code gave me, so I flipped through its menus: status, service. Journey log. Everywhere it had been since it had been built five years before. A total of eight thousand kilometres. Eight thousand! The sheer waste of it irritated my environmental sensibilities. Most cars averaged around five-hundred thousand a year, pretty much in motion all the time they weren't charging. This one just sat in Cloake's garage waiting until it was needed.

I downloaded the log to my phone. Could have been that Cloake had been lax with his security. Could have been he was dropping more breadcrumbs for me to follow. But I had my own breadcrumbs. I called Sanderson home security. Eventually I was put through to a harassed young man.

'Hi, I've lost the data from my doorcam video feed. Do you get a stream of it?'

'Yes sir, we keep the last three months data on file. I'll need the account name and address.'

'Sure. It's registered to Dr E B Fallon. I'm pinging you the address now.'

His face turned to one side, presumably checking his files. 'That account expired two years ago, sir.'

I knew how these things worked. Nobody threw away data they didn't have to. There was always the chance of making money from it. 'So you're still receiving the feed but not raising alarms. Can I reactivate the account?'

'You are not Dr Fallon, sir. I can't send you the file without her express authority.'

'Yeah, she said you'd want the passcode.'

'Not enough, I'm afraid. What is your relationship to the account holder?'

I could have pinged my ID and told him it related to an investigation, but that would have slammed the door shut until I could get a warrant.

'I'm her husband,' I said. 'She's out of the country now and one of the neighbours saw a suspicious character. Look, she messed up, accidentally wiping the memory when she tried to log in remotely to check. I said I'd sort it out. I have the passcode. I really want to clear this up before she comes back, and I'd rather do it without calling the police and wasting their time.'

He hesitated. 'One moment.' He turned away again, back to his own monitor. He frowned, chewed his lip. 'There's a fee for reinstating the account, and I will need that passcode.'

The bill that appeared on my phone was not, under the circumstances, excessive, but neither was the last slim reserve in my account. I authorised the payment and took out the card that had been lodged behind the controller and read out the passcode. 'Twenty-three, twelve, forty-seven.' It sounded like a date, could have been someone's birthday two days before Christmas, about the same age as Alice, as far as anybody could tell.

'Okay. On its way.'

My phone pinged, signalling the arrival of the message. I hung up.

The video was twenty seconds long. One visitor, three weeks before. He rang the bell, peered in the windows, and wandered away again. I'd seen him before. My last sight of him he was base jumping from the top of One Canary Wharf after shooting Big Bennie Thacker with my Glock.

CHAPTER 5

Saturday 16th November: Knocking on Doors

Entanglement is not for everyone. Some people are unable to reconcile their many concurrent lives, leading to that plethora of conditions made infamous by the overenthusiastic use of the early implicitins.

Cerasthesia is a condition that afflicts all the newly entangled to some degree. There are some unfortunate enough never to get past it. For them, the sensations of all their lives mingle and overlap into a paralysing chaos.

Some of the entangled, the monomaniacs, in their quest to reconcile their lives strive to live the same way in every world, inevitably failing as the realities diverge, as the circumstances in which their lives are framed change beyond their control.

The polymaniacs are the reverse. The need to make every life different, to never do the same thing twice, becomes all-consuming. A polymaniac will change their profession, their name, their appearance, their lifestyle, their gender, even their morality between their many lives. They are ever restless, hedonistic, but ultimately the saddest of all individuals, living on the borderline of sanity.

Each of us who are entangled find our own position on the spectrum between monomania and polymania. I myself tend towards the polymaniac; I engage in different professions, pastimes and relationships in my many lives. I write this text in one life but I would never have the patience to transcribe it in different realities. Fortunately I have a close friend who sits much closer to the monomaniac side. A man who by entanglement and business acumen has accumulated substantial wealth. He now divides his time between good works and restoring old road vehicles. He has promised that when this book is finished, he will read it in the world in which I write it while transcribing it in all the others where he is able.

—A K Amari - *The Measurement Problem, A Guide to Entanglement*

Sunday was a slow morning. I'd woken late after working into the early hours trawling the administrative fluff that Soames had sent by express courier, on a bead. Why he did that rather than send me an encrypted message was a mystery. It was a most tedious stack of memos, org charts, personnel files, purchase invoices, accounting audits. I had it all indexed and cross-referenced in minutes, but without knowing what I was looking for I had no search strategy, so I read at random, flicking from one thing to another, following a thread then veering off at a tangent whenever something grabbed my attention. I'd gone to bed on a stomach full of reheated lasagne and a head full of names and dates.

By the time morning came it had all congealed in my mind into something of a picture of that department at VGT. The people, the projects, who joined, who moved on. Alice's history there followed two projects, *Ambystoma* then

Furcifer, where she worked with Erica Fallon. Odd names, all the project names were like that. A search over my morning coffee told me these were Latin names for kinds of lizards.

Lizards. That's what Erica Fallon had kept in those glass tanks in her barn.

The Genetic Therapies Division was a hangover from VGT's early days before they made their money on implicitins. Ambystoma had yielded some useful advances on regeneration therapies; Alice had been full of enthusiasm when she first joined them, always wanting to tell anyone who would listen about the exciting work she was doing. Project Furcifer had delivered nothing marketable before it was sold off to a small privately held company called *Exercitus*. Doctor Erica Fallon chose to leave rather than work for the new owners. Alice was already in The Grange by the time the sale went through.

There was nothing in the files to tell me where Erica Fallon had gone. I found nothing on the net published under her name in the last three years, no mention of her professionally or socially.

Halfway through my second coffee, Baxter rang. Yeah, I was supposed to keep her informed.

'You're supposed to keep me informed, DI Drake.'

I grimaced. 'Nothing concrete on the DRC or Red Claw, ma'am. I saw Cloake, he fed me a line but I've got movement records from one of his cars that I'm following up.'

'Is that all?'

I gritted my teeth. So far I hadn't crossed any red lines, only grey ones; I hadn't exactly broken into Erica Fallon's barn. I hadn't misused my service authority in getting the doorcam footage. 'There's something else going on here. Something relating to VirGenTech.'

Her steely eyes turned steelier. 'Keep your personal interests out of this, Drake!'

'I have a photo of our Canary Wharf flier.'

'How? Have you run it through the PNR?'

'Of course. No match, but I know who he was looking for: A Doctor Erica

Fallon, former VGT researcher who vanished without a trace three years ago.'

Three slow nods while she digested that. 'Has to be the Erica that Big Bennie Thacker was looking for. There'll be some reason *Rdeča Kremplja* want her, and if they do, so do we. I'll get Harris on to tracking her down. You concentrate on the Wyndham case.'

'Thacker thought I knew Erica. This is a whole new angle on red Claw with some weird entangled shit going on. I've got leads to follow and a hunch I'm onto something.'

A *tsk* of irritation. 'No Drake. I suppose I should be happy to see some commitment from you, but Fallon worked for VirGenTech. You have too much of a personal interest.'

In a way she was right, but she was one person who was on shaky ground with that accusation.

'I think there's a connection between Erica Fallon's disappearance and Alice. I want to find her before Red Claw do. If I learn anything about Alice that's a bonus.'

'Enough! There's to be no personal crusades on my watch, Drake, and that's an end to it.'

I don't think I'd ever heard her raise her voice before, but it didn't matter. The hypocrisy of her words lit the fuse on my frustration.

'Your watch *is* a personal crusade.' I realised I was shouting. Too late, damage done, I didn't bother to moderate my tone. 'Everyone knows Red Claw killed your family.'

I hung up, seething. I stood and paced my small lounge, anger at her words mixing with guilt at my own. I'd only just calmed myself enough to sit when my phone rang: Baxter.

I answered. 'I'm sorry ma'am. I'll put in a transfer request right away.'

Her stern face glared from the screen. 'No you won't.' Her nostrils flared. 'I'll let you run with this on one condition.'

This was new. Compromise was a thousand miles from her style. I nodded.

'We have too many leaks in our department and in the service as a whole. Everything you do is your eyes only and if you find anything that might lead us to Vidmar's identity, you bring it immediately to me and no-one else. Do you agree?'

'Yes, ma'am.'

'Good. Look for Erica Fallon. Harris can take Wyndham. But watch your step. Now, what do you need?'

'A warrant for access to Doctor Fallon's bank and tax records and a forensic sweep of her home.'

'No forensics. The more people know about this, the more chance of a leak back to *Rdeča Kremplja*. We don't want to lead them to her. Your eyes only. Understand?'

'Yes, ma'am.' I gave her a firm nod. 'I want to track down her contacts, people she used to work with, so I'll be spending time in the field. If it's my eyes only you'll have to cover for me with the rest of the department or they'll wonder what I'm doing.'

Her eyebrows scrunched for a second, but she gave me a forced smile. 'I'll get you the warrant you need, Drake, and for cover, you'll be officially on a leave of absence because of the deterioration in your sister's condition.'

The connection dropped and I let out a long heavy sigh of relief. She'd given me carte blanche to follow my hunch. My hunch was that there was something very odd about Erica Fallon's disappearance. A moment later my warrant arrived. Carte Blanche, an on-demand warrant. I could demand records on anyone or anything. The catch was that every time I used it the details would be recorded, signed, and added to the blockchain and Baxter, the authorising judge, and someone in the conduct oversight department would be alerted. If I didn't have a solid justification I'd be in big trouble. It also meant that if the judge or the assigned oversight officer were bent then Red Claw and Vidmar would know where I was looking.

*

The tax office said she hadn't worked since leaving VGT in October three years before, the bank that she hadn't touched her account since the February after that. The UBI was still trickling in, enough to cover the taxes and services on the barn. Someone had to know where she'd been, what she'd done. Alice knew her, but anything she could tell me would be tangled in the events of other worlds. More likely to sow confusion and I had enough of that in just one world.

Finally—finally—I got a picture of Doctor Erica Fallon from the passport office. I stared at it for a long, long time. Mouth too wide, thin lips, nose too pronounced to be any kind of classic beauty, but there was something about her, something that made me want to know her better. Idiot; how could I know her better when I didn't know her at all. I might have seen her with Alice some time. But no, I'd have remembered. The other thing I got from the passport office was that she hadn't left the country. At least, not legally.

I summoned a car and clattered down my steep stairs out into the miserable winter drizzle, the kind of rain that floats more than falls, that soaks right through any clothing and feels colder than ice on the skin. Waiting outside the dim light of Kay's hairdresser shop, the only sign of life was the large wolf spider in the corner of the window. It got me thinking about how few customers Kay had, wondering how she'd managed to hold out so long before taking the relocation.

A car hummed to a stop behind me and unlocked its door with a muted *clunk*. I gave it the first address. The home of one Frank Wilson, senior administrator of the Genetic Therapies Division in VGT back then. He was another who had declined continued employment under the new owners. Once more out on the M11 heading north.

Forty minutes later the car pulled up outside a modest forties family home on the outskirts of Cambridge. Red brick, machine-laid in once-trendy curves, windows with curved glass in rounded frames. Not a straight line anywhere, like a lop-sided cartoon beehive. Looked pleasant enough but must have been a nightmare to live in. The door, nicely asymmetrical and leaning slightly off-vertical, would be somewhat disconcerting if you came home after a couple of beers too many. I pressed the bell and waited.

'Yes?'

The voice from the intercom was female, clipped. Unfriendly.

'Mrs Wilson?'

'Who wants to know?'

'Detective Inspector Drake.' I pinged my ID.

Another minute. The door opened: a smallish, youngish woman with shortish, brownish hair in some disarray. 'What's it about?'

'I'm looking for Frank Wilson. Is he in?'

Her lip curled. 'No, he isn't in. He hasn't been in for the last three years. What's he done?'

A small person appeared behind her, tugging at her fingers. I'm no judge of kids' ages, but this one was walking, sucking a thumb. About a metre in height.

She picked him up. 'What is it, Marko?' He wrapped his arms around her neck.

'I'm trying to find someone he used to work with,' I said. 'Did you ever meet any of the people at VirGenTech? Erica Fallon?'

'Nap time, little guy.' She gave me a quick look, and her hand went to push the door. 'Sorry, no.'

'Alice Drake?'

The door stopped half-way to the frame. 'Yeah, I knew Alice. Just a minute… What did you say your name was?'

'Lewis Drake. Alice is my sister.'

'Shit, that's tough.' Her hand ruffled the little boy's hair. Mark? Marko? She stepped back and pulled the door wide. 'Come in.'

She headed for the stairs, straight-edged and even, with a hint of a curve on the flight, and pointed me in the direction of the kitchen, not much bigger than the one in my little flat, but there was room for a table with a couple of chairs in what might have been a corner, if this house had had corners. I took the liberty of filling the kettle.

'Hope you don't mind,' I said when she appeared again. 'You seemed like you were ready for a coffee.'

She ran a hand through her hair and busied herself with cups and coffee. Instant.

'So what happened to Frank?' I asked over the rim of a steaming mug.

'He took off,' she snarled. 'Told me he'd had enough of this life. Time to move on, he said.' She raised her eyes to the ceiling. 'Marko was fifteen months old.'

'You knew Alice?' *Knew* sounded wrong. It wasn't like she was dead.

'She was one of the team working on Marko's treatment. It was a miracle, three months treatment saved him years of surgery. They published a paper on it.'

'What was the treatment for, Mrs Wilson?'

'Call me Jane. Jane Seymour. Like Henry's number three. I don't use Wilson.' She swiped at her phone. A wall panel next to the table lit up with an image. 'Marko was born with Velocardiofacial syndrome.'

It took me a moment to realise it was a newborn baby's face. A gap led up from the top lip to the nose: cleft palate. 'Wouldn't standard regen therapies have worked?'

'It's a genetic disorder. Regen grows according to the plan in the genes. They had to fix the DNA first.'

'*In Vivo Phenotype Reprogramming*.' That was the paper Alice had published with Erica.

'That's it.'

I'd always pictured Alice sitting in a lab full of incomprehensible machines performing abstract magic with bits of DNA. I never knew she worked so closely with real peoples' real problems. This is what she could do with Project Furcifer, and it had been buried. 'Did you know anyone else on the team?'

'I met some of them, I mean, they were Frank's work colleagues.' Her fingers sprang to life again, flicking through images on her phone. 'We had a bit of a celebration for Marko's first birthday. A bunch of them came.'

The screen changed to a video: grass, trees, a fence, blue sky, sunshine, people milling about, bottles and glasses, food, a barbecue.

Alice with a wine glass in her hand, laughing and touching the hand of Doctor Erica Fallon, who nearly choked on her drink with laughter. The image froze.

'That's Frank.' Jane pointed to a figure standing in the background by himself, a beer in his hand and a dour expression on his face. Dark hair with a pronounced widow's peak, below average height, prominent chin. 'As always not entirely there. But a real charmer when he wanted to be.'

'And that's Erica Fallon.' I pointed in my turn. 'That's who I'm looking for.'

'Yeah.' She shrugged. 'I recognise the face but I didn't really know her.'

'Can you put names to any of these others?'

'Some of them.'

The video resumed.

'That's Sam…' A figure approached Frank Wilson, engaged him in a long and thoughtful conversation. 'I forget his last name.'

There was only one Sam I'd seen in the pile of fluff. On a part-time contract, from the clinical side, a genuine medic specialising in regeneration therapies. 'Dr Samuel Okorie?'

'Yes, yes. That's him. He quit afterwards. Objected to the new owners.'

'Why?'

'He was working for the betterment of the human condition.' It sounded like she was quoting Sam's own words. 'Didn't want a job with a defence contractor.'

The elephant in the room, the one I hadn't seen, stampeded. 'I see.' Perhaps Erica had left for the same reason, but that wouldn't explain why she'd vanished.

'He died later that year.' Her eyes tracked down to her hands, resting on the table edge. 'A car ran him over.'

I was still digesting *defence contractor*, so it took a moment for her words to sink in.

'Ran him over? Cars don't do that. Not since… I don't know. Before you and I were born!'

'It was big news, a feral car hit him as he crossed the road. The company that owned it had gone bust and its records got lost. The car carried on driving around picking up passengers. Missed out on a recall for a brake problem.'

Three years ago. I wasn't paying much attention to the news back then. Other things on my mind. Alice on my mind. A vague recollection stirred, Vittoria talking about it. Scratch Dr Samuel Okorie from my list of interview candidates. I had plenty of others to work through.

'Would you mind sharing that video with me, Jane?'

I summoned a car and took my leave of her.

'How is Alice?' she called after me at the door.

I hesitated, not really knowing how to answer. Not with any kind of short answer. 'I have hope,' I said, and gave her a farewell wave as I climbed into the car. She watched from the doorway until the car pulled away.

*

Jeong Song, lab technician, lived in a flat on the fourth floor of a mansion block dating back to the late nineteenth or early twentieth centuries. Solid brick with stone embrasures and quoins. Genteel shabby. Low rent, high maintenance.

The door opened on its chain revealing a thin slice of a dark-haired, dark-eyed face.

I pinged her my ID. 'Ms Jeong? I'm trying to locate someone who you used to work with at VirGenTech, on Project Furcifer.'

'Show me your clearance.'

'Clearance?'

'State Security Act, 2054. I can't talk to you about Furcifer unless you got clearance.'

'It's not about the project, I'm looking for…'

She slammed the door in my face. Her final words came from the intercom. 'I can't talk to you. Go away.'

And so went my afternoon. Ms Jane Seymour's stale breadcrumbs were the most I got from anyone. Two people had moved without updating their registered address, one had died, two more refused to talk to me and five were out, or pretending to be out. Word had spread.

I took a car to the former VirGenTech building, an anonymous three storey glass and concrete block in an industrial park on the edge of Cambridge. A random scattering of windows shone bright in the gloom of the grey November dusk. The sight of the building jogged a memory. I'd been here before, with Alice, to give her moral support for her interview for a summer internship after her second undergraduate year. Back then there hadn't been a three-metre-high security fence topped with razor wire around the compound, there hadn't been a uniformed security guard sitting by the gate giving me suspicious looks. There *had* been a board by the entrance with *VirGenTech* emblazoned in two-metre high letters. In the last of the meagre daylight I found the pair of concrete slabs in the grass with the rusting remains of posts cut off at ground level: all that was left of that sign. Now there was no name, no hint as to who worked in this building, or what they did here.

The guard put his phone down as I approached the gate. He wouldn't let me in without an appointment, told me to contact their liaison department, on Monday.

A motor whined, wheels turned on tarmac behind me. My car, departing. It was Sunday, demand was supposed to be low. There was no reason for it to go. Cold, damp, tired, hungry and frustrated, I pulled out my phone and stabbed at the screen to summon another. Ten minutes I waited, peeking at the screen three times a minute, looking for an update. Finally, a car turned onto the road where I stood shivering in the perpetual drizzle. Lights bright, it hummed to a gentle stop by the kerb and the lock clunked. I pulled open the door and almost fell in, pulling it shut.

'Well, Detective Inspector Drake. You have been making a nuisance of yourself.'

The car moved off, and I stared at the shadowed figure in the diagonally opposite seat, a dark shape in the car's unlit interior. Flickers of passing street lights picked out a well-built male, short neatly-trimmed beard, deep black hair.

'I take it you're going to tell me to stop.'

'Consider it a strong recommendation.'

The car turned off the industrial estate onto an unlit road. The nav screen was off.

'Sure, but you need to give me a clue.'

'A clue?'

'Yeah. What, precisely, am I doing to make a nuisance of myself? Is it about

Frank Wilson? Doctor Fallon? The Docklands Redevelopment? Elijah Cloake?'

He didn't answer.

'Project Furcifer?'

'Don't play games. You'll lose.'

The car slowed and turned. Lights of an oncoming car picked out a signpost on the corner leaning in towards the hedge. Might have been an overlooked original or a neglected retro addition to give an old-world feel for the tourists. Didn't matter, the angle of it kept it unreadable in shadow.

'What I don't get is why a treatment for genetic disorders is a matter of national security. What are you, MI5? MI6?'

He didn't answer.

I'd been jumping to conclusions. Jeong Song's earlier mention of the State Security Act had me thinking of spooks, so I'd assumed this guy was a spook.

'Or Red Claw?' I reached for my Glock.

'STOP!'

The car did as it was told, tyres screeching as it braked to an abrupt halt. My abrupt halt came a fraction of a second later when my face hit the headrest of the rear-facing seat in front of me. A metallic taste hit my tongue. The Glock was plucked from my hand.

'Resume.'

The car moved off, with a little more care for its passengers this time. I couldn't see in the car's dark saloon, but it was a pretty good guess the Glock was pointing at me.

'State Security Act 2054, Drake. You're on formal notice.' My phone pinged. The notice was there, authorised, validated, incontrovertible. 'You understand what that means?'

I knew what it meant. Prosecution, trial in a national security court if I revealed any state secrets to anyone. It was up to me to figure out what might or might not be a state secret.

'I understand.'

'We're going easy on you, Drake. You're being manipulated by Cloake. He thinks he's been clever by giving you a set of unclassified VGT administrative records but we can still prosecute him on his intent to have you delving into things you shouldn't.'

'He's entangled. Do you think he doesn't know that? Do you think he cares that much if you lock him up?'

'I want to know what his game is.'

'Let me know if you find out.'

A flicker of light from a phone lit his face. From the angle I could just make out the display, the graphs, the colours. It was Argus, same as we used in the interview rooms. This car was set up with the monitors, IR video, voice analysis, breathing and heart-rate monitors. I'd been pretty honest with my answers.

'Here.'

The car slowed to a gentle stop.

'You might have a long and illustrious career before you, Drake, or you might have a very short one, then who would pay for Alice's care?' He leaned over and opened the car door. 'It's up to you.'

I stepped out into the darkness and drizzle onto a narrow verge of long wet grass overhung by a tangle of dripping branches and brambles from an overgrown hedge. My hand on the car door held it open. 'Did Samuel Okorie make a nuisance of himself too?'

There was a fraction of a second, a hesitation. 'You're fishing, Drake. You need to stop.' He tossed my Glock after me, sending it spinning into the roadside hedgerow.

I slammed the door as hard as I could and the damper slowed it to a gentle clunk as the lock engaged. Just about summed up my day. Here I was once again in the cold, the dark and the wet. The car's tail lights vanished around a bend as my hand groped in my pocket for my phone. Gone. It must have fallen out in the spook's car.

No phone. Everybody's nightmare. No way to call a car, no way to call for help, no way to pay for anything. On top of that I had no fucking clue where I was.

Oh yeah, no phone, no GPS, no navigation.

Ten minutes fumbling in the pitch darkness in the dripping hedge to find my

Glock—I counted myself fortunate that in the end I *did* find it. Losing another would have been embarrassing to say the least. An imaginary coin-toss had me heading back the way the spook's car had come, along a narrow lane between fields and hedges. The thin drizzle turned to light rain as I walked. After ten minutes I wondered where the spook had been going.

What the hell. Another ten minutes and I was back where I'd started, twenty minutes wetter. I kept walking, shrinking back into the hedge at the sound of tyres on wet tarmac ahead. Bright light dazzled me when a car came round the bend. It zipped past without slowing. I caught a glimpse, two passengers. One of them might have had a beard.

The road felt familiar but there must have been hundreds of miles of road like it, and besides, I'd been plagued with déjà vu and odd feelings these last days. Still, a bend to the right, an old metal farm gate to the side, and at the T-junction I knew to turn right. A kilometre further on I saw the gates and I knew where I was.

I was still weighing up whether it would be prudent to climb over when I heard tyres again on the road behind me. The gates swung open as the car approached and I slipped in ahead of it. It pulled past me on the drive. A figure in a coat and hat waited under the lights between the two columns of the portico of The Grange.

'Cecilia,' I shouted as she reached to open the car door. I jogged the last few metres.

'Lewis? What are you doing here? Where's your car?'

'Long story. Can I use your phone? Mine got lost.'

'You're soaked.' She looked up at me, blinking away the drizzle. A little shake of the head and a quiet *tut!* then she opened the door. 'Get in.'

I could have kissed her. Well, to be honest I often thought that when I saw Cecilia, but you get what I mean.

She took the rear-facing seat in front of me. 'And you're bleeding, Lewis.' She pulled a tissue from her bag and dabbed at my split lip.

I took it from her and continued my own dabbing. 'Just off duty?'

'Yeah.' She slumped back in her seat. 'Long day.'

'If I can borrow your phone, I'll call a car and get out of your hair.'

She smiled a tired and crooked half-smile. 'Let's get you warm and dry first.'

The car wound its way through those back lanes, emerging onto a main road, and turned off into a complex of nineteen-sixties or seventies semis and terraces. There weren't many of those still standing and still habitable.

Her front door opened onto a staircase, a maisonette not much bigger than my flat above Kay's hairdresser shop. She pushed me into the bathroom, handing me a towel. 'Shower,' she said. 'Throw your wet clothes out here and I'll dry them. There's a dressing gown on the back of the door. I'll make coffee.'

I did as I was told, emerging ten minutes later feeling warm and dry and awkward with a floral dressing gown that was several sizes too small stretched around my frame. I stopped dead at the sight of the print on the hallway wall. Waves of blues and greens like the memory of a fading storm. This was a print; I was pretty sure the one in Erica Fallon's barn was the original.

'Coffee?' She stood in the kitchen doorway holding out a steaming mug, a frown on her face.

'Thanks,' I said. 'Who's the artist?'

'Beate Messer.' She turned and led the way to the small table by the kitchen window and lifted a laundry basket from one of the two chairs so we could sit facing each other. A roller blind shut out the darkness, but the cold wind managed to find its way past the ill-fitting window frame. The tumble-dryer rumbled and rattled under the counter.

'Beate Messer. I haven't heard of her.'

'Minor local celebrity, turn of the century.'

I took a sip of coffee, then another. It was good coffee.

'That's good coffee,' I said.

A half-dozen utensils stood in a ceramic pot by the hob, a packet of oats beside it held closed by a clothes peg. A scattering of magnets held scraps of paper to the door of the fridge, and a small whiteboard read *olives, salad (misc), mushrooms*. There were no other knick-knacks of any kind, no pictures on the walls.

'Lived here long?'

'A little while. It's kind of temporary.'

I stopped studying the room, and studied her instead. She held my gaze, and took a sip when I did.

'I guess you've got plans, the two of you.'

'Two of us?'

'The engagement ring?'

She let out a nervous laugh. 'Yes. Plans. Yes.' Her left hand dropped to her lap and her eyes followed it.

'Sorry,' I said. 'I'm a nosy cop. Force of habit.'

I got her half-smile back, and her eyes, for a second. 'That's okay.'

I put my mug down and sat up a little straighter, leaning my forearms on the table. 'Did someone leave The Grange ten or fifteen minutes before I arrived?'

'Yes,' she said. Her mug went on the table and her posture mirrored mine. 'Dr Stebbins-Reese. He's trying a new protocol using a quantum random number generator to set the treatment times so that Alice gets the inhibitor at different times in different worlds. It seems less stressful for her.'

'I think that was Alice's idea.' *You're breaking me up, blocking me in every world at the same time*, she had said. 'Have you heard her talk about the people she worked with on Project Furcifer? Frank Wilson? Jeong Song? Dr Okorie or Dr Fallon?'

She leaned back on the chair, and looked, well, not out of the window, because it was dark outside and the blind was down, but in that direction. She held that pose for half a minute before facing me again.

'She's scared, Lewis. There's something she knows in Omega, that she can't remember when she's on the inhibitor. She's terrified she'll remember and say the wrong thing. You know how she is. Most of the time she can't tell who's in the room with her, and she says things meant for people in other worlds. She's frightened she'll say the wrong thing to the wrong person.'

'Who is she afraid of? If I knew that I might be able to protect her.'

'It's not who she's afraid *of*, Lewis. She's entangled—death in one world won't bury her secrets. It's who she's afraid *for*. She's afraid for you, Lewis. You, and… and Erica Fallon.'

The tumble-dryer ground to a rumbling stop and emitted a desultory beep.

*

Cecilia lent me her phone so I could order a car to take me home and a replacement for my own lost phone. In clothes crisp and warm from her dryer I was carried towards London, stewing in my own thoughts. Her words brought me full circle back to Alice, back to the events that had destroyed her life and ruled mine for the past three years. Three years of bitterness towards VirGenTech and towards the entangled still seethed beneath the surface. Bitterness I had never known until they took Alice from me. Alice, the only family I could remember.

Three weeks ago, I'd learned that Alice wasn't just catatonic, she was entangled more deeply than anyone. I hated the entangled. I loved my sister. The miles passed under the car's wheels while I tried to tame the demons of my own preconceptions.

My crisp warm clothes had cooled and softened and the rain had finally given up by the time I got home. A replacement phone was waiting for me in the parcel box, charged and preloaded with all my account access. It was ten pm; four hours I'd been without access. Plenty of time for the spook to have had the lost phone hacked. Perhaps it hadn't fallen from my pocket in the car, perhaps he'd lifted it when he leaned across to open the door.

Five minutes later, sprawled on my cheap lumpy sofa with a dram of the Linlithgow in my hand, I concluded that Cloake had anticipated my account would be hacked and that all the files he sent me, deleted. They had been. That was the first thing I checked when I turned on the new phone. That was why he had sent them on a bead, by courier. I turned the bead over and over in the fingers of my left hand. The problem was that my phone, my desks, home and work, even my TV were likely to be compromised. If I plugged this bead in to any of them I might find its contents deleted before I could even open anything. I still had the video of the celebration for little Marko Wilson given me by Mrs Wilson, aka Jane Seymour, and the journey log I'd copied from Cloake's Saqqaf.

I needed help but Baxter wasn't taking calls so I pinged her a meeting request. *Somewhere discreet*, I said. It came back right away. Noon, the next day, at Marek's.

My living room window looked out onto the street and at Kay's house opposite. I'd figured out what was going on: Kay's psychic abilities, a hairdresser's shop with no customers. And there was her surprising competence at dealing with the entangled that she'd shown with Stephanie. I hated the entangled, I hated the drugs, those who made them, those who sold them or used them, legitimate or black market. The microwave in the kitchen dinged. I stood by the window and ate one slow forkful of Kay's lasagne after another. I had no interest in the little people, they weren't hurting anyone more than they'd hurt themselves. And I liked Kay. She was a good friend.

The answers to my puzzles, the keys to this case, lay in other worlds. If I could find Erica Fallon in one world it might help find her in another. My sister was entangled, Cloake was entangled. He had his agenda, had his games, but Monica Wyndham admired him. I couldn't trust that judgement; she was too like my imagination of an unremembered mother. I didn't know if I could trust my own judgement. But when it turned into a battle between doing something and doing nothing, the something was bound to win out.

I dropped the dirty dish in the kitchen sink and walked slowly down the stairs and across the street. Kay answered the door right away, her face clear of its usual overlay, the skin of her cheeks covered with faint patina of light and dark spots. It took me a second to register and to understand what I was seeing; these were the scars from an infection of the virus Vaccinia 2048-Epsilon, from the early years of the plague war, when it used to take weeks to develop specific vaccines and anti-virals for each new pathogen. She must have been very young.

'I need to ask you a favour, Kay.'

'What is it, Lewis?'

'Don't be alarmed.'

She tilted her head, the doubt visible on her face.

'You're not psychic are you, Kay? You're sensitive, and I think you have something that makes you more sensitive.'

'Lewis…'

'Do you have any gammas? I need to blur the boundaries. I need to know what's happening elsewhere.'

'It's not that simple, Lewis.'

'Please, Kay. I need this.'

Her lips pursed and she nodded. 'Go back home. It's best done in a familiar environment. I'll be with you in a moment.'

Less than five minutes I waited before the doorbell rang. I hit the door release and Kay's heels clumped up the stairs. Her eyes homed straight on the glass on the coffee table.

'No alcohol, it's not a good idea when you aren't used to it.' She picked up the glass and downed it in one. 'Good god! How do you drink that stuff?' She pointed. 'Sit.'

I sat in the centre of my small couch. She pushed the coffee table out of the way and pulled up the footstool to sit facing me with her knees brushing mine. From her small bag, she pulled out a clear resealable bag and took out two black, oval capsules.

'You said you wanted gammas. You don't. Gammas won't tell you shit, you're only sharing with the alternates that diverge after you take them.' She held up one of the capsules between thumb and forefinger. 'This is a delta. With one of these, you share the minds of your alternates, you know what they know, you feel what they feel.' Her fist thumped my chest, my heart. 'In here.'

Her eyes were pinpoint sharp, piercing.

'That's not always good, Lewis. You understand me?'

'To be honest, no. But I hope this'll teach me.'

'Good answer. Hold out your hand.'

She dropped one of the capsules in my palm, and I slammed it into my mouth and swallowed.

Kay did the same. 'It'll come on slowly. It starts with the selves that are here in this room now doing what we're doing and it'll spread from there to more distant realities. Ones that diverged from this one further back in time. If you were to keep taking them it could go right back to when you were born or even before. You could be living all the worlds where there is someone that is recognisably you.'

'How many?'

'You can't count them, Lewis. When you swim in a river you don't count the water molecules, it's a stream with currents and eddies that flow and divide and merge.' Her hands moved as she spoke, turning and flowing like the eddies of the river she spoke of. 'There are wide, deep channels where all the water goes one way, and little rivulets, thin as strands of cotton that flow in another direction altogether.'

'Thin.'

'What was that?' said Kay. And she didn't say it, just leaned back and raised an eyebrow.

'Alice said I was thin.' My voice resonated, like I'd spoken a thousand times at once.

Kay leaned forward and took my hand with her right. 'Which hand am I holding?'

'Left,' I said. 'No, right.' I closed my eyes. My hand was warmed by the gentle touch of hers. I could see it, feel it, the right *or* the left, at the same time.

'Separate them in your mind. Concentrate. Tell me only in the threads where I'm holding the left.'

I tried. I looked at her hand holding my left, and opened my mouth to speak. Before the words left my mouth I was looking at her holding my right. 'I… I can't!' Panic at the loss of control rose like bile in my throat. 'What's happening?'

'Relax, Lewis. You're suffering cerasthesia, confusing senses and actions between worlds. It may pass, it may not, but either way you're in a safe place and I'm here with you. Roll with it.'

Her thumb rested in my palm, her fingers stroked the back of my hand, bringing back the memory of the touch of those fingers on my cheek, on my lips. Her lips on mine, the soft smoothness of her breast under my hand. The feline beauty the mottling of her skin lent her nakedness.

'You and I! When was that?'

She gave me that salacious smile, the flirting look. 'Lewis, it's happened dozens of times in one thin reality or another. Just two lonely people taking comfort in each other.' The grip on my right hand shifted to a tight grasp. 'It's alright. I know how you feel. You've told me more than once about the lovely, unattainable Cecilia.'

I'd barely been able to admit those feelings to myself. It was a shock to remember that in the quiet darkness of my bed I'd revealed them to Kay. Most recently on Tuesday night. It started with talking with her over beer and lasagne. Telling her about my experience at Marek's had raised questions but brought some comfort. At the end I saw her down the stairs to the door. She stopped in the doorway and gave me a kiss on the cheek, lingering a second as her hand found my waist. 'When I relocate you could come with me,' she whispered, but at the same time she hadn't spoken: she'd reached up to the back of my neck, reached up on tiptoe to kiss me. I'd taken her hand and led her back up the stairs.

'Which memory is mine?' I murmured. 'Which is the other?'

She shook her head gently. 'They're all yours. You aren't looking through windows into other lives. There is only one *you*, with many pasts, many futures. It's only now you begin to see them. For now you're only seeing lives that diverged over the last few days. Think about what else happened this week.'

'Yesterday I went to interview an entangled.' Nine o'clock, Soames had told me to be there. The car drove along that long drive, the deer ambled along the margin of the wood and I was sitting on the chesterfield in Cloake's library with my head in my hands, shaking with rage and sorrow. Cloake sat next to me rubbing my back, trying to calm me.

'What the fuck?' I mumbled, unpicking the memories. After my arrival the memories shattered into a dozen, a hundred, a thousand diverging fragments. Cloake questioning me in subtly different ways. That meeting followed so many fine threads, so many variations, so many questions, so many answers. What he told me was carefully constrained, but he prised from me everything about my life in a few short minutes. Two things were consistent in all my memories of that meeting, two things that surprised him: the VLA logs that had implied he'd met Wyndham, and the fact that I did not know Erica Fallon.

In every thread I was sent away in the Saqqaf with the promise that I would receive the VGT files. After that, those strands braided together in my memories into a thick bundle, more or less the same. I couldn't tease them apart.

Before Cloake there was Canary Wharf. My hand in Kay's turned cold and damp. My pulse raced when I thought of it, standing facing the empty chair, imagining the blowtorch burning through my shirt, my flesh, but it was only the memory of a fear, not of a reality. Not of a reality I could see.

'If I died…' Kay's face swam before my eyes, an overlay of a hundred Kays. *Focus!* Slowly her face resolved. Still and clear, a hundred separate, clear images, all with lips tight, eyes screwed up. 'I won't remember realities where I'm already dead, will I?'

A silent shake of the head.

'Thursday, I was on a raid. I was kidnapped for a time.'

'I told you to be careful.' She closed her eyes, held them shut for a moment.

'There's a thread where you didn't come home. You haven't been seen since.'

Sitting in Marek's, my death in other worlds had been traumatic but I'd felt nothing like it since, but I'd never felt anything like it before, and I must have died somewhere, at some time. Cloake's words came back to me: *To suffer such violence in such a thick stream of realities… you surely felt it.* Thickness was the key. In Marek's I'd felt my death in a wider swathe of realities than were left to me.

No-one likes to confront their own mortality. Thinking about it always left me with a hollow feeling. I had that feeling then. I'd had it after Marek's on Tuesday. I steeled myself to recall what I could of what happened then. I was looking for differences. Every memory I had of that morning I was sitting in Marek's. There were minor variations—Marek saw me, rushed over full of concern. There were one or two other customers doing their best to ignore my odd behaviour. The other constant was the stranger in the alley. In the darkness and with the hat pulled low I could see nothing of the face, but the timing their appearance, turning and leaving again, were the same in every world.

I drifted, lost in memory, slumped back on the sofa, only vaguely aware of Kay's watchful gaze. The diverging past stretched from days to weeks to months. All of them I lived in this upstairs flat above Kay's hairdressers, with occasional nights where our flirtations turned to physical passions. At work the casework followed similar patterns but there were differences in detail. Poor Marlowe was killed in a raid, replaced by the eager young Wilkins, or he wasn't. Others came and went. There were constants: DCI Baxter, Harris, Alice catatonic at The Grange, Cecilia caring for her.

I went back further, looking for I don't know what. 'When the delta wears off, will I remember these other lives?' I asked Kay at one point.

'Whatever you bring to mind now, you'll still remember it afterwards.'

Vittoria. Thousands of times, thousands of ways she told me she wanted a divorce, only months after we married. 'How can I be here for you when you don't open up to me?' she said again and again at different times, different places, different worlds, in the weeks after they gave Alice the treatment and sent her to The Grange. Alice was always at the heart of my replies, softly spoken, hurled in anger. Vittoria was right, a distance had grown between us after that.

'You never open up to me,' she said as we sat in the car on the way from Cambridge. We'd been to see Alice in her flat. Two weeks before it happened, we'd only been married a month. The distance was already there. I'd been latching onto to Alice as my excuse for not loving Vittoria enough, but I was wrong.

I hunted for the trigger; what went wrong? The years before we were happy enough together as far as I could remember, but those memories were still singular, one thread. There was a moment, a few weeks before the wedding. We were about to leave our flat to some event Alice had invited us too. Vittoria didn't want to go. She never got on with Alice, but she insisted I go anyway. I'd called a car and waited. Half an hour later my phone bleeped a notification—technical issue with the car, the replacement would be another twenty minutes. I cancelled it.

That moment, there was an *absence*, a place where a memory should be, a dark emptiness. I cleared my throat of an irritation.

'Every life I'm here, now,' I said. 'The last three years have been mostly the same. Does that sound right?' The irritation turned into a discomfort. My throat felt half-blocked. I tried to cough but there was nothing there.

'It's unusual. Your sister, she said you were thin?'

I nodded. I tried to cough again. It hurt deep at the back of my throat, rough and heavy like I'd been swallowing ground glass. My chest ached and a humming, buzzing noise invaded my ears.

'It could be that in any worlds that are different to these, you haven't survived.'

I could barely hear her—the noise, hissing, buzzing, clunking. 'What? How?' I squeezed the words out past the blockage in my throat. I couldn't swallow, couldn't cough. Whatever was there I couldn't get rid of it.

'Lewis? Lewis, what's wrong?'

Her words barely penetrated the buzzing. My chest and throat convulsed in painful retches.

Help me. The words formed in my mind, but I couldn't speak.

CHAPTER 6

Sunday 17th November: Donahue

'How many?' is a question we often hear. It's the wrong question. A theoretical physicist might talk about the Hilbert space that represents all the possible states of the universe's quantum wave function and the subset of those that contain you as an individual. If you press hard enough some may tell you the number is infinite, others might give you a vague number so preposterously large that it is meaningless to talk about it. We do not count the grains of flour in a sack, we speak of how much it weighs. Just so, in speaking of realities a better question than 'How many?' would be 'How much?' but there is no scale to weigh realities.

The entangled experience these divisions according to the laws of probability. Those branches in the fabric of the world that are caused by improbable events will affect a small cluster of realities, those that are likely will affect a much larger cluster. The common vernacular for these is thin *and* thick. *A* thick *reality is one that is wide and deep and easy to see.* Thin *realities are harder for us to focus our attention on.*

Everyone experiences a multiplicity of worlds, for modern science tells us that this is a prerequisite for consciousness. However, for those who are not entangled, they experience such a narrow slice of all the realities that all seem identical, so it feels like a single universe. The day-to-day experience of the unentangled is one of many worlds, but a thin, uniform one.

—A K Amari - *The Measurement Problem, A Guide to Entanglement*

In the beginning was the sound. Its hissing filled the emptiness, its end joined to its beginning with a heavy *clunk* to create an eternal unchanging cycle of being. The sound was all. There was nothing to make the sound, nothing to hear it. It existed, had always existed, would always exist, endlessly repeating, alone, independent, complete. The sound was the entirety of existence.

The light followed. White, uniform, invariant. The bright glare followed the sound. To follow, there must be an ordering. First one thing, then another.

There was time.

Unmeasurable time, a second, an eternity of the sound and the light.

Next came the awareness. The awareness of the sound and of the brightness. Awareness without thought, without question, without answer. Awareness without consciousness.

Last came the self. Awareness of the sound and the light coalesced within the self, leading to awareness *of* the self that heard, that saw.

The self remembered. It remembered a name. Its own name.

'Lewis?'

Kay. 'Ungh!'

The pale light of dawn's approach filtered through the small window of my bedroom accompanied by the sound of pigeons cooing from their customary spot on the flat roof of the ground floor extension. I lay on my bed, fully clothed. Kay was leaning over me searching my face, my eyes.

'What happened, Lewis?'

'I don't know.' The coughing, the pain, the noise. I cleared my throat. No pain, no soreness. I took a deep, easy breath.

'It was like you were having some kind of fit. You passed out. I didn't know whether to call an ambulance, but I didn't want to get you in trouble over the delta.'

I hauled myself up to sit on the edge of the bed.

'Are you alright?' She reached out to rest her hand on my arm.

'Yeah. I think so.' I patted her hand. 'You did the right thing, Kay. I'm fine, Sorry if I scared you.'

It took me a while to persuade her I really was okay, but eventually I managed to shoo her out of the flat, with lashings of thanks and copious reassurances of my health and sanity.

'It takes a few days for the delta to completely work its way out of your system.' She hung on the doorstep to tell me. 'You'll get flashes of it coming back, especially under stress. Be careful.'

'I will, Kay. I will.'

'And you might have dreams.'

'Dreams. Yeah. okay.'

She crossed the street, looking back several times. I waited for her to reach her door before I closed my own, so I could relax, slump down on the bottom step of my staircase. I'd learned nothing, nothing to tell me what I should be looking for. The need for coffee drew me stumbling up the stairs into the kitchen. Nine thirty, a couple of hours before I needed to leave to meet Baxter. The bead with Cloake's VGT files tempted me, but it wasn't worth the risk of trying to load it, so I sat with my coffee and worked my way through the thirty odd minutes of video of the celebration for Marko that Jane Seymour, the former Mrs Wilson, had shared with me. Alice and Erica were enjoying themselves, enjoying each other's company, close, touching, eye contact, smiles. Then bending down together to make a fuss of Marko when he tottered towards them.

Doctor Samuel Okorie figured in the picture three times. Once in a passing shot, talking to a tall, slim woman with paper-white skin and silver-grey hair, the pair of them similar in age: late fifties, early sixties. They stood close, his hand on her arm. Another time he was in the background of Alice's laughter. The third time in deep and earnest conversation with Frank Wilson, Okorie gesticulating forcefully, Wilson calm and imperturbable, nodding slowly in apparent agreement.

A records search found The Road Traffic Accident Investigation Branch report on Okorie's death: a tragedy ultimately caused by the demise of a rental company during the dying throes of the plague wars eighteen years earlier. So many died leaving businesses and personal affairs in such disarray that records were lost. Even after all that time there were still thousands of vehicles on the roads whose owners were untraceable. They were still driving, picking up passengers, banking the fees to pay for recharges and routine maintenance but missing out on recalls and manual inspections. The report recommended that more resources be devoted to tracking and eliminating feral cars. It never became a priority. No-one was going to win votes or make a profit from hunting them down.

Half an hour left to kill before it was time to leave. Beate Messer, the artist who had painted the canvases in Erica Fallon's house, turned up on an index of artists of the late twentieth and early twenty-first centuries. Her work had something of a following. Collectors were willing to pay significant, if not vast, sums for her pieces. She was born in Germany but moved to England in the nineteen-eighties and settled in Cambridgeshire with her partner and their son. There was a photograph of them outside their newly built barn-style home in 1997. Beate Messer, her partner, Michael Fallon, and their five year old son, Jacob. I found nothing on Erica Fallon's family history. Jacob might have been her father later in life, or her grandfather, or Beate and Michael could have had other children later.

*

My research sucked me in so much I was ten minutes late leaving home. Traffic soaked up the contingency in my timing so it was five past twelve when

I reached Marek's. Baxter didn't seem too perturbed by my tardiness. Two cappuccinos sat on the table before her. She pushed one over to me.

Cappuccino. Too much milk, too much froth, just too heavy. I took a sip out of politeness. 'I'm straying into someone else's territory, ma'am.' I gave her a summary of my discussion with Jane Seymour, the video, the account of my meeting with the bearded spook, and of the vanishing files. 'The fact they went to the trouble of wiping them from my account tells me there's something important in there.'

'And how does that help us?' she said. 'Have you asked Cloake to send them again?'

I smiled, and pulled the bead from my pocket. 'He's entangled. He expected it.' I clunked it down firmly like a *go* stone. It sat between us. Baxter's move.

'You'll need a dark machine to read it safely. Disconnected from any network.'

'There won't be anything on our supply list, nor anything off the shelf commercially. Can our techs rustle something up?' I asked that more in hope than expectation. Any standard kit has at least a dozen ways of networking built in: infra-red, bluetooth, greentooth, vis, five cellular protocols, three WIFI bands, ultrasonic... Cut all those out and you've got to hack the software so it doesn't sit waiting forever for some server in Casablanca or Ulaanbaatar to check its license.

'I wouldn't trust them to get it right.' She lifted her cappuccino from the table, set it down again. 'Or to keep it quiet.'

'Special Branch would have something, or MI5. But the spooks are the ones blocking me.'

She sat back, sipped her coffee, gave me those three slow nods. 'Red Claw have their own technicians. We seized three machines in the Canary Wharf raid.'

'Nice to know something good came of it, but how do we get one out of the evidence locker?'

She lifted the bead from the table, turning it over between her fingers. '*We*, don't, Drake. *You* will wait for a package to be delivered.' Gripped between her finger ends, the bead made a firm *clunk* again as she put it down and slid it across the table towards me.

'Yes, ma'am.'

She knocked back the last of her cappuccino. 'I'm coming to the view that someone has something to hide, not only the intelligence services.' She waited for me to agree, like she was telling me something I hadn't already figured out. 'Wilson disappeared, Okorie dead, and Fallon gone into hiding. She must know something.'

I was still trying to keep an open mind on that last one, whether her disappearance was voluntary, but I was way ahead of the game here. Time to let Baxter have the last word.

'Okorie's accident was thoroughly investigated. If there was anything suspicious about it, it was well hidden, and it was three years ago. Wilson, too, the trail has gone cold. Concentrate on Fallon. Red Claw are looking for her in the person of the Canary Wharf base jumper. We need to find her first and find out what she knows.'

'Yes, ma'am.' It was close enough to my line of thinking, but the spooks worried me, Red Claw worried me, Cloake worried me, and I was puzzled by our base jumping friend.

She stood and walked to the door, which squealed as it opened. I half-turned to Marek. 'Can I get a macchiato here please, Marek?' I pushed the lukewarm cappuccino away, and the door squealed again. A shadow loomed from behind my back.

'Detective Inspector Drake? Come with us, please.'

Two of them. Big guys. Their plain-clothes did nothing to hide their official status, nonetheless they each pinged me their IDs. Their demeanour suggested I was not being offered a choice.

*

Heading west along the Victoria Embankment we passed knots of protestors making their way towards Parliament Square for Winston Saïd's anti-entanglement rally. One straggle-haired old man in a heavy coat clutched a placard with a crudely painted burning cross accompanied by the words *Exodus 22:18*. After a long summer of protests and riots they no longer needed to bother with the full quote. Everybody knew it: *Thou shalt not suffer a witch to live*. All kinds of crazies objected to entanglement but the religious fundamentalists were the worst.

The protesters mostly stuck to the broad ground-level pavement, occasionally spilling onto the road, causing the traffic to slow and veer around them. Above, the new raised walkway by the flood wall was crowded with the people of London walking the embankment where they could once again see the river. They shimmered and shook in my vision, blurred and overlapped so I couldn't see how many there were. Just as Kay had said, the delta was coming back under stress. Notwithstanding the silence of my two burly escorts, I knew where we were heading before the car swung in through the security gates leading to Curtis Green House, a nineteen-thirties neoclassical hulk that had for a while been more commonly known as New Scotland Yard.

In through a side door, up two floors in the lift and along a dingy corridor, a discreet pointed finger or inviting open-palmed gesture directing me at every turn. Escort number one tapped on a door and entered. 'DI Drake to see you, sir.'

He stepped back and held the door open for me. The man behind the desk wore a uniform with a superintendent's crown on his epaulettes. The board on his desk read *Donahue*.

'Thank you for coming, DI Drake, please take a seat.'

'No problem, sir. How can I help?' I'm all for the friendly, polite approach whenever possible so I tried really hard to keep any sarcasm out of my tone. The brief glare I got suggested I wasn't entirely successful. The shimmering was getting stronger.

'You work for Baxter, Organised Crime.' His words were out of sync with the movements of his mouth.

'Yes, sir.' I could feel the pulse in my neck beat faster, stronger. The rhythm fragmented.

'You get on with her?'

'I have a good working relationship with DCI Baxter, sir.' I had to focus, I had to hold it together.

He opened a manilla folder that lay on the desk in front of him. Even in this digital age, the manilla folder still ruled in these halls of hallowed bureaucracy. He took an A4 sized print from it and passed it over to me. 'Take a good look at this, Drake.'

The face was the Canary Wharf base jumper. The image was the one I had taken from Erica Fallon's doorcam video, the one I'd fed into a PNR search. Cogs whirred. The PNR had told me there were no matches, but had alerted Donahue to my search, ergo: the jumper was on file, but his record was classified.

My mind span off in tangents: this plain unlabelled room, this desk clear but for the folder and the name board, the face in the picture of a man who was part of Red Claw, who had kidnapped me, then killed Big Bennie Thacker. I felt giddy with the pace of my mind, my *minds*, spinning new threads and following each idea to its conclusion.

This was what Kay had meant, flashes of the delta coming back under stress. I balled my right hand into a fist to shut out the tremors and my focus came back, clear and sharp.

A second or two since he'd slid the photo across the desk, Donauhie tapped it with his forefinger. 'Tell me what you know of this man,' he said. His face was impassive, almost bored.

'Very little, sir. This image cropped up in relation to an investigation.'

'What investigation?'

I took a deep breath. 'With all due respect, my orders are that it's my eyes only. I can't say more without DCI Baxter's authority.'

His eyes narrowed. I waited for the outburst. I didn't care, I had the focus, I was totally in command of myself and Donahue, whatever his department, was not in my direct line of command.

'Your department, Drake, leaks like a sieve. I've seen your case reports. Red Claw know everything you do before you do it. Like the fiasco at Canary

Wharf when you were abducted. Tell me about that.'

'If you've seen all our reports, it's all there,'

'Your report makes no sense. Why did he kill this interrogator, Thacker?'

The question confirmed my suspicion. Donahue already knew that the base jumper was the same man as in the photograph. 'I've been wondering the same thing, sir.'

'Your report says they were looking for someone. Who and why?'

'I can't say, sir.'

'I could have you dismissed from the service, Drake.'

'May I speak frankly, sir?'

He folded his arms and nodded.

'This is your undercover agent in Red Claw.' I tapped my forefinger on the A4 print. 'He isn't reporting back to you. He's turned, or he believes his line of command is compromised, or he's playing his own game for his own purposes. The last fits with my suspicion that he's entangled. Is that right?'

Donahue stared at me, still as a rock. Still as a wavering, shimmering rock. My focus fell apart.

'The entangled soon learn to hide their condition, Drake, unlike you. It's written all over your face. It surprises me, you with your views on entanglement. Why aren't you out there with your friends?' His hand waved vaguely towards the window overlooking the embankment where crowds of protestors were still heading towards Parliament Square.

'They aren't…' I began, and I was there: Winsford Saïd himself shaking my hand, clasping my shoulder like an old friend, then climbing onto the back of a truck that formed an improvised stage on the road outside the palace of Westminster. The gathering crowd pressed around and he raised a megaphone to speak to them, to speak to me. I waited with breath held to hear his words.

It went as quickly as it came and I was in Donahue's office once more. 'They aren't my friends, sir.'

His nostrils flared and he glared at me from beneath a furrowed brow. 'There's no bigger security risk than officers taking illicit implicitins. I ought to lock you up until it's out of your system.'

His clenched right hand slapped into his cupped left. 'If Chameleon crosses your path again, I want to know about it.'

'Chameleon. Yes, sir.' A code name. At least I had some kind of a name for him now.

'Get lost now, Drake. Get back to your *leave of absence*.'

I was up, at the door, grasping the handle when he said one last thing. 'We haven't had this conversation, Drake. You will tell nobody.'

I opened the door and left.

*

I walked out onto Victoria Embankment deflated by Donahue's words, confused by the flash of the meeting with Winsford Saïd. Speeding cars weaved around me as I wandered across the unmarked black tarmac of the road, then up the steps to the walkway. There had been a time, not long after Alice's failed treatment, when I'd got involved with the protests. In my first meeting an evangelical spoke, advocating the murder of all the entangled. No-one objected, no-one was outraged. They mostly didn't agree, but they were prepared to accommodate that viewpoint. I walked away and never looked back. Perhaps in some world that evangelical hadn't been there and perhaps I was seduced. These were my thoughts as I strolled north, past the Hungerford Bridge, and stood for a while watching the incoming tide eddying past the piers of the long gone Waterloo Bridge.

I'd taken the delta thinking it would reveal things I knew in other worlds, that secrets here were known there, but I'd learned nothing. What had happened in Donahue's office opened the door to another side of entanglement. I'd followed so many chains of thought in a few seconds and put together a picture far more quickly than I could have by my simplex self. This was a power of entanglement that I hadn't considered, the ability to look at a situation from many angles at the same time.

My phone pinged. A message from Harris: *Are you at home? I have something for you.*

There in fifteen, I answered, then ran down the nearest steps to the road level and called a car. On the way I looked up Superintendent Donahue on the personnel database. Several groups reported to him. Traffic services: that would be vehicle hacks and sabotage. Event security: crowd control at football matches and protests, and so on. Nothing I could see that would require placing undercover operatives in Red Claw, or reading our department's reports. Conduct Oversight is like that. No-one in the service admits to working for them, no-one's files say they do. The fact that he revealed himself to me in that interview told me how concerned he was about the activities of his agent, Chameleon.

In ten minutes I was back home picking at a bunch of grapes, waiting for the kettle to boil, when my doorbell rang. Harris came up my stairs clutching a tattered cardboard box. 'Baxter said I was to hand you this in person and ask no questions.'

He held out the box and I took it.

'So, I'm not asking any questions.'

'Thanks, Jack. Better that way.' I took the box into the living room and plonked it on the table. When I got back the kettle spouted steam and clunked to a stop. 'Tea? Coffee? Beer?'

'Coffee. Instant,' he said. 'I've seen what passes for beer in your fridge.'

I tutted. He smirked. A snob when it came to beer, yet he drank instant coffee. I spooned, poured, stirred. 'You ever come across a Superintendent Donahue?' I handed him the mug.

He gave me his longest long, cool look. 'I'm not the only one who shouldn't be asking questions.'

'What do you know?'

'I know you didn't say anything to me about Donahue. I'm already out of my depth here, Lewis. This mysterious box, now Donahue…' He clunked the steaming mug onto the counter and a spray of coffee leapt out. 'Listen, don't mention Donahue to anyone else, okay? Anyone at all. In the service or outside.'

'Okay.' I leaned back against the counter. 'Any progress on Aiden Harcourt?'

'He's so hard to find, or find anything about. I could go to Tripoli, track down his father, but is he relevant to the case?'

'Wyndham's memorial tomorrow. He might turn up there.'

'You going?'

'Leave of absence.'

He picked up his coffee. 'Yeah, I'm asking no questions.' He took one sip and put it down again. 'Gotta go, things to do.'

At the top of the stairs he turned back to face me. 'I don't know what you've got into, Lewis.' His voice was calmer. He clapped a hand on my shoulder. 'Remember me when you need someone to cover your back, okay?'

'Okay, Jack. I appreciate it. I will.'

He bounded down the stairs two at a time and out the door without looking back.

Tea, Assam, loose-leaf, brewed a full five minutes before pouring. Thus fortified, I returned to the living room and opened the cardboard box. Inside was an ISP, an *Isolated Secure Processor*. It looked like something you see in old movies, like a *laptop*. It folded open to reveal a screen and a keyboard. The only openings I could find in the casing were the memory bead dimple and a standard charger socket. I plugged in a charger cable and hit the power button. Nothing happened. I stared at it, lifted it up, closed it, opened it, tried again. Nothing. It took another stare for the penny to drop. I unplugged the power and pressed the on button again. My respect for the builders' paranoia crept up a notch. It wouldn't work while being charged so no data could leak over the mains power lines. I turned the thing over and gave it a closer examination. The casing was perfectly sealed. No seams, no joins, no screws holding it together. I wondered what might happen if I tried to cut it open. Curious, but not so curious that I was going to try it.

Sadly, the software was crap, like something out of the last century. I could open a document and read it. I could make notes, but not index them. I could kind of search for stuff if I had the wording and orthography exactly right. As for intelligence, my toaster had more smarts. I cursing the damned thing in annoyance and it began to shimmer.

There were a hundred documents I needed to read, a thousand. My eyes ran down the list; this one, and this, and this. I opened them, barely conscious of what I was doing. I read them. I read *all* of them, all at the same time. There was one, an audit report, due diligence on behalf of Exercitus, the defence contractor that bought the Genetic Therapies Division: 472 pages long. I typed a page number and started reading. I typed 472 distinct page numbers and in 472 separate fine-grained realities I read the page. Most of them said nothing; the document read like someone had decided for form's sake that they needed to have an audit but nobody was going to read it. Nobody cared, due diligence or not this sale was going ahead. There was an appendix, an inventory of the major capital items included in the sale. My so brief perusal of the accounts and purchase records raised a hundred discrepancies in the inventory. Many of them had been annotated, noted, signed off, ignored.

But why did the purchase record show four Regenesys 5101 Tomographic Resonators, at four million a time, when the inventory mentioned only three? I picked up my phone.

'Search...' I said, and stopped. I was focussed again, the room was still, my mind singular. So easy to get carried away in the uninhibited moments of entanglement. To search for anything about what I'd found would be to give myself away to the spooks. I would rather not know what would come of that after the last little chat with the bearded man in the car.

'Cancel.'

Too much of it related to technicalities way beyond me. Lab equipment, machines, chemicals. I had no idea what was important, but Alice would, if I could engage her attention long enough to tell me. That problem would wait until tomorrow. Problems now were food, and a safe place to keep this dark laptop.

I called Kay.

'Lewis, how are you feeling?'

'Fine, Kay, just fine. Wanna help me finish off your lovely lasagne?'

Beer, reheated lasagne, G&T for her and single malt for me. A companionable, calming hour with an old and trusted friend. She took the foil-covered baking tray with her when she left.

CHAPTER 7

Monday 18th November: Bullets

For millennia, people have found ways to enter different mental states through meditation, starvation, pain, or drugs, and many have reported feeling deep within themselves the unity of all life. Evolution tells us how this is so: every living thing on Earth shares a common ancestor. In the broadest sense we are all one and every mind is entangled.

In the early days of entanglement some people, those who had a heightened sensitivity or who received an excessive dose of alpha implicitins, came to experience this unity directly. For them there are no boundaries, the furthest, most distantly related alternates are as accessible as the closest. Further means divergence further back in time, less common structure of brain and mind and genes. In short, they participate directly in the awareness of every alternate of every living thing on Earth. This is the Omega State. Those who attain it become lost in the vastness of experience, become unable to communicate with those around them, unable to care for their own needs. They are invariably institutionalised, and usually have limited life expectancy.

—A K Amari - *The Measurement Problem, A Guide to Entanglement*

The light was constant, bright and white, uniform in my unfocussed eyes but for a blurred disk of greater brightness. The noise filled my ears, hissing and whirring and clunking, and other things, new things: footsteps and clattering, voices raised above the din, though there was no sense in their words. My throat hurt like I'd been swallowing sandpaper, like there was something stuck there. My chest hurt with every breath.

Timeless, the dream might have lasted seconds or hours. The sights and the sounds and the sensations filled the dream, but there was no response to them; no thought, no feeling, no comprehension, no plan, no intent, no desire, no need. I was there, but I was not there. My alarm plucked me from it, leaving me filled with disquiet that rested with me while I showered, dressed, ate a hasty breakfast and ran down the stairs to catch the car I had called, pausing on my way out to place a grape under the doormat.

I flicked between newsfeeds as I was carried north once more. The bishop of York had demanded that medical experiments with implicitins in brain-dead patients be banned. A junior foreign minister in London stated that there was no truth whatsoever in the rumour that MI6 had been using a secret mind control technology on the spy Hubert Neuville, recently found dead in his cell in Paris, cut to a middle-aged woman: '*ce n'était pas lui, dans la tête, ce n'était pas lui*', helpfully subtitled *Mme Neuville: it wasn't him, in the head, it wasn't him.*

I was half-way through a long piece, an interview with a consultant at King's College Hospital about research into the use of delta implicitins to improve the outcome of regeneration therapies for patients with brain damage through stroke or injury, when the car pulled through the gates at The Grange. Five to nine. I went straight in.

'Cecilia here?' I asked the guy at the desk as I signed in. *Henry*, his name tag read. Big beefy guy, crew cut, missing earlobe. New. I'd never seen him before.

'Haven't seen her.' He didn't seem that interested.

'Tell her I'm here if you do.' I finished signing my name and looked up at Henry's indifferent expression. 'Don't worry, I know the way.'

Alice's room was close by, second on the left at the front of the house. I tapped on her door and edged it open. 'Alice?'

'Lewis!' She jumped to her feet, bounded across the room and embraced me.

I wormed out of her grasp so I could breathe. She was here, all here in this world. 'Have you had a treatment already today?'

'Yes, Dr Stebbins-Reese is randomising the treatment times. Before, it was happening in every world at the same time so my mind was disintegrating.' She looked around me at the door. 'Lewis, is Beets here?'

'I don't know Beets, not in this world.'

She shook her head. 'I can't imagine you without Beets. Oh, no. It was that awful Veronica. Are you still with her?' This last said with a sly smile on her face.

'Vittoria, and no. That didn't work out.' An old joke. She'd never liked Vittoria. She'd got the name wrong once by accident and so Vittoria was ever after Veronica to her.

I held her hand and guided her back to the corner with the little table and the bucket chairs.

'You should find Beets.' She sat, and squeezed her eyes shut. 'No. You shouldn't.' Her hands clenched into balled fists. 'It's there when I'm whole, I know it all, but when I'm here, it's just fragments, and I don't know which world this is.'

'It's okay, Alice. Tell me about Beets. Is she someone you worked with?'

She lowered her eyes. 'I don't want to talk about her. I don't want to lose her again. I don't want to lose you again.' She held her hand over her knee, fingers outstretched, studying the nails.

'Let's talk about other people then.' I wanted to keep her talking simply for the joy of it. This was the most coherent she'd been since Stebbins-Reese had begun his treatment. I wanted to keep her talking, but steer her away from irrelevances like Beets and on to the things that would help me with the case. 'I met Jane Wilson the other day, Jane Seymour she calls herself now, and Marko.'

Alice's face lit up. 'Marko! Such a handful. I remember his first day at school.'

Three years she'd been at The Grange, since Marko was a toddler, barely walking. On his first day at school Alice had been lying catatonic in this room, in the Omega State. She remembered Marko's first day at school, but it was somebody else's memory.

'Jane said you worked a miracle. You and Sam Okorie.'

'I'm so glad. You should see Sam, bring him to visit. He's such a lovely man.'

'I'd like to, Alice.' I bit my tongue. 'I don't think I can.'

'There was an accident, he died. Was that this world?'

I nodded silently, glad I didn't need to explain. 'Jane showed me the photo. What Marko looked like before. I remember when Marlowe at work got hurt, they had this machine they used to stimulate the viruses that triggered the regrowth. I guess you had something like that for Marko's face?'

'It's much more complicated than that. We had to fix the genes first, and it wasn't just his face, his condition affected the heart, liver, other organs. We had to use a full-body tomographic resonator. VGT bought one for the project. We had it installed at Addenbrooke's Hospital where Sam worked. That's where we did Marko's treatment.'

'I guess it's still there at Addenbrooke's. Did VGT only buy one?'

'There was talk of buying more for the next phase of trials, but I don't know whether it happened. Was that this world? Frank would know.'

'Frank Wilson?'

'Marko's dad. Funny little man. He looked after the admin. Sometimes I couldn't understand what he was saying, he'd lapse into this thick accent.'

'Accent? What kind of accent?'

'I don't know. East European. He said he'd changed his last name when he settled so he could be more English.'

'Is that why the little boy is Marko? I thought at first it was a nickname.'

'Yes, that's it. And Frank used to spell his name with a C. F-R-A-N-C.'

Franc, Marko. Getting her to talk about her work was bringing her right into the world, breaking through the barriers. I would have really enjoyed it, except I felt such a shit trying to wheedle information out of her. 'I was trying to find Frank Wilson. I don't suppose you can remember what happened to him, from Omega?'

She closed her eyes and took a deep breath. 'It's easiest with things I want to remember. You, Beets, Marko. All I get when I try to think of Frank is fear and confusion. As if something bad happened to him.' She shook her head. 'I don't want to talk about him, about any of them. It's too dangerous.'

'Why is it dangerous?'

'Beets found out, and she told you, and now you're both dead.' Her head dropped. Her shoulders slumped.

'We'll just talk. You warn me off if it's getting dangerous.'

She looked at me with her head tilted. She wanted to.

'Why were the VGT projects named after lizards?' I said. Fishing for something, anything, safe.

'Lizards?'

'Ambystoma?'

'Oh, Ambystoma isn't a lizard. It's an axolotl, an amphibian. It can regenerate lost limbs. That was my first project. The old tissue regeneration techniques only worked on new injuries. We made it work on old scars and abnormal growths, reabsorbing them and rebuilding without surgery.'

'Furcifer?'

Her mouth turned down. 'I never liked that name. It's the wrong name. It wasn't only about appearances. You don't see the change in Marko's heart or liver.'

'So what's a furcifer.'

'A chameleon.'

My phone rang. I muted it. It rang again, one of *those* calls. *Sorry*, I mouthed to Alice as I picked it up. 'DI Drake,' I said, then I listened.

After I finished listening I put the phone back in my pocket. 'I'm sorry, Alice. I have to go. I'll be back as soon as I can. Say hi to Cecilia for me.'

I kissed her cheek and hurried out. There was a car already pulling in through the gate for me.

*

The forensic bots hadn't finished their sweep yet. Still a fresh crime scene and they didn't want it contaminated any more than it already had been. I had to wait on the gravel drive outside the long low wall of dark glass. A young Detective Sergeant from Cambridge CID waited with me. Harbin was her name. The deer watched warily from the edge of the wood beneath a low sun that shone with a sickly yellow light.

Soames sat, head in hands, on the sill of the incident van, ignoring the cup of tea he was being offered.

'Your DCI Baxter called us as soon as the incident was logged.' Harbin's breath misted before her face. 'I guess she had a flag on Cloake's name.'

'Most likely,' I said. That's exactly what Baxter had done. Now my very short leave of absence was over. She'd seconded me to Cambridge for this case but my search for Erica Fallon was still my eyes only. I didn't like that. I didn't like having to help people while holding back, but what I didn't like didn't come into it. 'Any idea when it happened?'

'Not yet. The butler had the weekend off, left Saturday morning, arrived back this morning and found him.'

'I was here Friday to talk to him about our case.'

Harbin gave me a furtive sideways glance. 'What were you looking into? Anything that might give us a lead?'

Her boss, DI Gallicoe, was in the van with the forensics guy. The cynic in me thought he'd sent his attractive junior to find out my interest in the case. Screw the cynic: she was just being friendly with a bit of shop talk. What the hell, save them and me a bit of time. I gave her a less furtive look.

'I've got three possibles for you.'

'Three motives?'

'I was looking into the murder of Sir Roger Wyndham. We have reason to believe he was involved with Red Claw, a gang working mainly in Docklands. There was evidence to link Cloake to Wyndham. I spoke to Cloake, checked it out, and the link was spurious. A false trail.'

'So how does that help?'

'It's a false trail deliberately laid. Someone was trying to link Cloake with Wyndham and Red Claw, so who, and why?' The fake log data for the Silver Dawn had me puzzled. The only result I could see was to get me here talking to him and now he'd been killed. I couldn't figure out cause and effect. There was another link between Wyndham and Cloake: Monica, Lady Wyndham, widow of one, friend of the other. If I let Harbin and Gallicoe work that one out for themselves I'd get a chance to talk to her first.

'Wyndham, Red Claw. okay, next one?'

'Cloake gave me some information that someone didn't want me to have. I got warned off, maybe he did, too, and maybe he didn't take the warning.'

'Red Claw again?'

'Much worse. Someone in the intelligence community. If they're behind, it and you get close, you may find your investigation shut down and yourself shifted to traffic duty. You'll want to park that one until you've eliminated the other two.'

'And the third?'

'Revenge. His decisions put my sister in an institution. That's where I was when you called. But I'm coming round to the view it wasn't his fault. I didn't kill him.'

Her eyebrows crinkled.

'Saving us all a little time, DS Harbin. I'd rather you eliminate me as a suspect first so you can move on. You should get someone in to interview the victim.'

'Interview? He's dead, sir.'

'He's entangled, dead in this reality. Another entangled might be able to speak to him in another.'

None of the motives I'd enumerated for Harbin stood up. The only evidence for the Red Claw link was the spurious VLA log for the Silver Dawn. The spooks were a more interesting possibility, but to kill him outright was a little heavy-handed. I'd expect something a little less obvious, like a feral car running out of control. Or they'd just have him disappear, like Erica Fallon or Frank Wilson.

The low sun reflected off the dark windows. An orderly line of forensic bots scuttled from the door, wielding their various instruments and carrying their racks of samples in sealed vials and bags. We filed in, DI Gallicoe, DS Harbin, and me.

Cloake was in the library, slumped forward on his desk. One bullet had entered above the left eye, the other at the back of the head. The assailant had entered the room while Cloake was at his desk, fired one shot as he approached, then walked round behind him to fire the second to make sure.

'Red Claw's assassin does this,' I said to Gallicoe. I'd been too hasty ruling out that connection. 'Two shots, second one to the back of the head. I'll lay odds they're ten point two mil. Usually the cartridges are left at the scene.' I had his attention. 'You might have to pass this one to us in London.'

'Let's not jump the gun, DI Drake. We'll wait for pathology.'

'Did forensics find any cartridges in here?'

'No.'

'Have you checked the services area? A cleaning bot might have picked them up.'

'The thing is, we may not be the Met's finest, but we know how to do our jobs.'

Half the desk surface was a panel set almost seamlessly into the old leather. The surface was active, but suspended, showing slow moving grids intersecting in a moiré pattern. He'd been dead way longer than any reasonable inactivity timeout. I caught Gallicoe's eye and reached for Cloake's right hand. 'May I?'

'Sure. Forensics are done.' Gallicoe was more interested in the books on the shelves than anything else.

Even through the latex gloves I could feel the coldness of the hand. The fingers moved with only a slight stiffness. I placed Cloake's right forefinger over the reader and the desk lit up. The wallpaper was a diagram, cross-section of a low dam with a road on the crest and turbines within. Spread over the surface were a few open documents. The *AD Trust Articles of Association—Draft*, I knew from Cloake's file he ran a string of charitable trusts, so I swiped that to one side revealing a calendar entry for the following day at two pm: *Stebbins-Reese*. In the top corner of the desk the padlock and shield icon of his security system blinked red. A tap with my forefinger opened it. A grid of video feeds popped up, all shut down at around the same time. One of them looked down on the desk from the corner of the ceiling where the dark dot of the camera lens was just visible. The last few minutes of the view showed Cloake working at his desk unperturbed as the time stamp in the corner ticked away the seconds of his life.

'Saturday evening or Sunday morning,' I said.

Gallicoe stopped his perusal of the shelves. 'How do you work that out?'

'Six pm Saturday, the last security video recording shows him sitting here.' I lifted Cloake's arm from the desk and his hand hung limp. 'And rigor mortis is nearly gone so he's been dead over twenty-four hours.'

'Anything from his security after that?'

'No.' I flicked back to the system log. 'All went down with error codes around that time, probably hacked. That also fits the Red Claw MO.'

Harbin rooted around in the waste bin by the desk. 'What's this?' She held up a square of greenish fabric, a couple of centimetres on a side. Two thin wires trailed from it.

'It's a bug.' The man in the doorway wore a neat suit. His beard was black, neatly trimmed, the same beard I'd seen from the flickering of passing street lights on Saturday evening after being picked up outside the former VirGenTech building. 'You'll find three more in there.'

Gallicoe lifted a book from the shelf. A square of the green cloth binding had been neatly cut away. 'You're Tamboli?'

He pulled out a phone and pinged an ID.

I checked mine. *Govind Tamboli, Exercitus Ltd, Chief Security Officer.* 'And you are here in what capacity?' I asked, not really expecting an answer.

He smiled.

'Relax, Drake,' Gallicoe said. 'Word from above is we're to give him our full co-operation.'

Exercitus was a defence contractor. No surprise that MI5 or the MOD or whoever would plant one of their own in charge of security.

Tamboli walked along the bookshelf, plucking three more books, all with neatly cut bindings. 'Curious, isn't it, Drake? He finds and takes out all our bugs then sits at his desk and waits for his killer. Why would he do that?'

It was interesting that Tamboli hadn't figured that out. Cloake was entangled. Death in one world is no big deal: an acceptable sacrifice to learn something or provoke a response. The urge to enlighten him was eminently resistible. 'Why were you bugging him?'

He tilted his head to one side and gave me an appraising look, a sardonic smile on his face. 'We keep an eye on people who might know too much. We'll be keeping an eye on you, Detective Inspector Drake.'

*

Parkside Police Station in Cambridge was a rotting concrete monstrosity that should have been knocked down and rebuilt decades ago. The tea they provided was a similar quality, but Soames didn't seem to mind. Gallicoe had been adamant; this was their investigation, they would do the interviews. Tamboli and I watched on the monitor in the adjacent room.

'Of course he has enemies, in business, in politics,' Soames said in answer to Harbin's obvious question. 'I don't know who might have wanted him dead, but Mr Cloake knew he was in danger.'

'What makes you think that?'

'Before I left on Friday he changed his will, asked me to witness it.'

'I wondered if it might have been you people at first,' I said to Tamboli, listening with half an ear to the drone of Harbin's questions and Soames' answers.

'Huh!' He shifted in his seat. 'Entangled. It's all a game to them. When he sent you those files he played by the letter of the rules we set him, but not the spirit. We had words. He wasn't going to do it again.' He gave me his shiny-toothed smile. 'My money's on your Red Claw link. How's that going?'

'Fishing, Mr Tamboli?' I reached to turn up the audio volume on the monitor. Harbin was asking Soames about Cloake's private cars. 'Not so well,' I said. 'Dead ends.'

'Well if you…'

'Shh!' I held my palm up.

'Yes. That's right, he always uses… used the Saqqaf himself, for safety.'

'Safety? What do you mean?'

'Well…' Soames looked down at his hands, back up at Harbin. 'I don't suppose it matters any more. I know it isn't strictly legal, but you know, he is… was a wealthy man. He had the contacts to get an off-the-books patch, so it doesn't log its movements with the VLA, and it has certain behaviours to assist if an authorised user is in danger of kidnapping or such like.'

'It's been ghosted?' Gallicoe cut in. 'Don't worry. The thing is, we can get the log from the vehicle itself.'

'Well…' Soames looked like he wanted a hole to crawl into. 'He deleted the log. Well, he told me to delete it.'

I eased the volume down again. 'I have no desire to step on the wrong toes, Inspector. Nothing Cloake sent me was classified. I'm not interested in your secrets, only in Red Claw. Let me talk to the Project Furcifer personnel.'

'Not going to happen, Drake.'

'Whatever Exercitus are doing with Furcifer is going to come out anyway. If not in this reality, then in another. There are more entangled all the time.'

He gave an expansive shrug, hands palm up at shoulder height. 'Not my concern. Or yours.'

I hadn't expected anything different, but perhaps the change of subject had distracted him from what Soames was saying.

They wound up the interview after that. I followed Tamboli out of the room to see him dash down the corridor to grab Gallicoe by the elbow and whisper urgently in his ear. Gallicoe stared at him, glanced back at me, then led Tamboli down the hall and into an office.

'Grab some lunch?' Harbin appeared beside me. 'The canteen here's pretty grim but there's a half-decent Bulgarian place five minutes away.'

*

It was reassuringly busy, but not packed. Harbin ordered banitsa. The service expense account paid for my Meshana Skara.

'I had a word with Gallicoe,' she said as the waiter retreated with our orders. 'With what you said about your possible motive he says we have to check your alibi and all.'

'Of course.'

'He wants me to conduct the interview, if that's okay with you. He says it would be good experience.'

Either that, or he thought she would be able to get under my skin. I could have demanded a more senior officer, but it didn't seem worth the trouble. 'That's fine.'

After that we talked a little about Cloake, a little about Red Claw, more about incompetence and corruption in the upper echelons of the service, until the food arrived.

Half her banitsa gone, she pushed flaking pieces of pastry around her plate. 'I have the advantage on you,' she said. 'Gallicoe had me look over your file this morning.' She continued in a softer voice, 'sorry about your sister. Must be hard on you.'

'Thanks.' I finished chewing a meaty chunk and swallowed. 'Even it up, tell me about yourself.'

'Not much to tell. Graduated four years ago.'

'Already a DS. Not bad going.' I stabbed a piece of steak with my fork. 'Married? Partner?'

A coy smile. 'You know how it is. All the good ones are taken.' And she looked back down at her plate. Some particular taken one on her mind. She gave a little shrug. 'And sometimes it doesn't work out. You know about that, though.'

Yeah, she'd seen my file. 'Vittoria was one of the good ones. I wasn't.'

'What happened?'

'I don't know. For a while I blamed her for not being supportive when I had to deal with Alice. I realised recently I was already drifting away from her before it happened.'

'Does she know that? You can't leave her thinking you blame her.'

I opened my mouth to argue, then closed it again. She was right, I'd been a bastard to Vittoria, piling my unjustified resentment on her.

We had departed the station as DI Drake and DS Harbin. An hour later Lewis and Meera walked back to Parkside in an amiable silence, me feeling stuffed after a meal far more substantial than I was expecting. As soon as we walked in, Gallicoe called Meera into his office so I was left with a spare desk and a few minutes to myself. One thing I had to do before anything else was send a message to Vittoria, an apology. I agonised over it for a moment, started drafting a long screed, deleted it and just paraphrased what I'd said to Harbin. The pathology report came through while I was writing. I skimmed it for the important details: time of death between six and ten pm on Saturday, the two bullets recovered now with ballistics. That made two murders, Wyndham and Cloake, with a common factor: Lady Wyndham. I called her but she didn't pick up. It was Monday, the day of the memorial service for Sir Roger. I left her a message to call me back. A message arrived from Vittoria: *Back in the UK next Monday, let's meet and sort this once and for all.* A weight lifted from me in that moment. Her and me, no lawyers. She wouldn't have said that if she didn't mean it.

Meera emerged from her tête a tête with DI Gallicoe to lead me to the interview room. As we entered, she paused and turned to me. 'This is just the job now. Nothing personal. okay?'

'It's okay, Meera. Go for the jugular.'

Gallicoe bustled in a moment later.

Recorders started, IDs formally checked, Gallicoe activated Argus to watch and listen for those subtle shifts of voice or expression that might indicate an untruth. He sat back with arms folded and Meera launched straight in with a picture of Alice lying vacant in a hospital bed, shortly after her entanglement treatment.

'Is this your sister, Dr Alice Drake?' she said.

Hardly a controversial question. 'Yes.'

'Please describe her condition.'

'At the time this image was taken she was believed to be in a catatonic stupor. It was more recently discovered she was in the Omega State.'

'Do you know the cause?'

'Yes. She'd reacted badly to a course of implicitins.'

'Why was she taking implicitins?'

'She wasn't taking them, they were being administered intravenously.'

'I'm sorry.' Meera's words were accompanied by a professional sympathetic smile. 'Why was she receiving this treatment?'

'She had agreed with her employer to enter their entanglement programme.'

'Permanent entanglement?'

'Yes.'

'That's a big step, and an expensive one. They must have held her in high regard.'

'They did.'

'What went wrong?'

'I don't know.'

'The screening process for these programmes are extensive, the protocols very cautious. Did someone make a mistake?'

'I don't know.'

'The wrong formulation? The wrong dose?'

I sighed, closing my eyes for a moment. I knew the game. I'd sat on the other side of the table often enough.

'I don't know.'

'You must have been very upset.'

'Very.'

'How much have you spent on legal fees and court costs trying to sue VirGenTech, DI Drake?'

'I haven't been counting.'

She looked down at her pad. 'At least two-hundred and forty thousand. All your savings and most of your salary.'

I shrugged. I hadn't been counting.

'It cost you your marriage, didn't it?'

'That wasn't going to last.'

She put down her pad and looked me in the eyes. She had such a cool interview technique. 'Did all of that make you angry, Lewis?'

'Yes, it did.'

'And now, VirGenTech have stopped paying for Alice's care.'

I couldn't help but twitch at that, but there was no point trying to hide it.

'How are you going to cope?'

So many options. There are always people willing to pay for favours of someone in the service, but that wasn't really me. I could take a second job if I could find one, or quit the service, fall back on the UBI and look after her myself. But here, now, answer the questions, answer only the questions, don't volunteer more. It's up to the interrogator to expand the scope. 'I haven't decided yet.'

Gallicoe's lip twitched. Meera's curled up a touch as she looked down at her pad. She knew the game as I did.

'Who do you blame for Alice's condition?'

That was a good question. One that I didn't have a prepared answer for. It was also one I couldn't help but expand on. 'I suspect someone is hiding the truth of what happened to Alice. I would like to find out what, who, and why.'

'There's a conspiracy?'

I nearly said yes. In my own mind I'd assumed it, but I didn't really know. 'A conspiracy means more than one person is involved. I don't know if that's the case.'

Gallicoe shifted in his seat and glared at Meera.

She glanced his way, then looked me in the eyes. 'DI Drake, please listen to this recording.'

Alice Drake was one of our star researchers, I wanted to keep her in VGT so

I encouraged her to apply for the entanglement programme and I authorised her acceptance.

Tamboli no doubt provided that, a recording from my meeting with Cloake. Meera waited for a reaction, I waited for the question.

'Who was speaking?'

'Elijah Cloake.'

'How did you feel when he said that?'

'He wasn't telling me anything I didn't already know.' I wasn't convinced by my attempt at nonchalance. There was no chance Argus was.

'Yes, but how did it make you feel?'

'Angry, for a moment.'

'Angry enough to kill?'

'With all due respect, DS Harbin, I've had the same training as you. We both know that to kill another person is not easy. Only someone who *has* killed in anger could answer that question accurately and honestly.'

Gallicoe's hand slammed on the table. 'That's what we're trying to establish, Drake.'

I looked at him.

He half-rose, leaning towards me, knuckles of his fisted hands pressing on the table. 'Well?'

Out of the corner of my eye I saw Meera shake her head.

'I'm sorry,' I said. 'Was there a question?'

'DI Drake,' Meera cut in. 'Where were you between eighteen hundred and twenty-two hundred hours on Saturday evening?'

The next hour was far less entertaining as I catalogued my vague and uncorroborated movements in the company of the man I now knew as Govind Tamboli, then with Cecilia Watts. The absence of any phone trace was noted from the time that I *alleged* my phone had been lost until I turned on and registered my replacement phone at my flat. Argus found no cause to doubt my account, but without independent corroboration I was still on shaky ground.

After Gallicoe had given up his pressing and table-slamming and terminated the interview, I followed Meera out of the room. She watched Gallicoe's retreating back.

'I'm sorry, Lewis, I don't know what's got into him. This morning he was saying it's just a formality.' She reached up behind her head and pulled the stick from her barrette. Thick black hair cascaded down her back.

'Tamboli got to him,' I said.

With a deft movement she had her hair coiled and pinned back up. 'Why, what's his game?'

'Good question.' I was hoping it was nothing more than another way of suggesting I keep out of his hair. 'I should try and get hold of Cecilia Watts. A statement from her will clear this up.'

'Do you need any help with that?'

'Should be okay. Just need to make some calls.'

'There's a room along here you can use.' Her hand on my arm guided me to a small office with a table and four chairs. I sat, she hung in the doorway with a hand on each side of the frame. 'I'm off-duty in an hour. Will you still be here?'

Surprise caught my tongue. It took me a moment to unravel my thoughts. 'Not today. There are things I have to do.'

'Yeah, sorry.' She leaned back to glance each way along the corridor. 'I guess that was kind of inappropriate.'

'No, I really have things I have to do.' I took out my phone. 'Swap personal numbers?'

We swapped. She closed the door with a smile on her face. It took me another moment to re-ravel my thoughts. I shouldn't have done that; it really was inappropriate given the case, my situation, my commitments. I couldn't pin down why it didn't feel right. It just didn't.

They always answered the phone promptly at The Grange, always within three rings. I'd lost count by the time I heard a gruff voice answer: 'Grange.'

I was pretty sure that was the same Heavy Henry I'd met that morning. 'Cecilia Watts, please.'

'She isn't here.'

'Do you know how I can contact her?'

'No.'

'Do you have her address or personal number?'

'I can't give out that information.'

I pinged my ID. 'Police business.'

'Got a warrant?'

I did have a warrant, I had a carte blanche warrant, but looking for a witness to give me an alibi didn't fall in its scope, and anyway, I didn't need it. 'If you hear from her, tell her I called.'

The tax office obliged; a name and an employer were enough to get an address. I called a car and stepped outside to wait for it. Somewhere behind the dismal darkening clouds, the sun was setting.

My car pulled up to the kerb and I got in. I knew roughly where Cecilia lived from when she had taken me there, dried me, warmed me, and let me use her phone to call a car. If it had been booked on my account I'd have the record and I'd know the exact address. I didn't have that but I knew which part of the city it was, and I knew when my car pulled away from the kerb and made the first turn that it was heading in the wrong direction. It stopped outside a burned out shell in a row of nineteen-thirties semis. *Kind of temporary*, she'd said about the maisonette.

I consulted the map and redirected the car to my best remembered guess, hoping I'd recognise the street. I did recall that hers was second from the right-hand end of a terrace by a corner.

They liked to build estates big in those days, with dozens of identical blocks on identical streets. The first five doorbells I rang got me responses ranging from politely unhelpful to thoroughly abusive. The sixth got me no answer at all, but the flower beds outside looked familiar. I rang at the next door, heard nothing, so tapped lightly on the glass. Still silence. I was half way to the neighbour on the other side when the door opened behind me, revealing the archetypal little grey-haired old lady with apron and spectacles.

I jogged back towards her. 'Your neighbour,' I said. 'Is she Cecilia Watts?'

'Yes.'

'Have you seen her?'

'Oh no. She moved out this morning.'

*

While my car zipped past a row of shipping containers on their dollies in the freight lane of the M11 I called Meera. She answered on the first ring and promised to have someone look into Cecilia's whereabouts in the morning. Kay was my next call.

'I'd like to see you tonight, is that okay?'

'Oh, yes,' she said. 'I'll put on something special.' An actress she was not. I didn't know whether to laugh or cringe at her performance.

After that I distracted myself with the news feed. Police in France were conducting forensic investigations at the Neuville estate. A post mortem had been conducted on Hubert Neuville but the findings had not been released. A deepening depression north of the Azores had been tagged as storm Lesley. Property prices above the ten-metre contour were breaking post-war records. I got drawn into a long piece about migration from low-lying areas and the rising population of young adults, the post-war baby-boom growing up.

I opened the door to my flat and stepped over the doormat onto the bottom step. Under the mat was a sticky purple grape skin, one more stain on the old floorboard. Upstairs, everything appeared exactly as it had when I left that morning, except for the drawer where my pack of blank memory beads lay. The wrapping had been pulled back a little. It must have been a hell of a tricky job to pull them all out, read them and then slide them back into the wrapping without tearing or creasing it more.

After a shower I checked everything I was changing into for bugs and trackers tucked behind labels or sewn into seams or lining. I soon tired of that and gave everything a couple of minutes in the microwave to fry the circuits. Once dressed in pleasantly warm clothing I poured out half my remaining Linlithgow, a meagre dram, and stood by the window sipping it. The sky was clear, I could even make out a few stars through the grimy glass and sky glow. Kay's downstairs light was on.

She answered the door as soon as I rang, put her arms around me and treated me to a long, languid kiss, long enough to be sure that any rats set by Tamboli's people to watch from the shadows got the picture. Inside, she picked up the baking tray from the hall table and peeled back the foil like she was opening the lid of a chest of gold doubloons. I lifted out the laptop and the bead. She turned off the downstairs light and I followed her upstairs to her bedroom.

'I can't thank you enough, Kay.' I leaned back against the bedroom door to close it.

'Are you kidding, Lewis? I haven't had this much excitement ever, in any life.' With considerable care, she rearranged the various pots and jars and tubes and brushes on her large dressing table to leave a small clear space in the centre just wide enough for me to lay the laptop.

She lay on the bed watching me, but I guess the excitement of looking at my back while I searched and read was too much. The muted snoring didn't distract me half as much as the watching silence had. Without the multiplex view that the deltas had given me my progress was slow, but I knew what I was looking for.

I found it, first in a security audit document, then in half a dozen others. The signature of one Govind Tamboli, security consultant. He'd been in on the Exercitus takeover from the beginning.

Kay stirred when I sat on the bed next to her about midnight. 'I'm done,' I said.

She stretched and pulled herself up to see me to the door, giving me another long kiss on the doorstep.

'Don't overdo it,' I said. 'You'll freeze.'

I resisted the temptation to look for rats as I crossed back to the front door of my flat. Mine for one more week.

CHAPTER 8

Tuesday 19th November: Cranfield

There are many formulations of implicitins with varying characteristics. Conventionally they are grouped into generations: alpha, beta, gamma, delta. From alpha to gamma, the effects become less long-lasting. Alphas take that door between our alternate selves that stands ajar, and smash it wide open, breaking the door from its hinges, permanently and irreversibly. Betas and gammas have shorter term effects and expose a narrower range of alternates. With betas, only alternatives also entangled are joined. With gammas, only those realities that branch after the drug is taken. Gammas are commonly sold on the black market for use in sexual encounters, the famous two-person orgy.

Deltas are a more recent development, combining the short duration effects of betas and gammas with the broad scope of alphas. As with alpha implicitins, delta subjects share in all the knowledge and experience of their alternates, even if those alternates are not entangled.

—A K Amari - *The Measurement Problem, A Guide to Entanglement*

There was the rasping discomfort in my throat, the feeling I wanted to gag, the pain in my chest each time the air was forced into it. There was the noise, the whirring of fans, hissing of pumps. Loud footsteps on a hard floor. The noise was so loud I couldn't hear what Erica was saying. Two macchiatos sat on the table between us. Her hand reached to grasp mine. Her lips moved but I couldn't make out her words. I watched her lips, and I saw the shape they made, the tongue behind her teeth descending as the mouth closed.

Alice. Something about Alice. It was a dream within my dream of the place of noise and light and emptiness, a dream of being in Marek's café with Erica, or a memory.

The noise grew louder, a squealing sound, an ill-fitting door scraping across a tiled floor. Erica's eyes went wide. Her hand let go of mine as she pulled back from the table.

My hand was on the Glock as I turned, it was in my hand and raised when I saw the figure standing by the door, dark coat, face shadowed by the brim of his hat. I hesitated. Fifteen years in the service and I'd never before fired in anger, only ever at the range. I hesitated and I saw the muzzle flash of his gun.

A bright light shone in my eye, making me squint. It moved away and back, away and back. A vague shadowy figure held a torch, shining it in my eye.

A smell of plastic and disinfectants, the noise of fans and pumps, loud footsteps on a hard floor. An insistent beeping…

My hand reached out to cancel the alarm and I was awake in my room, in my flat. For a moment my mind was numb, empty. The morning light leaked around the curtains. I smelled the damp from the walls, I felt the cold draught from the window on my face. A memory of a discomfort made me cough to clear my throat. I washed and dressed and made a pot of tea, all the while wondering whether they were memories, dreams or visions, and whether there was really any difference.

I needed to clear my head, I needed air. I needed to walk. The Docklands Light Railway took me to Bank station from where it was a short stroll down to Southwark Bridge. The rising sun shimmered in reflection on the Thames as I crossed to the South Bank. The raised embankment path led me westwards, past the steps down to the Globe Theatre, past the fading glory of the Tate Modern. I circled round the back to Park Street.

Half a dozen times in the last six months Cloake's Saqqaf had dropped him on Park Street and collected him an hour or more later. One corner of the crossroads where it had stopped was a building site, the next a down-at-heel vegan restaurant, then a shady-looking family planning and gene editing consultancy. The fourth was a two-storey, nineteenth century, yellow brick building with a glossy black painted door and whitewashed lintel. A small brass plaque read *The Gillibrand Institute*.

An environmentalist organisation, lobbying for measures to accelerate global cooling and to mitigate the damage caused by the excesses of years gone by. One of Cloake's interests; he'd given money to help those worst affected by flooding. It didn't seem likely that he'd been killed for trying to help farmers whose fields had washed away in distant parts of the world, but it tied in with another trip he'd made with the Saqqaf, to TU Delft, the technical university. Nobody understood flood defences better than the Dutch, and TU Delft was one of the top centres in the Netherlands.

He could have flown. Anyone wealthy enough to own a car, a fleet of cars, could certainly afford to fly, unless his environmental ethics stopped him. Even short-haul electric aircraft used a lot of energy. Long-haul though, there was little choice. Twice he had travelled to Heathrow airport and half a dozen times to the smaller one at Cranfield. I called Meera.

'International travel,' I said. 'Where has Cloake been in the last six months? We should check the airlines, charters, Border Force records.'

'Already done, Lewis. He's flown twice to Bangladesh, and left the country once by the tunnel, destination unspecified. His passport checked but no vehicle record, which fits with his favourite car being ghosted.'

'Fourth of October?'

'Yes. The tunnel.'

'He was going to a conference in the Netherlands. Bangladesh, was that commercial or charter?'

'Commercial. British Airways from Heathrow, first class. And we've been checking his communications in the days leading up to his death.'

'Anything interesting?'

'Five past six in the evening of the murder he made an encrypted call via an anonymous proxy in Bangladesh.'

A call routed through a foreign country with no data extradition treaty. No way to know who he'd spoken to. 'okay. Thanks, Meera. I'm going to check up on something. Might catch you later.'

So, Cloake spent a lot of time at airports, but very little time flying. Heathrow had thousands, tens of thousands of passengers. Cranfield was strictly charter. Private planes, a handful of flights in a day.

An hour later I was in a car weaving its way through a grid of straight narrow roads between low office buildings and long hangars, to finally come to a halt by a two-room prefab shack with a small plaque on the door: *Cranfield Airport Customs*. The lone occupant, balding, overweight, would have been eligible for retirement if he'd wanted it. His eyes opened as the door closed behind me.

'DI Lewis Drake,' I said, marching up to his desk. I offered my hand to shake. 'My apologies for disturbing you, but I'm hoping you can help me with a murder case.'

His handshake was firm and brief. A gesture invited me to sit. 'ID?' He took out his phone. I took mine out and pinged him. He had the courtesy and professionalism to respond in kind: Reynolds. I didn't seriously expect to find an imposter wearing a Border Force uniform in possibly the quietest point of entry into the country, but good to be sure.

I showed Reynolds the picture of Cloake. 'This man has been here six times this year. I believe he was meeting someone off a flight.'

'Names are all on the system, DI Drake, arrivals and departures. Why did you come all the way out here?'

Reynolds was here working the most tedious job in all the Border Force. The single pip on his epaulette was a lowly rank for his years.

'I have a carte blanche warrant for this case,' I said, 'but sometimes, to do your job, you have to ask questions, dig into things that are going to upset people, people with friends who can end a career or push you into a dead end. I could be chasing phantoms, but I need to be sure before I make it official.'

He didn't swear at me, or show me the door. He just looked at me, so I waited.

He pursed his lips, rubbed his bristly chin. 'Dates?'

'August tenth, September eleventh, October seventeenth.'

His fingers worked the desk. The display set up so only he could see it.

'No flights.'

'Which day?'

'All of them. No flights.'

The breath escaped me in a rush as I tried to work out why Cloake would come to an airport on a day when no-one was flying. I wanted that fuzziness, that blurry, out-of-sync world view that let me think of a hundred things at once, to figure this out.

Reynolds remained resolutely in focus, rheumy grey eyes fixed on me. 'How long have you been in the service?'

'Fifteen years.'

'And you're digging into things that are going to upset people? You should know better after fifteen years.'

'It's personal. What's it to you?'

'What is it to me?' he mumbled. He scratched his head and stared at the screen on his desk a good half minute before straightening up and looking me in the eye. 'Four years ago,' he said, 'I was a senior officer at the Heathrow freight terminal. I saw something odd. Shipments coming in and going out by road, all labelled, checked, logged. But some cases were coming in by road, and then going out again with new labels. Pharmaceuticals for export became imported cosmetics without ever leaving the warehouse. Now, why would they do that?'

'You reported it?'

'I reported it, then it never happened. I was dropped two ranks and sent here.'

'Black market. The pharma company was selling on the black market and needed the export paper trail. I guess the incoming cosmetics went back out as pharmaceuticals?'

'Okay, you're not so dumb. What do we do now, DI Drake?'

'Check flights the days before and after.'

His fingers worked again. 'August ninth, one flight incoming from Athens with a single passenger, Ms Felicia Fame. Ring any bells?'

'She was a teen celebrity twenty years ago. My sister used to follow her. More recently something of an environmental activist.'

'Then the same plane departs for Tripoli. Again, one passenger. Lady Wyndham.'

I sat up. Reynolds cracked the beginning of a smile. 'August eleventh. Lady Wyndham returns, Ms Fame leaves. Curious. Shall we check the CCTV?'

I hunched round so I could see the monitor. My host, Reynolds, climbing the steps of a small plane. 'I check passports before they leave the aircraft.' A moment later, he leaves, then a woman in a short felt jacket crosses to the terminal building followed by a small blue case. She looks like Felicia Fame, twenty years older than I remembered. A truck arrives with fresh electrolyte for the plane's flow batteries. Reynolds touched the fast forward; the time display skipped about thirty minutes. The fuelling truck is gone, a woman in a long coat and wide-brimmed hat walks away from the camera followed again by a small blue case. She climbs the steps and enters the plane, the door closes, the plane taxis away.

'You don't check the passports of departing passengers?'

'When they arrive in the terminal building.'

'So, there's nothing to stop someone getting off the plane as Felicia Fame, swapping coats with Lady Wyndham and getting back on the plane?'

'Detective Inspector Drake, I have a job here, it isn't a great job, but it pays enough to keep me and my wife fed, and my son in education accumulating degrees until he can find something useful to do. I have learned not to see things I'm not supposed to see. Now, you—you haven't been here, I haven't seen you or spoken to you. But you know, these records, this CCTV, it's all on the Home Office system. It's nothing to do with me if you go back to your office and look this all up and draw your own conclusions.'

'Thank you, Sergeant Reynolds. If you and I ever do meet, I should like to buy you a drink.' I offered my hand again and he shook it, firm as before.

'DI Drake,' he called as I was half-way through the door. 'There's no camera out front, but some passengers get picked up by a shuttle belonging to the Montpellier Hotel, even on days when there are no flights.'

I drew a picture. Lady Wyndham fakes leaving the country and books into the hotel. The next day the Saqqaf brings Cloake to the airport, than he takes the shuttle to the same hotel. A very spacious, comfortable shuttle, it turned out. Leather upholstery, mini-bar, full entertainment suite. Overkill for an eight minute journey. It pulled into a circular drive before a Georgian mansion, elegant simplicity in its façade, graceful proportions in the structure, grandiose interior. The concierge looked down his nose at me. I guess I didn't look like their usual clientele. I pinged him my ID, which was enough for him to at least deign to speak to me.

'What can I do for you, Detective Inspector Drake?'

'I need to see your register and CCTV.' I took in the perfect marble floor, the sweeping curve of the staircase, the chandelier.

'That won't be possible, sir, unless you have a warrant.'

I gave him my full attention. 'I have a warrant. I could use it, and let it be widely known that I was here, or you can let me take a discreet look.' On the wall behind the reception desk hung a tall dark portrait, presumably of the Georgian gentleman who had built or owned this place. He didn't look like he approved of my presence any more than the concierge did.

'I'll need to speak to the manager, sir. Please wait in the office.'

He didn't grab my arm to drag me from the reception area, but I got a strong feeling he wanted to get me out of there before any of the paying guests might be exposed to my presence. I sat where he pointed in the small office and waited. Five minutes. I spent the time reading a little more of Amari's book.

'Who the fuck are you and what do you want?' The manager stood tall and broad and dark in the doorway in his three-piece suit and northern accent.

I pinged him my ID and the warrant, without activating it. 'I believe you've had Ms Felicia Fame staying here three times in recent months. I'd like to see the CCTV to confirm it, and I want to know if she had a visitor.' I pinged him Cloake's image.

He gave his phone a long look, his fingers flicking between the documents I'd sent, glancing at me each time. The look on his face turned from stolid to grim as he eased himself through the narrow gap into the space behind the desk and sat.

'Our guests expect privacy. Why should I tell you anything?' The face went from grim to sour.

'This man has been murdered. Your guest might be in danger, too. I want to confirm her identity. You've seen the warrant. Do I have to explain why I'd rather not use it?'

'Sad days,' he said. 'So much corruption.' He woke the desk, scrolled through a list and picked an entry. His wall screen lit up, a view from behind the concierge desk, a woman with elegantly styled hair in a blue felt jacket that did not look right on her.

'That isn't Felicia Fame.'

The manager shrugged. 'She's whoever she wants to be, mate. So long as the bill gets paid.'

'And who paid the bill?'

'Your dead man there. Cloake. Creepy fellah. Unsettled me.'

'Entangled,' I said. 'Thanks, you've been very helpful.'

We both stood.

'She's in danger, you say?'

'Yes.'

'Should I say anything when she's here next?'

'Are you expecting her?'

He nodded. 'Next week.'

'If you hear from her, tell her to call me.'

Another nod. 'What about the others?'

*

One of Cloake's cars falsely reports meetings with Sir Roger Wyndham, and Sir Roger winds up dead. Cloake has a series of carefully concealed meetings with Monica Wyndham and two directors of the Flood Management Commission: Artur Darbinyan and Elroy Harland, then Cloake ends up dead. I was puzzling over that en route back to London when the phone rang. It took a second for me to place the face. Last I'd seen it, it was blurred across realities.

Superintendent Donahue.

'Drake, there's a gap in the serial numbers in the evidence log from the Canary Wharf raid. Something got pulled.'

Unusual, but it happened sometimes. The numbers are assigned by the bots when they bag something. The blockchain log is updated later. If someone decided something already bagged isn't evidence, that fact should be logged and signed off to account for the gap. Donahue wouldn't be wasting his time on this if it had been.

'I don't know anything about that, sir.'

'I'm not a complete fool, Drake. I'm not accusing you. Look over the list, tell me if you can see what's missing.'

'I was out of action a lot of the time, sir. I don't know if I'll be much help.'

'Good God, man. Just look at the bloody list. If you see anything, tell me.'

'Yes, sir.'

He hung up. My phone pinged with his message. I opened it, skimmed down. I knew what I was looking for. ISPs: *Isolated Secure Processors.* They were on the list, two of them, logged sequentially. Baxter said they'd found three. The third was never logged, no gap in the serial numbers. Baxter had sidelined one on the raid. A fortunate stroke of prescience on her part, unless she had some plan for it. So, that wasn't what Donahue was looking for. I went through that list three times before I saw what was missing.

My Glock, the Glock that Chameleon, the Canary Wharf base jumper, had taken from me, used to kill Big Bennie Thacker and left behind. The Glock that I had watched the sterile claw of a forensics bot place in an evidence bag.

I called Meera. 'Anything from Ballistics yet?'

'Hi, Lewis. Yeah, I'm reading the report now.'

'The bullets that killed Wyndham were ten point two mil, I'm expecting the same for Cloake.' That was the answer I wanted. It had to be Red Claw's assassin.

'Mmmm, hang on.' Her eyes ran zig-zags as she read down the page. 'Okay, here we are, both slugs were nine millimetre hollow point. Isotope analysis matches Union Cartridge, Herstal or Barnaul.'

'Nine by nineteen Herstals?'

She screwed her face up. 'Yeah. Could be.'

Nine by nineteen hollow-point Herstals, standard issue in the service.

'Still no cartridges found at the house?' The cartridge would confirm the type, and the imprint of the firing pin should have the microscopic serial number of the weapon that fired it.

'Nah. Search turned up nothing.'

Cloake killed by bullets that might be the same type issued to us. My Glock, missing from evidence. Might have been some oversight by the forensics team or a bug in the bot's firmware. That calibre, that size of bullet is common enough. Come to that, nine mil Glocks are common enough but the whole thing got me twitching. If someone was trying to frame me for Cloake, they'd have left the gun there, or if not the gun, the empty cartridges stamped with the serial number engraved on the end of the firing pin.

'I'll call you back, Meera.' I hung up and dropped the phone in my lap. I needed to think. Do something or do nothing.

I picked up my phone again and my fingers hovered over my contacts list. My heartbeat picked up, pounding in my temples, pulsing in my neck. The phone shimmered and shook in my hand. I swiped and found Baxter's link,

Harris's, Meera's. All swam in my vision, superimposed. Stress again, bringing back the delta, cerasthesia.

Focus dammit! My fingers clenched and I gritted my teeth until the phone stayed still again, stayed in focus.

I've got your back, Harris had said. I called him. He picked up straight away, in a car.

'Harris, Canary Wharf. Did you see the forensics bot bag my Glock, the one used to kill Bennie Thacker?'

'It'll be in the evidence log.'

'Did you see it?'

He hesitated. 'It was all a bit of a rush. My first thought was for your safety, then there was the base jumper.'

'Did you see the bot collect the Glock?'

'You know how it is, Lewis. If they put me in an interview room with Argus, I couldn't say I did.'

'I get you, Harris. Thanks.' He had my back. He'd cover for me if he could, I didn't doubt, but it wouldn't help me if Argus caught him in an untruth. 'Any news on Aiden Harcourt? Was he at the memorial?'

'No, neither was the widow. The daughter last saw her on Saturday evening.'

Saturday. The day Cloake was killed. 'She didn't report her missing?'

'No, she told her she was going away for a while, didn't say where or why.'

'Her husband and her friend both murdered. She thought she might be next.' Except on Saturday Cloake hadn't yet been found.

'The other thing the daughter told me, you know she's been on location for a shoot, at Woburn Abbey?'

'Yeah.' I knew the place, magnificent stately home, mostly eighteenth century, and I knew where it was, outside of Milton Keynes. 'The hotel—Wyndham was visiting his daughter.' More confirmation that the link to Cloake was a red herring.

'That's it,' Harris said. 'There were two other surprise no-shows at the memorial, directors of the Flood Management Commission.'

'Have you got the names?'

'Yeah, I have Artur Darbinyan, he's the CEO, and Elroy Harland, financial director. Ring any bells?'

'They've been meeting with Cloake. Have they gone to ground, too?' Pieces of the puzzle were clicking. 'Cloake's been having secret meetings with them *and* he's been visiting the Gillibrand Institute.'

'Gillibrand Institute. Flood management. You going to talk to them?'

'Yeah, I need to. But first I need to have another look at Cloake's house. Have to wait until tomorrow for the daylight. Damn these short winter days.'

I slumped back in my seat and closed my eyes. Nothing made any sense, but the tension had eased. All was still and focussed again when I opened my eyes. The delta flashback had worn off. I remembered that I'd told Meera I'd call her back but wasn't sure whether I already had. I opened up my call log to check, then hit her link.

'Hi Lewis,' she said, bright and cheerful. 'I'm looking at the traffic records.'

'Traffic?' I said, but I knew what she meant. Déjà vu.

'Yeah, Cloake's estate is in the middle of nowhere. VLA records show only forty vehicles moving within five kilometres of the estate on Saturday afternoon and evening. One of them might be the killer's.'

'Good work, Meera.' It was what I thought she'd say. I was too distracted. I should have thought to suggest that sooner. 'Listen, I want to have another look at the scene.'

'Sure. You're on secondment so I'll need to come with you. Were you thinking now?'

'Dark soon. I'd rather do it in daylight.'

'Tomorrow then, but are you still coming to Parkside this afternoon? It would be good to have another pair of eyes on the traffic.'

A glance at the nav showed I was only fifteen minutes from home. Forty from Parkside, then I'd have the trip back again in the evening unless I stayed over somewhere. No change of clothes, no toothbrush. 'I'll get there early tomorrow, Meera. We can have a look at the traffic data before we head out to the scene.'

'Sure. Eight am. I'll be here.' She hung up.

Bright as a button, Meera Harbin. Competent, efficient and easy company. I thought about calling her back and redirecting the car to Cambridge, but I was held back by a nagging feeling that I shouldn't. Too much going on in my life. It wouldn't have been fair on her to drag her into it.

CHAPTER 9

Wednesday 20th November: Scene of the Crime

As an analogy one can imagine an intelligent amoeba with a good memory. As time progresses the amoeba is constantly splitting, each time the resulting amoebas have the same memories as the parent. Our amoeba hence does not have a life line, but a life tree.

—Hugh Everett III

Anyone can make a quantum event manifest as a perceptible change in the world by invoking a quantum number generator to guide a decision; there are sites on the internet for the purpose. Flip a quantum coin to decide whether to have pizza or Chinese for dinner and both realities will exist. But only the entangled will experience both and judge which was the better choice.

With practice, the entangled can focus on ever finer filaments of the world and create tangible differences where there were none before. They can act in ways that carry a high risk and learn from the result. Even a fatal outcome in a thin reality may be a small price for insights they can then apply in wider worlds.

Against this ability to create divergences is the natural tendency of our conscious selves to converge on comfortable thoughts, habits and behaviours, to divide our worlds into fewer, thicker strands. Even where natural divergence creates large scale changes—sunshine in one world, thunderstorms in another—our thoughts tend to converge where they can.

—A K Amari - *The Measurement Problem,*
A Guide to Entanglement

Hiss! Clunk! Hiss! Clunk! There was the white disk bright above me fixed in my vision, a clattering of metal on metal and vague green shapes moving in the periphery of my sight. Something had happened, something terrible, but I couldn't remember what or where or to whom. I couldn't remember who *I* was, only that I was lost in noise and light, lost in the pain and the raw discomfort of the tube through my mouth and down my throat, and in the dryness in my unblinking eyes.

The frustration of not knowing rose up. I felt rather than heard the strangled sound trying to escape my blocked throat. The green shape at the edge of my sight jerked, became larger, looming over me. There was green, and there was a pale oval, two darker spots. I struggled to focus. A face, skin so white, eyes so dark, and silver-grey hair cut short. Thin pale lips moved but I could hear no words over the noise.

A soft, cool hand touched my cheek springing me from the dream. Meera

Harbin's long black hair hung down, half concealing her face and her small dark breasts.

'Coffee?' She bent to give me a light kiss on the lips. The lingering nutty scent of her hair filled my nostrils.

I reached round and my middle finger explored the dimples at the small of her back. 'Mmmm!'

She kissed me again and stood, raising her arms to sweep the hair back over her shoulders, standing long enough for me to admire her slender form. As she headed towards the bedroom door her lustrous thick hair swung gently above her shapely bottom, revealing a deep black birthmark to the left of her backbone. She plucked her dressing gown from its hook as she passed through the doorway, gracing me with a wicked smile over her shoulder.

The alarm jerked me awake; my arm shot out to shut it off. It was dark and cold, and the eternal odour of damp hanging in the air placed me firmly back in my flat above Kay's shop. *You might have dreams*, Kay had told me. She said nothing about dreams within dreams. The noise and light and the silver-haired woman in green were a continuation of the dreams I'd been having. Stranger than I can describe but thoroughly dream-like. There was something familiar about that face, the short silver-grey hair and pale skin. Dreams are like that. The mind borrows from people you've known or met to build the story.

The Harbin dream was different, clear as crystal. It felt real, down to the soft sense of languid release, the desire for more, the inexplicable undercurrent of suppressed guilt that stayed with me even as I washed and dressed. It felt more real than standing in the grotty little kitchen of my flat waiting for my coffee machine to finish doing its job.

Eight am at Parkside, she'd said. I found her at her desk, totally absorbed, black hair held coiled to the back of her head with the stick barrette. She turned at the sound of my feet scuffing on the stiff blue carpet tiles. 'Hey, Lewis. Pull up a chair. Let me show you something.'

A map of the roads around the Cloake estate filled her screen. The house lay at the centre, the long drive stretched southwards then bent southeast through the avenue of lime trees.

'This is the traffic in the area between six pm and ten pm.' She tapped the *play* icon, and dots whizzed around the roads. Some stopped for seconds or minutes before moving off again. Nothing entered or left the Cloake estate. 'Do you see it?' She turned to me, teeth white and even, eyes sparkling.

'Nothing went into the estate. Nothing stopped near it.'

She faced the screen again. 'Look, this road that runs down the east side by the woods. It's a narrow country lane, single track with passing places. I'll play it again, slower.'

The road she was pointing at ran along the top of a low ridge beyond the woods that covered the eastern edge of the estate. There were two passing places along the road. One vehicle turned onto the lane heading north while another came in the opposite direction. The first car pulled into a passing place to wait for the second, then carried on after it had passed.

'It was only stopped for a moment Meera, not long enough for…'

'You're missing the point. Look at the second passing place. Why didn't the southbound car pull in there? It was closer to the point where they'd have met.'

The penny dropped. Cars are constantly talking to each other, exchanging position, speed, preferred route information, optimising the traffic flow amongst themselves. 'There was already a vehicle there, no room for another.'

'That's it. A car that hasn't uploaded its logs to the VLA—ghosted—but these other two vehicles must have been talking to it to co-ordinate their movements. If we're lucky one of them will still have its registration number in its cache memory.'

Every time she looked at me brought that morning's dream back. It was most distracting. 'Where are they now, those cars?' I said, trying to swing my attention back to the task.

She drilled down on the display through to the VLA records. 'This one's a public rental currently in a charging station in Glasgow.'

'That much travel, our mystery vehicle will be long gone from its cache.'

As I spoke she was already pulling up the record for the other. She leaned back and folded her arms, looking smug. With good reason. A farm utility vehicle currently parked in a shed two kilometres from the Cloake estate. It hadn't moved from there since the night of the murder.

We both spoke at the same time. 'Put a block on it,' I said. 'I'll put a block on it,' she said, and laughed. She locked it down and sent a request to the traffic department to send someone out to retrieve a copy of its cache memory.

*

Meera booked out one of the Parkside squad cars. We sat facing each other all the way out to the Cloake estate. Mostly I talked as she asked me about Alice, oozing sympathy and concern, leaning forward to touch my knee when I spoke of my first sight of her lying blank and motionless in the neurology wing of Addenbrooke's Hospital, and of the guilt I had felt at having seen so little of her in the years before.

The gates were still open when we arrived but the uniformed guard had been replaced by a drone armed with a pulse gun that could stop a car dead. It stepped aside at our approach. The deer were on the lawn again, but skittish. The car slowed as the herd broke into a run across the driveway in front of us. As the last of them passed, Meera asked, 'What are we looking for, Lewis?'

'A nine millimetre Glock, Met police issue. I suspect someone used it to kill Cloake then planted it to frame its owner, or two cartridges fired from said Glock. Or both.'

'They swept the house. Found nothing.'

'Yeah, that's a puzzle.'

The car pulled up on the gravel drive. Another drone guarded the front door but stepped aside when I pinged it my ID. There was a shimmer in its outline.

Meera's footsteps crunched on the gravel behind me. 'That's cold, Lewis,' I heard her say, but when I turned to ask what she meant, she walked past, through Cloake's front door. I must have imagined it.

The entrance hall was a mess. All the trees and shrubs had been lifted from their planters and the stones and soil dug out and piled on the dying carpet. I checked each pot and planter anyway, but found nothing. I took my Glock out. Not *my* Glock, the replacement I'd been issued after Canary Wharf. Meera took a sharp intake of breath. I gripped the gun by the barrel and held it out to her. 'They're trying to frame me, Meera, but they messed it up. If there's anything to be found here I'd rather you and I find it. You take me in if you have to.'

She took the weapon from my hand, weighed it in hers a moment then handed it back. 'You're okay, Lewis. Something doesn't smell right about this.'

'This is what you're looking for.' The voice came from behind me. I span around. Nobody.

'Did you see him?' I said.

'See who?'

I hurried to the entrance to the long corridor and looked both ways. Nobody. I turned to see Meera standing, walking towards me, an echo in her movements; the delta was coming back and I was hearing voices from another world.

'Services,' I said, trying to hold my focus on the here and now. 'Your DI Gallicoe said they'd been checked but let's have a look.' I knew the corridor to the right of the hall led to the library, bedrooms, reception rooms and garage. I headed left. The first door opened on a large modern kitchen. All pale woods on the floor, cupboard doors and worktop. The high, tinted-glass window looked out onto the drive. The place was spotless, flawless, like a showroom. On the other side, at the rear of the house was a small but comfortable suite of bedroom, lounge, small kitchen. Some clothes folded on a chair in the bedroom. A dishwasher in the kitchen with its door open, half-loaded. Soames' quarters. The next door on the right, again at the rear of the house, was the services, with a pile of half-sorted laundry by the washing machine. Cleaning bots sat at their charging stations, all deactivated—standard procedure for a crime scene. A door at the back led to a rear lobby with a rack of boots and wellingtons, coats on hooks, gardening tools and a row of refuse and recycling bins. A heap of small metal items lay on the table: tin-cans, a worn screwdriver, broken door-spring.

'Did the forensics bots do this, Meera?'

'No, it was found this way. Soames must have been in the middle of sorting the recycling before he left on Saturday.'

'No, those are top of the line bots, they sort it and bin it themselves. Someone tipped out the bin to look for something.'

'The killer?'

'Or someone else. If you came here sometime, say, on Sunday, to look for spent cartridges, you'd start in the library, but if you didn't find them there…'

'You'd check the recycling in case a bot picked them up.'

'Let's have another look in the library.'

It was as I'd last seen it, with the notable absence of Cloake's body.

I crossed the room towards the desk, miming a gun with my forefinger. 'Bang!' The cartridge leaping from the chamber would have fallen and landed under the table or the settee where I had sat with Cloake. I scrunched down to look: clean and clear. Not a speck of dust, and no cartridge. I carried on around the back of the desk and aimed my finger at the back of Cloake's imagined head.

'That's cold, Lewis.' Meera folded her arms tight across her belly. 'People who could do that…'

'Bang!' I said. The cartridge would have arced out to land on the floor by the window. If it *had* landed there it was gone now. The corner of my eye caught a movement in the trees at the far edge of the lawn.

Meera sauntered up to stand close to me, her eyes following my gaze. 'What is it?'

The woods were a good half kilometre away and there was no sign of movement. 'Could have been a deer.' The rest of the herd were way over on the other side of the grounds.

Meera's quiet gasp pulled my attention from the woods. By the time I turned around she had her pistol in a solid two-handed grip, aimed at the figure silhouetted in the doorway.

'Hands up!' she commanded.

He raised his hands, slowly and deliberately, and stepped forward into the light. His left hand held a gun, gripped by the barrel. 'This is what you're looking for,' he said.

'Hello, Chameleon. Is that my Glock?'

Meera's grip on her gun did not waver. 'Put it down, slowly.'

'Relax, DS Harbin, I'm on your side.' He paced the length of the library, arms raised, and placed the gun on the desk. 'I have the spent cartridges too.'

'Is he?' Meera glanced at me. 'On our side?'

'He's an undercover in Red Claw working for a Superintendent Donahue. If he meant us harm, we'd already be harmed.'

'More a freelancer than undercover, and I blew my cover at Canary Wharf. Donahue was not pleased.'

One more glance at me to confirm, then she holstered her gun. 'How do you know my name?' My gun and the cartridges went into her jacket pocket.

He looked from Meera, to me, and back at her. 'Because Lewis introduced us half an hour ago. There's some divergence going on here. How come you're so late getting here in this reality?'

Divergence—that explained the voices. Fragments leaking through from those other realities, but only fragments.

I shrugged. 'Can you tell me why we were here earlier in the other one.'

Again he looked at Meera, then at me, like he was weighing something up. 'We're wasting time. Let me answer the questions you've already asked.'

'But we haven't...' Meera started to say. I stopped her with a hand on her shoulder. 'He means questions we asked in another reality.'

Chameleon nodded. 'Just so. First, yes, I do have a name but you don't need to know it, Chameleon will suffice. Second, after Elijah was killed, he told me…'

'But he's...' Meera broke off without finishing. She figured it out: he's dead but he's entangled.

'Elijah said he was alone in the house, and would likely not be found until Soames came back Monday morning. I thought it worth a look before the scene was disturbed. That's when I found the Glock. Not the Red Claw assassin's usual weapon, and that one usually leaves only the cartridge cases.'

'Did you know it was mine right away?'

'I suspected. Donahue got the serial number from records, and he said it was never logged in evidence at Canary Wharf.'

'So why? Why did they kill him with my gun?'

'The immediate result would have been to frame you for the murder if I hadn't recovered it. What Vidmar intended beyond that, I can't say.'

'Elijah couldn't ID the killer?'

'No, he was masked. But tall, male, two metres tall, around ninety kilos.'

'Why did Elijah take out Tamboli's bugs?'

'So he could call his friends and warn them without being heard. He knew what was coming when his security system went down, and he was afraid they might be next.'

'The encrypted call through the anonymous proxy,' Meera said.

'Monica Wyndham and the FMC board members, that's who he called,' I added. 'Do you know where they are?'

'Yes.' His attention was wandering, his eyes looking past my shoulder, like Alice when she was losing focus, or so I thought. 'Yes, I do,' he mumbled, 'but that's another thing you don't need to know.' He stepped around the desk and up to the window. 'There's someone out there,' he said. 'In the trees.'

'I can't see anything,' Meera said. I made another attempt to scan the tree line, but with the shifting and shimmering of the delta coming back it was hopeless.

I heard the crack, saw the window glass flex and vibrate for a fraction of a second. 'Down!' I yelled. Meera stood there, a blank look on her face. I grabbed her around the shoulders and dragged her down to the floor.

'Lewis!' she shouted.

There was a faint crazing on the glass, a darker smudge at the height of Chameleon's head. These windows were tough.

'Lewis! What are you doing?' She pushed me away and shuffled back until she was pressed against the bookshelves. I looked back at the window. Clean, clear, unmarked.

Chameleon looked down at me, an eyebrow raised. 'Have you been taking implicitins, Lewis? Betas? Gammas?'

'Deltas, two days ago,' I said as I stood.

He crouched down to Meera's level. 'He's not going crazy, slightly entangled is all, a touch of cerasthesia.' He offered a hand to help her to her feet. 'But someone is out there, and did take a shot. We should leave.'

Meera pulled out her phone. 'I'll call the squad car to the door.' She tapped and swiped and looked out of the window. The car lurched into motion, away from us, up the drive. It turned the bend and its hi-viz stripe flickered between the grey trunks of the lime trees.

She drew her weapon. 'Someone's fucking with us, Lewis.' The resounding *ker-chunk* as she chambered a round underlined her words.

'Garage.' I pointed to the door to the hallway. 'Come.'

I sprinted across the library and into the corridor, Meera's and Chameleon's footsteps behind me.

Chameleon stopped me with a hand on the shoulder, looking up at the glass skylight. 'Whoever's behind this is creating divergences. Best if you don't. Keep your focus and get out of here. I'll find you again.' With that he turned and ran back towards the services wing.

I hesitated for a second before dashing with Meera to the end of the corridor, to the plain sprung door to the garage.

'Nice car, Lewis.' That was Meera's voice, but not this Meera. I felt an itch between my shoulder blades. Meera pulled up beside me, two-handed grip on her gun. I had my hand on the door handle. She nodded: *ready*. I pushed the handle down and barged the door open. We sprang through together, me covering to the right, her to the left. I motioned her to keep out of sight and cover the room. She crouched behind the Silver Dawn. The door of the first car, a Guangzhou, was locked. I took out my phone and pinged it with the police override. Still the door didn't open. It wasn't only the Saqqaf that Cloake had hacked; every licensed vehicle should respond to the override.

Same result with the Samsung next to it but, as I stepped past it, the lights of the next car flashed and the door locks issued a barely audible *clunk*. I hadn't even invoked the override. The Saqqaf, Cloake had authorised it for my use and never revoked.

'Nice car, Lewis.'

She'd already said that. 'Get in. Now.' It might have been a memory crossing the boundary or a shift in the light, but I turned and looked up through the skylight. He was dressed in black and holding an assault rifle, the shadowed face invisible behind the glare of the sun on the glass. Before I could raise my gun he fired and ducked below my line of sight. At such close range his shot punched a hole in the reinforced glass. Meera cried out and fell to the floor.

I pulled open the Saqqaf's door, grabbed her by the upper arms and dragged her in to lie prone across the saloon floor. Who knew what damage I was doing.

'Saqqaf! Nearest A&E!' I shouted. The door slammed shut and the car leapt from its bay and out under the rapidly rising roller door. Gravel flew behind us as it swerved around the side of the house, then accelerated across the grass onto the drive. A muted thud from the back window was followed by a succession of others. Our assailant had turned his weapon on full automatic, but the car was up to it.

The Saqqaf spoke in a slightly accented synthetic voice. 'Emergency protocol engaged, estimated time of arrival at Addenbrooke's Hospital, twelve minutes. A&E have been alerted.' I was thrown sideways as we turned the corner into the avenue of limes. Ahead, the drone stood square in the gateway, its raised pulser flashed and the Saqqaf lost speed, but was still travelling fast enough to hit the drone with a massive crunch. It flew up, metallic claws flailing at the bonnet until it smacked into the windscreen and rolled off to the side. Half a ton of steel and composites and it didn't even crack the glass. The only scars it left were a pair of gouges in the paintwork of the bonnet.

Meera cried out with the jolt of the impact. She sucked breath between her teeth.

We turned on to the road and sped up. The Saqqaf had only slowed to take the corner, its shielding good enough. A small voice inside me screamed its horror while my combat first aid training kicked in. Most injuries were treatable with modern regen techniques provided the casualty's condition could be stabilised. Blood loss was the thing that could kill her, and she was losing a lot. I lifted her arm so I could pull the jacket sleeve off. The Glock and one cartridge dropped from her pocket as I wadded it up.

'Am I going to make it, Lewis?' Her voice was small and distant beneath the pounding of my own heart.

The entry wound was right over her spine. So much blood, so much, but steady, not pulsing. It hadn't hit an artery. 'Yeah, you're going to make it, Meera.' I pulled up her top to expose the wound and pressed down with her wadded-up jacket to stem the bleeding, ignoring her squeal of pain.

She gasped and moaned, but after a few moments her ragged breathing slowed to something near normal. 'Who was it, did you see?'

The fact she could speak astonished me. The training kicked in again: *Still conscious, good. Too much internal bleeding, blood pressure would drop and she'd pass out.* 'I don't know.' I shook my head, kneeling beside her on the floor of the car's saloon. I lifted my hand a second to get a better position and saw the deep black birthmark to the left of her backbone, exactly like the one I'd dreamed. I pressed down again and she whimpered. With my free hand I took her hand and I closed my eyes.

When I opened them again I was kneeling beside Meera's lifeless form on the concrete floor of Cloake's garage holding her limp hand.

'Lewis?' I looked up. Harris stood in the doorway from the house, dressed in a black flak jacket, assault rifle in his hands. 'I'm sorry, Lewis. I was too late.'

Meera's ragged gasp brought me back to her in the Saqqaf.

'Nearly there,' I said in a soft voice of futile reassurance. Somewhere in the deepest recesses of my awareness I had a dim apprehension of Harris's form, speaking, but I couldn't focus on him, not without abandoning Meera. I couldn't focus because he was *thin*.

Jack Harris was well below male average height. The shooter I'd seen through the skylight was a tall guy, but that was another reality, might not even have been the same shooter. In this world the hardened glass of the skylight had saved her. At such close range the shock wave from an assault rifle bullet's impact would have instantly pulped her insides otherwise.

I gave up trying to work it out when the Saqqaf turned into the entrance to the Addenbrooke's Hospital complex. They were waiting between the concrete pillars outside the emergency entrance: two medics, a gurney, a long-armed lifter. They shooed me out of the way so the bot could lift Meera out with delicate care onto the lowered gurney. Her jacket, my Glock and the cartridges were left behind. The car pulled away a moment later, as any car would in the emergency drop-off zone.

I trailed her and the medics through the sliding glass doors, trying not to lose them, trying not to get in the way. I was ignored through the reception area filled with the patiently waiting public sitting in hard resin chairs with their various ailments and injuries. A green-suited figure blocked my way when I tried to follow through the doors at the back. He led me into a small windowless room off the reception area and sat me down. The green-gowned man introduced himself as Dr Green. I almost laughed; my nerves were all over the place.

My ID served as answer to some of his questions, but he did want what I could tell him about the injury for the surgical team.

'How is she?' I asked ten minutes later when he'd finished with his questions. 'Will she be okay?'

His fingers flicked at his pad. 'Scan shows a spinal cord injury. They're stabilising her before beginning surgery, but she's in the best place. This is the country's leading centre for neuro-regeneration.'

I heard the words but I lost the meaning at 'spinal cord'. My head span, my ears buzzed and I could see only Meera lying on the floor of the Saqqaf; the blood, the wound, the birthmark. I heard her cries of pain.

'… but it's likely to be some weeks before she's fully recovered.'

My eyes focussed again on Dr Green. 'But will she be okay?'

'Yes, yes, that's what I've been trying to tell you. She'll make a full recovery but it will take time. She'll need many hours of regen in a TR.'

The relief at his words drained me. I sagged in the chair. I felt a prickling in my eyes and my mind went blank, allowing idle curiosity to take my tongue. 'What's a TR?'

'Tomographic Resonator. It's used to control the tissue regeneration process.'

'Like a Regenesys 5101.'

I got the indulgent smile of the expert speaking to someone out of their depth. 'That kind of thing, yes, but we use Unigen machines here.'

'You did have a Regenesys 5101 once. Sam Okorie was using it for an experimental treatment.'

'Okorie? I've heard the name but he was before my time I'm afraid.'

The door swung open with a bang. 'Drake, I got an alert from Meera's tag. What happened? How is she?' Gallicoe's face was the colour of beetroot, his breathing short and heavy.

His sudden presence brought it home to me like a hammer blow—I had a problem, a serious problem: the Saqqaf would be heading back to its home, with Meera's jacket in the back, with my Glock and the two cartridges. Soon, if not already, Cloake's house would be swarming once more with an incident response unit.

While Dr Green repeated to Gallicoe what he'd told me, I pulled out my phone and opened up the link to the Saqqaf.

Error 503: service unavailable.

Could be that the response unit had already found it, disabled it, and opened it up, but given how uncooperative Cloake's cars were to police overrides, I'd have thought it would take longer. Either way, there was nothing I could do about it.

Dr Green gave us directions to the neurosurgery department and made himself scarce. Gallicoe launched himself in the direction of the hospital's innards, following Green's directions.

'Are you coming?'

'Thought you'd want me back at the Parkside station for a debrief.'

His hand paused on the metal plate on the door.

'Standard procedure,' I said.

'Fuck procedure, this is Meera. Give me the rundown as we walk. Formal interview tomorrow.'

The wedding ring on Gallicoe's hand, his severely distracted manner, Meera's comment over lunch: *all the good ones are taken*, all added up. I wouldn't have thought he was her type. As we made our way through the maze of stairs and corridors I recounted the story of the day's events—leaving out some details, details like other worlds, details like Chameleon and Harris. In the waiting area we found a vending machine that offered something vaguely reminiscent of tea. Gallicoe was bold enough to risk the alleged coffee.

'The thing is, Drake, it doesn't add up,' he said. 'Why did the squad car leave, and why did the gatekeeper drone try and stop you?'

'Had to be someone in the service instructed them.' Harris was in the service and Harris was there at the scene, at least in some reality. He might have been there to watch my back, but someone had to have sent him. If you'd asked me before then who I could trust, Harris would have been top of the list. There had been a divergence, that was clear. The birthmark on Meera's back that I'd seen in the car was the same I'd seen in my dream that morning. It was no dream. The previous afternoon, in some thin reality I had diverted my car to Cambridge, met Meera, and stayed the night with her. We had arrived at the Cloake estate earlier than in this world, and I had heard and seen echoes: *That's cold, Lewis, This is what you're looking for.*

I drained my paper cup and sat in one of the moulded resin chairs opposite the vending machine. Gallicoe, pacing up and down, came to an abrupt stop. 'Is she going to be okay, Drake? You were there, you saw…'

'They say she'll be fine. Now sit down before I dislocate my neck.'

Gallicoe was halfway through giving me the run-down on the Cambridge office politics when Dr Green pottered along with a tall, slender, silver-haired woman in tow, attired similarly in the green medical gown. We stood, and I tried to figure out where I'd seen her before.

'Ms Harbin is being prepared for surgery, now. Ms Elland'—Dr Green gestured to the silver-haired woman who offered a reassuring smile—'will manage the surgeon. She is our most experienced neurosurgical consultant.'

She offered a hand to shake, Gallicoe first, then me. 'I've been here long enough that I was wielding the scalpel with my own hands when I started. But don't worry, that was a long time ago.'

She sat us down. 'I've studied the scans and reviewed the surgeon's program. I'll be watching closely during the procedure. It isn't often we have to intervene.

The machines make far fewer errors than us fumble-fingered humans used to.'

Gallicoe was on the edge of his seat, fingers twitching. 'Will she be alright?'

Ms Elland switched her expression from soothing blandness to serious professional. 'It is a serious injury. In decades past she would have been confined to a wheelchair for the rest of her life. This surgery is the first step. We remove tissue that is too badly damaged to heal without scarring, including the shattered vertebra, which we'll replace with a temporary scaffold so that the regeneration can proceed smoothly. The full treatment will take some weeks but I am confident she will make a complete recovery.'

'When will we be able to see her?'

'After surgery she'll be in ICU for observation. You can see her there, but just for a few minutes. Tomorrow, if all's well, she'll be moved to a neurology ward.'

'Someone should be here when she comes out of it. Will you stay, Drake? There's paperwork I need to deal with, and I'd like to update the squad in person.'

'Be glad to, Gallicoe. Until you get back here.'

I sat, I read Amari, I drank the thin, brown liquid from the vending machine and ate sandwiches from the small shop by the main reception. A hand on my shoulder woke me. Ms Elland.

'You can see her now.'

She led me along bright, echoing, empty hallways in desperate need of fresh paint, up stairs, more deserted corridors, to a swinging double door with battered metal panels at waist height: ICU. The noise hit me as soon as she pushed the door open. Fans and pumps, beeps and buzzes, scurrying footsteps and voices, bright lights. I'd expected intensive care would be a silent oasis of peace and calm—I guess *intensive* counted for more than *care*. Meera was in the third bay on the left.

'Five minutes,' Ms Elland said as she pushed me forward.

'Hey, Meera. How are you doing?' I know. But I couldn't think of anything that wouldn't sound lame.

'Your Glock, Lewis. It was in my pocket. Where is it now?'

'You don't need to worry about that, that's my job,' I said, and I was worried. 'Gallicoe's worried about you.'

'That's his job.' There was a touch too much bitterness in her voice.

'I told him what happened, but I left some things out.'

'Like?'

'Chameleon.'

'You want me to leave him out, too?'

'It's your call, Meera. I might be wrong about him. They've no reason to suspect anything of you, but if they ask with Argus watching I don't want you to get yourself in trouble.'

She closed her eyes. 'You know, it's all such a blur in my mind. Before I got shot it was just you and me. After, I blacked out. How would I know whether there was anyone else there.'

Ms Elland knocked. 'Time's up, Mr Drake.'

I reached to squeeze Meera's hand. 'You'll soon be dancing again.'

'That'd be a miracle. Couldn't dance before.'

Ms Elland led me past the open door of the adjacent bay. I stopped when I heard the noise, a rhythmic *clunk, hisssss, clunk, hisssss*. The sound of my dreams of light and sound—*A face, skin so white, eyes so dark, and silver-grey hair cut short. Thin pale lips moved but I could hear no words over the noise.*

'Mr Drake?' Ms Elland stared at me with her dark eyes beneath silver-grey hair cut short. This was my dream, lying in an intensive care bed in Addenbrooke's hospital under the care of Ms Elland. Not a dream, another reality.

'Sorry, bad memories.' Memories or dreams. 'Have you worked here a long time?'

'Most of my career.'

'Did you know Sam Okorie?'

Her turn to stop dead. She looked at me like she noticed me for the first time. 'Dr Green said you were asking about a Regenesys 5101. What's this about?'

It was a loose end in an inventory, that's all it was. But four million is a lot to sign off without reason. 'It may be relevant to my current case. Do you know what happened to it?'

'It went back to VirGenTech as far as I know.'

'I'd like to find out. There'll be records.'

'You'll need to speak to the admin section.' She pushed open the swing door for me. 'End of the corridor, left, down two floors for the exit.'

'Did you know Sam well?'

'Are you another one?' she said. 'I thought you'd all given up. Isn't it enough for you that he's dead?'

'No, Ms Elland. I'm not another one, I'd like to know what happened.'

'End of the corridor, left, down two floors. Goodbye Mr Drake.' She turned her back and strode away, the heels of her flat shoes clacking on the shining tiles of the corridor.

End of the corridor, left, down two floors. I took out my phone and was about to call a car when it rang. Gallicoe. My heart was in my mouth as I answered, but if they'd found my Glock in Cloake's car I wouldn't be getting a courtesy call—they'd be here to take me into custody. I picked up.

'Drake, where did you send the Saqqaf?'

'Nowhere. Isn't it back at Cloake's house?'

'That's the thing. Why would it go anywhere else?'

I didn't like his tone, like he didn't believe me. But to be fair, in his place I wouldn't have believed me either. I gave him an awkward silence, which he broke.

'How's Meera?'

'I spoke to her for a minute. Good spirits. She can have visitors tomorrow.'

'Good, good. By the way, that car she issued a block on, traffic have been out to read the cache. The reg number of the vehicle it encountered belongs to a van that was scrapped fifteen years ago.'

The dead end didn't surprise me. It would have been too easy. I stepped out into a dark and cloudy evening and called a car to take me home.

CHAPTER 10

Thursday 21st November: Addenbrooke's

Every possible reality exists: every possible past, every possible future.

The naïve argument from this is that there is a world where you are god-emperor of all the world, or where all humankind lives in an idyllic paradise or an abominable hell.

No.

That you can imagine a world does not mean its existence is possible. For a reality to reach a state in which you are god-emperor of all the world there must be a way, a sequence of possible events, however unlikely, that lead to that state. In particular for it to be you, *who is god-emperor, we must start from one of the possible states in which* you *exist.*

I experience worlds where the conditions in which most people live are considerably better than in this one, others where the sum of human suffering is far greater, but no paradise and no hell.

—A K Amari - *The Measurement Problem, A Guide to Entanglement*

I dreamed again of the place of bright lights and perpetual noise and the rasping in my throat. I knew I was dreaming, and I knew where I was in this dream. My chest rose and fell in time with the *hiss! clunk!* of the machine that breathed for me.

Two figures loomed over me dressed in green. I struggled to bring them into focus. A wisp of grey hair was escaping from beneath her cap. There was grey, too, in the fine eyebrows. The creases in the corners of those eyes deepened.

'Is he awake?' the other one said. His hair was as grey as hers, his skin as dark as hers was light.

'Lewis?' she said. 'Blink if you can hear me.'

I had to think about how to do that, I had think about where my eyelids were and how to get them to move. I couldn't. I couldn't move at all, but my chest rose with the hiss of the ventilator.

'I don't think he is.' She looked away, at something to my side and above. 'It looks like REM sleep. I'm surprised to see even that. Do you think it's the deltas?'

My eyes blinked of their own accord, but she wasn't watching. Under the fingers of my right hand there was a crease in the sheet. My middle finger pulled back and followed its edge.

She looked at me again. I couldn't blink.

Clunk! My chest fell. My mouth was dry, filled and blocked by the plastic tube. My throat was sore and the tube made me want to gag. My chest hurt with every forced breath.

'Pulse is rising,' he said.

'There's *something* going on in there, Sam.' She watched my eyes.

I couldn't blink. The ventilator hissed. My chest rose.

Footsteps echoed, getting louder. They stopped by my bedside. Another green-suited figure.

'It's time, Ms Elland.'

'No! We need to give the implicitins more time to work. There *is* more brain activity.'

'Ms Elland, when you first proposed giving delta implicitins to brain-dead patients you assured the ethics committee it was a time-limited data gathering exercise. This patient is brain-dead and he's tying up an ICU bed. Those are random neurons firing. It signifies nothing. We'll extubate and put him in a side room until he passes.'

The ventilator clunked, and was silent. An alarm sounded.

I blinked. The cracked ceiling of my bedroom was grey in the morning light. My arm stretched out of its own volition to cancel the alarm.

Ms Elland and Sam Okorie. It was them in the dream. They had figured large in my life in recent days and they were both medical practitioners. Natural, then, that they would figure in a dream of an intensive care bed like the ones I'd seen. Except that I'd been dreaming of that place for days without knowing what it was.

I knew now where I'd first seen Ms Elland. First things first, I dragged myself out of bed, acutely aware of every movement of my body, how it obeyed my orders without question. To the kitchen, to the coffee machine. Beans ground, pressed, loaded. I found Jane Seymour's video on my phone while I was waiting for the water to boil. I skipped forward to the first appearance of Sam Okorie. Jane Seymour hadn't said anything about the woman standing close to Doctor Okorie, very close. Ms Elland. Not just work colleagues. He, a specialist in regenerative therapies, she in neurology. The camera panned and settled on Alice and Erica. Erica talking, Alice laughing. Their words were lost with distance.

Baxter called while I was pouring the coffee.

'Gallicoe needs you in Cambridge this morning for a debrief on yesterday's events.'

'Yeah, I know. Did he give you the rundown?'

'Sketchy. One assailant, a DS from Cambridge injured. You didn't get a look at the gunman?'

'Nothing identifiable.'

She nodded, slow, three times. 'I've asked him to keep me informed.'

'Do you know where Harris is? He isn't answering his phone.'

'He's been in Tripoli since Tuesday. I sent him to track down Aiden Harcourt.'

Harris couldn't be in Tripoli if he was at Cloake's house when Meera was shot, unless that was only in the reality where Meera died.

'Have you had any confirmation that he arrived?' I said.

'Leave it, Drake. Just do your job and let DS Harris do his.'

*

Foreign DNA in brain of dead French spy Neuville. That was a typical headline in the lowbrow news that morning. I closed the feed when the clock ticked past nine. I was caught in a traffic swarm, still twenty minutes to Cambridge. I called Addenbrooke's. They put me through to the admin section straight away when I pinged my ID.

'How may I assist you, Detective Inspector Drake?' A bland voice, androgynous, obsequious.

'You can put me through to a human.'

'Certainly sir. Please state the name of the person with whom you wish to speak.'

I sighed. Typical NHS, phones answered by a system that must be thirty years old. 'I would like to know what became of a Regenesys 5101 tomographic resonator used by Dr Sam Okorie in association with VirGenTech plc approximately three years ago.'

'You need not consult human staff, sir. Such records are accessible to me.'

'Good, send the data to this device, please.' I tsked in irritation at myself. *Please!* I was talking to a dammed machine.

'I cannot do that, sir, without proper authorisation.'

'That's why I want to talk to a human.'

‘Certainly sir. Please state the name of the person with whom you wish to speak.’

I sent a copy of my carte blanche warrant. ‘Is that sufficient authorisation?’

‘No sir, unless you activate it.’

That’s why I wanted to talk to a human. There was no way this machine was going to care if my enquiries were on or off the record. As soon as I authorised it, the fact I was asking the question would be on file and coded in the blockchain to be seen by Baxter, the issuing judge and the conduct oversight officer. I opened the warrant and my finger hovered over the *authorise* button, as I wondered whether I was making a mistake.

I authorised the warrant and the answer came back, plain and simple. The machine was collected on the instructions of VGT and shipped to Heathrow en route to a hospital in Ljubljana. The VGT shipping document was signed by Frank Wilson, Jane Seymour’s vanished spouse, Marko’s father. I was looking up the phone number of that hospital when my phone rang. That was not a coincidence.

‘Still fishing, Drake? Regensys 5101?’

‘Good morning, Mr Tamboli. I didn’t know your people had hooks in the warrant blockchain, too.’ I smiled. He didn’t. ‘Please don’t misunderstand me. I’m not interested in how you used Furcifer’s phenotype reprogramming technology to alter Hubert Neuville’s brain so he’d spy for us, or how your people had Sam Okorie killed, or drove Dr Erica Fallon into hiding. I am only interested in tracking down Frank Wilson, the VirGenTech admin who was working for Vidmar to give him Furcifer’s technology. That should be as much a concern to you as it is to me.’ I was feeling good. I’d put all the pieces together in a moment. I wasn’t one hundred percent sure that all of it was right, but I was pretty sure I had most of it.

Furcifer, the chameleon that changes colour. The project name was wrong. It wasn’t about appearances, it was about the depths, the insides. What deeper than the brain, the mind. The endless official denials that the deceased French spy Hubert Neuville had been subject to mind control. Okorie wanted no part of Exercitus, the company that had bought Furcifer, but he knew too much, as did Erica Fallon. As did Alice.

I wanted a reaction. I was hoping for an acceptance that Vidmar was a threat, and that I could work with them to negate it.

He stared from the screen, eyes wide. His jaw worked a moment, then a hand rose to stroke his beard. The mouth opened and let out a small strangled sound, then a snort like a small explosion. Then he let go, laughing like a loon. Violent eruptions shook his face for a full minute before he hung up.

I could only assume that something I'd said had been wide of the mark. I was to learn, in time, that all of it was stupendously, wildly wrong.

The car dropped me at the entrance to Parkside Police Station. Gallicoe was waiting in the lobby by the front desk. As I entered, a pair of drones glided across the lobby to block the door behind me.

'Detective Inspector Lewis Drake,' Gallicoe said

'Gallicoe?'

'I am arresting you on suspicion of the murder of Elijah Cloake.'

*

I was stewing in the interview room for thirty minutes before Gallicoe came in with a uniformed DI I hadn't seen before. He started the recording.

'DI Gallicoe,' said Gallicoe.

'And DI Smith,' said the other. 'Interviewing Detective Inspector Lewis Drake.'

'DI Drake,' Gallicoe began, 'look at the image.'

I looked at the wall display. 'It's a discarded cartridge, I'd guess nine mil.'

Another image, a magnified view of the base of the cartridge, *Herstal* stamped in an arc around the indentation made by the firing pin. The image zoomed until the microscopic serial number machined into the end of the firing pin appeared. Clear as day, all nine digits.

'Do you recognise the serial number?'

'Yes. It's the firearm that was issued to me, and taken by forensics after the operation at Canary Wharf last week.'

I knew what was coming next. The evidence log that Donahue had sent me.

'This is the list of items recovered during that operation. I can't see a Glock. Can you?'

'No. Can you see the gap in the sequence numbers where it should be?'

He didn't rise to the bait. I didn't want him to ask me where it was now, because I'd have to lie, and Argus would know.

'The thing is, this cartridge was found on the floor of Cloake's garage yesterday. It wasn't there after Cloake's murder. Why didn't you take it with you then?'

'I've lost you. What do you mean?' I knew exactly what he meant. He'd got carried away with his own story of what had happened.

'You killed Cloake, two shots, but you left one discarded cartridge behind. Did someone disturb you?'

'I've never killed anyone in my life, DI Gallicoe.'

Smith gave Gallicoe a nudge. Argus believed me.

'So you went back to recover the cartridge but DS Harbin insisted on coming with you.'

'I went back to look over the scene again. It had crossed my mind that no cartridges were found there, and DS Harbin suggested she might be able to help. Any news on who shot her?'

'That isn't the subject of this interview, DI Drake.'

'Because it had to be someone on the force. Someone who had the authority to send Harbin's car away and to override the drone at the gate. Someone who was able to take my Glock from evidence and kill Cloake with it.'

He hesitated for a fraction of a second. 'The thing is, Drake, you're here to answer questions, not ask them.' He glanced at Smith, who shrugged. Nothing I'd said raised flags on the monitor.

'You used Cloake's Saqqaf to take DS Harbin to Addenbrooke's yesterday?'

'Yes.'

'Why the Saqqaf?'

'It was the first one that would open for me.'

'Where is it now?'

'I don't know.'

'DI Drake, tell me where you sent it.'

'I didn't send it anywhere. We reached Addenbrooke's A&E, I went in with Harbin. It drove away. I assumed that once the emergency was over it would return home.'

'We will find it, DI Drake, and its log will tell us what you commanded it. You're only making it worse for yourself by concealing evidence.'

I shrugged.

'Did you leave the murder weapon in the Saqqaf? Did you send it to hide somewhere until you could get back to it?'

It was considerate of him to ask me two questions. I chose to answer the second. 'I did not give the Saqqaf any instruction.'

'Where is the Glock now, Lewis?'

If I said I didn't know, Argus would raise an alarm. Even now it would be picking up my rising stress, stress that lately always tripped the implicitins, but now everything remained resolutely focussed, life on a single track. I needed a way to answer this question without incriminating myself.

'I can't...'

A loud rap on the door stopped me. It opened before Gallicoe could respond.

'Stop this farce, Gallicoe. Drake didn't kill Cloake. I was at Canary Wharf and I saw his weapon taken into evidence.'

I'd never been so happy to see Baxter's face.

*

Once more she'd ordered me a cappuccino before I could object. I took a sip out of politeness. We were at the back of one of those once trendy, chrome and glass coffee bar chains with over-priced coffee made from third-rate beans that had been roasted until the only flavour left in them was bitter charcoal. At least the milk in the cappuccino softened that.

'It's not over, Drake. Their story doesn't make sense, but neither does yours.

This Govind Tamboli could have cleared you with a word. What do you know about him?'

'You know he hit me with a State Security 2054 notice the other day?'

She nodded.

'He wants to keep me away from what Exercitus are doing, but he's gone past being obstructive. It's like he wants me locked up.'

'You haven't tried to run a search on him?'

'No.' I'd done some dumb things, but not that one.

'Good. That would've set more red flags flying. I'll make some discreet enquiries.'

'Thanks.'

'You need to show some progress. Find Erica Fallon and we might discover what this is all about.'

'I was on the track of a missing tomographic resonator.'

'I'll save you some time. I checked when I picked up the warrant blockchain. It's where it's supposed to be, in Ljubljana.'

'Why Ljubljana?'

Baxter looked at me and shook her head. 'VGT decided it was surplus to requirements. Frank Wilson asked for it to be donated to the hospital in his home town.'

Marko, Franc. Jane Seymour had spoken of his accent, but hadn't said where he'd come from, just Eastern Europe. Ljubljana, Slovenia.

'Anything else?' she said.

There was. I wanted to know why Harris was at Cloake's house when Meera was shot but I couldn't think how to broach it. The last time I asked her about Harris I'd been slapped down. I picked up my coffee and put it down again.

Baxter spoke first. 'I've something you should know.'

'Go on,' I said.

'Our mystery man from Canary Wharf is an undercover agent working for a Superintendent Donahue. His codename is Chameleon. I have reason to believe that either he's playing a double bluff, or Donahue is in the pay of *Rdeča Kremplja*.'

'Donahue,' I said without thinking. 'There has to be someone in our department too. Someone who could have lifted my weapon before it was logged in evidence.'

'It isn't as simple as that, DI Drake. The forensic bots should have updated the log as soon the gun was bagged. More likely there's a mole in forensics who hacked the bot.'

'Unless the log was altered afterwards.'

'I checked the log myself. The blockchain is valid. It hasn't been altered.'

'Unless by someone entangled.'

'Ah, yes. The superhuman abilities of the evil Entangled.'

I let it go. I didn't think Cloake was feeding me BS when he told me he could have done it but I didn't know for certain.

Lunch was past overdue. After Baxter left me in the café, I abandoned the almost untouched cappuccino and went on a quest for a sandwich, en route tapping and stabbing at my phone to get Wilson's file from the tax office. The records I'd got from Cloake only covered his career in the Genetic Therapies division. The tax records told me that prior to that he was at VGT's head office in London, as import/export co-ordinator.

Import/export. It might have been a coincidence but I had to be sure. I abandoned the sandwich hunt and called a car.

*

Sergeant Reynolds' eyes opened and he sat up. The door to the Cranfield customs office closed behind me on its spring. One raised eyebrow was his welcome and his question.

'Import/export,' I said, and sat by his desk.

'What about it?'

'The pharmaceuticals. VirGenTech implicitins?'

He pursed his lips and nodded.

'Who signed the forms? Do you remember?'

'I don't need to remember.'

'Look, I promise I'll keep you out of it, but I need to know. I could search company records but that would be recorded on the warrant blockchain.'

'Yeah. No-one has secrets, they can't hide the records, and you can't hide looking for them. Not when everything's online.' He reached down and his desk drawer rattled on old sliders as he pulled it out. 'I should have erased this years ago. Hell, I should never have made the copies in the first place.'

His hand on the desk made a firm clunk. When he lifted it away, there was a memory bead. 'I don't need to remember. It's all there.'

*

On the way back home I called Kay. 'Hi. I'd like to see you this evening. Is that okay?'

'Shall I put on something special?'

'Oh yes. That would be wonderful.'

She opened her door wearing a particularly slinky number. I ran up the stairs to find the laptop awaiting me on her dressing table.

Import/export—Reynolds' dataset included thousands of shipping dockets, invoices and customs declarations. With the feeble software on this machine it would take me weeks to sort it out, to confirm my suspicion.

'Kay?'

She lay across her bed in a seductive pose. 'Yes, Lewis?'

'Do you have any more of those deltas?'

She sat up straight. 'I don't know if that's a good idea.'

'I'm out of good ideas, Kay. There's only bad ones left.'

She rummaged in a drawer and pulled out the resealable bag with the black capsules. There was a marking on them all, light blue lettering: *VGT*. 'Are these the same ones?'

'Yeah.'

'I never noticed the mark. These are VirGenTech originals, not knock-offs.'

'Nobody else knows how to make deltas. Only VirGenTech.'

I swallowed the capsule and turned back to the laptop.

Her hand rested on my shoulder. 'Lewis?'

I looked up; sad eyes, pouting lip. 'What's up, Kay.'

'I'm leaving tomorrow,' she said. 'There's a spring tide on Saturday, a storm forecast. I've got a van coming to move me before we flood again.'

I took her hand in mine. 'That's good, Kay. Where are you going?'

'Brighton, I've never been but I'm happy there in another life. I thought I'd give it a try.'

'I'll come visit when this is all over.'

She smiled and nodded and dropped her eyes. 'You'll be alright in the flat until Monday. After that they'll come and board it up. Have you arranged anything yet?'

'Been busy. Shouldn't be a problem though.' One more thing to worry about. There'd be plenty of places available, but finding one that was reasonably habitable was another matter.

She opened the bag once more and took out another two capsules. 'Just in case, Lewis. But be careful. Too many, too soon can mess you up. Not everyone can take it.'

I made a start while I waited for them to kick in. I read, looking for dockets for implicitin shipments. Even stepping through one at a time it didn't take long for me to find one with Frank Wilson's name, then another. Almost without noticing I found I was reading several at once, then dozens, then hundreds. A pattern fell into place, of small, low value shipments of alpha implicitins, then betas, and—the real money-spinners—gamma implicitins. Reynolds had marked dozens of the shipments, matching by date, size, weight, to supposedly imported cosmetics. With the benefit of the parallel view that the delta gave me I found hundreds more. Implicitins relabelled as cosmetics going to dozens of recipient companies. I used my phone to check on public company records, owners and directors of those companies, and the layers of shell companies that held them.

I blinked and I was on a hard bed in the dark and cold. My hand reached to feel a rough brick wall next to me.

I blinked again and I was lying on my back in a bright room with clinical white walls. Monitors beside my bed showed squiggly lines and gentle flashes of lights. It was quiet here. My throat was still sore but the tubes were gone.

'He's breathing independently, and there *is* neural activity. Look at the EEG, Sam.' That was Ms Elland's voice, somewhere to the side of the room. Vague movements registered in the corner of my eye.

'It doesn't seem possible.' A man's voice. 'He was brain-dead. You saw the scans. You saw what he lost.'

'We have to regenerate the damaged tissue.'

'That's outside of the protocol. It was hard enough getting ethics approval for this.'

'It's unethical not to. If he was brought in off the street with these responses we'd do it, no question.'

I wanted to see their faces. I strained at my eyes, and they moved for me. I saw his silent face, Dr Sam Okorie.

'Do it for Alice, Sam. Remember Florence? So long we'd planned to go, and I could hardly prise you out of our room, you were so desperate to finish the paper you'd started together before her accident.'

'Can you hear me, Lewis?' Dr Okorie shone a light in my eye. I squinted against the glare. The light moved away and back.

'Stop doing that!' I shouted. I tried to shout, I tried to raise my arm to push the torch away. What came out was more like 'Stnn nnn' accompanied by a twitch of my hand.

Ms Elland's hand restrained Dr Okorie's. 'Blink for me if you can hear, Lewis.' A voice in calm and soothing tones.

I squeezed my eyes shut and opened them again to see her smiling down at me.

'Once more.'

I guess she wanted to make sure it wasn't a coincidence when I blinked the first time.

'I told you, Sam.'

'I'd never have believed it.'

She looked up at Dr Okorie. 'We have to tell his wife. Is she still in London?'

'She's due for discharge from St Thomas's tomorrow. We'll handle the rest of her treatment here as an outpatient.'

Tell his wife, she had said. My hazy memory dragged up a name—*Vittoria*, but I couldn't put a face to it, then I remembered she had gone. I was still puzzling over it when Ms Elland demanded my attention, and then began a long and tedious sequence of being pricked with pins and stroked with feathers, blinking when I felt anything, which wasn't much. Then being asked to try and move various parts of my body. Ms Elland erupted in raptures of joy at every little twitch of a finger. Speech didn't get far.

I lay in the hospital bed. I sat in Kay's bedroom before the laptop. I was one person in both places, and yet in the bedroom I remembered, I knew who I was, I knew how I had come to be there. In the bed I could hold only fragmentary memories, incoherent wandering thoughts. But from that broken body, there was a memory, a memory of sitting in Marek's Café with Erica Fallon, and turning to look down the barrel of a gun.

There was another self. A hard bed, a cold dark room. I'd felt that self momentarily before waking in the hospital but I couldn't find it now. Thin. It must have been a thin version of my life.

All this time I was reading, researching, correlating the files on Reynolds' bead. The trail of the implicitin shipments disguised as imported cosmetics changed over time. The earliest went to companies ultimately owned by Frank Wilson. Soon though, he became more discreet, ownership structures more complicated, layered with false names, intermediary agents. Without using the warrant I couldn't trace them all, but a handful led me back to the same few names, the same few addresses. One of those addresses was the small house in Cambridge where Jane and Marko still lived.

Wilson vanished from Reynolds' files the same month he appeared in Cloake's. He transferred from import/export to genetic therapies as the first *in vitro* tests in the Furcifer programme were showing promise. Dates of the transfer, of his marriage to Jane Seymour, of Marko's birth: it seemed too much of a coincidence that his own child would be born with a disorder that made him an ideal test subject for Furcifer, unless Wilson had deliberately engineered it.

The trail ended three years ago when he vanished, when the Genetic Therapies division was sold to Exercitus, when Sam Okorie was killed, when Erica Fallon disappeared. When Alice was lost in the Omega State.

I'd drawn a picture of Wilson's rise within Red Claw beginning with the first small shipments of the earliest alpha implicitins. The rewards for those who took them could be great but so were the risks. Their effects were rapid, intense, and irreversible so there were no repeat sales, hence the small volumes. Over the years as the pharmacology advanced to less dangerous variants, and as Wilson developed his distribution network, the volumes increased. There was an echo here of Cloake's rise to power and influence within VirGenTech. In those years at the heart of the black implicitin trade Wilson must have been tempted to use them himself.

Three years ago Wilson vanished. Three years ago a power struggle within Red Claw had left docklands littered with corpses, ending with the Leven Road massacre. Vidmar had emerged as the new leader. Coincidence? Maybe. Circumstantial? Definitely. But I knew it in my gut; this was how Frank Wilson had risen to become the Vidmar who now ran Red Claw.

CHAPTER 11

Friday 22nd November: Beets

In some of the lives I live I conceal my entanglement. In some it suits my purpose, in some it is unsafe to be openly entangled. The advantages that entanglement brings provoke resentment and hostility amongst some of the unentangled.

In every world there are individuals, organisations, movements, political parties that align themselves against us. Their motives are varied and complex: religious dogma and simple bigotry underlie much of their hostility, but there is also a genuine and deeply felt fear of the unknown. Some with political ambitions see an opportunity in whipping up fear and distrust to build a following. Nothing new there.

A common trope amongst all these groups in all the worlds is the conspiracy of the entangled. The supposed objective of this conspiracy is nebulous, changing from world to world and day to day, but most commonly it is said that the entangled wish to subjugate, enslave or exterminate the unentangled population.

I would like to state clearly and definitively that I am *a part of a conspiracy of the entangled. In fact, I am a part of several different conspiracies, with different objectives in different worlds. There are many other conspiracies, some have objectives that align and some that conflict with my own. Face it, conspiracy—acting in concert with others of like mind to achieve an objective—is an inescapable aspect of human politics and commerce and has been so throughout history. We, the entangled, are no different in that respect.*

As for world domination, the subjugation of the unentangled—well, I have come across one or two megalomaniac entangled with tendencies in that direction, but most of us are not sufficiently credulous as to allow them to succeed.

—A K Amari - *The Measurement Problem,*
A Guide to Entanglement

A jarring, clanging bell woke me, but when I opened my eyes it was just the insistent inane melody of my phone alarm. If I'd been dreaming, I couldn't remember it. If all my dreams were built on waking experiences in other lives then I'd been asleep everywhere.

My phone rang before I'd even made it to the bathroom: Baxter. I answered voice-only for the sake of modesty.

'Drake, any developments?'

'I've a hypothesis for you: Frank Wilson is Vidmar.'

She frowned. 'You have some reason for suggesting that?'

'It's complicated, but yes.'

A pause. I was beginning to think the image had frozen when she spoke again. 'So where does that lead us?'

'Wilson vanished three years ago. No trace, no records of him leaving the country, not legally, not under his own name, so if I'm right he's operating under a new identity. I want to do some digging in Ljubljana.'

'No.' Her answer was instant. 'You keep on Erica Fallon. I'll see what I can find through my contacts in Slovenia.' She hung up. I'd hit a nerve: she had a very deep and personal reason for chasing this one herself, and I was content to stick with finding Erica—she was much closer to Alice.

Ms Elland came to mind while I showered and shaved. Hostile to me in this world, but I was somewhere between a patient and an experimental subject in that other world, the world where she was on more than friendly terms with Sam Okorie. She'd said something about time they'd spent together at a conference, and a paper he had been writing with Alice.

While the coffee was brewing I leaned against the kitchen counter with my phone in my hand, searching. Medical conferences, there were hundreds every year: different subjects, specialties, venues. Two or three times a year Dr Samuel Okorie would appear at one or another, presenting papers or participating in discussion panels. Aspects of regeneration treatment was his topic. His last appearance was July three years ago, two months before Alice's illness, three months before his death.

He'd had to finish a paper alone so Alice must have been already ill. Perhaps in this world he didn't make it to the conference Ms Elland was referring to. I skipped back through those he had attended in earlier years and found the Regenerative Therapies Conference the previous October in Berlin, and the year before that in Lisbon. The same conference took place two weeks after he died, in Florence.

Remember Florence, Sam? That's what Ms Elland had said.

I typed a short message and sent it. My phone rang as I poured my coffee. 'Thank you for calling, Ms Elland.'

'How do you know about Florence, Detective Inspector Drake?'

'You were heard mentioning it to Dr Okorie.'

'No. That never happened. We were careful.'

'In this reality you only planned it. There are worlds where he didn't die. Where you did go to that conference with him.'

A hundred expressions flashed across her face in seconds. I waited for any one of a hundred questions I thought she might ask. I hadn't thought of the one she chose.

'Are you going to tell my husband?'

I could have threatened to, but I didn't want to alienate her more. 'No. I just wanted to get your attention.'

'You have it. What do you want?'

'Before he died, Sam Okorie was writing a paper with Alice Drake. I want to know what that unfinished paper was about.'

'Your people were hounding him about it and you're telling me you don't know?'

'I wouldn't be asking if I knew.'

'He vowed he'd never finish it, destroyed all the copies. Then…'

'Then he died?'

'I always thought they'd killed him. The police, the security services, Exercitus.'

'Perhaps not Exercitus. It might have been someone else.' Someone with access to the VGT network who could steal, then delete all of Alice's data including her copies of the draft: Frank Wilson. 'Was it about phenotype reprogramming of a living brain? Something that could be used to control people.'

'What? No! Regenerating brain tissue is hard enough as it is. So often it leads to disabilities, personality changes, all kinds of problems. It's an absolute last resort. We're experimenting with delta implicitins to try and improve outcomes, but that's just at the research stage. With phenotype reprogramming you're talking about changing the structure of a living brain, far harder than regeneration even if you could overcome the rejection problem.'

'Then what was Sam and Alice's paper about?'

'Alice's paper with Erica was quite brilliant, but it described only part of the work, creating the viral vector that injected the DNA repair and stimulating the regeneration under the resonator. The second part was managing immunocompatibility. Back in the years before regeneration they used to transplant organs and give patients drugs to suppress the immune system or the transplant would be rejected. With phenotype reprogramming the same thing can happen. Too big a change and the host rejects the new tissue. Sam and Alice worked out how to ensure the modified tissue did not provoke an immune response. Sam was going to finish Alice's work and publish, but Exercitus leaned on him not to, then, I don't know what happened but they lost Alice's records, so they came to Sam for what he had. He destroyed it rather than let them have it. The knowledge died with him.'

'Not in every world, Ms Elland. I've seen him, and you.'

'Do you know…' She stopped and caught her breath. 'Do you know how it turned out? Sam and me, after Florence?'

'I saw you, heard you talking for a few moments. I got the impression the two of you were close. That's all I know.'

One step forwards, two steps back. If what Ms Elland said was correct, then Furcifer was not about mind control by reprogramming brains. Rumours and stories and conspiracy theories. Mme Neuville's assertion *'ce n'était pas lui, dans la tête, ce n'était pas lui.'* was the desperation of a distressed widow. Those government denials of mind control technologies had been carefully drawn to give the story credence. Made me wonder what were they distracting attention from, what Exercitus was really up to.

'If you find out more, DI Drake, I'd be grateful to know.'

'If I find out more… Tell me, any news on Meera Harbin.'

'she'll be in the resonator for her first session this morning. I don't anticipate any difficulties but it'll just be the first of many. she'll be back on the ward by noon if you want to visit.'

*

First, I had to see Alice.

Stebbins-Reese was there. He beckoned me in and carried on fussing with his monitors.

Alice sat in her chair radiating serenity, hands dangling from the ends of the chair arms. The skullcap, with its mesh of fibres and sensors, wrapped her scalp. I thought her eyes followed me as I crossed the carpet towards her. She tilted her head a little as I stooped to kiss her cheek.

'Hi, Sis.'

Her smile stretched a fraction. 'Lewis, you're so full of surprises.'

'Surprises?'

'You were hollow...' Her mouth stopped in the middle of forming the word as she searched the room. She'd lost me again. Then her eyes landed on me, clear and steady. 'You were dead. An empty vessel, but now you're spilling into it, filling it more each time you dream. They're going to regenerate your brain, then you can live again there, too. Beets will be so happy.'

'I know Beets in that world?'

'You know Beets in every world.'

'I don't know her in this world.'

'I know what you know better than you know yourself.'

I couldn't make sense of that. I'd have said she was wandering again, speaking in other worlds, but she was looking straight at me with a rare focus. I cast a glance in Stebbins-Reese's direction.

'It's the new formulation,' he said. 'Low dose capsules on a time release. She can stay on the cusp for a sustained period now.'

Alice picked up a blister pack from the table and handed it to me. Eight blisters, four empty, the others each containing a small pink capsule. The foil of the pack was printed in the repeating pattern of the VirGenTech logo. 'It comes and goes. Sometimes I see and feel it all, but it's a little more remote. I feel less of everyone's pain, but more of my own. I think I might become angry.'

'Angry with who?'

'Vidmar. I don't want to be angry, but I have to protect you and Beets. He switched my meds, gave me a massive dose of alphas instead of betas.'

'Vidmar? Or Frank Wilson?'

'Yes, those are his names, but he has so many others.'

'Where is he, Alice?'

'Not where. Who. I know. I know what you know, and I know what I know, but so many names and faces. I don't know which is which.' Her eyes wandered again, then turned to me once more. 'Without the inhibitor I would know which, but without the inhibitor I wouldn't be able to tell you.'

'Alice? Alice?'

Stebbins-Reese gave me a curious look, then glanced at his monitor. 'Looks like she's still here,' he muttered.

Alice's hand, resting on the arm of the chair, turned and her finger curled, beckoning me closer. I bent my head to her and she whispered in my ear. 'There are secrets, Lewis. One he wants to hide and one he wants to know.'

'Who? Vidmar?'

'Govind Tamboli.'

'In this world? What secret?'

She jerked back away from me, eyes wide, biting her lip. 'I… I don't know. The doctor knows.' She nodded towards Stebbins-Reese. 'Don't you, Doctor?'

'What's that my dear? Know what?'

'I've seen you through his eyes. He knows you… He knows you in the worlds where they listen. Is this one of them?' She reached up and lifted the skull cap from her head. Stebbins-Reese cast her an exasperated look as she stood and strode towards the head of the bed and lifted the framed print from the wall above. She turned it around. Tucked into the bottom corner at the back was a small dark rectangle with two thin wires stretching along the frame edges.

Stebbins-Reese looked at Alice, a puzzled expression on his face. He opened his mouth to speak. I tapped him on the shoulder and put a finger to my lips. He nodded and sat quietly while I joined Alice for a closer look. It was the same as the bugs Meera Harbin had found in the bin in Cloake's library.

I took the print from Alice and hung it back in its place. *He knows you in the worlds where they listen.* That sounded like another congruence. Tamboli was involved in the bugging of Cloake's house, and Tamboli's car had collected Stebbins-Reese from The Grange last Saturday.

Alice closed her eyes and lowered her head. 'Lewis?' she murmured. I took her hand and guided her back to the chair, where Stebbins-Reese lifted the skull cap back onto her head.

'She's drifting,' he said when he turned back to the monitor. 'Focussing on our world is an effort for her, but each time she's a little sharper and holds it for a little longer.'

'Is this a cure?'

'It isn't so simple. Alice has been in the Omega State for so long now that her personality is spread across more realities than you or I can imagine. To permanently deprive her of that would lead to a deep psychosis, and might well kill her, at least some of her.' He shook his head. 'No. She will never be the way she was before. The best we can hope for is to manage the condition so that she can live independently. And it would be wrong to try; she has seen and lived more than you or I could imagine. Cutting her off from all of that would be like taking the soul of an eagle and stitching it into the body of a worm. I can think of nothing more cruel.'

I looked at her, sitting with that beatific smile, hands drooping over the chair arms. Generations had sought what she had but found only the slimmest echo. The false unity of psychedelics or schizophrenia, the harsh disciplines of asceticism, meditation, religious fervour.

'Good progress today.' Stebbins-Reese eased the skullcap off to reveal her shaven head. He packed his instruments in his bag.

I bent to kiss Alice's cheek. 'I'm going too.'

He paused at the door. 'Do you know where Cecilia is? She hasn't been here the last couple of times I've come.'

'I was wondering that myself,' I said.

'She's gone home.' Alice's voice was firm. She was looking at me.

'At her flat?'

'No. *Home*.' She closed her eyes and she was gone.

Stebbins-Reese and I walked down the corridor towards reception, each of us with our phone out to summon a car. We signed out and waited together by the portico in the crisp November sun.

'You left here last Saturday with Tamboli,' I said.

'You have him to thank for my being here to help Alice. He's the one who first made me aware of her case.'

'And what is he expecting in return?'

'Exercitus has a problem that Alice and her friend Dr Fallon know how to solve. When and if Alice is well enough, they would like to speak to her.'

'To solve that problem?'

'Or to help them find Dr Fallon.'

'You had a meeting scheduled with Elijah Cloake. What was that about?'

'I was quite clear with him. Patient confidentiality. I wasn't going to talk to him about Alice.'

'What did he want?'

'He'd heard about my work and he was setting up a foundation to help victims of implicitins. Ah! Here's my car.'

*

Reception at Addenbrooke's directed me to the wing where Meera's room was. I found my way through the maze of echoing, shabby corridors, now bustling with the comings and goings of nurses, doctors, visitors, and porterbots shuffling patients to their various destinations. I literally bumped into Ms Elland as I turned the last corner.

'Hi,' I said. 'Is Meera out of regen yet?'

She smiled, pointing back the way she'd come. 'Third on the left.'

I saw the shimmering in her profile as she walked past, the telescoping of the corridor into a hundred others not quite lined up. I waded through the distortions to the door, tapped, and entered.

The head of the bed was raised. A grey plastic brace around her shoulders disappeared with the rest of her beneath the covers. I was pretty sure she was lying very still. The twisting and writhing were my viewpoints.

'That looks hideously uncomfortable, Meera.'

'Believe me,' she said, 'it's worse than it looks.'

I sat in the hard chair and took in the rest of the room: monitors by the bedside, the window looking out on the concrete wall of the adjacent block, the discoloured patch on the wall facing the foot of the bed. Something had been attached there once and removed. The new paint didn't quite match.

My perspective shifted. It was me lying in the bed looking at that discoloured patch on the wall, looking at the glass and concrete through the window.

A knock on the door. It opened, pushed by the end of a crutch, followed by its partner. She swung in on the pair of them and stopped at the foot of the bed.

'Lewis?' Her voice cracked. She hobbled closer and bent over me, her face filling my vision, tears streaming from those beautiful green eyes.

Erica Beate Fallon. My wife.

'Hi, Beets,' I said but it came out, 'Hnnn, Buh.'

She kissed my cheek, pressed her face against mine and sobbed into the pillow. Her hands wrapped my head and her hair tickled my nose.

'Lewis?'

A voice, bringing me back.

'LEWIS!'

Meera swam into focus, propped up in her back-brace.

I sat with Meera making small talk. I lay in the bed with Beets sitting beside me squeezing my hand so hard it hurt. And I puzzled over Erica Fallon, Beets; I knew her so well, and not at all. I knew every detail of her face: Wide mouth, narrow lips, light green eyes, pale cheeks, the crooked half-smile. But there was something strange, something different about her.

I lay on the hard bunk in my holding cell in Parkside Police Station wondering how the hell I was going to get out of there.

Like the night before, the part of myself in the cell was unaware of the others. Where I sat by Meera's bedside, Baxter had interrupted Gallicoe's interrogation and given support to my story, and last night, I'd taken another delta. Where I lay in the bed with Beets next to me they'd been dripping deltas into my veins. In the cell, I'd been arrested on suspicion of murder, interrogated, locked up. Baxter hadn't come in that reality; that was the point of divergence. My self in the cell was blind to the others because I hadn't taken another delta. There I knew nothing of what I'd learned since the divergence.

Meera looked up at the sound of the door opening behind me. 'Here comes trouble.'

I turned. Chameleon was standing in the doorway.

'Someone's created a divergence, Lewis. You, in Parkside, you need to be careful.'

Where he spoke I knew he was right, but in the cell I had no idea. In the cell, I heard footsteps echoing down the corridor.

*

Where is the Glock now, Lewis?

That had been Gallicoe's killer question. I couldn't tell him without incriminating myself.

I can't say had been my lame answer. He'd pushed at that for an hour before formally charging me and having me taken to a cell. Then this morning, another two hour session in the interview room.

All night I'd alternated between pacing the cell and lying on the hard bunk, not sleeping, but dozing with strange unremembered dreams scratching at my consciousness.

Baxter knew the Glock had gone into evidence, or should have done. Gallicoe claimed he'd sent her a message to confirm or deny, but had no response.

The last remnants of my lunch lay on the tray by the door, waiting for them to come and collect it. Some bland curry of unidentified vegetables and vat-grown chicken pieces. I'd eaten what I could. Nothing better would be coming and I needed to keep up my strength.

Hearing footsteps along the hallway, I stepped back against the wall of my cell. Beeps of key-codes being entered, the clunks of bolts being drawn back. The door swung open.

'Lewis, let's get you out of here.'

Harris.

'How? I've been charged.'

'Baxter knows your gun went into evidence. Now Red Claw's moles think you're out of the picture she wants to keep it that way, get you back in the field without Vidmar knowing.'

Jack Harris was the one person I could trust without question, but I had a bad feeling about this. I stepped out into the corridor and Harris's hand on my back propelled me towards the barred gate at the end. 'There's a cover story for the locals,' he whispered. 'We're taking you to Bishopsgate station for questioning about the Wyndham murder.'

An ARO with helmet and black visor waited by the booking sergeant's desk, assault rifle at the ready. My shoes and belt were returned to me. Harris signed the authorisations while the ARO pulled my arms behind my back and zipped a restraint on my wrists. My trepidation grew to distinct uneasiness. An ungentle shove sent me stumbling towards the door.

We were half-way to the exit when a voice called from behind us. 'Hey, just a moment...' Harris and I both turned to the desk sergeant, who waved a sealed transparent bag with my phone in. 'What am I supposed to do with this?'

The ARO strode back and snatched the bag from his hand.

A squad car waited in the courtyard. Harris pushed me in. I took the rear-facing seat, Harris followed and sat opposite, the ARO next to him. These guys with their black body armour, black helmets, black visors, they'd almost seemed part of the furniture, part of the equipment. With this one sat silently in his seat, the helmet brushing the roof of the car, the assault rifle held across his body. I'd never realised until then how they looked to people on the receiving end of their talents.

Harris looked pretty stone-faced himself.

'Any chance of cutting this tie, Jack?' I squirmed half-round in my seat.

I got a flicker of a grin from him. 'Sure thing, Lewis.' His hand delved into his jacket pocket, pulled out his lock knife and unfolded the slim blade. I twisted round in my seat so he could reach, and I felt the tie part.

The ARO lifted off his helmet. Sergeant Elphick, the one who'd been with us at Canary Wharf. His granite face was scarcely less intimidating than the dark visor. He did condescend to give me a brief nod of acknowledgment before handing me the plastic bag with my phone in it. I slipped it into my pocket.

'So... Bishopsgate?' I said as I leaned back, flexing my fingers to get the blood flowing. The iron gates of the University Botanic Garden zipped past on my right.

'No, that's the story we're giving the locals.' Harris gave me his most engaging grin. 'You're going to escape custody.'

I watched the houses fly past, nineteen-forties semis on one side, early twenty-first century rabbit hutches on the other, though these ones looked still lived-in. We ground to a halt at the approach to the Trumpington charging station, caught behind a queue of empty cars waiting to turn across the traffic into the entrance. As we sped up again a sleek black number pulled out to join the traffic behind us. Sleek, black, except for the gouges in the paintwork of the bonnet.

'Any luck in Tripoli?' I asked Harris.

His eyes flicked sideways to Elphick next to him. 'Baxter tell you I was there?'

'Yeah.'

'Waste of time, but I know why Wyndham was killed.'

'So do I: secret meetings with the Flood Management Commission, taking control of Jazila, the flood defence contractor, buying land in Essex. He was planning to build a barrage across the Thames estuary. Was he buying land in Kent, too?'

'No, but the widow was. How did you figure it out?'

'I met a confused entangled in the street outside my flat last week. She said something about a barrage, that they never built it in this world. My guess is the widow persuaded Wyndham, and she got the idea from Cloake. Cutting off the sea that far down the Estuary would recover all that land that's been abandoned. Rebuilding would be cheap and easy. The government money for Docklands redevelopment would dry up, Red Claw's power in the Isle of Dogs broken.'

'That's motive for Cloake's murder, too.'

'None of which helps us find Vidmar or the assassin. Did you find out who was first at the Wyndham crime scene?'

'Yeah, two of the local uniforms. They checked he was dead and called it in.'

'Were they wearing body armour?'

He clenched his teeth in a grimace. 'No.'

Elphick sat still as concrete, in his heavy boots and body armour.

We were nearly at the junction with the M11 to London when the car pulled a sharp right and bounced along cracked and pitted tarmac between blocks of crumbling flat-roofed town houses. The Saqqaf followed at a respectful distance.

'What's up, Jack? Where are we going?'

The car pulled into a courtyard surrounded by pale brick apartment blocks and stopped by a graffiti-covered wall punctuated by broken windows. Elphick put his helmet on, stepped smartly out and stood by the door with his rifle half-raised.

'Here, Lewis. This is as far as we go,' Harris said.

This spot, abandoned crumbling buildings all around, screened from sight in all directions, looked like an execution ground. If not for Harris's open, friendly face I'd have been scared for my life. Even so, a shiver of apprehension ran through me as I climbed slowly from the car and stood by the impassive Elphick. Harris got out after me.

'You managed to overcome us in the car, Lewis. There was a struggle and you got away. okay?' Harris turned to Elphick. 'Make it convincing.' He tilted his head back like he was waiting for a fist on his chin.

The black-clad figure moved his black-gloved right hand from the rifle and into a pocket. In a fluid motion he pulled out a black snub-nosed pistol and shot Harris in the chest. The faceless helmet turned to face me. He dropped the pistol and raised the rifle. 'Run.'

I twisted and ducked and ran. I felt the concussion of the first shot whizz past my ear. I angled to my left and sprinted, stumbling at the sound of the second shot. A whine of motors, a screeching of tyres and a rattling spray of crumbling tarmac came from my right as the Saqqaf hurtled round the corner. Elphick got off a single shot at it before its sleek, low front scooped him from the ground. His head hit the windscreen and he somersaulted onto the roof before sliding off behind it.

Behaviours to protect an authorised user. That's what Soames had said in his interview after Cloake's murder. He was on the mark when he said it wasn't legal. I hadn't realised it was even possible to make a car do that.

Elphick lay on the ground, his left leg bent forward at the knee at an unnatural angle. He raised himself up on his right elbow and stretched towards the assault rifle that had fallen a short distance from him. Harris was on his knees, bloody hands pressed against his chest.

My left leg caved beneath me as I tried to sprint back to get to the rifle first. My elbow, then my shoulder hit the ground hard and I rolled. The rifle in Elphick's hands swung to aim at me. One more gunshot echoed between the derelict buildings all around and Elphick slumped down. The black sole of his boot half a metre from my face had a small green square set into the instep with a number standing proud. Twelve.

Harris dropped the snub-nosed pistol and fell forward.

I scrambled over to him and rolled him over.

'Said I got your back, Lewis,' he gasped through clenched teeth, then his features relaxed and the breath sloughed from him in a fading whistle.

Blood pooled beneath Elphick's neck where Harris's shot had found the narrow gap between helmet and collar. Their tags would be sending alarms; the place would be swarming in minutes. It seemed Vidmar wanted me dead, and history told me that being in custody did not put people out of Vidmar's reach. I tried to stand but my left leg gave way again with a wrenching pain in the calf. My hand grasped the muscle and felt the hot stickiness. That second shot, when I fell. 'Sorry buddy,' I whispered to Harris. 'I need to borrow your knife.' I found his slim-bladed lock knife in his pocket. The snub-nosed pistol lay where Harris had dropped it. I picked it up, reached up to open the Saqqaf's door and stumbled in. The car was moving before I'd even hit the floor.

'Motorway,' I said, 'towards London.' The M11 was close. First priority was to get some distance. Second was to become untraceable. I still had my phone. I'd need to ditch that. One call to make first, which went straight to Baxter's voice mail.

'I must be getting close. Elphick tried to kill me. He's dead but he got...' Words failed me. Jack Harris, my closest friend from the Hendon training college. Back then neither of us knew who we were, me with my missing past, and him before he was him. I stuffed those thoughts away to deal with later. I had to find the one responsible: Elphick was dead, but Vidmar was the one behind all this.

'He got Harris,' I snapped. 'I'm going off-grid for a while. I'll be in touch when I have something.'

My eyes landed on the pistol on the seat next to me. I picked it up for a closer look. Beretta, old. I pulled the clip and plucked out a cartridge, a little fatter than the standard nine mil we used, maybe ten point two mil. Elphick, two metres tall, size twelve boots, carrying a ten point two mil pistol, wearing Kevlar body armour: had to be Red Claw's assassin.

I opened the window and threw my phone out. I pulled up my trouser leg to have a look at the wound. A glancing shot that had torn a groove in the skin and muscle underneath. Lucky—a bullet from that assault rifle would have half-torn the leg off if it hit square. I undid my shirt, pulled it off and used Harris's knife to slice off the sleeve. A good, sharp knife, slender blade. The sleeve was long enough to tie around my leg, tight, to try and stop the bleeding.

My tag would have detected the shock proteins from the injury and transmitted an alert. Harris's knife wasn't sterile but beggars can't be choosers. I raised my left arm and probed with my fingertips until I found it, a small hard lump half a centimetre across. I cut over it and worked the blade beneath, cutting around and under until I could pull the pellet out, stopping several times to let out a few choice words—it hurt a hundred times worse than the gunshot to my leg. My tag, by then transmitting alerts that it could no longer detect my pulse, followed the phone out of the window.

The phone, then the tag. Breadcrumbs pointing the way towards London. It was possible I'd been tagged in some way while I was locked up. Nothing I could do about that until I could get a change of clothes, or a microwave to delouse the torn and bloody rags I was wearing.

'Saqqaf, off at the next junction, keep to the quietest roads.' There was only one place I could think of to hide out where I could take the time to deal properly with my leg and figure out what to do next. I gave the car the address and ten minutes later it pulled up to the gates at Erica Fallon's faux-barn.

*

'Whaaa nnnh nnnh.' Beets didn't understand. It was killing me, not being able to speak, not being able to move enough to even gesture.

'WHAAAA NNNNHHH!' My hand squeezed hers as I tried again. I could squeeze my hand, progress of a kind.

'What happened?' she offered tentatively.

I could have cried. I squeezed my eyes shut, squeezed her hand to tell her she had it right.

'It was another officer, Elphick, he shot us both. Laila got there too late to stop him.'

'Gahhhh!' *Please, Erica, tell me what happened.*

A flicker of emotion, then she pulled herself together and put on her detached scientist voice. 'Elphick came into Marek's, he shot you in the head, and as I got up he shot me…' Her hand reached down to her hip. 'I was on the floor, Elphick was about to finish me off when Laila arrived. She came to see me the next day at Kings. They'd already told me you were brain-dead, and they wanted you…'

Her detachment failed. She wiped her eyes with the back of her free hand and sniffed. 'They had your consent form to use your body for research, but they still asked me. Laila came after. She couldn't stop saying she was sorry, if only she'd got there a minute earlier. I was the one trying to console *her*. I mean, it wasn't her fault.'

Her green eyes were rimmed in red, her face blotchy, creased, tear-stained, her hair straggled around her ears, but then she gave me that crooked half-smile again. I'd never seen anyone so beautiful.

She stroked my cheek. 'she'll come and see you as soon as she can.'

I vaguely wondered who this Laila was, but it didn't seem important. Only Beets was important and there was something different about her. The few fragments of memory of that life couldn't give me a reference point for me to figure out what.

*

'I'm watching Parkside, it looks like trouble. Where's Harris taking you?'

Meera squinted a look of confused curiosity at Chameleon.

'They say they're taking me to Bishopsgate, but I have a bad feeling about it.'

'I've lost sight of you. Is the car heading in the right direction?'

'So far, just turned onto Trumpington Road, the A1134, towards the motorway.'

'Good, good. I sniffed its registration as you left the station. I've set the Saqqaf to follow. It's on charge at Trumpington.'

'Passing the Botanic Garden. Did you take it offline after it dropped us at Addenbrooke's?'

'I thought it best. I can engage its kidnap protocol if things start looking dodgy.'

'What does the kidnap protocol do?'

'What *is* going on?' Meera looked at each of us in turn.

... a sleek number with deep gouges in the shining black paint of the bonnet pulled out to join the traffic behind us.

'Whatever it can. Run the squad car off the road if it has to. If you get away, I've a safe house, I'll meet you there.'

I was about to agree, to ask him for the address. 'I can't. I took another delta last night. I can see that self, but there, I was already locked up, no delta. I can't tell that self anything.'

'Shit,' he said. 'Yeah. I should've realised, delta flashbacks don't normally come so long after.'

'What the hell is going on?'

I could feel Meera's frustration. Chameleon and I looked at each other. 'It's complicated,' he said.

'They've turned off into a derelict housing estate.'

Meera looked at me in open fascination as I gave a running commentary:

Harris, shot by Elphick, Elphick shooting at me, the Saqqaf hitting him. My hand went to my armpit as I felt the pain of the knife cutting out my tag.

'He… I've figured a safe place to go,' I said.

Chameleon hunched forward in his seat. Meera looked like she would have hunched forward, too, but for the brace.

'Where?' Chameleon demanded.

Memory erupted in an image, a face with green eyes, a crooked half-smile. That scrambled brain in the other world couldn't provide me a reference to figure out what was different about Beets but now I had it. Everything fell into place: Project Furcifer, phenotype reprogramming, the spy Neuville, how Vidmar was hiding and how Erica Fallon had been hiding.

'Shit. NO! I can't go there. If they're tracking me I'll lead them straight to her.'

'Where, Lewis? Lead them to who?'

'Shit! Shit! We have to get there. I'm calling a car.' I grabbed my phone.

'The Saqqaf's here, outside, but we can't do anything. It's another reality!'

'She'll be at the same place in this reality. If Vidmar follows me to her in that world, he'll know where she is in this.'

She's gone home, Alice had said. Cecilia had gone home. I knew Beets in every world, Alice was right, it was just that in some worlds she had another name, another face.

Cecilia Watts.

The eyes were the same pale green. The shape of the face was different but the way she wore it was not: the crooked half-smile, the tilt of her head, the way her lips moved as she spoke, the subtle inflections of voice. She'd changed her appearance, changed her identity, but Cecilia was Erica. She'd used phenotype reprogramming, the fruits of project Furcifer, to take on a new identity, just as the spy who had replaced Hubert Neuville had done. Just as Vidmar had done. In the world where I lay paralysed with Erica at my bedside, Vidmar had replaced Winsford Saïd. In other worlds he could be anyone.

My self seeking shelter at Erica's barn didn't know that Cecilia was Erica, or that she had gone home. That if I'd been tagged I would lead them straight to her.

*

The Saqqaf sped away down the lane with a faint hiss of tyres on tarmac. I limped in through the open gate and round the back of the barn. The key was still under the plant pot. I let myself in and the door clicked shut behind me.

I'd seen a first aid kit in the back of a kitchen cupboard but I couldn't recall which. I started at one end of the line of units, lowering myself on to my knees, and shuffled along as I opened one cupboard after another. I don't know why I was being so careful to be quiet, to not disturb anything, but as I gently closed the third door I heard the softest noise. Someone else trying to be quiet.

'Don't move. I have a gun.'

I knew that voice. I turned my head. She did have a gun, held unsteadily in two hands, wavering in the general direction of my head.

'Cecilia? What are you doing here?'

'I could ask you the same, Lewis.' She let out a deep breath and put the gun down on the worktop. 'What the hell happened to you?'

I must have been quite a sight, sleeve ripped off, blood soaking into my vest from under my left arm, bandage around my leg. I'd left a smeared trail of blood across the tiles of the kitchen floor. 'Got in a fight,' I said. 'Needed somewhere to hide.'

She helped me up onto my feet and wrapped an arm around me to support me out into the hallway, into the study. She pulled aside the rug to reveal a trapdoor. The cellar. There had been another house here before the barn was built. An old house with a cellar, another of those things I remembered even though I'd never known.

'Can you manage the ladder?'

'Sure.'

She went down first and I sat on the edge of the opening and eased myself down to rest my good leg on the tread and half clambered, half hopped down.

The light was bright, clinical, the walls whitewashed to a uniform brilliance but for one bare wall stained by damp leaching in and streaked with a rust-red smear from a metal hook. A bench down one side held pieces of machinery, lab equipment. A shelf unit at the end was crowded with bottles and boxes. There was a small medical lab down here.

She had me lie on a couch, pulled off my right shoe and sock, dropped them on the floor and cut away my trouser leg with a pair of scissors.

'What's going on, Cecilia? How do you know Erica Fallon?'

She spared me a glance. 'I thought you'd figured that out.'

I gritted my teeth at the sting of alcohol as she cleaned the wound.

'It's shallow, I can stitch it,' she said.

She opened a drawer under the bench and came back, ripping the wrapping from one of those curved needles. I have a thing about needles. I looked away while she threaded it.

'What do you mean, figured it…' That's when my eyes landed on the wheeled stand, a machine with arms that arced over and under, big enough to slide around a couch like the one I was sitting on and cover about half a metre of its length. I wouldn't have known what it was but for the angled logo embossed on its side: *Regenesys 1101*.

'That's it,' she said. 'That's how I hid.'

I looked at her, really looked. At her face, at her cheekbones, her delicate elfin chin. At her pale green eyes. There was no similarity with the face in the passport photo, the woman talking and laughing with Alice in Jane Seymour's video. But then there wouldn't be. 'You're Erica Fallon. Project Furcifer *is* all about appearance.'

'That's what Exercitus wanted it for.' Her graceful fingers rose and fell as she stitched. 'I didn't understand at first. Alice was spiked, then Sam was killed. I had to hide before Exercitus got me too, and I had to look after Alice. It was easiest to become someone else. I knew how to deal with the rejection so I searched the public missing persons database from the war and found a name and genetic profile of someone around my age: Cecilia Watts. I didn't have a full body resonator so I only changed my face.'

'Exercitus wouldn't want you dead. They're floundering trying to reproduce your work.'

'Yeah, I worked that out when I saw the news about Hubert Neuville. He wouldn't have had his immunosuppressants after they locked him up. I'd pity him but I wonder what they did with the real Neuville.' She cut the wrapping from a bandage and began winding it around my leg. 'So if it wasn't Exercitus, who was it?'

'Vidmar,' I said. 'Frank Wilson. And he did have a full body resonator. He had the one from Addenbrooke's shipped to Slovenia before he disappeared.'

'Frank Wilson.' She stopped winding the bandage. 'It fits. He had access to all our files, even the ones on rejection. He could have deleted them.' She snipped and tied off. 'Sit up, let's have a look at your armpit.'

I sat and raised my arm. My shoe lay on the floor by the couch. 'What's that?' I jumped down and picked it up. The heel was loose. I pulled at it to reveal a small cavity, a hard half-centimetre bead within. A tracker.

'Shh! Do you hear something?' Cecilia/Erica whispered.

A shadow moved on the edge of the open trapdoor. Something fell, hard, clunking as it bounced off a wooden tread of the ladder, hitting the stone floor with a loud crack.

Grenade.

*

We ran down the corridor. Meera's voice shouted after us. 'Drop by again!'

I'm not slow, but I barely kept up with Chameleon, reminding myself with every step that I hadn't been shot in the leg. Through the maze of hospital corridors, taking flights of stairs three steps at a time, down to the main entrance where the Saqqaf waited. As it pulled away, Cecilia was helping me down from the ladder. 'She's got a lab in the cellar,' I said.

The roadside houses had given way to fields when I spotted it. 'There's a tomographic resonator. She used it to change her face, that's how she's been hiding.'

'Phenotype reprogramming,' Chameleon said. 'That's the trick Vidmar used.'

My other self figured it out a moment later, while Cecilia tied off the bandage. Not Cecilia. She was Erica.

'Oh, shit,' I said. 'They put a tracker in my shoe.'

'I suspected as much. They were going to let you get away, even if the Saqqaf hadn't come to your rescue.'

'Why? Now I know.'

'It's a throwaway tactic when you're entangled. Create a divergence, do something different in some thin reality, see if you learn anything. They'll clean up the mess afterwards. Vidmar won't know you've been taking deltas, he knows how you feel about entanglement.'

'I went to one protest meeting.'

'In this world, but in another you're one of Winsford Saïd's closest confidantes. It's an easy mistake for an entangled to read too much into someone's behaviour in one reality.'

A shadow moved on the edge of the open trapdoor. Something fell, hard, clunking as it bounced off a wooden tread of the ladder, hitting the stone floor with a loud crack.

Blackness hit me like a granite block, a void, an absence. I came to, gasping for breath on the floor of the car.

'Lewis, are you alright? What happened?'

'It's too late,' I shouted, taking a tight grip at the neck of his shirt. 'She's dead. I'm dead.'

'No, we're nearly there. It's not likely Vidmar was ready to move this quickly in this reality, he wouldn't have had any reason to.'

I pulled myself back up into the seat and lurched sideways as the car made the sharp turn through the open gate, then lurched the other way as it braked and span a half turn. Chameleon ran to the front, rang the bell and hammered on the door as I sprinted around the side, grabbed a drainpipe to swing around to the rear of the house, jumped a row of plant pots and landed by the back door. The key was still under the dead chrysanthemums. I opened the door to

Cecilia's terrified face and the neat little pistol held in her shaking hands.

I raised my hands, palms out, placatory. 'We've got to leave,' I said, 'they know you're here.'

She licked her lips. The gun carried on shaking. 'How do I know you're not one of them.'

'No time to explain. Trust me or shoot me. Pick one, Erica.'

Her green eyes went wide. Slowly, she lowered the gun.

*

Erica sat by my bedside, holding my hand and talking about something and nothing. I'd frightened her with a spasm when the grenade had gone off. I wished I could have explained it, but she calmed down in time and then my dinner arrived to distract her. They raised the head of the bed so I was a little more upright and Erica fed me soft, flavourless mush with a plastic spoon, like she was feeding a baby.

The Saqqaf stuck to the back roads, weaving along narrow lanes that I didn't recognise and emerging into a derelict industrial park. Great steel sheds with panels torn and falling down from rusting girders, bare frames of glass frontage. Faded grass-stems and waist-high tangles of bushes and brambles grew in erratic rows along the cracks and pits of the tarmac and concrete aprons where once hundreds of cars would have been parked during the busy working days.

The car passed the sturdy pylon of a wind turbine, still turning, and pulled around the back of a faded blue oblong building to a loading bay, a concrete platform with six roller shutters. One raised high enough to crouch under. Cecilia/Erica followed Chameleon in and I lagged behind. She cast worried glances over her shoulder at every turn, at every noise of metal creaking. I hadn't said much since we'd left the barn, my mind was more in the hospital, with the other Erica beside me squeezing my hand, feeding me.

Chameleon led us through a cavernous warehouse where the icy wind whistled through the cracks and openings in the building's thin shell, past rows of grimy steel vats tall as a three storey house. A tangle of dried and broken pipework as thick as my thigh linked it all together. At the end a metal staircase clanked beneath our feet as we climbed to a catwalk. One side looked out onto the domed tops of the vats, the other side was a row of rooms with glass windows and doors. Most were empty but for dust and grit. One had broken tables and chairs, dark streaks on the walls where the rain had penetrated, a whiteboard with writing and diagrams in faded reds and blues.

He stopped by a door labelled *Hansford Harcourt, General Manager*, and grasped the handle. 'Toilets and washbasin in the next one along, the water still works, at least it did when I was last here.'

Cecilia squeezed past him on the catwalk where he'd indicated. Chameleon opened the door and turned on the light, a single bulb in a pendant fitting with a wide conical shade.

'Power? In this derelict?" I said.

'There's a battery bank downstairs fed from the wind turbine. The batches would spoil if they lost power.' Batches of what, he didn't say. It hardly mattered. A battered electric fan heater lay on the floor. Chameleon flicked the switch and it whirred and rattled.

A small table stood in the corner with two office chairs. A thin mattress and sleeping bag lay by the far wall. The edges of a window frame were not quite concealed by a white composite panel held by screws at each corner. To keep the cold out or the light concealed.

I leaned against the edge of the table and crossed my arms. 'How long have you known Frank Wilson was Vidmar and that he'd changed his identity?'

He rolled one of the chairs over by the wall nearby and slumped into it. 'About three weeks. Erica figured it out. She's the key.'

'You could have told me.'

'We didn't want to distract you. Erica's the key, but in these worlds she disappeared. Elijah said we should give you the data we had but not our preconceptions and I trusted his judgement. It worked didn't it?'

'It worked?' I jumped to my feet and glowered down on him in his chair. 'I led them straight to the barn, to where she was hiding. I died there, but I'm still here, like I didn't die at all but Erica hadn't been taking implicitins. In that world she's dead and gone forever because of me!' As I towered over him with my fists shaking by my side I remembered how easily he had outmanoeuvred me in Canary Wharf when I tried to jump him. He looked up at me, a face of quiet passivity and I knew if my anger rose further he could put me in my place again.

'It's the measurement problem,' he said at last. 'Whatever you do, however well-intentioned your actions, all possible futures are real. It will always end badly in some strands of being.'

It sounded like a quote from Amari's book. His words didn't heal the hurt but they broke the tension. I allowed myself to relax, back away.

'What about the bigger picture? Where does Donahue come in?'

'In other worlds he's been instrumental in uncovering Red Claw's links to police and politics. But with phenotype reprogramming we can't be sure Donahue in this world is really Donahue. Everyone is suspect.'

I gave him a long hard stare. 'By "we" you mean you, Elijah Cloake, and Monica Wyndham. Is this is all about building a barrage across the estuary?'

'It's bigger than that. Vidmar is using phenotype reprogramming to adopt different identities in all the worlds where he exists. We've been trying to unmask him in each one, but he has learned to cover his tracks well. We think Erica has found a way to find him in every world. Vidmar knows this, so he's trying to kill her, and you, everywhere, but in these worlds where she disappeared, Elijah thought you were the best bet to find her. Vidmar must think so too, or you'd already be dead.'

'Who faked the VLA logs for Cloake's silver ghost?'

'That must have been Vidmar, but if he hadn't, Elijah was going to find a pretext to bring you to him. Vidmar wanted you to get the VirGenTech files, he wanted you to find Erica as much as we do, but he's been taking the initiative every step of the way, keeping you off-balance, watching you. You only needed to make a mistake in one narrow reality and reveal Erica's location. Killing Elijah and framing you for it was one more way to keep the pressure on. That was his mistake. That's where he lost the initiative. Elijah anticipated it, sent me a message and waited for them to kill him, so I could gather up the evidence.'

'It was only dumb luck that I found her,' I said. The barn, the cellar, the grenade. Dumb bad luck.

'Not really. You and she are close in other lives. It was only a matter of time before you figured it one way or another. Those feelings, they always leak through.'

'If Erica knows, why didn't you or Elijah ask her?'

'Not easy from the internment camp. The anti-entanglement movement is powerful in that world.'

'Ask me what?' Erica slipped into the room and leaned back against the door. Erica. I was getting used to the fact now, she was Erica, not Cecilia. It was almost like I'd always known. It was why I'd always been drawn to her.

'You,' I said, 'but a different version of you. Three years ago Frank Wilson shipped a Regenesys 5101 to Slovenia and used it to change his identity. He deleted all the files on preventing rejection in phenotype reprogramming and spiked Alice and killed Sam Okorie. He's the one you've been hiding from, and you apparently, in this other world, worked out how to find the identity he'd taken.'

'That was clever of me. Any idea how I did it?'

*

'What is it, Lewis? What's wrong?' Erica stood by my bedside leaning on one crutch, stroking my hair and cheek with her free hand.

I was there with them. Me, Chameleon, Erica as Cecilia in that derelict factory office in Cambridge. I was here, in this hospital bed, Erica leaning over me. She had discovered that Vidmar in this world was Saïd. She must have told me but this body's memories were so fleeting, snatches of events, feelings, familiarity were all that were left. I couldn't form the words to ask her.

The door behind her swung open. Sam Okorie appeared at the foot of the bed. 'Has he been like this long?'

'A few minutes,' Erica said. 'Something's upsetting him.'

He leaned over me so his face filled my view. 'Lewis, we're scheduled to start your first treatment, but we can't do it in this agitated state. I know this must be hard for you, but you need to calm yourself.'

I blinked so he'd know I understood. I didn't want to miss anything important. I didn't want to delay the treatment either. I needed to communicate and any improvement might help. I closed my eyes for a moment to concentrate on my breathing. Slow, regular, deep breaths, ignoring the sounds of movement around me. I opened my eyes again as Erica's hair brushed my cheek. She kissed me on the lips and straightened up. 'I'll be here when you're out of therapy.'

A porter rolled into the room, hooked on to my bed, and wheeled me along to the regen therapy room where Sam Okorie put my head in a clamp so it wouldn't move. 'So, Lewis. Your improvement so far is due to the delta implicitin treatments linking you to your functioning consciousness in other worlds, which stimulated neural plasticity and reprogramming of the undamaged part of your brain to take over some of the function you've lost. What we're doing now is to heal some of that damage. It's going to be a long, slow process. Many sessions over weeks to rebuild what you've lost, and even if things go well it could be months or years before you're fully recovered, so don't be disappointed if you don't notice an improvement straight away.'

I squeezed my eyes shut.

He put me under a machine much like the one in Erica's cellar. I saw flickering lights at the edge of my vision but no other sign that anything was happening. An hour later they wheeled me back, and I didn't feel any different. Tired was all, very, very tired.

I was almost asleep when a hand took hold of mine. I opened my eyes. Erica. I blinked and closed them again.

*

'I have some deltas,' I said in the gloom of the derelict factory office.

Erica/Cecilia looked up. 'No. No way. I tried it once, I was lost for three days. You wouldn't believe some of the things I saw. It was a nightmare.'

'It gets some people that way.' Chameleon stepped forward before I could argue. 'Too many lives all jumbled together, no control.' He looked at Erica and she nodded. 'Chances of her learning anything useful are next to nothing.'

'They're in my flat anyway. I can't go back there now after what happened to Harris and Elphick.'

'That was another reality, Lewis.' Chameleon's face was in mine, his hands gripping my upper arms. 'Nothing happened in this one. You're not on the run.'

In my mind I knew he was right. In that reality I was dead, killed by a grenade with Erica in her cellar. But the escape, the deaths of Harris and Elphick, were as real to me in memory as anything I'd ever experienced. It made me feel like I had to hide but in this reality Baxter had arrived during Gallicoe's interview, confirming my story. In this reality I was never locked up. Here I was still working the case.

'Then I should go back. Vidmar will be watching me, now he knows I found Erica in one reality.'

'He'll come up with some other way to put pressure on you, keep you off-balance,' Chameleon said. 'That worked for him with the fake breakout. Question is how? What's your weak point?'

Erica's eyes met mine. She knew as I did. Three years living as Cecilia Watts, caring for her, three years seeing me come to visit her every day that I could.

'Alice,' we said in unison.

'We have to get her first,' I said, 'protect her.'

She straightened and swept her hair back behind her ears. 'From midnight there'll be two on duty. They'll be dozing in the staff room by two am. It's always quiet until the early shift comes in at six.'

'Three am, then. We'll be in and out in five minutes, then back here.'

She nodded. Chameleon pursed his lips. 'We should create a divergence.'

'A diversion?' Erica looked at him with a puzzled expression.

'A divergence,' I said, 'we don't do the same thing in every reality. What are you thinking?'

'We don't need to win in every thread. If we find out how to identify Vidmar in one, I can spread that knowledge to every one where I survive, but if we're all in one place in every world, he can kill us in all of them.'

'I want to keep Alice safe in every reality.' I expected an argument, I expected him to remind me that death in one world is not a serious matter for the entangled.

'Agreed, but we diverge. One stream you go with Erica, the other, you stay home and I go.'

So I left them in that little office in the abandoned factory and trudged past derelict warehouses and offices and workshops through the dark November evening and onto Stourbridge Common. A storm was building, the overlong grass of the common and the branches of the trees whipping back and forth in the gusts. By the time I crossed the Green Dragon Bridge over the river Cam, the darkness of a stormy November dusk had turned to full night. I resisted the temptations of the eponymous pub on the other side of the road and summoned a car, a safe distance from the safe house in case anyone tracked where I was picked up.

Emotionally and physically drained, the low whine of the motors, the rush of the wind and the hissing of wheels on tarmac, all lulled me to sleep within minutes of reaching the M11. I was woken by the agitated beep of the car telling me I'd arrived. It was still windy, it was still raining. The windows of Kay's house were dark. The street light picked out the large black *Closed* notice in the window of her shop. I dashed through the downpour to my front door. Inside, the hallway light flicked on revealing a foil-wrapped tray on the second step of the steep staircase. Kay, she couldn't leave without one last kindness. I lifted the precious gift and climbed the stairs, into the flat, into the kitchen. Peeling back the foil from the top revealed a substantial cottage pie. A note on top read *220°C, 1/2 hour. Come and visit me in Brighton when you can. Love, Kay.*

I lifted the ceramic tray from the foil and put it in the oven. Only when I turned back to the worktop did I notice the black rectangular slab resting in the foil.

The laptop went into the fridge, wrapped once more in the foil.

I needed to sleep, so I resisted the urge to make coffee. I would need a clear head, so I resisted that last drop of the Linlithgow that sat in its bottle eyeing me up from the table in the corner of the living room. I needed to eat something, so I sat on the sofa with a glass of water and my own thoughts for company while I waited the interminable half-hour for the cottage pie. I was in bed by nine pm with a warm, full belly, hoping but not expecting to sleep. Tomorrow was going to be a long day.

CHAPTER 12

Saturday 23rd November: High Tide

Death comes to us all. For the entangled it comes many times. It is almost always an experience of sufficient intensity that it demands our attention even when it happens in the thinnest of realities. Intense, but not final. We lose that thread of existence, but the memories are retained, the shared self that experienced that life continues.

This is the hardest thing for the unentangled to understand. All of those instances of my self that live their varied existences are part of the same 'I.' It is 'I,' not 'we' who experience those lives, and when a part of me dies, I endure.

There may be physical pain as death approaches. There may be emotional pain of separation from those we know only in that reality, or the knowledge of the pain our parting may cause to those close to us, but we endure.

So, while death is not something we choose lightly, there are times when it is useful to follow a path that for an unentangled would be reckless.

One day, all the instances of my self will age and die in their turns and I will become thinner as there are fewer and fewer of me of ever greater age. There is a suggestion in quantum theory that the truly random ravages of entropy will leave an ever diminishing part of myself living indefinitely, but we believe that consciousness itself is rooted in the quantum nature of reality. Even if my body persists there may come a time when my existence is too thin to hold my mind. Entanglement is too new for any of us to have reached that point yet. No-one really knows.

—A K Amari - *The Measurement Problem,*
A Guide to Entanglement

The alarm woke me with a start in pitch darkness. The wind howled, the rain lashed against the windows, distant thunder rumbled. I reached for the bedside light and flicked the switch. Nothing. Power was out. No toast, no coffee. I washed and dressed with only my phone for light. Cold stale muesli for breakfast followed by the black capsule from the resealable bag washed down with a glass of water. My third delta in a week. So far the lives I'd seen were all recent divergences, but if I kept taking them I'd see more and more lives, lives that had split from this one in the more distant past. I could get lost. The thought scared me but there was no way I could sit and wait in this flat not knowing what was happening to my other self after I diverged.

Amari talks about creating divergences, how with practice the entangled could do so at will, thick or thin, two worlds or a thousand. I'd done it myself almost unconsciously while reading Cloake's data and Reynolds'. Now I needed strands of reality where I could choose different actions and I had not developed that skill. The internet was the answer: there are a hundred quantum random number generators online, a thousand. I picked one and asked for a random number between one and two, a flip of a quantum coin that would create the divergence as both answers came back, each in a separate world. If the answer was one, I would go, two, I would stay, and Chameleon would go.

Looking back I remember both selves but in that interval before the delta kicked in each of my alternates was unaware of the other. Each of me messaged Chameleon and one of me settled for a long wait.

The other climbed out of the back bedroom window onto the flat roof of the ground-floor extension, dressed in dark trousers, hoodie, boots. My matt-black coat weighed down by the Glock in the right pocket. It was two fifteen am, and I was more awake than I had any right to be after less than five hours sleep.

Outside was as dark as a cave, wet as a monsoon swamp. The howling wind caught me and my feet slipped on the slick, wet roof. I hit the felt with a jarring impact to my hip and crawled to the leeward side of the roof, grasped the gutter edge and lowered myself down, praying it would hold. My feet were only three feet from the ground when it cracked, dropping me into ankle-deep, ice-cold water.

Three houses separated mine from the end of the terrace. I waded through back gardens overgrown and flooded, climbing broken-down fences and catching my feet in tangles of dead brambles and unpruned roses. The last garden had a gate leading into the alley, rotten timbers hanging from rusted hinges that gave way at a modest shove. The wind curled around the corner of the boarded-up convenience store at the end of the terrace. Hard rain and salt spray blinded me as I sprint-waded across the road, hoping the downpour would cover me from any rats that Tamboli's people might have set to watch my flat. The narrow alleyway opposite provided some shelter, so I jogged the hundred metres to the next street. The black shape of the Saqqaf was almost invisible in the darkness, waiting where I'd told it, a street away from any surveillance.

The Saqqaf sped through the dark streets, swift and silent, all lights extinguished, to the Shadwell gate. Another five minutes and I was on the motorway. No traffic but the shipping containers on their dollies trundling along the freight lane at a sedate hundred kph. They might have been stationery behind the clouds of rain and spray as far as it looked from the Saqqaf's saloon.

At two forty-four am the Saqqaf came to a stop at the loading bay. Chameleon watched as Erica scurried from the half-open roller door and bundled into the car.

'Let's see the map,' she said. 'We're going in by the service entrance.'

I switched the screen to navigation and she zoomed in to The Grange. A short distance east of the main gate a side road extended northwards, and from there a track led to the back of the building. 'There's a gate here with a keypad. Four digit code.'

'Do you have the code?'

'No, but Chameleon said we don't need it.'

Yeah. Dumb of me to even ask.

Beyond the dark and derelict industrial park that housed the safe house, the Saqqaf whisked us through the illuminated streets of the Cambridge suburbs and back again into the darkness of narrow lanes. With headlights extinguished we drove through a limitless limbo with only the faint hum of the motors and the splash of invisible rain and spray for company, swaying to one side or another as the car turned corners that we could see only on the nav display.

My heartbeat picked up as we turned the last bend towards the lane and slowed. The window slid down to reveal the keypad on its post. I pulled out my phone and opened up the quantum random number generator and set the range: from one to 9,999. The result came back as four fuzzy blobs. Ten-thousand distinct realities—too many for my small mind to separate. I showed it to Erica. 'Key in that number. If the barrier opens, read the number back to me, loud and clear. Only if it opens.' In each of ten-thousand realities Erica read a different number, leaned out and her fingers moved in a shimmering blur pressing every digit four times. Ten-thousand realities; in one of them, the gate opened. A thin echo of her voice said, 'One, three, nine, seven.'

'One, three, nine, seven,' I repeated, loud and clear. Erica punched the numbers, a green light flashed and the car rolled forwards with a crunch of gravel, lurching and splashing through the ruts and potholes of the worn track.

We slowed to a halt and Erica leaned forward to peer through the windscreen. 'Something's wrong.' She fumbled for the door and stepped out. The rain had stopped, the wind fallen to a strong breeze that rustled the tree tops all around. Faint shadows moved in the sky where the glow of the lights of Cambridge caught the rushing clouds. The shape of the house was a blacker silhouette in the darkness. Not a single light showed. Power was out here too, or it had been cut.

'Wait.' I caught her arm before she could run in. 'A place like this must have a standby power supply.'

'The stable.' She led the way across the rutted gravel to a single story building. I followed her in to total darkness.

'There's a breaker somewhere.' Erica's whisper was loud in the enclosed blackness.

I lit a torch. Behind her were the stacked power cells. On the wall next to her the big chrome handle of the breaker was in the *off* position. I reached behind her and turned it. The hum of electric power filled the room and light edged in through the doorway behind us.

I bolted out of the stable towards the house. Light flooded onto the puddled, weed-strewn gravel from the windows at the rear and the wide-open back door. Inside was the kitchen: shining white tiles and steel counters overlain by the thick odour of burnt grease. From there a swing door led into a dark communal dining area, then into a corridor. Lights at the far end lit the reception desk, half-hiding a dark shape on the floor. That could wait; Alice's room lay on this ground-floor corridor.

Her door was open, held from closing by a still, booted foot. The foot, the leg, the body lay on the floor, a pistol in his hand, blood pooling from the wound below The Grange logo on his uniform. It was Henry, the new receptionist.

Alice was gone.

Ten minutes I spent searching the entire building: upstairs, downstairs, outbuildings, kitchen, storerooms, common areas, infirmary, offices, staff rooms, residents' rooms. There were two more dead, both in staff uniforms. The one by the reception desk was armed. Erica didn't know him, but the last was a nineteen year old trainee.

'Maurice!' she cried when she saw him lying on the staff room floor. I held her for a moment. She sniffled into my shoulder then pushed me away.

I almost had to drag her out of there. 'Someone has to stay to mind the residents until help arrives,' she said. Only the sound of approaching sirens persuaded her. As we turned out of the gate the ambulances and squad cars flashed past the end of the lane towards the main entrance.

The Saqqaf ghosted its way back to the factory. Erica got out first. I had to get out, too, to protect Erica. I had to leave, to find Alice.

'Lewis, come on.' She reached in and rested her hand on my arm. The wind had picked up again, whipping her hair around her face as she crouched by the car door. Heavy raindrops drummed on the car roof.

'We need to make plans, Lewis.' Chameleon hunched behind her, speaking to me over her shoulder, his hand on his forehead shielding his eyes from the rain.

She'd been kidnapped, not killed. That meant they wanted something and sooner or later Red Claw would be in touch. It was Red Claw behind it, had to be.

The heavens opened as I pulled myself out of the car. We sprinted to the loading dock through waves of rain thick enough to swim in, vaulted onto the platform, and ducked under the shutter. The wind had been coming from our right, south west, when we left for The Grange. Now it came from the east. A spring tide in an easterly gale. There'd be a mighty storm surge coming up the Thames Estuary with the high tide if this continued.

Five forty-five am and we were back in Chameleon's hideout. Everything I'd touched since this started had led to failure, death and pain for others. Erica killed by the grenade in her cellar, Harbin dead or paralysed, Cloake dead, now Alice kidnapped.

I felt the weight of Chameleon's hand on my shoulder. 'Remember, Lewis, whatever they do, Alice is entangled, as entangled as it is possible to be. They can hurt her, even kill her in these threads of reality but she carries on, undiminished.'

His words held no meaning for me. I was not comforted.

*

I did my best to look away as I was quickly and efficiently cleaned by the gentle ministrations of the mechanical nurse, distracting myself trying to make sense of that strange nightmare of running around an old building, an old house or nursing home, looking for someone, desperate in my search.

The door of my room was pushed open by the end of an aluminium stick. 'Beet-thh.' I said as she stumped into my room. The crutches were gone, just the one stick to steady herself.

'Bee-eet-thhhh!' I had to say it again, simply for the joy of being able to.

'Oh no.' She smiled. 'We're not going to be able to shut you up now.'

There was something I needed to know, something I needed to ask Erica, and I was waiting. Waiting in the disused factory in Cambridge, waiting in my flat in docklands. Waiting for me to ask. Fighting through the fog in my mind, I half-raised my forearm and gripped her hand as she sat next to me.

'Need... neeeeed... athhhk.' I had to think about how to make the sounds, how to make my mouth and tongue move, like I knew the theory of how to talk but hadn't mastered the skill.

'What do you need, Lewis?'

'Ow... ow...' I knew what I wanted to ask her, *How did you find Vidmar's identity*? I had to find the words, I had to make my mouth speak them.

'Ow... f-f-f-f... ngggh! AAAAARGH!' My left hand clenched a handful of bed sheet, my right hand gripped hers and my eyes squeezed out tears of frustration.

'Ow y... y...' I raised my right hand from the cover and curled the fingers. Gritting my teeth I stretched out the index finger and pointed. '... y... y...'

She grasped my hand. 'How did I...?'

I squeezed my eyes shut, and open. *Yes.* 'Ow f-f-find…'

The eager pleasing smile dropped from her face. 'You don't remember? How could you not remember?'

I smiled at that, tried to smile. Some of my muscles seemed to work but I suspect it was more of a toothy leer. 'Brain f-f-fucked.'

'You want to know how I found Vidmar's identity?'

I squeezed my eyes shut once more.

'The Viradyn.'

'nhhh?'

'A few weeks ago, Alice started talking but at first none of it made sense. "There are tigers." That was the first thing. Later she started mumbling about Vidmar.

'You'd talked about him often enough in the last couple of years so I tried to ask her. Sometimes she'd say something: "Who is he? Which world is this?" Finally, I was visiting her one evening—you were working late—she sat bolt upright, eyes wide open, looking right past me. "It's in the Viradyn," she said. I knew what she meant. The Viradyn DNA sequence editor. It's the machine we use in the lab to prepare the regen viruses. I found the one Vidmar used in a storeroom in the lab. We'd replaced it with a newer model. These machines keep a full audit of everything they've prepared in case of problems later. The DNA profile he'd used was still in memory. I took a copy and you matched it with Winsford Saïd's DNA from the PNR database.'

*

Four paces across the living room of my flat. Four paces, turn, four paces, back and forth, willing myself to speak in that other world, to make Erica understand me.

The Viradyn.

I stopped my pacing and hesitated for only a second. I no longer cared if Tamboli had bugged my flat, what he might hear or see. I marched straight to the kitchen. The jars in the fridge door clanked together as I pulled it open. I peeled the foil from the laptop. My fingers drummed on the kitchen worktop while the machine ground through its interminable startup sequence.

*

'The Viradyn DNA sequence editor!' My outburst shattered the cold silence of the factory office. Chameleon and Erica both looked at me in blank surprise.

'The machine Vidmar used to prepare his regen virus still has the DNA sequence he used in its memory, it's in a storeroom in the Project Furcifer lab.'

'Another reality?' Chameleon said.

'Yeah.'

'It might not be in the same place in this world.'

'Wait,' I said. In my flat in the kitchen, my fingers drummed on the worktop. In the abandoned factory I stood still and closed my eyes. 'Wait.'

I'd seen the Project Furcifer lab the night Cloake was killed, the night Tamboli warned me off. The anonymous block surrounded by security fencing, cameras, armed guards. It belonged to Exercitus now.

The laptop was ready. I opened the inventory and searched for *Viradyn*.

I opened my eyes. Chameleon and Erica were watching me.

'There was a Viradyn machine as part of the sale to Exercitus.'

'If we can get our hands on it, and if the memory hasn't been wiped,' Erica said, 'we can get the DNA profile from it. How would that help?'

'I can run it against the PNR database. Anyone employed in any state office, anyone who has ever been arrested, immigration records, medical records. It covers about eighty percent of the population and even if we don't get an exact match we're likely to find family members by statistical correlations. It's our best lead. We find Vidmar, we can press him to tell us where Alice is.'

Chameleon folded his arms. 'He's entangled. What can you threaten him with?'

'I'll worry about that when we find him.'

Tamboli had pinged me his ID at the Cloake crime scene. I grabbed my phone, found the card and placed a call.

He picked up on the first ring. 'Drake. Two of my men are dead. What do you know about it?'

That confirmed what I'd already figured out: Henry and the other new guy at The Grange where Tamboli's plants. 'Red Claw took Alice,' I said. 'You want to find her as much as I do, and I know how to find Vidmar, but I need your help.'

His face twitched, something between a sneer and a snarl. He was more concerned about getting Alice back than he was about his people. That suited me, even if his motive was pure self-interest.

'How do I know it wasn't you rescuing your sister from our evil clutches?'

'What have you got to lose?'

Another twitch, a derisive snort. 'What help?'

Five minutes later I was in the Saqqaf tearing through the quiet pre-dawn streets of Cambridge to the Exercitus building.

I was pacing the front room of my flat.

My phone rang. In the Saqqaf and in the flat—Baxter. I picked up. 'Hello ma'am.'

'DI Drake? I have some disturbing news.' Her voice came with an echo of a fraction of a second.

'What is it?' I stood motionless in my front room. I sat frozen in the back of the Saqqaf, convinced she was going to tell me they'd found Alice's body but she gave me all the bad news I already knew.

'We're putting everyone onto this, Lewis. I'm calling everyone in, we'll be ready to do anything that's needed to get her back.'

Lewis. She called me Lewis. She never used first names for anyone, ever. 'Thank you, ma'am,' was all I could answer.

'Will you be at home? I'll send someone for you.'

'Yes,' I said. 'No.'

Her lip twitched, like she was tempted to indulge in a sympathetic smile but couldn't quite muster the emotion. 'Which is it?'

In the flat, in the car. Concentrate, focus, separate my selves,

'Yes, ma'am. I'm at home,' I said in the flat, and in the Saqqaf, 'No ma'am.

I'm in Cambridge. I was following a lead on Erica Fallon. It might be relevant.'

I resumed pacing my living room while the Saqqaf pulled up at the entrance to the Exercitus compound. Tamboli stood in a smart camel-hair coat under the floodlight by the barrier.

'Nice car,' he said as I got out. 'How did you come by it?'

'Long story.' I stormed past him to the pedestrian gate. The uniformed guard looked past my shoulder. I looked back at Tamboli. He nodded, the gate opened and he followed me through.

'Did you find someone?' I asked as he caught me up.

'Jeong Song. Lab tech. She knows all the equipment.'

There were procedures to get me into the building. ID verification, authorisation. I had to leave my phone. No unauthorised devices allowed on the premises.

Jeong Song waited beyond the security gate. I recognised her from Cloake's personnel files, and from seeing a two-centimetre sliver of her face through the chained door of her apartment.

'I'm so sorry, Mr Drake.' The chagrin on her face looked genuine enough, but then, she'd have known Alice, before. 'Anything I can do to help, but I don't understand…'

'You're understanding isn't needed, Ms Jeong.' Tamboli beat me to the punch. 'Just your co-operation.' He cocked his head sideways in my direction and raised an eyebrow.

'I'm looking for a machine, a Viradyn DNA Sequence Editor.'

She nodded, turned on her heels and marched ahead through a pair of double doors into a darkened corridor. Harsh white lights flicked on as she entered with me right behind and Tamboli bringing up the rear. The rapid clack-clack of her heels on the tiles, the soft squeak of my right shoe, the heavy clump of Tamboli's Oxfords echoed along the long windowless passage. After all this time it was too easy.

Too easy. I should have known. The clack-clack of Jeong Song's heels slowed. She held her pass up to a scanner and pushed open a door. I followed her into a long room kitted out as a laboratory. The faint glow around the window blinds of the coming dawn was drowned by the lights flicking on to their glaring laboratory brightness. Benches lined the long walls and stretched along the axis of the room. Fume cupboards, centrifuges, a dozen other kinds of incomprehensible equipment were laid out at regular intervals. Everything was clean, bright, unblemished.

New.

Jeong Song laid her palm on the top of a cream-coloured cube half a metre on a side with a display panel, slots, grilles, buttons. She smiled a smile of proud, proprietary ownership. 'Viradyn D27B. Latest model, four megabases per second. Eight of them in *this* lab. What are you planning to do with it?'

'That's not the one.' I leaned back against the opposite bench. I knew what was coming, but I had to ask. 'There was one on the inventory when Exercitus took over. Where's that one?'

'That one?' She raised a hand to her mouth and cast her gaze to the side. 'Let me have a look.' Three steps back and she turned to face a wall monitor. A few gestures and the screen flickered with a succession of forms and tables.

'Here we are, Viradyn D07A. Obsolete, decommissioned February after the takeover.'

'Disposition?' Tamboli asked.

'Sent for disposal on your order, Mr Tamboli.'

He shrugged. 'Ah, well. I can't be expected to remember every docket I sign. So, why are you looking for it, Drake?'

'That machine. The clue to Vidmar's new identity is recorded in its memory.'

'Then you're out of luck. Equipment disposal here is under MOD security protocols.'

'Meaning?'

'It's been scrapped. Memory removed, wiped and slagged in a furnace.'

*

The deep thrumming of heavy motors rattled the living room window of my flat. The wind had dropped, the rain stopped, and the water in the street had drained away, at least until the afternoon high tide. The armoured bulk of an

APC eased to a halt outside and a slight figure in a dark raincoat jumped down from the rear door and strode to my front door.

Harris. I let him in.

'How are you bearing up, Lewis?'

'Okay, thanks, Jack. Just waiting. Can't do anything else.'

'One of the reasons I'm here.' He followed me into the living room. I collapsed into the armchair while Harris looked down at me. 'We got a message from Red Claw. Baxter thought it better I bring it to you in person.'

He flicked the display from his phone to my wall screen. Alice, strapped to a chair much like I had been in Canary Wharf. Her eyes were closed tight and she rocked back and forward, twisting her head from side to side and emitting a high and wavering keening, broken only momentarily each time she took a breath.

Harris's jaw dropped. His shock wouldn't help, neither would my rage. That part of me screamed from deep down where it could stay until it was of some use.

'They've given her an inhibitor,' I said. 'She's cut off from the life she's known. No longer in the Omega State. Not even entangled.'

The camera pulled back to reveal a man standing next to her dressed in jeans, heavy jacket, a balaclava hiding his face, a pistol in his hand. The floor beneath was concrete, the wall behind smooth and white with discoloured paint peeling in patches and a rust-red streak running down. Stark shadows from a bright light to the left of the camera angled across the floor and onto the wall. The rock-steady viewpoint suggested the camera was on a tripod.

'This is a message for Doctor Erica Fallon,' a synthetic voice-over began, drowning Alice's soft wails. 'You have information we require. Contact us at this anonymous remailer.' An address appeared at the bottom of the image with a dot EEEU domain—Eastern Europe Economic Union. 'Alice Drake has been given enough inhibitor to cut her off from entanglement, her suffering is real, her death will be real.' At this, the standing man unfolded his arms and pointed his gun at Alice's head.

'The wall behind them has water damage,' I said, 'could be somewhere in the flood zone.' There was scarcely a building in London east of the Tower that hadn't been flooded at some point. It was a huge area. I could kid myself that there was something familiar about that wall, but one rusty streak, one patch of crumbling discoloured plaster looks much like another. 'Has forensic image analysis picked up anything?'

'Nothing useful. The frames have the camera serial number and model embedded. It's a mil-spec unit so all the other metadata is encrypted. The light is from a white LED work light, about twenty centimetres across, mounted a metre from the ground, like a builder or decorator might use. The man in the balaclava has hazel eyes, brown hair, about one point eight metres in height, eighty kilos, resolution isn't good enough for iris identification. There's no sign Alice has been injured.'

Not physically, but *like taking the soul of an eagle and stitching it into the body of a worm*, Stebbins-Reese had said. 'I guess Baxter's going through channels to get a trace on that remailer.'

'Yeah, but you know how long that takes. When I left she was fighting a losing battle to stop Superintendent Donahue taking charge of the case.'

A flurry of rain rattled the window. The wind was picking up again, the next front coming through. I gazed unseeing at the heavy low cloud over the rooftops. 'Donahue. He knows there's a leak in our department. He sees all our files.' I gave Harris a hard look, hard as I could knowing he'd died protecting me. 'I think he has a plant in our department.'

Harris looked down at his lap.

'You never went to Tripoli. I told you I was going to Cloake's house. You were there when Meera was shot.'

'Donahue's orders. He said he knew all about Aiden Harcourt and he was a red herring. He thought you were in danger and someone was trying to frame you. Told me to watch out for you. I was in the woods, but the gunman was already lying in wait. And after, he had a car waiting nearby.'

'I don't know who in the service I can trust, Jack. Anyone could be in Vidmar's pay.' Anyone could *be* Vidmar. I didn't want to say that out loud.

'Do you trust me?'

'You. No-one else.'

'Baxter? Donahue?'

'No-one.'

I picked a pen and notepad from the sideboard. 'The gunman you saw at Cloake's. Two metres, about eighty kilos, size twelve boots, body armour?'

'Could be the same one.'

I wrote the name on the notepad, *Elphick*, and passed it to him.

'How do you know?'

I clenched my teeth and grimaced. The same gesture Harris had used when he didn't want to talk about Tripoli in the car with Elphick. The APC was still parked in the road. 'Why the APC?' I asked.

'Flood water's rising. It was either that or a boat. Baxter thought you might want to come to the station to wait for news. Do you know where Erica Fallon is? We should get her in protective custody until this is over.'

I had to think about that. In the flat with Harris I'd left her at the factory with Chameleon. At the Exercitus building with Tamboli I'd left her at the factory with Chameleon. I didn't know who I could trust, but if I couldn't trust Chameleon, Erica and Alice were both already dead.

'She's safer where she is than she would be in custody.'

Harris joined me by the window. 'Weather's getting worse and there's a high spring tide this afternoon. Let's get you back to the station while we can.'

*

'So.' Tamboli folded his arms. 'Do you know where Erica Fallon is? We should get her in protective custody until this is over.'

'She's safe,' I said. 'Safer than she would be in custody.'

Tamboli let out a soft grunt. 'What about Cecilia Watts?'

That caught me off-guard. 'What about her?'

'Stebbins-Reese told me she never turned up for work on Monday, hasn't been seen since. We believe she was working with Red Claw. She knew where Alice was and who was on duty.'

'Not Cecilia,' I said. 'There were four staff on duty last night including your two plants. Only three dead at the scene. Who was the other one? I'm guessing they were Red Claw's insider.'

'You *are* full of surprises, Drake. How do you know that?'

'I was there. I suspected Alice wasn't safe at The Grange, but I got there too late. *We* got there too late. Me and Cecilia Watts.'

'I could arrest you, you know? The State Security Act has some conveniently imprecise clauses about impeding security operations.'

'You know she went into hiding because she believed your people spiked Alice's treatment and killed Sam Okorie?'

'I don't know why she'd think that.'

'Because of the ham-fisted way you leaned on Sam Okorie. But that's beside the point. She knows now it wasn't you. It was Vidmar.'

'It all comes back to Vidmar doesn't it. Will she talk to us now that's been cleared up?'

'Once Alice is safe.' Maybe she would, maybe she wouldn't. I didn't care.

'Do you have any idea where they've taken her?'

'I'm hoping you might help me with that. I'll need my phone.'

He led the way out of the lab, back to the reception area. As I'd hoped, Baxter had tried to call me, and she'd forwarded me the hostage video that Harris had shown me in the other world. Tamboli watched it with me.

I opened the metadata. The phone asked me for the key file to decrypt it.

'That's military spec encryption.' Tamboli confirmed what Harris had said. 'Send it to me.'

I sent the file, happy for once that I was dealing with spooks.

*

The sound of the wheels turned from a rumbling over old tarmac to a splashing wake as the APC headed into a dip in the road on the approach to the Shadwell gate.

'Tide's rising,' Harris said, more to himself than to me. 'Good thing we didn't wait.'

He didn't venture outside the wall so often or he'd have known it was too early for the tide. That would come soon enough; this was the volume of rainwater overwhelming the drains.

They'd already closed the gate in anticipation of the tide but they opened it for us. The APC rolled through under the railway arch and we had to wait again while the outer gate closed before they'd open the inner.

As soon as I walked in from the lift lobby Baxter came and shook my hand. 'Please, Lewis, I need a quiet word.' She led me to her office. The eyes of Harris and the rest of the squad followed us. Baxter closed the door and gestured for me to sit.

'I'm so sorry, I feel responsible for this. I allowed you to pursue this case even though it impinged on your personal life. That was a mistake.'

'Thank you, ma'am. But it isn't your fault. This is Vidmar's game.'

'Is there anything you can tell me that would help? What's Vidmar's motivation?'

'He believes that Alice and Erica Fallon know something that can be used to identify him. He's using Alice to flush out Erica. He wants to kill them both.'

The trouble was that what Alice and Erica knew wasn't enough in this reality. The vital link in the chain had been broken with the destruction of the Viradyn machine. As long as Vidmar didn't know that, he was on the back foot.

'You know where Erica Fallon is now?'

'I can't say that I do.'

She actually smiled at that, one of those cold, off-centre smiles, like she appreciated what I was saying even if she didn't like it.

Baxter hunched forward over the desk. 'You know Superintendent Donahue is taking the case. I've had to promise him our full co-operation.'

'Do you know what he's doing?'

'He's trying to get GCHQ assistance on the video metadata, they're the encryption experts. Though I wonder why the metadata wasn't stripped. It's easy enough.'

The same thought had occurred to me, but I kept my silence as in the other reality I was hustled out of the Exercitus building by Tamboli towards a waiting APC, completely black, without the usual markings. As we sprinted towards it through the rain, the rear door flew open, and a man dressed in black body armour, without insignia, reached out to pull me in. Another waited inside. Tamboli followed on my heels.

Dim red light filled the interior as soon as the door closed. Bench seats on either side gave enough room to seat ten. The forward end held a block of storage lockers and a rack of automatic rifles and grenade launchers.

Baxter steepled her fingers and gave me her long, piercing look. 'How are you holding up, Lewis? Waiting for news is a killer for the nerves. You seem to be handling it well.'

If all I had been doing was sitting around waiting for news I would have been crawling up the walls, but at that moment the APC was pulling away. Tamboli briefed his two agents. 'Decrypt gives us a location on the Canary Wharf estate.' He pulled up a plan and pointed. A former clothing store at the Cabot Square end of the main shopping concourse, lower level. I was itching to tell Baxter or Donahue, but if Tamboli and I were being led on a wild goose chase or into a trap, let it be only that world.

'I'm bearing up,' I said to Baxter. 'Any other leads? Anything on Frank Wilson?'

She grimaced. 'Another dead end.' A flick of her hand and an image appeared on her wall: a view from a surveillance camera looking along the crowded platform of a railway station. One face, walking towards the camera, circled: Frank Wilson. 'I asked my contacts in Ljubljana to run a search on Wilson's face. This was taken at the railway station three days after his wife reported him missing.'

'Anything after that?'

She flicked the image to another, the internal camera of a car, Wilson the only passenger. 'He was taken to a gated residential compound outside the city.' The next image was an aerial shot—a substantial country house, the grounds surrounded by high walls. 'He went in and was never seen to leave.'

'Never seen to—doesn't mean he didn't. What do we know about the property?'

'Ownership is tied up in trusts and offshore holdings too dense even for

Penfold to disentangle, but there were other interesting visitors in the following weeks.' She pulled up a grid of images, six faces, all in car interiors.

'That's Big Bennie Thacker,' I said, 'Snips Sullivan, and… the rest of them, all of them killed in the Leven Street massacre. Is there more?'

'They sent me hundreds of images. These I picked out by cross-referencing against our files of known or suspected Red Claw members.'

'Perhaps I should look through the rest of them. I need to be doing something.'

'Later. Right now Marlowe is running traffic analysis looking for unexplained perturbations in the area of The Grange. The kidnappers will have used ghosted vehicles but there's not much traffic at that time of night. You'd be most use helping him with that.'

So I did. I pulled a chair over to Marlowe's desk. He was floundering with no idea what to look for. First task was to set the search window.

'What was the last contact you had from your people at The Grange?' I asked Tamboli in the back of the van as it hurtled down the M11 towards London.

'They reported in at two am. All quiet then.'

'Narrow the search window,' I said to Marlowe. 'Two am to three thirty.' Three thirty was when Erica and I had arrived. 'Three kilometre radius.'

He gave me a questioning look. I gave him a *just fucking do it* look and he did it. The map zoomed into the road network around The Grange, the lane that passed the front gate and the side road that we had taken to the service entrance. At the western edge of the circle another road met the lane from the south. That was the one I'd walked along in the rain the night Tamboli had picked me up and dumped me, forever ago. A week ago. Only a week.

'Now look for any vehicle movements. Anything at all.'

He did. There was nothing. Not a single registered vehicle movement. Middle of nowhere, middle of the night. Whatever vehicles they'd used had been ghosted, as I expected.

'Widen it. Five kilometres.'

That brought in part of the industrial park that held the Exercitus building. A road led from there out to the Cambridge ring road, the streets of the residential district inside. Now we had hundreds of movements: traffic around the ring road, vehicles coming and going. Many from one particular building in the industrial park. I reached over to select it and hit the query key. A label appeared. *FPS Logistics Distribution Depot.*

'One at a time,' I said to Marlowe. 'I want to look at every vehicle that stopped for more than a few seconds. We'll start with these in the housing district.'

He sorted them all into a list and we went through them one at a time, checking the journey log for each one, who owned it, who rode it, where from, where to. We picked through the night-time movements of forty-seven Cambridge residents each travelling to or from a place of work, an airport, a night club, to or from their homes in that little estate in Cambridge.

'What are we looking for?' said Marlowe after number thirteen.

'I'll know when I see it.'

The Industrial area came next. A handful of cars collecting or depositing workers, then a constant buzzing of small vans arriving, waiting, shuffling around the FPS Logistics depot, being loaded for delivery rounds. A stream of dollies arrived from the ring road, mostly from the direction of the motorway. They drove into the depot, stayed there a few minutes, dropping containers of packages, then heading off to a charging station.

'What's that one doing?' Marlowe flagged a dolly that stopped by the side of the estate access road and remained stationary for five minutes.

The log said it had dropped its container at FPS but gross vehicle weight still said five tonnes. Too heavy for an unladen dolly, too light for a fully loaded container. 'That's it. Where did it go next.'

We followed its route on the map, all the way down the M11, into London, through the Bromley-by-Bow flood gate and onto the Isle of Dogs. It vanished from tracking when it entered the low level loading bay under one of the buildings at the eastern end of the Canary Wharf complex. Corroboration of Tamboli's decrypt of the video metadata.

I walked to Baxter's open door and knocked. She looked up from her screen and beckoned me in.

'The traffic data gives us a trail,' I said. 'It *looks* like they left The Grange in a ghosted car, then switched to a freight container on a dolly down to Canary Wharf.'

'Donahue's on the road with four APCs now, heading east on Upper Thames Street. He has a decrypt on the video metadata that says the same thing.'

'I don't think she's there.'

Baxter raised an eyebrow and steepled her fingers.

'It's too easy. Red Claw are never so lax, leaving metadata on a video, using vehicles that could be tracked. Plus, there's a spring tide this afternoon. Docklands is going to flood if it hasn't already. It's a diversion, maybe a trap.'

*

'It's too easy,' I said to Tamboli as the APC sped through the underpass of the M25 interchange. 'This is a diversion, maybe a trap.'

His neatly bearded face curled into a grin. 'Why do you say that?'

'Red Claw don't make these kind of mistakes.'

He smiled and his teeth flashed in the red light of the APC interior. 'Drake, never ascribe to cunning that which can be adequately explained by foolishness. We're nearly there. We'll check it out.'

As we slowed at the end of the motorway to join the city streets the thrumming and hissing of tyres on wet tarmac was drowned by the rattle of rain and hail on the steel body. The nav display on the bulkhead showed our steady progress to the Bromley-by-Bow flood gate. The gates were closed when we arrived. A sluice in the gate opened, water flooded out and splashed down a drainage grill in the road surface. When the torrent had subsided to a trickle the gate slid open and four cars and a light van drove out. The APC crept forward into the lock and stopped before the high outer gate. A display on the gate read *0.27m*, barely deep enough to reach the wheel rims of the APC. No-one else was foolhardy enough to want to drive out into the flood zone so the inner gate closed behind us. The sluice in the outer gate opened and water rushed in.

We advanced through the flooded streets of Poplar heading south towards the Isle of Dogs. From above and around, the wind and the rain howled and clattered. Motors whined beneath the floor and the rushing sound of the wake raised by the vehicle's broad tyres surrounded us.

After a couple of sharp bends the APC climbed a ramp. The hiss of tyres on wet tarmac replaced the splashing wake as we climbed to the raised ground level of the Canada Wharf complex, the roof over the top of the flooded car parks and malls. When the APC stopped, the front left slit window gave me a rain-blurred view of the lower floors of One Canada Square, where I had been briefly questioned by the late Bennie Thacker. Through the front right window I made out the bridge that carried the track and the platforms of the Docklands Light Railway station over the road.

'It pains me to say it, Drake, but you're right about a number of things.' Tamboli stood as the vehicle slowed to a stop. 'Red Claw don't make those kind of mistakes.' He turned and nodded to the black-clad guards. They seized my arms and forced me to lean forward on the bench. Their grips were too strong to resist as they pushed my hands behind me and zip-tied my wrists together around one of the steel supports of the back-rest.

Tamboli crouched to my eye level. 'Your meddling is becoming inconvenient, but I do believe you know where Erica Fallon is and you will tell me, eventually.' He straightened. 'But first I have to deal with Superintendent Donahue.'

A hammering on the rear door drew his attention. A minion opened it and it slammed back on its hinges, caught by the wind. A man in ARO uniform jumped in and helped the minion to pull the door closed.

The newcomer lifted the helmet from his head. Elphick. Elphick was working for Tamboli, and it was Tamboli that had brought Stebbins-Reese in to treat Alice so that he could find Erica, to solve the phenotype reprogramming rejection problem, or so I had thought.

'All ready?' asked Tamboli.

'Everyone's in position. When Donahue gets here the rising tide will cut off their retreat along Westferry Road.' Elphick squeezed past me to the nav display. He pointed to the raised roundabout at the western end of the complex. 'We have teams with rocket launchers in these buildings—' I followed his fingers as he pointed to the four corners of Cabot square, '—the underground levels are flooding so no escape that way and we have machine guns set up in the entrances to the buildings.'

Tamboli stroked his beard. 'They could run for the North Dock footbridge.'

'We've mined the bridge, and we have snipers in the buildings on either side. They run that way and we've got them.'

Donahue was on his way with four APCs. He'd come by way of the Shadwell gate, and along Westferry Road. He would be doing the same in this world and in the one where I waited in the Bishopsgate station.

*

I sat at my desk playing through the video of Alice suffering in the chair. Again and again I played it. The wall behind her evoked a sense of familiarity that might have been memory, or might have been a seepage from some other reality that, without context, would be meaningless. Tamboli's words in the APC pushed that question from my mind: *It pains me to say it, Drake, but you're right about a number of things*. By the time I was strapped to the bench I was at Baxter's door.

'Tamboli!' I shouted as I burst in. 'Search for his face in your Ljubljana dataset.'

'Do you have an image?'

His ID was still on my phone. I pulled it up and flicked the photo to Baxter. He ran the search and an image flashed up: Tamboli, neatly trimmed black beard, sitting smug and relaxed in the back of a car *leaving* the Ljubljana house. The date stamp was March, four months after Frank Wilson arrived.

'He's Vidmar.'

Baxter raised a sceptical eyebrow.

'It all fits. The tomographic resonator—it was in that house, not the hospital. Frank Wilson had dealings with Tamboli before he disappeared—he could easily have got a DNA sample. He used phenotype reprogramming, the technique developed by Alice and Erica, to change his physical appearance. It takes time, four months should be long enough.'

'DI Drake.' She smiled. 'Lewis. The link to Tamboli is interesting but you may be getting ahead of yourself. Let's concentrate on finding Alice now, and we'll come back to this afterwards.'

I was right. I knew I was right. Baxter was humouring me and I didn't have time to start trying to explain about the deltas and what I was seeing in other worlds. I took a deep breath. 'I need some air,' I said and stormed out, heading straight through the office to the lift. The indicator said *B*. It would be a minute at least before it reached me from the basement level. Beyond the glass door Harris sat at his desk, looking at me. He half-rose. I shook my head and he hesitated. I turned and pushed through the door to the stairs and ran down three at a time. Four flights with one-eighties at each floor and half-way between. I had my phone out dialling the number as I dashed across the lobby. It was ringing as I pushed through the door into the storm.

'Chameleon!' I shouted against the wind as he picked up. 'Canary Wharf is a trap, Tamboli wants to wipe out Donahue's squad. Tell him before he gets there.'

'Who's Tamboli?'

The question floored me. Chameleon hadn't heard about him.

'He's Vidmar.' It all added up, Vidmar was always one step ahead. Tamboli worked for UK intelligence, worked for Exercitus, working for Red Claw. And he had been looking for Erica all this time. His access to intelligence resources, back doors into the Met's systems, would tell him everything about Donahue and his troublesome unit, everything he needed to lure then into a trap and wipe them out.

The phone was back in my pocket before Harris emerged onto the street.

'I needed to get out of there,' I said. 'Go back in. I'm going to Marek's. I'll be back soon.'

I was drenched by the time Marek's door screeched before me.

'There's a man who loves his coffee,' Marek said as I dripped on his tiles. 'What can I get you?'

'Macchiato.' I slipped off my coat and hung it on the stand. My phone rang before I'd sat down.

'Donahue is holding by the Shadwell gate,' Chameleon said. 'Tell me what you've got. I'll relay it to him in this world and that.'

*

The wind, focussed by the narrow gap between skyscrapers, was strong enough to shake even the eight tonnes of steel and ceramic armour that made up the APC. Every now and then I thought I felt a tremor that came up through the chassis, the springs, the wheels. The road beneath us looked like the ground between buildings but was the concrete roof over the shopping complex that extended between them. That high tide would be ripping through, sweeping away the last of the naked mannequins and empty shelves.

'What are they doing?' Tamboli railed. 'They should be here by now.'

The four dots on the display had been blinking in the same spot by the Shadwell gate for twenty minutes.

'Relax.' Elphick sprawled on the bench opposite. 'It'll be some jobsworth refusing to open the gate. Okay, here we go. They're moving again.'

We all watched the display, Tamboli, Elphick, the two minions, and me. Donahue's squad was coming, slow and cautious.

Donahue knew it was a trap but the APCs continued on their route, turning onto Westferry Road and up the ramp to the roundabout and onto West India Avenue. They took both lanes, two abreast towards Cabot Square. Two turned left, two right, and they came to a halt, two each on the north and south sides of the square.

If I could have stood up I'd have seen one of them through our vehicle's forward slit window, but restrained as I was, only the bridge carrying the raised Canary Wharf DLR station over the road was in my line of sight. A train slid in from the north. No-one else noticed, their eyes were all fixed on the APC. The train shoudn't have been running. It was called the Docklands *Light* Railway for a good reason: trains were light in weight, running on exposed high-level tracks. They always shut it down in high winds, like now.

'What's going on over there?' Tamboli turned from the window towards Elphick, who muttered into his radio, listened.

'No activity. The vehicles have stopped. No-one's got out.'

'Take them out,' Tamboli snapped.

'Take them out,' Elphick repeated into his radio.

Rocket launchers, like Elphick had said. I didn't hear them launching. I guess the wind drowned that sound, but I did hear the detonations and I felt the APC tremble with the shock waves. The distant blast, the heavy impacts of debris falling back to the ground, were followed by a sustained crashing and splintering. Through the small window I saw a rain of glass shards blown out of the buildings around Cabot Square, twisting and tumbling in the wind.

The four dots on the display winked out.

Elphick held a hand to cover his ear and the earpiece within. 'All targets eliminated.'

Tamboli was still standing, peering out of the forward window, his fingers *tap-tap-tapping* on the bulkhead. It did me good, seeing him uneasy, relaxed me. I tried another tentative tug at the zip-tie around my wrists. No luck.

'Let's take a closer look.' Tamboli swung into the driver's seat and unlocked the manual controls. The screen lit up with the forward view and the APC rumbled into a slow crawl, past the tower to our left, then beneath the DLR bridge. When we stopped, the station on the bridge was once more visible, this time through the rear slit-window. Flickering shadows moved behind the translucent glass panels that hid the station platform. It might have been detritus swirling in the wind, but I didn't think so.

Red Claw had set their trap around Cabot Square ahead of us. From the station and the bridges of the DLR behind us Donahue's armed squads could make pincer sweeps along the edges of the docks to north and south. The APCs that Tamboli's people had taken out were like the one I was sitting in. No doubt Donahue's people were carrying the same rocket launchers. I had to hope Donahue had got the message about where I was.

Tamboli weaved the APC between the larger pieces of debris of Donahue's APCs. He stopped close to the first of the twisted wrecks. The armoured shell was ripped open. The wheels on one side had sunk into a crack in the roadway beneath.

'You three, get out and check the APCs.'

'There'll be no-one alive,' Elphick said.

'I want to know if we got Donahue. Go.'

They zipped up, each took a rifle from the rack and huddled by the door.

'Ready?' Elphick said. The other two nodded. Elphick pulled the handle and they all leapt down. The wind and rain howled in. I doubt it was ten seconds before that door slammed shut again, but I was soaked. Tamboli marched back from the relative dry of the forward end and engaged the locking bar. I turned my attention back to the forward view screen; Elphick and the two others jogged towards the splintered carcass of the APC, weaving and sidestepping through the fragments of twisted metal. Elphick clambered up between the sunken wheels and poked his head through the rent armour.

'No-one here.' His voice crackled through the radio.

'Donahue? Try the next one.'

'No.' Elphick climbed back down. 'There's no-one at all. The APC was empty.'

Of course it was empty. They'd all left the APCs at Shadwell and Donahue had pulled strings to get a DLR train running. I tried to figure it out, how long since that train had pulled in? How long for Donahue's unit to work their way from the train to where the action was? If it had been my plan I'd have monitored the APCs' cameras to see where the rockets were launched from and I'd be closing in on those positions from within the various buildings.

Tamboli's fingers tap-tap-tapped on the bulkhead. He stood, looking through the slit window, down at the screen, at the controls, back out of the window.

A momentary lull in the wind brought a second's silence, broken by a loud crack. Tamboli jumped.

'What's the matter, Tamboli?' I said. 'That was just something falling from one of the towers.'

He turned and glared at me. Another loud crack, and on the screen behind Tamboli I saw Elphick raise his rifle, aiming up at one of the buildings to our right. He fell in a hail of gunfire.

Tamboli was in the driving seat before Elphick hit the ground. The screen switched to the rear view and the APC exploded into motion in reverse. A bright flash from the DLR bridge washed out the screen. I hunched down as best I could with my hands tied behind me, twisting to keep my back to the rear of the carrier, knowing it would be futile if the rocket hit us.

It didn't, but the blast lifted the rear of the eight-tonne van from the roadway then it slammed down again. The wind tore away the smoke and dust to reveal a chasm behind us where the rocket had blasted a hole, an opening into the darkness of the mall below. Tamboli switched the viewscreen forward and we lurched into motion again. The wheels of the wrecked APC ahead of us had sunk deeper into the cracked roadway. As we accelerated towards it, it leaned more. A deep and spreading crack slanted across the road.

'It's collapsing,' I said.

'Shut your mouth, Drake. The foundations go down a hundred metres.'

He was right. The foundations for the skyscrapers did. It was going to take worse than this to bring them down, but the eager tide pouring through the shopping mall beneath us had been eating away the foundation, tearing at the concrete columns that supported the roof. The rocket fire had shattered that roof's own strength.

We stopped, lurched, a distinct lean now to the van. A gentle alarm beeped. *Unsafe surface. Please vacate the vehicle. Unsafe surface. Please vacate...*

A ripping tide, decades of neglect and corrosion, rocket strikes, and an eight-tonne APC were too much for the concrete deck. The bench on which I sat fell away beneath me, the tie around my wrists pulling me down. Tamboli's feet left the floor, his arms waved desperate circles as the van rolled around us. The roof became a wall became a floor. My head connected with the side of the van when it hit bottom and I blacked out.

When I came to I was hanging by my wrists from the back support of the upside-down bench, half-kneeling on the roof of the upturned van, in salt water up to my armpits and rising. One rear door lay open, beyond it, lapping water. A few metres away the water splashed and foamed under a cascade from the gutters above. The diffuse light picked out a concrete column, cracked and leaning. Tamboli was gone.

The steel floor above me rang with the staccato rhythm of pieces of the roadway raining down on it. The cracked column leaned more and shattered, raising frothing waves as the crumbling concrete fell and the steel reinforcement twisted and buckled. The tie dug into my wrists as I tugged and twisted to try and free myself, then the concrete deck above slammed down. In any other kind of vehicle I'd have been instantly crushed. As it was, the floor above me buckled under the impact, forcing me down so my head was barely above the water, then the whole carcass lurched, the nose dropped and the rear door rose up, above the water level; a moment's respite.

In a slow, grinding motion the APC slid, then dropped. The floor beneath the vehicle gave way and it fell through to the next level down. Water cascaded in through the open door. I took one last desperate breath as the torrent tore at me, battering me against the sides of the van. I held my breath and braced my feet against the wall of the APC and pulled desperately at the tie around my wrists. It dug deeper into my flesh but I felt the bench support move. I slid my wrists up the bar as high as I could and the tie caught on something, something hard. My fingers probed and found it, a jagged edge, the end of a burst rivet that had held the bench against the van's frame. With my lungs ready to burst, I yanked the tie across the sharp edge, once, twice. On the third go it parted. I pushed with my legs as hard as I could towards the open door above me. The air in my lungs rushed out as I ascended.

I broke surface and took a great, gasping breath. The water was still, the tide now slack between flood and ebb. Lashing rain fell through the opening in the roadway above and in the grey light that filtered down I could see only water and the nearer concrete columns. No way up.

In Marek's café I pulled up a plan of the Canary Wharf complex. I was at the northern side of the old Cabot Square car park. At the far side, the south, was a stairwell, a way out. I swam into the dark towards it.

A flash, and the crack of a gunshot echoed through the darkness. I held myself still and my legs dropped through the water and found the solid floor. As slow and quiet as I could, I rose to my feet in waist-deep water and waded to the cover of the nearest pillar. Another shot. Two more. I strove to peer through the purple blotches left in my vision by the flashes. Another exchange of fire began. Assault rifles were firing somewhere in the darkness. Closer at hand there was the more high-pitched crack of a pistol. A bullet struck the pillar that sheltered me and ricocheted away with a spinning whine.

Water splashed, movement in the shadows, a dark shape took shelter behind a nearby pillar. In the muzzle flash from his pistol I caught a glimpse of his face—one of Tamboli's guards from the APC. During a burst of covering fire from further along the line, he waded back towards my position.

A hail of automatic fire followed him. I picked out the helmet and uniform of one ARO, another beyond him. Between the scant details I could see in the flooded car park and the map before me in Marek's, I pieced together a picture of the tactical situation. Donahue's armed response squad was spread across the eastern side of the car park, sweeping west while Tamboli's men retreated towards my position. I took a deep breath and dived down to swim beneath the surface towards the stairwell. Making slow, careful strokes, I strove to avoid breaking the surface. With each stretch of my arms forward I felt for the next pillar, and failed to find it. The sounds of gunfire fell to a cacophony of muffled thuds in the murky water. The shock wave of a stray bullet cut through the water above my head.

With the breath bursting from my lungs I rolled onto my back, let my legs drop to the floor and eased my face up to the surface enough to open my mouth and take a gulp of air. A glance to either side told me I had missed my pillar and angled off into the no-man's land between the two sides.

The firing intensified, bullets flying scant centimetres above me. I dived down and swam again with more urgency and less caution towards the stairwell.

When I surfaced again, the ripples of my motion raised scintillating glints from the light of the stairwell. Behind, sporadic single shots fired from the cover of the pillars—Tamboli's men had paused their retreat and were holding their ground. I sank down behind the last pillar. A gentle kick and I drifted backwards towards the stairwell until my back scraped the sharp edge of a submerged step. I turned and crawled out of the water, towards the light, around the turn of the stairwell and ran into a heavy steel gate, locked and bolted.

'You won't get out that way.'

He stood on the steps behind me, a pistol in his hand. He beckoned me down, his eyes darting back and forth between me and the car park behind as he edged down the steps ahead of me. The gunfire intensified as I stepped back down into the water. The AROs were retreating now from gunfire to right and left. More Red Claw had come in behind them and now they were being pushed back towards the north side, beneath the chasm.

My captor raised a radio to his mouth. 'I've got Drake.'

Tamboli's voice crackled from the radio. 'Kill him.'

He raised the pistol. I dived into the water as he fired. In Marek's I let out a grunt of pain, my hand flew to clasp my lower ribs on the right of my chest but cold and shock hid the pain from me in the car park. I surfaced again to the sound of a volley of shots. I staggered to my feet to find my attacker face down in the water. Warm blood mixed with cold water ran down from my wound.

A dark silhouette waded towards me. 'Is he dead?' Tamboli's voice. I needed a weapon, and there was one somewhere nearby dropped by my assailant, if I could find it in the cold, dark water.

I dived down, I dived down in all directions, near and far. I couldn't count how many different paths I took, how many strands I separated that reality into, but in one my hand closed around the grip of the dropped pistol. Now I knew where it was, I dived again in all the other realities and my hand went straight to it. I climbed to my feet and the shimmering shape of Tamboli approaching solidified into a single perspective as all those realities converged again.

Surprise crossed his face as he stepped into the light. He raised his gun to shoot, but mine was already raised. I fired and he fell forward into the water, then the world turned black and I slid into cold, wet darkness.

*

I came to lying on hard dry concrete, my back against a wall. Uniforms crowded around me. Someone was pressing a pad against my ribs. I was on the landing in the stairwell, the steel gate above wide open.

Donahue squatted beside me.

'Alice,' I said. 'She's not here. It was a trap.'

'A trap,' he agreed, 'but we're taking the prisoners to your station at Bishopsgate for interrogation. Someone must know something.'

'Govind Tamboli, the Exercitus security chief, is down there,' I said. 'Have the DNA in his brain sequenced during the post mortem. He's Frank Wilson—Vidmar.'

The café door squealed. Harris stood dripping in the doorway. 'You okay, Lewis?'

My hand was pressed against my ribs. 'Donahue,' I said. 'He'll send his prisoners to us.'

'How do you know?'

I jumped to my feet and pushed past him. 'Come on!' I was out and sprinting through the puddles before he could ask anything else.

'Attention please, everyone.' Baxter was standing by her office door when I came in from the lift lobby, Harris close behind me. 'Superintendent Donahue has captured a number of Red Claw operatives and is sending them here for questioning. We'll divide up into pairs and use all six interview rooms. Our key objective is to locate Alice Drake.'

'Any news on Vidmar?' Harris shouted.

'Nothing.'

'Casualties,' I called out from the back. 'Did we lose anyone?'

Her gaze cruised the room. 'Thank you, Drake. We should take a moment to reflect on our fallen colleagues. Al Hadri, Jefferson and Elphick.'

I felt the darkness return as she spoke. I collapsed into a chair. In that other reality she would be adding my name to that list.

*

I wasn't allocated to one of the pairs conducting interviews—too personally involved, Baxter said—so I sat at my desk working through the files of all the detainees, matching faces and DNA against the files to confirm or deduce identities and to check on their recent movements, call records, known contacts, etc.

I got a DNA match with an immigration record of one Ignacij Novak entering the country four years before but the face on the file wasn't the same. Our man was a dark-haired low-brow bruiser but the photo had a narrow face, blue eyes, fair hair. My immediate thought was another phenotype reprogramming case, but falsified immigration records were nothing new. Money and favours changed hands, records were altered. An image search for the fair-haired man on the record gave me another name: *Kazimir* Novak. Ignacij Novak had no records of online activity or vehicle hire and his bank records were sparse to say the least, but a car rented on Kazimir Novak's account had travelled the previous morning to Cambridge. Kazimir himself was registered in a hotel in Edinburgh, had called room service and this morning had taken a car to a conference on smart roofing materials in the city.

I jumped up from my desk and headed for the stairs down to the third floor, to interview room four. I tapped on the door and entered—Harris stopped mid-sentence.

'Anything wrong, Lewis?' Marlowe said.

'I wondered if you two might want a coffee break. I can keep our friend company.'

Ignacij Novak's wrists were cuffed to the securing ring on the table. Such restraint was usually reserved for the most recalcitrant of our guests.

I sat and stared at him. He stared back, stone-faced, unflinching. He was locked up tight and I needed the key to open him up. There were a hundred ways to try and break someone like this, the trick is knowing which to use.

I had a lid on it, I thought. My anger, my frustration. I did have a lid on it, mostly. The room shimmered around me. Ignacij Novak shimmered with it. It might have been him, twitching and shifting, but when I strained to focus, he was still as a rock. It was me, moving and breathing out of sync in all those countless fine-grained realities that gave me a smear of superimposed viewpoints. I stopped fighting it and allowed myself to diverge.

I sat stock-still, staring him down.

I stood, knuckled fists on the table and leaned in and screamed vile abuse in his face.

I broke down, sobbing, begging him to tell me where Alice was.

I took the Glock from my pocket, the Glock that should have been locked in my desk, and slipped the magazine. 'What do you think? Is there a round in the chamber?' I pressed the barrel against his forehead. 'Where is Alice Drake?' He didn't even blink when I pulled the trigger.

Through it all, he sat unperturbed. I tried to pull myself together, to converge. I had to get out. Bit by bit, in one strand of reality after another I dragged myself to the door and grasped the handle, until I was mostly there, ninety percent, ninety-nine.

The edge of a tattoo showed in the gap where the top of his shirt was unbuttoned, the edge of a circle. I had a pretty good idea what it depicted but in a thin reality I reached and undid his next button to see: Chi-Ro, the superimposed first two letters of *Christ* in the Greek alphabet, in a circle with the alpha and omega.

In another world I asked him: 'Ignacij Novak, is yours the god of all the realities, or only this one?'

'There is one God. One world. All else is Satan's deception.'

'And yet you serve Satan's minion. The entangled Vidmar.'

He didn't rise to that.

'I understand the importance of loyalty. Loyalty to your benefactors, to your church. Most of all, to your family.' My hand rested on the door handle, but where I spoke the words I was still sitting, staring down Novak. 'I have a passing interest in architecture. Do you know anything about architecture? Do you know any architects?'

There was the faintest sign of a twitch in his left cheek. I slapped the magazine back into the Glock, rose to lean across the table. 'You're going to be locked up for the rest of your life and there's no threat I can make, no bargain I can strike that will change that. So I'm not going to threaten you or make a deal with you, but there is something you need to know.'

The twitch this time was more pronounced. The closest I was going to get to him asking.

'The woman you people took is my sister.' I pulled up the image from the immigration record, Kazimir Novak, the architect, Ignacij Novak's brother. 'If anything happens to her, I will kill this man.'

I stood and marched to the door and grasped the handle. He spoke in a voice of coarse gravel.

'She is in a cellar, in a house near where we took her.'

'Where?' I demanded and pulled up a map, but I knew where as soon as he said it. While I questioned him, while he confirmed what I knew, I left him there silent and alone and headed for the lift lobby. I took the lift down to the ground floor while summoning the Saqqaf. Outside, in the wind and rain I called Chameleon. Alice would need help in the worlds where I'd died, and in the world where I was still questioning Novak.

Also, in the worlds where, through some slip of concentration, my Glock did have a cartridge in the chamber, I stood looking down at Novak's head resting on his manacled hands while a pair of uniforms burst into the interview room and took the gun from my hand.

'I didn't mean to…' I mumbled.

'What was that, Lewis?' I was on the fourth floor, Harris looking into my eyes, face filled with concern. I didn't know how I'd got there.

'Alice. They have her in the cellar at Erica Fallon's house.'

Harris nodded. 'Come on, Baxter's office.'

Outside, rain falling on my phone turned Chameleon's face into a smeared mosaic. 'I'll call Donahue. Gallicoe too, he's nearer. We'll get her.' The Saqqaf's tyres splashed through the puddles towards me.

'You repeat what I tell you.' Ignacij Novak clenched his manacled fists. 'I thought you were a man who makes empty threats. You are no man. You are a demon.'

'Come with me, sir,' said the uniform. 'I'll let them know upstairs.' His colleague stared in dumb shock at Novak's lifeless form.

The uniform led me by the arm from the interview room. Harris had me by the arm as he led me to Baxter's office. In both places I stumbled as I stooped to climb into the Saqqaf.

I lived these realities all together, all confused in my mind.

'How many are there guarding her?' Baxter asked me in her office.

'How many are there guarding her?' I repeated to Novak in the interview room

'You should have thought to ask him that before you shot him.' The uniform nodded his head sideways towards Novak's corpse.

'Are you alright, Lewis?' On my phone's screen, Erica leaned forwards over Chameleon's shoulder.

'Two,' said Novak. 'You give them the password, *jastog*, when you knock on the trapdoor or they kill her.'

'Two,' I said, to Baxter, to Chameleon and Erica, to the uniform. I couldn't pull them apart. If I spoke, if I moved, if I did anything, I did it in all those worlds. 'There's a password, *jastog*.'

'Lewis, are you suffering from cerasthesia?'

Cerasthesia. That's what it was. I was overwhelmed by too many diverging realities, unable to act in any one world without doing the same in others. Now I was afraid, like I'd never been afraid. Alice would be safe, Chameleon would see to that. I was afraid for myself, afraid of the loss of control.

I found myself in the Saqqaf, Erica's eyes staring at me from Cecilia's face on the screen. It was she who had asked me. I nodded.

'Stay calm,' she said. 'Try to relax.'

'I'll call Gallicoe,' said Chameleon. 'We'll meet him at the barn. I'll see you there.' He hung up.

Baxter was already on the phone to Gallicoe.

'I need to get to Erica Fallon's barn,' I said.

The Saqqaf beeped in acknowledgement and the nav display updated. The surge of acceleration pressed me back in my seat as I joined the motorway.

'You're going nowhere Lewis.' Harris guided me to the chair by Baxter's desk and sat me down. 'You don't look well.'

Baxter hung up the phone. 'He's been under a lot of strain. I have to take some responsibility, I leaned on him too much on this case.'

The uniform led me to the lift lobby and pressed for lower ground.

'I need to get to Erica Fallon's barn,' I said as the lift door opened.

'I'm sorry, sir, but I have to take you to a holding cell for the moment.'

Baxter stepped out of the lift. 'He's been under a lot of strain. I have to take some responsibility, I leaned on him too much on this case.'

*

'Nee' ge' 'veca Fanh-nh barn.' My right hand shook uncontrollably under the covers.

'What was that, Lewis?' Sam Okorie's attention was fixed on the monitor by my bedside. He hummed and mumbled to himself as he worked the sensor array on my head. It itched.

Seemingly satisfied, he turned towards me. 'Good progress, Lewis. Plenty of synaptic activity in the regenerated areas. We're ready to move onto the next stage. He put up a graphic on the wall screen. My brain in 3D. The paths of the bullet in bright red, cones of yellows and oranges around it.

'This is the area we'll be regenerating tonight. We'll top up your delta implicitins now and introduce the next batch of virus. You'll be ready for the resonator in two hours. Eight pm.'

The personal care bot trundled in and lifted me, changed me, cleaned me while I sat in the Saqqaf on the way to the barn, in Baxter's office, on the bunk in the holding cell, sitting in the position the uniform had put me. Baxter had him bring in a chair and sat in front of me, her knees almost touching mine in the cramped, bright, cold cell.

'What happened, Lewis?' Her voice might have been gentle, but it reverberated from the tiled walls, giving it a hard edge.

'Tamboli,' I said. The personal care bot didn't react. 'Tamboli was Vidmar.'

She nodded. Slow, three times. 'It's going to be hard for a while, Lewis. I don't know why you had to kill Novak, but we're all behind you. You've had a rough time. You'll have to leave the service but we'll try and keep you out of prison. Any others involved, do you know?'

Baxter leaned forward over her desk with fingers steepled. 'Tamboli must have had others in the force working with him, passing intel on our operations.'

'Elphick. I don't know who else.' There had to be others. Elphick wouldn't have known about the first Canary Wharf raid until the briefing that morning.

I closed my eyes and leaned back. I didn't want to talk any more. I wanted to understand what I'd done, why I'd killed Ignacij Novak. Perhaps I'd made a genuine mistake. I had checked there wasn't a cartridge in the chamber but I was already fragmenting. Maybe in some strand I hadn't checked. Maybe I'd deliberately put one there.

Baxter stood and looked down at me in the cell. 'We'll talk more tomorrow. Get you some representation, some counselling.' I stared blankly at her feet. She left.

Baxter stood behind her desk. 'I'd like to call a medic for you, Lewis, but I guess you'd rather stay here until we have news.'

I tried to stand, but my head hit the roof in the Saqqaf and I fell back into my seat. Harris took my arm and stood me up and led me stumbling from Baxter's office to the rec room. I managed to stretch out on the couch and close my eyes. The Saqqaf surged through the M25 underpass.

Thirty minutes later I was stopped at a road-block half a mile from the barn, a squad car, two uniforms and a drone with a pulser.

The window slid silently down at my gesture.

'This road is closed, sir. Please instruct your vehicle to turn around.'

I pinged him my ID and he stepped back to call in.

'What's happening?' I asked his colleague. 'Have they made any move, tried to contact them?'

He hunched down in his raincoat, the drizzle trickling from the edge of his cap. 'We've set up a perimeter, put in a stinger to trap any phone calls. Now we're waiting for a negotiator.' He peered into the dark silence of the road ahead. 'Keeping everything quiet up there until they're ready to move.'

Keeping quiet met my approval. The negotiator didn't. We had the password;

someone could go in and surprise them. Someone, not me. In my current state I'd be as likely to mix up one world with another and shoot Alice, or Gallicoe, or anyone.

'Go ahead, sir.' The first uniform waved the drone aside. 'Slow and quiet, keep your lights off.'

I confirmed his instruction to the car and it did as he said, creeping silently along the dark lane until its way was blocked by another car a few metres short of the gate of the barn.

I got out and stumbled my way to where a cluster of shadowy figures stood.

'Lewis?'

Erica.

'Yeah, what's happening?'

'Gallicoe and Donahue are arguing over jurisdiction.'

'Is Chameleon here?'

'He's been waiting for you.' She took my hand and led me past the next of several cars. From further up the line a heated whisper carried across through the drizzle: 'You're out of your district, Superintendent Donahue. We will wait for the negotiator.'

'Who do we trust, Donahue? Gallicoe?' Chameleon spoke from the shadows of the hedge.

'Gallicoe was in deep with Tamboli but that doesn't mean he was turned.'

'It's his people surrounding the place.'

'Stinger's on?'

'Yeah. That's in Donahue's control. No-one's making calls in or out without his say-so'

'Let them argue. We'll take the back door. There's a footpath, a stile through the hedge a hundred metres back. Are you here everywhere? In the worlds where I'm still in Bishopsgate?'

'I'm here everywhere I can be, show me the way.'

I leaned against him and he helped me back along the lane to the stile, him shimmering and blurring under my own erratic movements. At the back of the barn, I lifted the plant pot, took the key and opened the door.

'Show me the trapdoor,' Chameleon whispered, 'then keep back. You're in no condition to get in a fight.'

I couldn't disagree. With exaggerated care I led him by torchlight from the rear boot room through the kitchen and into the dark hall. The study door was open, the rug pushed back against the wall.

I tapped on the trapdoor. '*Jastog!*'

'Še vedno je odprto, tepec!' a gruff voice rumbled. From behind us, from the far side of the hall, a toilet flushed.

The last vestige of coherence fled. I turned, rolling away from the trapdoor as torchlight loomed in the doorway behind us. Chameleon fired or I fired or we both fired. Chameleon was first to fling open the trapdoor and jump down. I fought my way through a chaotic blur, different perspectives in frantic superposition.

I couldn't trust my own perceptions, my own actions, but to fail to act would be the death of Alice. In the video she was tied to the chair at the back of the room, in front of the damp wall, so I leaned down over the lip of the trapdoor looking for the man, the movement in any other direction, and I fired and I fired and I fired until the magazine was empty and the Glock clicked with each pull of the trigger.

When the crashing echoes of the gunfire faded, all I heard over the ringing in my ears was a quiet keening. I turned and tried to climb down, but my feet in one world were not where the rungs were in others and I fell. Several times I fell, from high up or low down, onto bare concrete or into Chameleon's arms where he did his best to catch me.

Alice sobbed, still tied in the chair. I crawled to her on hands and knees looking from every angle to see if she was hurt. Chameleon cut her free, or handed me his knife from where he lay at the foot of the ladder. I held her with my eyes closed and she held on to me, still shaking while boots thundered on the floor above, voices shouted and uniformed officers swarmed down the ladder.

Eventually gentle hands prised us apart in one reality after another. A common theme took shape, Stebbins-Reese examining Alice, lights in her eyes, reflexes.

Erica was there. 'Lewis,' she whispered, helping me to my feet. 'She's alright, Lewis. She's going to be okay.'

Stebbins-Reese stood by a table on the other side of the basement. He picked up a glass of water, sniffed at it, stirred it with the spoon that still rested in it and the liquid became white and cloudy. The split cases of a dozen pink capsules lay scattered on the table top.

'They were preparing the next dose of inhibitor,' he said. 'Dissolving the capsules in water, they'd be very strong. Fast acting.'

I took the glass from him and downed it in one.

'Chameleon?'

'I'm here, Lewis.'

'Get the inhibitor to me in Bishopsgate.'

*

The porter wheeled me to the treatment room. Everywhere I looked there was the faintest shimmer. Even here in the hospital I was diverging. Cerasthesia would have been making its mark but all I could do was lie still and stay where I was put. It calmed me a little while I writhed and twisted on the couch in the rec room, and on the bunk in the holding cell.

Baxter came to me in the cell and in the rec room. 'Alice is safe. They're taking her to Addenbrooke's for a thorough examination.'

In all the chaos of my own divergence, her words rang through clear and strong and perfectly synchronised.

By the time I reached the treatment room, my selves in Erica's barn were fading. By the time the resonator started its work those selves were gone from me. An hour later, beneath the silent pulsing of the machine, I was vaguely aware of Chameleon's presence in the Bishopsgate rec room, Stebbins-Reese in the cell, each giving me a glass of cloudy water.

I emerged from the treatment exhausted, alone, *thin*. An insignificant remnant, physically and mentally, of someone I had been in lives now lost to me, hidden from me by the inhibitor.

CHAPTER 13

Sunday 24th November: Marek's Café

Before entanglement, each of the alternate versions of our selves lived separate lives in separate diverging realities. With entanglement, we learn that all those alternates are aspects of the same self. They are not, and never have been, separate. It is only the illusion of the simplex perception that makes us think so.

This raises an interesting question: how do we define whether an individual living another life in another reality is an aspect of the same person? After all, it is something of a truism to observe that you are not the same person you were ten years ago, so would you expect an alternate whose story diverged from your own ten years ago to be?

Perhaps we can suggest that all the versions of yourself that diverged from the time of your birth are the same individual. Simple enough, but how about from the time of your conception? Perhaps genetic identity is the key. That sounds logical, but in one world your embryo may have split to form identical twins. Are you the same person as both the twins? Also, the DNA in your cells is undergoing mutation all the time, an alternate may be subjected to a change in DNA early enough to have a significant effect on their development.

There is no clear and simple answer to these questions. All that can be said is that the unity is most profound between versions of an individual who are closer to each other in spirit, closer in the time since divergence, closer even in physical form.

There are no clear boundaries. As time goes on, each of us who have started this road of entanglement find that the breadth of perception increases, we join with the lives of alternates whose common history lies ever further back in time.

—A K Amari - *The Measurement Problem,*
A Guide to Entanglement

It might have been the long session under the resonator the previous evening or perhaps the isolation from all my selves who had cut themselves off with the inhibitor, but I slept long and deep. There was one dream, slow and gentle: I was sitting in the study in Erica's barn, a broad screen angled in front of me with the plans of a house, our new house. My fingers moved and the lines and angles shifted. It needed more space, more light in the living room. I thought of a house I'd seen or dreamed about, Diskret school, where the south-facing front was a wall of tinted glass and the ground around it rose up at the sides to form the grass-covered roof.

Too extravagant. The plot I had to work with was too small and it really wasn't my style—more like something my father might have designed. Something traditional was more to my taste. My fingers moved and the windows became a little wider, the rooms a little larger. Perhaps space to squeeze a fifth bedroom upstairs. More than we'd need but who knew what the future might bring.

The door opened behind me.

'Simon?'

For a moment my own name, Simon, sounded strange on Erica's tongue. She stood in the doorway, beautiful and majestic, though if I told her that I'd have my head bitten off. She stepped over to me as I stretched out my arm to curl around her waist. The other palm I placed on her belly and felt the kick. 'I've another idea for a name,' I said.

'Go on.'

'Alice.'

She laughed, and reached across to the bookshelf and picked up the dog-eared copy of Alice in Wonderland handed down from my mother. 'Yes, I like that.'

*

The bright sunlight of a crisp morning shone in through the window of my hospital room. My head was clearer than I could remember since I first woke from that emptiness, my other selves hidden from me by the inhibitor they had taken. My dream was no dream, but another life that had diverged years before, bringing impressions of memories of a mother and father lost to me when I was twelve. Simon, that must have been my name. So much was different, yet even in that distant life, Erica and I had found each other.

I lay still, enjoying the relief that it was all over. Vidmar as Tamboli was dead in those other branches of reality and Alice was safe. I had a lingering curiosity to know what would become of those other versions of me, but the thought of enduring again the chaos of cerasthesia was unnerving.

It dawned on me that I could feel pins and needles in my toes. Trying to wiggle them I got just a twitch, nothing more, but it was progress.

Outside my room the usual noise and clatter of hospital life continued. People walking, talking, bots and drones whirring along the passage. I was here, in this world, in this world alone, in this world that was not mine.

My only clear memory of this reality was of those few seconds before the bullet tore through my frontal cortex and into the cerebellum, some trick of neurology that kept the short-term memory when everything else was lost. The entangled say that each version of ourselves in all the diverging worlds are aspects of a single person, but it didn't feel that way to me. There was a point sometime in the pasts where the ancestor of those worlds diverged from this one. In this world I had met Erica, and my familiarity with her had leaked across the boundaries along with fragments of the backdrop of our lives: the barn, the key, the paintings of Beate Messer. In the past I remembered she was present as Cecilia. We'd shared a few words in passing when I visited Alice but I didn't really know her.

My nose itched. Without thinking I tried to scratch it and an unruly forearm wavered above my head before my hand fell and smacked me in the eye. The next ten minutes were spent straining to master control of a limb that flailed and jerked everywhere but where I wanted it to go.

I closed my eyes for a moment. When I opened them again Erica was sitting by my bedside, wearing Cecilia's face.

The same hospital, a different room, a different world. The window was to my right, not my left. The chaos of monitors and drips and cables was missing. After we'd rescued Alice from the barn, they'd brought me into Addenbrooke's for tests. At first they thought I'd had a stroke, then concluded it was a stress-induced psychotic episode. They'd given me sedatives and kept me in for observation.

'I think the inhibitor is wearing off.' I only said it there, free of confusion and cerasthesia.

Erica opened her small bag and took out a blister pack of pink capsules. 'Do you want one now?'

I hesitated. So far everything was clear. 'Keep them handy.'

Two worlds, then three. I sat in a car with wrists cuffed, Baxter in uniform beside me, a woman I didn't know in the facing seat. She had come while I was in the cell, we were on our way to a remand hearing.

It was simple; I'd killed Novak. In a desperate fit to get him to talk. That made no sense, he could hardly talk if he was dead. Still, it was simple, I'd killed him.

The solicitor—that's who she was, a human solicitor provided by the service union—she was trying to make it complicated. 'We'll ask the magistrate to order a psychiatric assessment, Lewis. With that we can hopefully demonstrate that you aren't a danger to anyone else and we can get you out on bail.'

I had nothing to say to that. It was enough to know that things were going better in my other lives, that Vidmar was dead, that Alice was safe.

'Any news about Alice?' I asked Erica.

'She's calm. Back in the Omega State. Stebbins-Reese wants to leave her there a while to recuperate before trying the inhibitor again. But how are you feeling?'

'I'm okay. The doctors said I can leave when I'm ready but I'll be signed off from work for a while.'

'Do you have anywhere to go?' Erica asked.

'I'll figure something out.'

'You can stay with me.' She looked at her hands as she spoke. 'In the flat. The barn's still a crime scene.'

'I don't want to intrude. You and I… in another life, but not this one.'

She looked up at me. 'Yeah, Chameleon told me about that.' She gave me her crooked half-smile. 'There's a spare room.'

She waited outside while I dressed. We had an appointment to make in London. Plenty of time.

*

The inhibitor hadn't completely worn off. Either that or the deltas they had given me as part of my brain damage treatment were passing from my system. For whatever reason those other lives faded to snatches, moments caught when my attention wandered. In a car on the M11 passing the Bishop's Stortford turn-off with Erica beside me, she said she'd got used to Cecilia's face and wasn't going to change it back. I sat at a table between Baxter and the solicitor as an elderly man droned interminably from behind his desk at the far side of the room.

Erica snapped me out of my mental wanderings, bursting into the room ahead of the breakfast trolley, and bending to give me a long and gentle kiss on the lips. She pushed herself up. 'How are you feeling this morning, my love?' Her eyes searched my face.

'Better.' The word came out strong and clear. 'Much... better.'

She brought a hand up to stroke my hair and kissed me again before pressing the button to raise the head of the bed.

She took my hand, I squeezed it and half-lifted the arm from the bed.

'Don't remember,' I said.

'What don't you remember?'

'Us.'

I didn't remember our past together, but I knew her face, I knew every nuance of expression. That tiny flick of the eyes downwards, a twitch at the corner of the mouth—what I'd said had hurt, but she was trying not to show it. I wanted to explain but every word was an effort. I squeezed her hand again, and the tension eased as her eyes met mine.

She fed me. I tried to do it myself but gave up when the first spoonful of porridge splattered on my cheek. Ms Elland appeared shortly afterwards to run some tests. She ushered Erica out.

Erica hovered in the doorway. 'Laila says she's on her way. she'll be here soon.'

'Laila?'

'Laila Baxter.'

DCI Baxter. The nameplate on her door read, DCI L Baxter. I never knew what the L stood for. First name terms with her subordinates was not her style.

Ms Elland looked up from the monitor she was studying. 'Go and buy her a coffee. We'll be an hour or so here.' She walked over to close the door and came back to the monitor.

I couldn't see the screen but I saw the frown on her face as her hand worked the controls, flicking up and down as if scrolling back and forth.

'Problem?' I asked.

'You've been showing high stress responses over the last twenty-four hours.

Heart rate and blood pressure elevated, cortisol and adrenaline levels increased. Were you in any pain?'

'Died.'

'What?'

'Some of me died, other world.'

'Are you still connected?'

'No.'

'I was planning to carry on with the implicitins a little longer but now I'm not so sure.'

It wasn't a question, but the way she looked at me was. If I agreed with her I wouldn't experience the cerasthesia again, but I would be disconnected from my real life. This, lying crippled in this bed, wasn't my life. This me was an interloper, an imposter, filling a void left by a dead man. My past life, the life I remembered, was shared with those other selves. I would have to be severed from them soon enough, but I wasn't ready for that yet.

'Don't stop,' I said. 'All over. All good.'

She gave me a long hard look before reaching for the meds trolley. 'Oral, fifty milligrams. We'll see how you get on today.' She twisted the cap off a bottle and tipped out a black oval capsule with the VGT logo in white.

After I'd swallowed it, washed down with a sip of water that Ms Elland held for me, she started on the tests. Skin sensitivity, reflexes. *Can you feel this? Push against my hand. NO, PUSH!*

Those other lives faded into my consciousness slow and dreamlike. I was back in my cell, hunched on the bunk with my arms around my knees. I walked with Erica down the alley to Marek's. Sharp cold air, blue sky above, but no sunlight penetrated this narrow canyon between the buildings. At the same time I walked with her up the same alley from the opposite end. She'd met me at St Thomas's hospital. They'd taken me there from the rec room after reports came through that Chameleon had rescued Alice. I paused outside Marek's door a few seconds to allow the convergence. From east and west we'd arrived, but in all those strands together, Marek's door screeched as I pushed it open and held it for her. Even unentangled, her movements meshed together between the streams, unconsciously converging.

'Macchiato, Marek.' She slipped off her coat and hung it on the rack. 'And two cappuccinos.'

Two cappuccinos. One for Erica, and one for Baxter. She'd be here in a moment. I was signed off sick but happy to have an informal chat to catch her up on details she'd missed. There would be formal reports and interviews later.

We made our way to the far side of the empty café. Erica sat with her back to the mirrored wall, me opposite, where I could see the door in the mirror.

She looked relaxed, an easy not-quite-smile on her lips. I knew her moods and expressions whichever face she was wearing. The thought echoed my earlier observations while I lay disconnected in this hospital bed. Shared thought, shared memory. If all these selves were the same person, then if I loved Erica Fallon in one world, I loved her in all of them. Even in the worlds where we'd never met.

'I don't know what you expect,' she said, but the tone of her voice was softer than the words.

I sighed. 'Do you remember, must have been a couple of months after you started at The Grange, when I asked you out?'

'I remember. It was two weeks, the fourth time we'd met.'

Her hands lay loosely clasped on the table, the fingers of her right fidgeting with the engagement ring. 'I was so afraid. After Alice, then Frank Wilson disappearing, Sam Okorie killed.' She slipped the ring from her finger. 'I didn't want to get close to anyone. Bought this stupid thing myself.'

I reached across the table and took her hand. 'I know.'

My phone beeped: A message from Chameleon. *Tamboli's post-mortem results coming through shortly.*

'Three cappuccinos.' Marek placed his tray on the adjacent table and lifted the wide china cups onto ours, one at a time, shimmering and shaking as he did. The cups on the table didn't line up, smeared amongst different places, overlapping.

'What is it? Because the order's wrong?'

'No. I'll be alright.'

A deep breath. I willed myself to focus and the cups separated. I could see the overlaps, but each in its own world. 'I'm alright.'

'You have the inhibitor?'

I took the blister pack from my pocket and popped out a pink capsule, split it in two, dropped the contents into a coffee and stirred.

The café door squealed. Baxter, in uniform, with the detective chief inspector's three pips on each shoulder. She weaved between the tables towards us in precise movements. Shimmers in the corner of my eye distracted me but when I looked back at her she was in sharp focus.

Her face twisted a little as she sat at the table end between Erica and me. It was something like a smile, but not enough to break through her stern demeanour.

'Thanks for coming, Lewis. I appreciate it.' She turned to Erica. 'Cecilia Watts—you work at The Grange, looking after Alice Drake.' She held out a hand for Erica to shake. 'I'm afraid I've been looking through everyone's files. Yours included.'

'Well, no.' Erica looked at me and smiled. 'It's got to come out some time. My real name is Erica Fallon.'

Baxter looked from Erica to me and back, and back again. 'She used the same trick as Vidmar to hide. Phenotype reprogramming to change her face, but only the face. Vidmar regenerated his whole body. Wilson was a little guy, one metre sixty. Tamboli must have been a good thirty centimetres taller.'

Erica gave me a look. 'It must have taken him months.' She raised her coffee cup to her lips. 'Painful.'

Ms Elland gave me exercises to perform while I was lying in bed, tensing and relaxing muscles one at a time. Feet, calves, thighs. Touching thumb to each fingertip in turn. I stopped when I realised I was doing the same on the bunk in the cell in Bishopsgate, and sitting in Marek's.

The cups on the table were losing focus. I wanted to reach for mine, with the inhibitor dissolved in it. Each time I looked it was in a different place.

Baxter sat, still and upright as ever. 'You've done well, DI Drake, but there are some things I don't understand. Like why was Cloake killed?'

'That's an easy one. He'd been working with the Flood Relief Commission on a project to put a barrier across the Thames Estuary. That would have killed the cash cow of government money for Docklands redevelopment that Red Claw was feeding on. What I had trouble figuring out is why Cloake allowed himself to be killed in this world. He was expecting it.'

Baxter's hand paused en route to a coffee cup. 'Go on.'

'The entangled don't fear death in one world, they continue in others. It was a tactical move, so Vidmar would think he'd won, but all Cloake's death did was pass control on to someone with the smarts and the clout to complete the job: Lady Wyndham.'

'And Sir Roger himself?'

'I'm not sure. At first I thought Cloake had set him up, faking VLA vehicle logs to make it look like they'd been meeting so that Vidmar would think Wyndham had betrayed him, but that doesn't feel right—the timing is backwards. We linked Cloake to Wyndham because Wyndham was killed, and Vidmar would only have found out about that after we had, through his mole, Elphick.'

'Elphick wouldn't have known, not his department. There must be another *Rdeča Kremplja* mole. Any ideas?'

'No. No idea.'

'We'll figure it out.' Three slow nods and she pushed herself back from the table. 'Excuse me a moment.' Her voice was oddly resonant. All around me the world shimmered and blurred with the overlay of countless worlds ever so slightly out of sync, but Baxter was sharp, like the foreground focus of a wide aperture photograph.

My phone beeped as she pushed through the door at the back of the café that led to the toilets.

*

The door of my hospital room opened and a uniformed female figure whirled in, two pips of a Detective Inspector on her shoulder. She beamed widely, one hand still on the door handle. 'Do you have any idea of the trouble you've caused HR, sir?' She trotted over to my bedside and sat down. 'They'd already processed your demise, now they're running round in circles trying to work out what to do.'

I stared, trying to place her while my hands mimed the motion of opening a message on a phone.

*

'It doesn't add up.' Erica leaned across the table. 'Thirty centimetres taller, that would have taken six months, a year.'

The phone fell from my hand onto the table. 'The post-mortem shows no other DNA in Tamboli's brain. He wasn't Vidmar, just another Red Claw mole.'

I was trying to focus through the cerasthesia to reach for the cup with the inhibitor when the confusion left me. I was in the hospital bed, with Laila Baxter in an Inspector's uniform smiling down at me. I was in the holding cell in Bishopsgate, and in Marek's café with Erica. All those places with all the rich and subtle variations of those broad streams of reality.

I reached across the table for the cup and slid it towards me as Baxter returned from the toilets. I took a long drink of cappuccino. As soon as she sat she picked up hers and almost drained it in one go. 'You've been in hiding all this time?' she said to Erica.

'Yes. After what happened to Alice, and then to Sam Okorie, it seemed wise, and it meant I was able to look after Alice. No-one suspected, until Lewis figured it out.'

'When did you figure it out, Lewis?'

'The first problem was understanding why she had gone into hiding. I thought, as Erica had—' I glanced at Erica, watching me, '—that Exercitus had spiked Alice's treatment and killed Sam Okorie. They were desperate for the solution to the tissue rejection problem, but that made no sense.'

'Go on.'

I paused to drink my coffee. Baxter raised her cup and finished it.

'Alice was spiked and Sam killed for a completely different reason: to conceal how Vidmar had changed his identity. A few weeks ago, Dr Stebbins-

Reese began treating Alice with the inhibitor. She began to talk and something she said was enough for Erica and me to work out what Frank Wilson, Vidmar, had done, and whose identity he had taken.'

'I don't follow.' She looked at Erica. 'If you knew who Vidmar was, why didn't you tell someone?'

'*I* didn't know. That was another me, another reality. Apparently in that world, Vidmar took the identity of Winsford Saïd.'

'I see. But in this world he replaced Tamboli.' She said it with a straight face.

As long as I'd known her Baxter always had to have the last word. I had to keep talking, keep *her* talking, give time for the inhibitor to take effect. 'Apparently so. The important thing is that Vidmar is entangled. He knew his identity had been exposed in that other world, but all he knew of how it happened was that it had something to do with Erica. He had to find her, and that is what this whole case has been about. The Thames barrage, Wyndham's murder, they were a side show. Vidmar led me to Cloake with the faked vehicle logs, knowing he would lead me to Alice and Erica. Knowing that in other worlds, Erica and I were close and I was the best bet to find her in this one.'

'It's a good story,' she said. 'And mostly right. I did have to get rid of Wyndham and Cloake because they were working on building the barrage. Your sister I spiked because she'd stumbled on to what I was doing. I thought the overdose would kill her, but at the time the result seemed sufficient.'

'And Sam Okorie?'

She smiled. Not the gentle laughing smile of DI Laila Baxter in the other world, but a malevolent grin. 'You may find this hard to believe, but it was exactly what it looked like. A tragic accident. A feral car that missed a recall.' She reached into her jacket and pulled out a Glock. 'One of those amusing little ironies. If it hadn't been for that, you wouldn't have changed your identity, Erica, and you would already be dead. But now I need to know, exactly how did you trace my identity?'

Time, I needed more time. I jumped in before Erica could answer. 'I knew as soon as I met the real Laila Baxter.' When DI Laila Baxter sat down by my hospital bedside, her red cheeks plumped from her grin. A face I knew so well but had never seen so filled with emotion. The face was the same, but the way she wore it was not. It all clicked into place. Phenotype reprogramming rebuilt Frank Wilson's body to a new gene plan. XY to XX, male to female, was just one more pair of chromosomes in that blueprint. 'You killed her when you took her identity in this world. I guess you had to get rid of her partner and children because they'd have known.'

She leaned back in her chair, the gun held casually in her hand. 'You are full of surprises, Lewis. You could only have met her in another reality.' There was a shimmering in the movement, an echo in the sound of her voice. She was losing her synchronisation in the streams of this reality. 'I didn't think you would ever take implicitins. You hate the entangled. In some worlds you're deeply involved with the anti-entanglement movement.'

*

I sat on my bunk counting the bricks of the whitewashed wall opposite, imagining each was another reality and in each one Vidmar had taken a different identity. In some the DNA sequence editor with the secret of Vidmar's identity in its memory might still be sitting on a shelf in the VirGenTech building. If she learned of its existence in one world, she would know in all of them, so long as she was entangled.

So long as she was entangled, she knew in this world everything she knew in Marek's café. Now she knew that I knew she was Vidmar, I'd have to be silenced.

*

'An inconvenient coincidence that you found me like that,' she said, and made that slow nodding motion, as she so often did in our conversations at the station. As Frank Wilson had done as he listened to Sam Okorie, caught in the background of the video of the party celebrating Marko's treatment. 'What I need to know now is how you found me in that other world, where I was Winsford Saïd.' She looked at Erica, then at me. 'I can split this world into a dozen lines, a thousand, a million, and you can watch her die in each one.'

'Tamboli knew,' I said. 'But he didn't tell you. Did you know he was going to betray you?' She was beginning to twitch, a nervous tic in the right cheek that lifted the corner of her mouth a couple of millimetres with increasing frequency and decreasing regularity, turning that part of her face to a blur in my vision. 'He may have been acting the faithful servant, but he wanted Erica and Alice himself, so he could unmask you.'

'An arrogant simplex fool. He thought he could take my place. His usefulness was wearing out.'

Erica's eyes met mine. I glanced down at the coffee cup and raised an eyebrow. She nodded; she'd seen what I'd done, and that we needed to play for time. 'I'm the one who figured it out.' Erica crossed her arms and leaned back. 'Why aren't you threatening to shoot Lewis while I watch?'

Baxter frowned, her twitching worse. 'Because, stupid woman,' she hissed through gritted teeth, 'you are not Entangled.' She raised the gun and pointed it in Erica's face. Her finger curled on the trigger. 'How many times do I kill her before you tell me, Lewis?' Her hand shook. 'How many… How many…'

'You can't do it, can you?'

Her wide eyes stared at me. 'What did you do?'

I dropped the two halves of the split capsule on the table. 'Put fifty milligrams of inhibitor in your coffee.'

The café door behind me screeched across the tiles.

*

The hinges groaned as the cell's steel door opened. Baxter stood in the doorway, gun in hand. There were no shimmers, no double images, all the worlds where I was in the cell, she was there. I had one chance. If she diverged she would find a way to get the truth out of me, as I had from Ignacij Novak. Now, now was the time to release my bottled rage. Screaming, I ran at her. I never heard the gun fire, never saw the flash. I must have been dead before my brain could even process the senses.

*

That life vanished from my experience like the fall of a black stage curtain. It was my choice, my action, that had led to it and there was no pain or shock. I blinked and Laila Baxter's face came into focus.

'You were the first at Marek's when I was shot,' I said. 'What happened?'

'We managed to piece it together afterwards. Vidmar was tipped off that you had identified him as Winsford Saïd.'

'Elphick?'

'Yes. He was supposed to be on the squad sent to make the arrest.'

'So Vidmar gave Elphick the order to kill me and Erica.'

'Yes. Elphick, and Harris.'

Her words hit me like a runaway steamroller. In all the confusion and uncertainty, Jack Harris was the one person I'd never doubted, never could doubt.

*

Baxter/Vidmar's hand waved incoherently, pointing at me, at the wall behind me, wavering towards Erica. In the mirror wall facing me Harris stood by the closing door.

I leapt at Vidmar and her gun fired, deafening in my ear. The weight of my impact knocked her backwards on her chair and my own momentum carried me twisting over her. The gun skittered along the floor towards the back wall. I lunged towards it but she pulled me back and tried to grab it herself.

I rolled on to my back. Harris stood over us both, pistol in his right hand.

*

'What Vidmar didn't know,' Laila Baxter continued, 'was that Harris was a double agent working for Donahue to identify Vidmar's moles. He was too far away so he called me when he got Vidmar's order, but Elphick was already at Marek's. I was too late.'

*

'Ma'am? What's going on?' Harris's eyes moved from Baxter, as he thought, to me.

'You have your orders, Harris. Follow them. Now.' She edged back towards the gun on the floor behind her.

'She's Vidmar!' I said.

'DCI Baxter? Vidmar?' The puzzlement on his face evaporated as Vidmar's hand found the Glock. She swivelled around.

Two shots rang out almost at the same moment. Vidmar lay dead from Harris's shot, and I felt the hot, red blood running beneath my shirt from Vidmar's.

On the floor of Marek's, I leaned back against the mirrored wall, Vidmar sprawled very dead in front of me. Now Harris was on his phone running through the usual *officer injured* routine. My shirt was sticky, red and sticky. Erica held herself together with admirable calm, pressing down on my wound.

Futile though. I could feel the blood pulsing out with every beat of my heart. My vision blurred and faded from grey to black.

*

I opened my eyes and Laila Baxter's face filled my vision.

'Sir? Are you alright?'

'Baxter?'

'Yes, sir.'

''s okay Baxter. I'm just confused.'

'So am I sir. The doctor, Dr Elland, she said…'

'It's Ms Elland, she's a consultant.'

'Yes, Ms Elland. She told me, that you're you, but not you. You might have a different memory of recent events, because of the implicitins.'

'She's right. The version of me that you know is dead. How long have you known me?'

'Two years. They'd promoted you to DCI and put you in charge of the unit while I was off.'

'Off?'

'On maternity leave.' She bit her lip. 'Don't you remember any of that? Do you know me?'

'You have two children?'

'Three now.'

'They're all well?'

She frowned. 'Why wouldn't they be?'

Erica chose that moment to return so I let the two of them talk around me for a while. This was my life now, these were the people close to me, but I was not the me that they knew, and other than that leakage of habit and familiarity between worlds, I did not know them. I did not know this Erica who was my wife.

CHAPTER 14

Monday 23rd December: North Laine

I live my many and varied lives with joy and with pain. I do what I can to make things better for the people who share these worlds with me, like anyone, entangled or not. What more can I do?

And yet, no matter what I do for the best, all possible futures are real. There are worlds in which my actions, however well-intentioned, cause pain. How hard it has become to do anything, knowing that in some slice of reality my plans will fail, that those I seek to protect and aid will suffer.

How do I measure my worth as a human being, knowing that the direct consequence of my actions is pain for others?

This, for me, is the measurement problem.

—A K Amari - *The Measurement Problem,*
A Guide to Entanglement

The news feeds helped me piece together what was happening in this world. Winsford Saïd's death and the revelation of his real identity was still causing ripples. I was watching a piece about alleged links between government ministers and Vidmar's enterprises when Jack Harris knocked on my door. He strode in with a real swagger, very much changed from how I'd known him, yet very much the same. No longer the Harris of boyish good looks.

'Great beard,' I said, and it was. Thick, dark auburn, but it had me puzzled.

He gave me a funny look, like he was puzzled, too. 'Shit,' he said. 'They told me your memory was screwed. I grew this over a year ago, after the treatment.'

A different world. Erica still worked for the VGT Genetic Therapies division. Project Furcifer had delivered on its promise and phenotype reprogramming was becoming commonplace for genetic disorders. So of course Jack Harris would go XX to XY to bring his body in line with his inner self.

He reached to clasp my hand in a solid grip. 'I'm so sorry, man.'

'What for?'

'I should have been there, should have had your back.'

He'd died for me at Elphick's hand in that derelict housing estate in Cambridge and he'd been there to save Erica in Marek's café.

'So many worlds, Jack. You always do the right thing, sometimes it doesn't work out. It's not your fault.'

He didn't stay long, but I hope I eased his conscience a little. I went back to the news—the Foreign Secretary had resigned over his close links with Saïd and pressure was mounting on other members of the cabinet.

The following days were an unending cycle of sessions in the treatment room that left me exhausted. Erica came every day, and there was a steady stream of visitors who thought they knew me, but the gulf was wide. I gave up trying to explain that the Lewis they knew was dead, and that I was another. Whether all those different versions of myself were really aspects of a single *me*, I still don't know. I'll leave that one to the philosophers.

Every day I called Alice at The Grange. Some days she was too disconnected to talk, some days lucid, and often confusing. I told her my worry; in those worlds where I'd died I never got a chance to sort out the service benefits with Vittoria, which meant the bills weren't going to be paid. She didn't seem concerned but couldn't tell me why.

One time she told me about my life in a world where the war had never happened, our memories never lost and we had the names given to us by our parents. There were no implicitins, no entanglement. Erica and I lived in her barn and I was an architect.

The first of December, Ms Elland was giving me the usual battery of tests when Sam Okorie burst in. 'They've arrested the Chancellor!'

Tests forgotten, we watched the press conference with the Chief Constable, accompanied by Superintendent Donahue. Enquiries were ongoing, further arrests could not be ruled out. The political soap opera was not enough to stop the work of Ms Elland or Dr Okorie for long, so I was left watching the growing wave of resignations. By the time Erica arrived the government had fallen and the opposition leader was at the palace being invited to form a minority government. We watched the drama unfold in silence.

Three days later Erica and I were watching the live broadcast as the new Home Secretary stood by the open gates of an internment camp, shaking hands with each of the entangled as they stepped out to freedom.

'She seems a good person,' Erica said. 'Do you know anything about her?'

'I interviewed her when her husband was murdered.' Said husband, Sir Roger Wyndham, was standing in the background at the internment camp gates. Erica raised an eyebrow.

'I guess she knows Elijah,' she said as Lady Wyndham gave a particularly warm handshake to Cloake.

The camera zoomed in on another familiar face in the line as he stepped forward into an emotional embrace with the Home Secretary. 'And here, her own son, Aiden Harcourt.'

*

The next morning I was sitting up with a tablet, reading prospectuses to kill time between breakfast and my next treatment, when a knock on my door was followed by that familiar face.

'Chameleon!' I hauled myself half upright to clasp his hand in mine. 'Or should I call you Aiden?'

'Things here are different to the world you knew.'

The world *I knew.* Here at last was someone who really understood who I was. 'Everything's different. I don't really know anyone here.'

He let go of my hand and sat next to the bed. 'You've got friends, Lewis, even if they have different memories to you. Don't push them away.'

'They aren't my friends. They're *his*. The Lewis Drake who died.'

'You would have done everything he did in his place, because you *are* him. This is still *your* life.'

'My life. So much I left unfinished. I don't know what's going to happen to Alice now I'm not there to pay the bills at The Grange.'

'That's covered.'

'How?'

'When Elijah learned there was no money to look after Alice he set up a trust to help those unable to care for themselves because of implicitins.'

'I so misjudged him. All of you, the entangled.'

'Not all of us. Vidmar is entangled, too.'

'Is? Not was?'

'In your worlds you unmasked him before he could find out about the Viradyn machine. That gave us time to get to it where it still existed, but there are worlds where it's gone. He knows about it now.'

'It was all for nothing, then.'

'No, not for nothing. So many futures have changed because of what you did. The barrage will be built, the killings and corruption stopped. You can't win every battle, but that doesn't mean it isn't worth the fight.'

'No more battles for me.' I picked up the tablet from where I'd dropped it on the bed, with the list of prospectuses on the page. 'I'm not going back to the service.'

'I guess you'll have sick leave for a while. There'll be time to make up your mind.'

'HR are tying themselves in knots. They already had me down as deceased.

I'm thinking of telling them they were right and I'm someone else.'

'Now Elland and Okorie know how to bring back someone from brain-dead it's going to happen again. The law is going to have to figure out what that means sooner or later.'

'Yeah, I'll leave that one for someone else.' I dropped the tablet back on the bed. 'How was it in the camp?'

'Tolerable. It gave me time to work on my writing.'

'Writing?'

'I use my father's name to publish. A K Amari.'

*

On the twelfth they discharged me. It would take months or years for me to make a full recovery. Regen had healed the physical damage to my brain, but so much was lost, I had to learn all over again to use my body. Erica took me home to the barn. I was reluctant but I had nowhere else to go. I wouldn't share her bed, though, it didn't feel right—we were strangers, but such intimate strangers, with every look, every movement, every word steeped in warm familiarity. And anyway, I couldn't manage the stairs with the crutches, so she made up the bed-settee in the snug for me. Late in that first night I woke as she climbed in next to me, sniffing and wiping her eyes. I held her and we slept, that was all. On that first night that was all, but there were other nights.

Slow and steady, careful delicate steps, we filled in the gaps for each other of our separate pasts. She told me we'd first met at that celebration for Marko. Elijah Cloake had heard Alice mention me and said she should bring me along. That day was the first time I met Erica and the last time I saw my then fiancée, Vittoria. As far as we could work out, that was where our worlds had diverged from their common past.

So it was that on Erica's birthday, the twenty third of December, we went on a day out to celebrate. She kept pace with me as I stumped along the narrow, crowded street, dodging around the little clothing stalls, pedestrians and cyclists. Everyone huddled in thick coats, woolly hats, scarves, gloves. The walking stick attracted some curious looks, but most people were kind enough to step out of our way.

Out of the corner of my eye I saw it in the window of an art gallery. I don't recall the name of the shop, there are dozens like it in the streets of Brighton's North Laine. Framed, behind glass, waves of blues and greens. This one was a print, limited edition, signed by the artist and labelled *Erinnerung an einen verblassenden Sturm*. The original still hung in the study of our barn. That picture always brought the other Erica, Cecilia, back to me. This Erica, the Erica on my arm, had offered to hide it away. But no, I'd said. I needed to remember. She had her memories of the Lewis that was lost to her, the Lewis that used to inhabit this body.

'The café's down here.' I waved my stick to point down the street. A little further along I saw the sign I was looking for.

'This is it,' I said. Erica pushed open the door for me and I edged my way through the narrow gaps between the backs of occupied chairs towards an empty table in the far corner. I peeled off my outer layers and stacked them with my stick against the window.

'I'm intrigued, Lewis.' She laid her hand on mine. 'Why this particular café?'

'Alice said we should come here,' I said, lowering myself gratefully into the seat.

The place was steaming with the crowd of people taking respite from the chill sea breeze, loud with the hubbub of chattering voices. Outside, it began to snow, thick heavy flakes like I'd never seen in England.

'I'm going to submit the application today.'

My words drew her gaze from the falling snow. 'Where?'

'Cambridge has a good school of architecture but I doubt I'd get in. I've found three possibles in London. Commutable.'

She hadn't tried to sway me but the relief was clear in her eyes. Architects are seldom victims of violence.

'The waitress at the counter over there,' she whispered, glancing sideways, 'she keeps looking at you.'

I turned to see her weaving between the tables towards us with her pad. 'I'm sorry for staring,' she said, 'but do I know you from somewhere?'

She had bright red lips, eyes shadowed in deep, dark shades of blue, geometrically precise eyebrows, cheeks a dusty pale darkened to brownish orange over the cheek bones, but I knew what she looked like beneath the make-up. I knew her name without looking at her handwritten name badge.

'In another life, Kay.'

—

ABOUT THE AUTHOR

David has been an avid reader of science fiction since his teenage years, back in the days when computers filled rooms, people were excited about space travel and dinosaurs roamed the Earth. He's always had a hankering to write stories himself and in the early 1990s he even had a go, but work, marriage, and children left him little time to develop the craft. The old WordPerfect files sat on a floppy disk gathering dust for decades.

A career in software development ended with retirement in 2017, and with the children grown he had the time and resources to engage in his passions, taking guitar lessons from a local teacher, and enrolling in a two year creative writing course with New Writing South in Brighton. During the course he started his first attempt at a novel: *The Long Fall*. The mistakes made in writing that bloated monster were as educational as the course itself. (He intends to revisit and publish it at some point.) Another novel, *When The Enemy Comes*, is in the editing phase.

The first publication success came in 2020 when Mythaxis published his short story *Winter*. Several others followed in various magazines. Recognition came when a draft of *The Measurement Problem* won the Science Museum SF Debuts Prize, a competition run as part of the London Science Museum's 'Voyage to the Edge of Imagination' exhibition in 2022/23. More recently his short story *Asylum* received the Kepler Award, sponsored by Cosmic Roots & Eldritch Shores.

When he's not travelling or hiking David lives in West Sussex with his wife and two cats, and from time to time one or more of his boomerang offspring.

More information on David and his writing can be found at:

www.sixwhits.com

To get in touch via social media of your choice please visit:

www.linktr.ee/whitmad

Printed in Dunstable, United Kingdom

65366618R00163